W9-DCJ-574

What Lies in the Woods

# What Lies in the Woods

KATE ALICE MARSHALL

FLATIRON BOOKS
NEW YORK

This is a work of fiction. All of the characters, organizations, and events portrayed in this novel are either products of the author's imagination or are used fictitiously.

WHAT LIES IN THE WOODS. Copyright © 2022 by Kate Alice Marshall. All rights reserved. Printed in the United States of America. For information, address Flatiron Books, 120 Broadway, New York, NY 10271.

www.flatironbooks.com

Designed by Susan Walsh

Library of Congress Cataloging-in-Publication Data

Names: Marshall, Kate Alice, author.
Title: What lies in the woods / Kate Alice Marshall.
Description: First edition. | New York : Flatiron Books, 2023.
Identifiers: LCCN 2022020886 | ISBN 9781250859884 (hardcover) |
    ISBN 9781250859907 (ebook)
Subjects: LCGFT: Thrillers (Fiction). | Novels.
Classification: LCC PS3613.A7746 W47 2023 | DDC 813/.6—dc23/
    eng/20220721
LC record available at https://lccn.loc.gov/2022020886

Our books may be purchased in bulk for promotional, educational, or business use. Please contact your local bookseller or the Macmillan Corporate and Premium Sales Department at 1-800-221-7945, extension 5442, or by email at MacmillanSpecialMarkets@macmillan.com.

First Edition: 2023

10  9  8  7  6  5  4  3  2  1

*For all the wild girls who search for magic in the woods*

What Lies in the Woods

There is a wilderness in little girls.

We could not contain it. It made magic of the rain and a temple of the forest. We raced down narrow trails, hair flying wind-wild behind us, and pretended that the slender spruce and hemlock were still the ancient woods that industry had chewed down to splinters. We made ourselves into warriors, into queens, into goddesses. Fern leaves and dandelions became poultices and potions, and we sang incantations to the trees. We gave ourselves new names: Artemis, Athena, Hecate. Conversations were in code, our letters filled with elaborate ciphers, and we taught ourselves the meanings of stones.

Beneath a canopy of moss-wreathed branches, we joined hands and pledged ourselves to one another forever—a kind of forever that burns only in the hearts of those young enough not to know better.

Forever ended with the summer. It ended with a scream and the shocking heat of blood, and two girls stumbling onto the road.

The way Leo Cortland told the story, he thought at first that the sound was some kind of bird or animal. His spaniel's ears perked, and she barked once, staring intently into the trees.

The truth was he knew right away that the sound belonged to a child. The story he told was a way to explain to himself why he stood for so long, unmoving. Why, when the spaniel lunged toward the noise, he hauled her back, wrapping the leash around his fist. Why he was starting to turn, to walk the other way, when the girls stumbled out of the woods, the two of them wild-eyed and whimpering and their clothes soaked with dark blood.

"What happened to you?" he asked, still in shock, still seized with the urge to get away.

One girl shivered and shook her head, wrapping her arms around her body, but the other spoke. Her voice was hollow and lost. "There was a man," she told him. "He had a knife."

"Are you hurt?" he asked, wishing that he had his gun, wishing that his spaniel had ever been a threat to anything but his shoes.

"No," the girl said. When he told the story, Leo would linger on this part. The way she stared right through him, like there was nothing but a ghost behind her eyes. "But our friend is dead."

This was the one part of the story that was Leo's and Leo's alone; after that, it belonged to everyone, and each found a different part to tell again and again, polishing it smooth. Some spoke of the bravery of the two of us who had stumbled to the road to find help, who despite the shock gave the description that would lead to the attacker's arrest. Others focused on the monster himself, fascinated by his wickedness and his brutality, the darkened corners of his soul.

Our parents always spoke of the moment they found out—of hearing that three girls had gone into the woods and only two had emerged, knowing right away that it was their girls, because it was a small town and because they knew the way the wilderness called to us, the way we slipped down deer trails and searched for the tracks of unicorns beside the creek.

Knowing that three of us had gone into the woods. Not knowing which two had returned.

Others spoke of the young man who found the last of us. Cody Benham was walking through the woods with the search party—three dozen men and women, most of them armed, all of them angry. He spotted the small form lying sprawled over the rotting hump of a fallen tree, as if she'd tried to climb over it with her last failing strength. The rain ran over her, rivulets of blood-tinged water tracing lines down to the tips of her pale fingers.

He didn't call out at first. He fell to his knees instead, all the breath going out of him. He pressed his face against her cold cheek.

Her fingers curled against the bark.

Some people talk endlessly of the miracle it was, when they carried that little girl, still breathing, from the woods. They praise her strength and her bravery. They remember the television image, the girl in a wheelchair with a scar twisting up her cheek like a knot in a tree, and how she nodded when the prosecutor asked her if the man who'd hurt her was in the room.

They told the story again and again, until they thought they owned it.

We tried to forget. We didn't tell the story.

Not the real one.

Not ever.

I tried to appear attentive as the couple across from me flipped through the binder of photographs, murmuring appreciatively. Normally, I'd say it was a good sign—except for the telltale tension in the bride-to-be's shoulders, and the way her eyes kept darting up to my face when she thought I wasn't looking.

My phone, facedown on the table, vibrated. I pressed the button to silence it without picking it up, resisting the urge to check who was calling.

"Your portfolio is really, really impressive," the bride said, fiddling with the edge of her paper napkin. "Really."

"I'm glad to hear that," I replied, mentally calculating how much I'd just lost on gas by agreeing to this meeting. I should have known better. The groom being the one to contact me, the way he'd specified, *I showed Maddie some of your photos,* when I asked if she'd seen the website.

"It's just," she began, and stopped. Her husband-to-be, an earnest-looking young man with a chin dimple and too much hair gel, put a hand on her wrist.

"Babe, it's exactly what you were looking for. You're always complaining about washed-out photos. You wanted someone who isn't afraid of color."

My phone started buzzing again. "Sorry about that," I said, picking it up to check the caller ID. Liv. I declined the call again and tucked it into my purse. Whatever the latest crisis was, and it was always a crisis, she'd have to wait a few minutes more.

"It's just," the bride said again. She bit her lip. "I'm sorry, I don't want to sound totally awful. Your photos are really, really—"

"Impressive," I finished for her, smiling. When I smiled, only one side of my mouth went up. She flinched.

"Come on, Maddie," Husband-to-Be said—I couldn't remember his name. It was probably Jason. It was usually Jason, for some reason. The ones who trotted me out like a surprise, as if to shame their partners into hiring me. It had mostly stopped happening since I tripled my prices, which magically turned my scars from a pitiable flaw to part of my edgy appeal.

"It's all right," I assured him. "It's your wedding day, Maddie. Everything should be perfect."

"Right," she said, relieved that I *understood*.

"And if anyone isn't perfect, you shouldn't have to have them there," I added. Her smile faltered.

"Your prices are very high," she snapped, turning pink. "Maybe you should consider lowering them. You might get more business."

I sighed. "My prices are high because my work is really, really good," I said, parroting her words back to her. "I make sure that my photo is front and center on my website because I don't want anyone to waste their time or mine. And now we've done both."

I stood, picking up the binder. My coffee sat untouched on the table, but I had only ordered it to kill time while I was waiting for them to show up twenty minutes late. "I hope you have the wedding of your dreams, Maddie. Jason, nice to meet you."

"My name's Jackson, actually," he muttered, not lifting his eyes past my chin. As I walked away I heard him whispering furiously to her. Just as the door swung shut, she burst into tears. I stopped on the sidewalk and shut my eyes, letting out a breath and telling myself to relax the muscles that had slowly tightened throughout my body.

The only thing worse than brides like Maddie was getting to the meeting only to discover that the client was a "fan." Not of my photos, of course. Of the dramatic story my life had become when I was eleven years old.

I pulled my phone out of my purse. Liv hadn't left a message, but that wasn't surprising. She hated being recorded. We'd spent enough time with cameras shoved in our faces, and the clips still lived on the internet under names like GIRLS FOIL SERIAL KILLER IN OLYMPIC FOREST and SURVIVORS OF "QUINAULT KILLER" ALAN MICHAEL STAHL SPEAK OUT.

Back then Liv had what her mom called "stubborn baby fat" and a round face made rounder by blunt bangs and a bob. In the years after, she'd sprouted up and slimmed down, and then she just kept vanishing by degrees, melting away until you could count the vertebrae through her shirt. She made sure there wasn't enough of herself left to get recognized.

I didn't have the option. The scar on my cheek, the nerve damage that kept the corner of my mouth tucked in a constant frown—those weren't things I could hide. Changing my name had cut down on the number of people who found me, but I'd never get rid of the scars, and I refused to try to hide them. I kept my hair cut short and sharp, and I always photographed myself straight on. I described my style as unflinching. My most recent therapist had been known to suggest I was using honesty as armor.

As if on cue, the phone started buzzing again. This time I answered, bracing myself to talk Liv down from whatever crisis the day had brought. "Hey, Liv. What's up?" I asked brightly, because pretending it could be anything else was part of what we did.

She was silent for a moment. I waited for her. It would come in little hiccup phrases at first, and then a flood. And at the end of it I would tell her that it was going to be okay, ask if she was taking her meds, and promise I didn't mind at all that she'd called. And I didn't. I was far more worried about the day she stopped calling.

"I'm trying to reach Naomi Cunningham," a male voice said on the other end of the line, and I blinked in surprise.

"That's me. Sorry, I thought you were someone else. Obviously," I said, letting out a breath and sweeping windblown strands of hair back from my eyes. "Who's calling?"

"My name is Gerald Watts, at the Office of Victim Services. I'm calling about Alan Michael Stahl."

My mind went blank. Why would they be calling me now? It had been over twenty years, but— "Has he been released?" I asked. I remembered the word *parole* in the sentence. *Possibility of parole after twenty years.* But twenty years was eternity to a child. Panic bloomed through me like black mold. "Wait. You're supposed to call us, aren't you? We're supposed to be allowed to testify, or—"

"Ma'am, Stahl has not been released," Gerald Watts said quickly and calmly. "I've got better news than that. He's dead."

"I—" I stopped. Dead. He was dead, and that was it. It was over. "How?"

"Cancer. Beyond that, I'm not able to share private medical information."

"Do the others know? Liv—I mean Olivia Barnes, and—"

"Olivia Barnes and Cassidy Green have been notified as well. We had a little more trouble getting hold of you. You changed your name." He said it like it was just a reason, not a judgment, but I stammered.

"You can still figure out who I am, it's not like I hide it, but it cuts down on the random calls and stuff," I said. I'd had strangers sending things to my house for years. Or just showing up themselves, ringing the doorbell, asking to meet the miracle girl and gape at my face.

"I don't blame you," he said. "Him dying, it'll get reported here and there. You might want to take some time off, if you can. Go someplace you won't get hassled. Shouldn't take long for the interest to die down."

"I'll be fine. It never takes long for some new tragedy to come along and distract everyone," I said.

He grunted in acknowledgment. "Ms. Cunningham, if you need to speak to a counselor, we have resources available to you."

"Why would I need to talk to a counselor?" I asked with a high, tortured laugh. "I should be happy, right?" The man who'd attacked me was dead. A little less evil in the world.

"This kind of thing can bring up a lot of complicated feelings and difficult memories," Gerald Watts said gently. He had a grandfatherly voice, I thought.

"I'll be fine," I told him, though I sounded faint, almost robotic. "Thank you for telling me."

"Take care of yourself," he said, a firm instruction, and we said our goodbyes.

I stood at the curb, my toes hanging over the edge, my weight rocking forward. There was something about that feeling. After the attack, I'd had damage to the membranous labyrinth in my left ear. I'd had fits of vertigo. Years later, after it faded, I would stand like this, almost falling, and that rushing feeling would return. But I was in control. I was the one who decided if I would fall.

I closed my eyes and stepped off the curb.

---

I was on my second glass of wine by the time Mitch came home. He dropped his messenger bag with the kind of dramatic sigh that always preceded a long rant about the soul-stifling horror of working in an office.

"You wouldn't believe what a shit day I've had," he declared, kicking off his shoes as he headed for the fridge. "Bridget is on my ass about every little thing, and Darrel is out sick *again*, which means that I have to pick up the slack. Fuck, all that's in here is IPAs. I might as well drink grass clippings."

"There's a porter in the back," I said, sipping my wine and staring at the wall.

"Thank God."

I picked out patterns in the wall texture as Mitch cracked open the beer and dropped onto the couch next to me. I liked Mitch. There was a reason I liked Mitch. In a moment I would remember what it was.

I ran a finger along the rim of my glass, examining him. His hair flopped over his eye, too long to be respectable by exactly a centimeter, and he maintained a precise amount of stubble. We'd met at the gallery opening of my ex-girlfriend, forty-eight hours after she dumped me for being "an emotional black hole" and then demanded I still attend to support her. Mitch had stolen a whole tray of fancy cheeses and we hid in the corner drinking champagne and waxing faux-eloquent about tables and light fixtures as if they were the exhibit. It had been a bit cruel and definitely stupid, but it had been fun. *This man*, I'd thought, *is an asshole*.

So of course I'd gone home with him.

"And how goes the wedding-industrial complex?" he asked.

"Fine," I said. I paused. "No, it wasn't. The bride didn't want a photographer with a mangled face."

"Bitch," he said matter-of-factly. "You're wasting your time with those people."

It was, more or less, what I'd said to her. But it meant something else, coming from him. "Today was a waste of time," I agreed. The whole thing felt so far away.

"You're better than this," Mitch said. His hand dropped to my knee, his head lolling on the back of the couch. "I mean, Jesus. You have actual talent. And you're spending your time on Extruded Wedding Product #47."

"I like what I do," I said evenly.

"It's beneath you."

"Okay." I wasn't interested in this argument, not again.

"All those women are so desperate to have their perfect day. I can't even imagine getting married. I just try to picture it, you and me at the altar and the tux and the floofy white gown, and it's like a complete parody. I don't see the point. Do you?"

"I don't see the point of marrying you, no," I replied, but he was already moving on. We were back to complaining about work—something about a jammed copier.

"I mean, *Jesus*, this job is going to kill me," he groaned when he'd finally wound down.

My glass was empty. I reached for the bottle on the coffee table and discovered that was empty as well.

"You polished that off by yourself?" Mitch asked, amusement with a rotten underside of judgment.

"An old friend of mine called today," I said.

"Bad news?" he asked. His posture shifted, canting toward me. Two parts comfort, one part hunger. That was the problem with writers. They couldn't help digging the edge of a fingernail under your scabs so they could feel the shape of your wounds.

My scars had climbed across the skin of half a dozen characters already. Sometimes he sublimated them into metaphor—gave a girl a faulty heart, a cracked mirror to stare into—but reading those stories, I could always feel his fingertips tracing the constellation of knotted tissue across my stomach, chest, arms, face. He'd gotten permission at first, but after a while it was like he owned the story just as much as I did.

The parts I'd told him, anyway.

"It was Liv," I said.

"Having another one of her spirals?" Mitch asked knowingly.

I bristled. I hated Mitch talking about her like he knew her. They'd never even met. "I didn't actually talk to her," I said. I needed more wine. The bottle hadn't been full when I started, and it wasn't hitting me hard enough to blunt the edges properly.

Mitch reached for my hand. I stood and walked to the kitchen, pulling another bottle of red down and casting about for the corkscrew. Alan Stahl was dead. He would never get out. He would never come after me.

He'd promised to. After he was sentenced, he'd told his cellmate he was going to get out and slit my throat. Part of me had always been waiting for him to show up at my doorstep, ready to finish what had been left undone twenty years ago.

I set the knife against the rim of the foil and twisted. The knife slipped, the tip jabbing into my thumb. I swore under my breath and just put the corkscrew straight through the foil instead, pulling the cork out through it. Wine glugged into the glass, splashing up the sides. The bottle knocked against the glass and almost tipped it, and then Mitch was grabbing it from me, taking my hand and turning it upward.

"Naomi, you're bleeding," he said.

I stared. The cut on my thumb was deeper than I'd thought, and everything—the bottle, the glass, the corkscrew, the counter—was smeared with blood. I wrenched my hand free of Mitch and stuck my thumb in my mouth. The coppery taste washed across my tongue, and instantly I was back in the forest, the loamy scent of the woods overlaid with the metallic smell of my blood, the birds in the trees flitting and calling without a care for the girl dying below.

When I remembered it, I pictured myself from above, crawling over the ground, dragging myself up onto that log. I didn't remember the pain. The mind is not constructed to hold on to the sense of such agony.

"Look at me. Naomi, come on. Look at my face," Mitch said, touching the underside of my chin delicately, like he was afraid I would bruise. I met his eyes with difficulty. "There you are. What's going on? If you didn't talk to Liv—"

"I know why she was calling," I said. I swallowed. It was mine until I said it out loud. Then it belonged to Mitch, too, and all the people he told, and the people they told. But of course the story already belonged to countless others—Cassidy and Liv and Cody Benham and whatever journalist found out about it first, and surely there would be some footnote article in the papers tomorrow, "QUINAULT KILLER" DIES IN PRISON.

"Naomi. You're drifting again," Mitch said. This was why I liked him. I remembered now.

"Alan Stahl is dead," I said. "Cancer. He died in prison. He's gone." If I could say it in just the right way, it would make sense. Everything would fall into its proper order, and I would know how I was supposed to feel.

"Oh my God. That's great news!" Mitch seized my shoulders, grinning. "Naomi, that's *good*. I mean, I'd rather he be tortured every day for another twenty years, but dead is the next best thing. You should be celebrating."

"I know. It's just complicated," I said, sliding past him. I grabbed a kitchen towel and pressed it to my thumb. The bleeding wasn't too bad. It would stop soon.

"It must be bringing up a lot of trauma," he said with a wise nod. And that was why I didn't like him.

"Can you stop talking like you know what I'm going through better than I do?" I stalked to the hall closet, pawing through it one-handed for a bandage.

"You've never really processed what happened to you. You shy away from it in your work. You need to confront it head-on. This is a perfect opportunity. Turn it into the catalyst you need to really dig in. You could do a series of self-portraits, or—"

"Oh, for the love of God, Mitch, will you let it go?" I said. I found the package of Band-Aids and held it under my arm while I fished one out. Mitch moved in to help, but I turned, blocking him with my body. "I don't want to turn my trauma into art. I don't want *you* to turn my trauma into art."

"You'd rather churn out identical images of identical smiling people and never create anything of meaning or significance?" he asked.

I slammed the closet door shut. "Yes. If those are my two options, I will take the smiling people. Who are not identical, and neither are the photos. They're *happy*, so you think they're beneath me. But you know what? It means a hell of a lot more to a hell of a lot more people than a story in an obscure magazine that doesn't pay and never even sent you the contributor copies." That was harsher than I'd intended, but I didn't back down. I couldn't. I was running blind through the forest, and the hunter was behind me. I could only go forward.

"I didn't realize you thought so little of my work," Mitch said stiffly.

"Whereas I knew perfectly well how little you thought of mine," I snarled back. Then I pressed the heel of my hand to my forehead. "I'm sorry. Can we just pretend that I didn't say any of that?"

"You're under a lot of stress." Translation: He'd find a time to bring this up when he could be the unambiguous victim. But I let him wrap his arms around me and tuck my head against his chest. I held my hand curled awkwardly, my thumb throbbing, as he made soothing sounds and stroked my hair. "Come on. Let's drink. It'll solve all our problems."

I laughed a little, surrendering. I'd have a drink, and we wouldn't fight, and Stahl would stay dead, and the past would remain the past, and no one would ever have to know the truth.

Then I heard it—the faint *buzz, buzz, buzz*. My phone was ringing in my purse. I maneuvered past Mitch in the narrow hall and got to it on the last ring. Liv—really Liv this time.

"Hey," I said as soon as I picked up, Mitch trailing behind me.

"Naomi. I've been calling all day," Liv said, fretful. I could picture her perfectly, folded up in the corner of her couch, wrapping her long black hair around her finger. "Did you hear?"

"About Stahl? Yeah. I heard."

"I can't believe he's dead." She sounded far away.

"I know. Liv, hang on."

Mitch was standing too casually halfway across the room. I held up a *Just one minute* finger and slipped back through the hall into the bedroom, shutting the door behind me.

"Are you okay?" I asked quietly when the door was shut. If I was a mess, I couldn't imagine how Liv was holding up. "Have you talked to Cassidy?"

"A little. She texted. I haven't . . . I wanted to talk to you first," Liv said carefully.

"About Stahl?" I asked.

"No. Not exactly." She took a steadying breath. "I did something."

"Liv, you're kind of freaking me out," I told her. "What do you mean, you did something? What did you do?"

Her words sank through me, sharp and unforgiving. "I found Persephone."

I hadn't opened the box in years. Through several moves, assorted boyfriends and girlfriends, and three therapists, the box had remained in the back of one closet and then another, collecting stains and dents.

The corner of the lid had split, and my fingers came away dusty when I opened it. Most of the box was taken up with the quilt that the school had delivered to me in the hospital—a square of fabric from each of my fellow students and teachers, signed with get-well wishes. It smelled faintly of disinfectant, and there was a blood splotch dried to dull brown at one edge.

*I am sorry you got murdered,* Kayla Wilkerson had written. *Almost* was added in with a little caret.

There were cards, too. Some from the same classmates, some from locals, most from total strangers. They'd filled many more boxes than this, but after years of guiltily hanging on to all of them, I'd grabbed a fistful to keep and shoved the rest into trash bags, holding my breath the whole time.

Below the cards was the binder. I paged through, not really reading any of the articles. I knew them all by heart. There were photos, too, of me in the hospital and after. Some were snapshots, others professional, and in none of them did I recognize myself, even knowing it was me.

Toward the back was a photo of the three of us. It must have been on one of the days of the trial, given the somber way the other two were dressed: Cassidy in her polished Mary Janes and Liv in a dress with a lace collar—the same one she wore to church. I was wearing a faded Bugs Bunny T-shirt and jeans with holes in the knees. That meant that it was early on. Not long after, someone had pulled my dad aside and told him some of the money that had been flowing in—donations, money from the few interviews I did and the many my dad did—better go to getting me decent clothes. Cassidy's dad, Big Jim, was the one who made sure that it all got collected up in a trust, ensuring it went to my care and medical bills rather than Dad's twin habits of drinking and collecting broken junk.

We were smiling. Someone must have told us to, because I couldn't imagine us doing it spontaneously. Cassidy had the bright, practiced smile of the mayor's daughter, used to being photographed. Liv's smile was barely a tug at the corners of her mouth, her hands knotted together and her feet crossed at the ankle. She always had a vague look in the photos around that time. In the weeks after the attack she'd gone into her first major spiral, but they were still scrambling for a diagnosis and the meds weren't right yet, leaving her disconnected from herself.

And of course my smile was pitiable. My cheek was still bandaged up—presumably not from the original wound, but from one of the surgeries to attempt a repair to the damaged nerves and muscles, which had been at best semisuccessful. The downward pull of one side of my face had only served to make me seem more sympathetic. So did the wheelchair, which it would take me a few more months to go without consistently, mostly due to pain and sheer exhaustion.

Sometimes when I couldn't sleep I still counted them. Seventeen scars. Seventeen times the knife had plunged into me and slid back out again. I still could not understand how I had survived. People had told me over the years that I'd been blessed, brave, determined, fierce. I hadn't felt like any of those things. Survival had never even crossed my mind as a possibility or a concept. I'd crawled across the forest floor because in my blood loss–addled brain, I was trying to get away from the pain, like I could leave it behind if I got far enough.

One of the stab wounds had nicked the side of my heart, not quite puncturing the atrial wall. If it had been a millimeter deeper or farther to the right, I would have escaped the pain after all.

The door opened. Mitch crept in with a hangdog shuffle. "I'm sorry," he said, sinking down cross-legged beside me on the carpet. "You're right. I'm an asshole. Completely useless. Can you forgive me?"

"Okay," I said, and then I flashed him a quick smile. If I sounded half-hearted, he'd keep up the *Please forgive me* groveling as long as it took. "You're not useless, and you're not an asshole."

"Yes, I am. I'm a horrible boyfriend." He leaned his head against my shoulder. I sagged. I didn't have the energy to make him feel better right now, but if I didn't he would keep this up all night, berating him-self for his supposed failures.

"It's okay," I soothed. "You're so stressed out, and I shouldn't have snapped at you."

"I'm sorry," he said again. His fingertips trailed down my arm and played across my palm, and I shut my eyes. What was wrong with me? Mitch loved me. He wanted the best for me. Why couldn't I love him like I used to? "Who's Persephone?" Mitch asked.

I jerked, startled, and realized that Mitch was looking at my hand—at the bracelet wrapped around my fingers. It had been in the bottom of the box. I hadn't even known that I'd picked it up. It was simple: a discolored nylon string, knotted into a loop and strung with plastic alphabet beads that had faded and chipped until the letters were almost unreadable. But not quite.

"No one," I said. I tossed the bracelet back in the box, disturbed that I'd picked it up without noticing. *I can't tell you more. Not over the phone*, Liv had said.

"Then why do you have her bracelet?" he asked with a little laugh. "Let me guess. Elementary school crush. Your BFF. Your babysitter."

"I don't even know why that thing is in there," I said. I should have gotten rid of it a long time ago. I crammed the binder and the cards and the quilt back in the box. The things in that box were the very last possessions I'd taken with me when I left Chester. "Maybe I should throw it all out. Move on."

"You know, I don't think I've told you how fucking amazing you are," Mitch said. "You were eleven years old and you put a serial killer away. They had jack shit on Stahl without your testimony. You were a pint-sized badass, and I think holding on to things that celebrate that isn't a bad thing at all."

I shook my head. I hadn't been brave, just obedient—and terrified. Not of Stahl, but of failing. The police and the prosecutors and everyone else told me over and over again that I *had* to do it, that it was all on me.

We'd all identified Stahl, but there were questions about witness contamination with Liv and Cass. They'd given general descriptions right away, but they'd seen Stahl on the news before the official ID. I'd been unconscious during the televised arrest, untainted. So while all three of us testified, my words counted the most. I *had* to do it. Otherwise none of his victims would have justice, and he was an evil, evil man, and did I want him going free?

"I'm going to go home for a while," I said. I hadn't been certain until I spoke the words out loud.

"Home? You mean Chester? Why?"

"You know. See my dad. See Liv and Cassidy."

"That makes sense," he said, nodding. "Go back to the beginning. Full circle and all of that. Get some closure."

*What does that even mean, you found her?*

*I'll tell you, but only in person.*

*I'm not going back.*

*We owe it to her.*

"Closure. Yeah. Something like that."

We met on the first day of kindergarten. This was, of course, completely inevitable; Chester Elementary only had one class per grade. I was well aware when I sat down in the front row between Olivia Barnes and Cassidy Green that I was the moat between two opposing armies.

Cassidy's dad, Big Jim, was the mayor of Chester and owned the last operating mill in town. One of the last in the whole county, in fact. Chester was a town that still sported signs reading THIS HOME SUP-PORTED BY TIMBER DOLLARS, but increasingly those signs were a lie. The blame for this fell, fairly or not, on people like Marcus Barnes and his wife, Kimiko.

Kimiko was a biologist, Marcus an environmental lawyer, and be-tween the two of them they represented everything Chester hated. Af-ter they moved to town, they woke up one morning to find a spotted owl, neck broken, dumped on their doorstep. They'd had their tires slashed while they were eating at the family restaurant in town, and Kimiko had fielded more than one racist and obscene call.

The truth was that by the time they arrived the era of plenty was over for the logging industry in the Pacific Northwest. The Olympic National Forest belonged to the owls, whether Chester liked it or not, and it wasn't Marcus and Kimiko Barnes who'd made that happen. But the grief and fear of a dying town didn't care about logic. Liv started that first day already an outcast.

Nobody hated me or my family the way they hated hers, but I was almost as much of an outsider as she was. I was the girl with divorced parents. The girl with holes in her clothes and a stale smell. Mom was a floozy who'd walked out and Dad was a lazy drunk who could barely hold down a part-time job at the bar, and no one expected me to turn out any better.

Of all the kids in Chester, Liv and I were the least likely to be friends with the mayor's daughter. But for some reason, Cassidy Green took one look at us and, much to her parents' consternation, decided that we were going to be best friends. Come recess she declared that we would play with her, and we were too stunned to protest. The adults tried to intervene, refusing transportation to playdates and lecturing Cassidy on her responsibilities as the mayor's daughter to keep good company, but they were too late—Cass had claimed us.

Soon enough our friendship turned downright feral. Forbid us to see each other and we'd spit and claw and sneak out into the woods until our parents relented. Eventually, they gave up trying to keep us apart. Cassidy was like that. She got an idea into her head and it took her over. Once Cassidy Green was fixed on a thing, there wasn't a force in the world that could dissuade her.

I might have been the one who discovered Persephone, but Cassidy was the one who made her ours.

---

I'd agreed to meet Liv and Cass at ten a.m., which meant stealing out of the apartment before Mitch woke up—an added bonus, given how things had gone last night. It had started with his suggestion that he come with me to "document" my return to Chester, and quickly turned into the fight I'd been trying to avoid. I'd said some vicious things— some I'd meant and some I'd said just to wound him. He'd laid out every one of my transgressions in return.

And now I'd left. I hadn't actually said the words—said that I was leaving *him*. But I knew I wouldn't be going back. I rolled into town feeling untethered. I wasn't sure if that was a good thing. Mitch and I hadn't been right for each other, but I'd never been good at being alone.

In the years since I'd left, Chester had been transformed, but you wouldn't know it driving through town—at least, not until you looked closely. The shops were the same—except that the grocery store displayed antiques in the front window, hoping to scrape together a few extra bucks each month, and the café was themed after a briefly popular but now-forgotten movie that had filmed nearby. The general store advertised rain ponchos for the hikers and campers who hadn't taken "rainforest" literally enough while they were packing, and there were national park passes in the windows of most of the cars parked on Main Street.

When we were growing up, Cass would have laughed at you if you suggested that she would end up living in Chester as an adult. Turned out the joke was on her, but as far as I could tell, she was happy. She opened the door in a flour-smudged apron with earbuds dangling from one ear. When she spotted me her face broke into a flat-out grin, and before I could even tense up she'd crushed me in a hug.

"Naomi! You're early," she declared, popping back and letting me catch my breath. "You look amazing."

I looked like a herked-up hairball. She looked like something out of a home and garden magazine, with her platinum hair swept up and her makeup immaculate. The apron was protecting a satiny maroon blouse and slacks. I wondered if she had a business meeting or if she always looked like this now.

"I made better time than I was expecting. I hope it's not a problem," I said.

She flapped a hand. "Don't worry about it. Here, follow me in, I've got cookies about to come out. Oh, take your shoes off at the door."

I obeyed, leaving them next to a neat line of pumps and walking shoes and cute little flats sized for a child. How old would Amanda be now? Eight, nine? Cass had gotten pregnant her senior year of college—

she and I turned out to have similar coping strategies, but I was luckier with birth control.

Senior year of college—crap, Amanda was almost twelve. Where had the years gone?

The house was pristine. Fresh flowers decorated the mantel. The photos were framed and arrayed with precision. There was a formal portrait of mother and daughter for each year, Amanda growing into a little carbon copy of her mom, a phenotypical rebuke of the father who'd never bothered to even send a Christmas card.

Cass had removed the cookies and set the tray aside to cool by the time I reached the kitchen. "Bake sale at school," she explained. She waved me toward one of the stools at the kitchen island, which looked like stylish steel spikes and were roughly as comfortable.

"Let me guess. You're the head of the PTA," I said, not sure if this was a compliment or a tease. Maybe both.

She wrinkled her nose. "God, no. I don't have the time. The lodge eats up every spare minute and then some. And we're wrapping up wedding season, which means I'm running around like a chicken with my head cut off. This weekend's father of the bride calls me three times a day, I swear. Complete control freak."

"Kindred spirit?" I asked teasingly. I'd handled my share of that kind of client. Even for Cass, once, back when she was pushing me to be the lodge's dedicated wedding photographer. It would have been a great source of income, but I couldn't handle that many return trips to Chester.

The nose wrinkle returned. "Oh, hush."

"I'm sorry, did you just say 'Oh, hush'?" I asked, an incredulous laugh rasping in my throat.

She snorted. "It's possible I've been doing this hospitality thing too long."

"When's the last time you said 'fuck'?" I asked her. "Come to think of it, when's the last time you *actually* . . ." I waggled my eyebrows at her.

"Too fucking long," she said, the old Cass breaking through with a grin. She busied herself cleaning up after her baking, neatly stacking tubs of flour and sugar, wiping every last speck off the granite countertops. She'd polished away her rough edges when she took over the lodge—turning it from a failing, structurally questionable relic of another decade into a thriving luxury getaway. But in a way, that was who Cass had been all along: she committed herself completely to the things she decided to care about, even if that meant transforming herself.

Once upon a time, I had been her project. Her mission in life had become getting me to graduation alive and relatively whole, and I wouldn't have managed it without her. Part of me was jealous of this life that had her full attention, now.

"So. Do you know what this is about?" Cass asked.

"Liv didn't tell you?"

"All she said was that it was important," Cass replied.

I hesitated. It seemed strange that Liv would tell me and not Cass—but then, I wouldn't have come to Chester if she hadn't. "Maybe we should wait for Liv to get here."

"Naomi." Cass gave me a level look. "I need to know what I'm about to get into. If this is one of Liv's delusions—"

"It isn't," I said, with confidence I didn't entirely feel. Liv's meds kept her even-keeled most of the time, but they weren't a guarantee.

"You're sure."

I shrugged. "You know Liv."

She sighed and swept a few crumbs off the counter into her cupped palm. "Better than anyone. Come on. I don't deserve to get blindsided, whatever it is."

I ran my finger along the scar that skated down the inside of my left wrist. That one didn't belong to Stahl. It belonged to Persephone.

"Liv said she found her," I said quietly.

"Who?" Cassidy asked. I didn't answer. Cassidy hissed out a breath. She didn't need me to say it out loud. "What the hell does that mean, she found her?"

I lifted a shoulder. "You know how she is about giving details on the phone."

"Because the NSA is definitely interested in Olivia Barnes's private conversations," Cass said in a biting tone and then shook her head like she regretted the words immediately. I couldn't blame her for being frustrated. I'd said worse, at times. "I thought this was about Stahl. About coming together to mark the occasion. If I'd known—"

"We should hear her out," I said.

"This isn't the time for this," she said. "Come on, now? When everyone's already talking about Stahl? And that podcast guy in town—"

"What podcast guy?" I asked, mystified.

She looked surprised. "He hasn't called you? I figured you'd be at the top of the list. He's doing one of those serious true-crime things. It's about Stahl—or one of the episodes is about Stahl, or something like that. I didn't really listen because I didn't give him the time of day. He's talking to all sorts of people, though."

"You'll write a whole book about it, but you won't give an interview?" I asked dryly.

Just when it looked like interest was fading, the Book had come along. Purportedly the first-person account of the attack constructed through extensive interviews with the three brave girls at the center of the case. Of the three of us, the author had actually only talked to Cass, but that fact didn't end up on the book jacket.

"You know that was my parents' idea, not mine," she said. "It's not like it was exactly pleasant for me to relive it all, either." She picked at a dried fleck of something on the countertop, not meeting my eyes.

I looked down at my hands. Sometimes I was glad that I was the one who had been attacked. People understood my trauma. It left its marks clearly visible on my skin. But Liv and Cass having to watch, forcing themselves to stay silent and hidden—that was worse, in some ways.

The doorbell rang. Cass jumped. "I'll get it," I offered, already sliding off the stool. I padded back down the hallway, time receding through the photographs as Amanda got younger, disappeared. I could see Liv's blurred outline through the frosted glass by the door. She was looking out at the street, shifting her weight nervously.

I opened the door, and she whirled around as if shocked that anyone had answered. Her dark brown eyes were wide and startled. She had her father's strong jaw and her mother's black hair, which tended toward frizz. She broke into a smile. "You came," she said.

"I told you I would," I reminded her, gently chiding.

I hesitated, unsure if she would welcome my touch. She stepped in, and I put my arms around her gingerly, finding myself taking inventory—thin, but not quite gaunt. Restless, but with a steady, clear gaze when she pulled back. Her nails weren't ragged and she hadn't been picking at her lips, which was rare for her. The tension I'd been carrying around in my shoulders eased just a bit.

"You look good," I told her, and meant it.

She grimaced. "You mean I don't look crazy."

"No, I mean you look like you're taking care of yourself. And you don't always, so you don't get to be annoyed when I notice."

"As opposed to how you always take perfect care of yourself?" she asked, giving me a skeptical look.

"Oh, shut up," I told her, and she laughed, her chin tilting up to bare her long neck, eyes flashing. She was beautiful in these moments, our Olivia.

"Liv! I feel like I haven't seen you in *ages*," Cass declared when we made it back to the kitchen, and I caught her giving Olivia the same appraising once-over that I had. She swept in for a hug, neatly plucking Liv from my side. "How does this keep happening when we live practically next door to each other? Can I get the two of you anything? Water? Have you eaten?"

Her voice was too bright, her smile too wide. Her anxiety thrummed behind the words. My own nerves were strained, ready to snap, but we both knew better than to push Liv. It would only make her shut down.

"Nothing, thank you," Olivia said. She bit her lip, fingers fidgeting with the seam of her jeans.

"Why don't we all sit down, and you can tell us what this is about," I said gently.

Olivia took one of the stools, and I sat next to her. Cass stood on the other side of the island, arms crossed loosely. I could tell she was restraining the urge to go into mother hen mode—she'd always been protective of us, the first to step up when we needed rescuing. Between the two of us, we'd kept her busy over the years.

Olivia took a breath. She ran her hands over each other as she talked, her tone animated and excited. "I know that we've all tried to put what happened that summer behind us," she started. "There are things we haven't talked about. And I understand why we couldn't. But that's changed, hasn't it? Stahl is dead now. He won't—he can't—get out." She faltered and looked up at us.

I put my hand over Liv's, wordlessly urging her to continue. She tucked her hair nervously behind her ears and pushed up her glasses, a tic that made her seem for an instant like she was eleven again.

"I started looking for her three years ago," Olivia said, speaking rapidly. "At first I couldn't find anything. But a few months ago I got lucky. I found her. I found Persephone." She looked at us triumphantly.

"What is there to find?" Cass asked roughly. "She's right where we left her."

"That's not what I mean," Olivia said, shaking her head rapidly. "I— I—"

"You found out who she was," I said. Olivia nodded, grateful, and smiled.

Cass scrubbed at that same spot on the granite with the side of her thumb. Her jaw was so tight a tendon flared. "We shouldn't be talking about this."

Olivia's smile collapsed into a small frown. "She has a family. People who have been looking for her. They deserve to know what happened to—"

"*Stop*," Cass said, looking up abruptly. Her eyes were bright with unspent tears. "Stop. We agreed we wouldn't talk about it. About her. Not ever."

"We were *eleven*," I said. Eleven, and terrified of what would happen to us if we told anyone about Persephone. It wasn't just about people finding out that we'd kept her a secret. There was the trial, too.

The police and the prosecutors had hammered it into us: if the jury had any reason to think we were wrong, if we gave the defense any way to make us seem unreliable, Stahl would get away with what he'd done—to me, and to all those women. I remembered being convinced that if we made a single mistake, he would get out and he would come after us. I'd had nightmares for years, waking up certain he was in my room, about to finish me off.

If they'd known the truth about Persephone, they would have thought we were strange, wicked little beasts—and we were. What little girl isn't? Of course we'd kept quiet.

We'd never told a soul about what lay in the woods, about those beautiful bones.

"We owe her," Olivia said stubbornly.

"We don't owe her a thing. We didn't have anything to do with . . ." Cass gestured broadly. "Any of that."

"Which means there's no reason not to tell," I pointed out, though my stomach was clenched with dread. I didn't want to know Persephone's name. I didn't want to know who she had been.

Cass bit her lip. "It's been over two decades. If anyone was waiting for Persephone to come home, they've given up by now. Is it really going to help anyone, after all these years?"

"Wouldn't you want to know? What if Amanda was the one who'd gone missing?" Olivia asked.

Cass covered her eyes with her hand. "Fuck. Of course I would. But, Liv, it's not that simple. What do you think Amanda's life is going to be like if this comes out? It would ruin me. People aren't going to want to hold their business retreat at a lodge owned by a woman who hid a *body* for twenty years. And good luck booking any weddings, Naomi."

"It's not going to be like that," Olivia said, tone turning desperate.

"God, I sound awful. Worrying about money, when . . ." Cass's voice choked off. "But seriously, Liv. What do you think happens when people start asking questions? I don't think any of us wants the world to know *exactly* what happened in those woods. Or after," she added softly, pinning me with a level look.

"Maybe it's time they did," I replied, voice hollow.

Her calm fractured. "Of course you're in favor of just blowing everything up. You're never the one who has to stick around to clean up the mess."

"What's that supposed to mean?"

"It means you've never tried to fix anything in your life. You just break it and leave," Cass said. There was a prickly anger in her voice that left my skin feeling raw. "You left us behind. Amanda doesn't even remember you."

"Can you blame her for wanting to get away?" Olivia asked.

"We were kids. People have shit in their childhoods. The point is to move past it," Cass said.

"Yeah, you've definitely moved past it. We're what, two blocks from your parents' old place?" I asked, my temper flaring to match hers.

"Better to be living with a shitty boyfriend and taking photos of people who are happier than you'll ever be?"

"Fuck off, Cass."

"You too, Naomi."

We glared at each other. Then she laughed, wagging her head. "It is so damn easy to fight with you. Always has been."

I let out a strained chuckle of my own. We'd scrapped constantly as kids, too. Quick to fight and quick to get over it. Even back then, my instinct had been to lash out and run at the slightest provocation, and Cass was always the one who hunted me down so we could patch things up.

Cass straightened up and walked over to the counter, plucking a half-empty bottle of white wine from its spot. "I'm drinking. Who's with me?" I glanced at the clock. Barely 10:15.

"Cass—" Olivia started.

"Well, I'm not drinking *alone*," she said, and took down glasses for all of us. She set them out and poured a splash into each. She took a sip from hers, shut her eyes, and stood there with the glass hovering an inch from her mouth. Then she opened her eyes, and they were clear and calm. "Listen, Liv. I understand what you're doing—I do. Really. It's not right, leaving her out there. But you've been thinking about this for years. We've only had a few minutes. Give us some time to catch up, okay?"

"I—" Olivia began.

"We need time to figure things out," Cass insisted. She glanced pointedly over at me, looking for backup. "We have to think about the consequences."

I took a swallow of my wine. Liv was right—it was long past time to tell someone about Persephone. Someone out there had to be looking for her. Mourning her.

But this wasn't something to do on a whim. We needed time to think.

*I* needed time to think. Because Cass was right—I didn't want people asking too many questions about that day in the woods. Persephone was a secret we all shared, but I had my own secrets, too.

"Please," Olivia said, her eyes fixed on her lap. There was an ache in my chest. I couldn't get a full breath.

"Let's just take a beat here," I said, hating myself for it. "Cass is right. We need to make sure we're going into this clear-eyed."

Olivia gave a tiny nod. She'd closed in on herself.

Cass sighed. "I'm sorry, Liv. You sprang this on us, and . . . and maybe you're right, and it's time. But if we decide to do this, let's be *smart* about it. I can make some calls, and we can talk to a lawyer, and at least make sure we wouldn't be opening ourselves up to some kind of liability. Okay?"

"Okay." It was barely a sound, it was so quiet. She lifted her eyes to the level of the counter, and even that seemed like a monumental effort.

Guilt worked its slick way through my gut. "Do you want to know her name?"

"No," Cass said immediately, and I was glad. Because neither did I. I wanted her to stay Persephone. Stay a myth, a story. Stay our secret. The instant she had a name, we'd have to admit that she was a person.

That she was more than the bones we'd found in the forest, and the magic we'd made from them.

We talked about inconsequential things after that. Cass's daughter, Amanda; the lodge; my work. Cass and I kept up the conversation while Liv sat silently, picking at the skin at the base of her thumb. Finally I put my hand on her arm.

"I should probably get going," I said. "Liv, can I give you a lift home?"

"Already?" Cass asked, more out of obligation than anything. We were all eager to call the strained gathering to a close.

"I'm wiped from that drive, and I should really drop by and see my dad," I said.

"We'll talk soon," Cass promised, and enveloped us each in a hug before letting us go. She kept her hand on my arm a moment longer than she needed to, giving me a look that I knew well. The *Make sure Liv's okay* look. She squeezed my arm one last time before letting me go.

Liv trailed along after me and got into the passenger seat without comment. She sat there, picking at that patch of dried skin. Liv didn't drive. It wasn't that she couldn't; she just hated it. She was a common sight on the side of the road around Chester, walking on the shoulder with her head down and her thoughts a million miles away.

I started up the engine. "I'm sorry," I said.

"For what?" she asked.

I shrugged. "For all of it."

"I know you don't want to lose business, but—"

"That's not what this is about," I said. It hadn't even entered in. I supposed I should have been worried about the impact it might have on my work, my sole source of income, but my reputation had always been made by things beyond my control. The idea that I had a say in any of it seemed faintly absurd.

"Then why?" Liv asked.

I took a left up the gravel road toward Liv's place and didn't answer at first. "That day, in the woods. The day I . . ."

"I know what day," Olivia said gently, saving me from having to finish the sentence.

"You saw Stahl." I said it like it wasn't a question. Like I didn't need the answer.

"So did you," she said, a small line appearing between her brows.

"Right," I replied, more sigh than sound. "Right. Of course."

The fingers of her right hand dug into the biceps of her opposite arm. She stared out at the trees, grown wilder in my absence. The town of our youth was being swallowed up by the forest it had tried to tame. "We need to do this," she whispered.

I pulled up in front of the metal gate that blocked the end of Marcus and Kimiko's drive. Discreet solar panels perched on top of the posts, and there was a pad to enter the combination. Back when we were kids it had been a chain and a padlock holding the gate shut, and Marcus would sit up most nights in the front room with his gun on his lap. Things had calmed down since then, but the habit of paranoia remained.

Once that fear was in your body, that knowledge that someone wanted you dead, it never entirely left.

The car idled. I knew I should tell Liv that she was right. We'd kept this secret long enough. But I was exhausted—from the drive, from the argument, and from years of knowing that every time Liv's name appeared on my phone there was a fifty-fifty chance of a crisis. She was stuck in this place where she needed me, but she wouldn't let me be there for her.

There was nothing left in me to give. Not today.

I touched her wrist lightly. It was the only way I ever touched Liv—carefully, afraid that she would run. Afraid that we would break.

There was something dark and strange in her eyes, more like anger than sorrow but not properly either. "I'll be here tomorrow," I said, ritual words I'd spoken many times before.

"So will I," she answered. We'd ended a thousand calls like that—with a promise. It wasn't *Never again*, but it was *Not today*, and we could string those days along one after another, a procession of sunrises we'd held on long enough to see.

I withdrew my hand. She gave a little shiver, and we sat for a moment, silent. "You want me to drive you all the way up?" I asked.

She shook her head. "I could use the walk." She opened the door and stepped out, unfolding her long limbs one by one, taking care with each movement like she didn't quite know how to live in her own skin. She paused, her hand on the door. "I love you, Naomi," she said, with the same deliberation.

"I love you, too," I told her, hanging the words on a smile she didn't return. She pushed the door shut and walked to the gate, slinging herself over it in a few practiced movements. I watched after her until she rounded the bend and disappeared among the trees.

The truth could hold until tomorrow, I told myself. We could have the questionable comfort of our secrets for a few more hours.

---

Dad lived outside of town, in the house where I'd grown up and where he'd grown up before me. It'd always been a wreck. My grandfather's sole talents had been cutting down trees, collecting crap, and ignoring his kids. Dad ended up with two out of the three and not the one that brought in a paycheck, so the place had only gotten worse over the years, especially after Mom took off—fed up with him and with me and with a town too stubborn to realize it was already dead.

A rusted-out Chevy Impala had joined the herd in the front yard. The piles of scrap metal, busted string trimmers, cracked bathtubs, and bent bicycles—all things he was going to get around to fixing up and

selling any day now—had crept out another foot or so toward the prop-
erty line, but otherwise it was the same old house.

The police car parked in the drive was new, though: a black SUV
with CHESTER POLICE DEPARTMENT emblazoned on the side. The
Chester Police weren't infrequent visitors to our place—they'd show
up every few weeks after Dad got drunk and drove into a mailbox, or I
got busted for shoplifting or fighting or minor acts of vandalism.

I parked off to the side as the front door opened. A short Black
woman in a Chester PD jacket stepped out. When she spotted me she
stepped off the porch and lifted a hand in a wave. I made my way over
with a sinking sensation.

"Are you Naomi Shaw?" she asked as I got close. She was even
shorter than I'd expected, but she looked like she could bench-press
three of me.

"Cunningham," I corrected her.

"I see," she said, eyes tracking to my scar. "I've just been talking to
your father."

"My sympathies," I said. "What's going on? Did he do something?"

"More like he didn't do anything," she said. "This is the third time
I've been up here and the third time he's promised me he's working on
clearing this place out so that it's habitable. I haven't seen any progress,
and it's past the point where I can turn a blind eye. Things have got to
improve. Rapidly."

"Good luck with that," I said, rocking back on my heels with my
hands in my back pockets. "That house has been a disaster for decades."

"It's dangerous," she said. "There are no clear walkways. If emergency services needed to get in to help him, they wouldn't be able to."

It wasn't that bad—was it? I hadn't actually seen the inside of that
house in what, five years? Last time I was here it was a junk heap, but
you could get around.

"So, what? Is it going to get condemned? I only ask because whatever he tells me, it's not going to be the whole truth, and I'd like to

know what I'm dealing with." I kept my tone casual. I felt like a pump-kin getting its guts scooped out by hand, fingernails rasping against my insides. This was going to happen sooner or later. But as long as it had been *later*, we could both ignore it. Could get along, in our own way, each of us steadfastly ignoring the other's sins.

"I haven't done anything official yet, but it needs to be cleared out at least enough to make sure there isn't any structural damage, and so that emergency response could get in if he got hurt or there was a fire. I told him I could give him thirty days before I had to report it."

"That's generous of you." I had a month to deal with it, then.

"That was three weeks ago."

"Of course it was." I raked back my hair, looking up at the cloud-scabbed sky. I couldn't deal with this. Not right now.

"Let me give you my card," she said, more gently this time. "I can get you some numbers, people to call. You can still get the place fixed up, but he'll need somewhere to stay in the meantime. With you, or—"

I laughed. She looked taken aback. "Trust me, no one wants that. I'll figure something out." It was more a statement of hope than fact. The idea of prying Dad out of this house wasn't an appealing one.

"It's not safe for him to stay here," she said firmly, underlining the point, and there was that look I knew—the *How could you let this hap-pen?* look.

"It wasn't always that bad," I said, gripped by the need to explain. "It was always a disaster, but it was livable. I don't come to Chester much. I didn't know . . ."

"Can't really blame you for not wanting to come back to the area too often," she said.

"You didn't live here back then, did you?" I asked.

She shook her head. "I'm more of a city girl. My wife wanted to live in the woods, though, so here we are. I've heard all the stories, of course."

"The ones where I get stabbed a bunch, or the ones where I'm an unrepentant delinquent?"

"Bit of both," she confessed. "I'll leave you be. You give me a call if there's anything I can help you with here."

I nodded. "Thanks," I said, checking her card, "Officer . . ."

"Chief," she corrected. "Bishop."

My eyebrows shot up. "Chief? What happened to Miller?"

"Retired, six months ago," she said, weight set back on her heels as she watched for my reaction. "Mayor Green and the city council brought me in from the sheriff's office."

I'd always figured when Chief Miller finally crumbled to dust, Bill Dougherty would inherit the job out of sheer inertia. He'd been Miller's number two almost as long as I could remember. Of course, Dougherty was the moral and intellectual equivalent of an untoasted marshmallow, so I could only assume Bishop was an upgrade.

"Welcome to Chester, then," I said genuinely, and she gave me a nod.

"Ms. Cunningham. Have a good day," she said, and marched off to her car. I tucked her card in my back pocket and turned to face the door, fighting the urge to get in my car and drive straight back to Seattle. Forget the house. Forget everything. Let bones stay buried and secrets unspoken.

Bishop's car crunched away down the road. I made my way up the steps.

Dad hadn't locked the door. Never did. Even after what had happened to me, he'd never shaken the belief that bad things just didn't happen in a town like Chester. The day he had to lock his door, he'd tell me, was the day he'd find a good rope and a strong beam and put himself out of his misery.

I pushed open the door, not yet stepping over the threshold. I knew exactly where Dad would be: in his chair, magazines stacked four feet high beside him, an avalanche of boxes, busted shelves, books, and God-knew-what filling every bit of the living room apart from a narrow path to the chair and sightlines to the TV.

Only there wasn't a path to the armchair. In a couple places the mustard-brown carpet showed through, but newspapers, magazines, Tupperware, and random detritus I couldn't identify covered most of it. The house smelled rank, like something had died in here. For a minute I was afraid it was Dad, until I remembered that Bishop had just talked to him.

"Dad?" I called, hovering in the doorway. Indistinct shifting and settling marked his movement, but it was a long time before he actually appeared. I was still unprepared when he emerged from the warren and we stood face-to-face.

He'd gotten old. Obviously he'd gotten older, but I hadn't expected that he'd get *old*. He'd withered like a dead beetle drying out in the sun. His hair had receded, baring flaky, red skin, and he stood canted like he was trying to find an angle that didn't ache. He wore a T-shirt and flannel pajama pants, both of them faded but relatively clean.

He looked me up and down with his pale, watery eyes and grunted. "Didn't know you were in town."

"Good to see you, too, Dad," I replied. I swallowed. "You going to invite me in?"

"No," he said. I crossed my arms; he grunted again. "Suit yourself." He backed up, because there wasn't room to step aside. I followed him into the gloom. He took a right, weaving his way between stacks of plastic grocery bags. I didn't know what was in them. I could only hope it wasn't perishable food.

"What are you here for?" he asked.

"Checking in on you," I said, balancing on one foot as I stepped over a spilled pile of magazines.

"Still alive, aren't I?" he asked.

"I crossed paths with Chief Bishop just now."

"Nice lady," he said, pausing to look at me. "Wants to evict me. Put me in a home."

I raised an eyebrow. "I can't imagine why."

"Sarcasm. That's all you've got," he muttered. "Are you here to tell me I've got to clean this place up? Because I've already heard it." He lurched his way toward the kitchen. I followed apprehensively.

I braced myself, ready for mold and rat droppings, but it wasn't as far gone as I'd feared. The stove had two burners clear, and there was enough room to maneuver. It smelled stale like the rest of the house but not foul, which suggested he wasn't keeping rotten food around.

"Clear off a chair, then," he said, gesturing vaguely at the kitchen table, which was buried beneath canned food and unopened cleaning supplies. The chairs were stacked with plastic cutlery and disposable plates and bowls. A line of full trash bags stood by the back door, ready to go out, a few flies zipping around them.

"I'm good standing," I said. I didn't really want to touch anything in here. "She said she warned you three weeks ago you had to get this taken care of."

"What's to take care of? It's my house, I live in it. Shouldn't be anyone else's business," he said. "You want a beer?"

"No, I don't want a beer. It's barely eleven," I said, deciding not to mention the wine I'd had already. He shoved aside a teetering pile of canned chili to get at the fridge. The cans tipped, banging to the floor and rolling everywhere.

"Jesus Christ, Dad. How can you live like this?" I asked.

"I do just fine," he said, extracting a can of beer with great discernment despite the fact that there was only one brand in the fridge. "And why do you care, anyway?"

"I care," I said, anger turning the words into a snap of teeth.

"I didn't ask *if* you cared, I asked *why*," he barked back.

I stared at him. He stared at me. It was always like this. He'd never once raised a hand to me, but we couldn't stop ourselves tearing into each other. When he was around and conscious, which wasn't often.

Anyone would have had a hard time knowing how to help a scared, wounded girl or the scared, angry teenager she turned into. Maybe Dad had never had a chance, but he hadn't even tried. The only emotion that got any reaction from him was anger, and so I'd clung to it. At least if we were fighting, it meant he was paying attention.

"You're my father," I said. "I care. Can't help it, apparently, and God knows I've tried."

He popped the tab on his beer and took a long sip. "I don't need charity."

"You need help," I said. "You can't clear this place out on your own. Please, Dad. Let me call someone, or—"

"What, you want to pay someone to take all my stuff? Throw it out like it's garbage?"

"It is garbage," I said, and knew immediately it was a mistake. There'd been the tiniest sliver of light under that door, but now it slammed shut.

"It's good stuff. Just needs some fixing up. Organizing," he said.

"It's not—" I stopped. There was no point. There had never been any point, any of the times I'd tried. "They're going to make you leave. You won't have a choice."

"We'll see," he said. "What are you doing back here, anyway? You didn't just come to see me."

"Cass and Liv and I wanted to get together," I said, letting the subject change, knowing it was the same as admitting defeat. "Mark the occasion, that kind of thing."

"You mean Stahl dying. Yeah, I heard about that. Cancer. Huh." He said it like he was commenting on the weather.

I made a sound of disbelief. "That's all you've got? The guy who almost killed your daughter is dead, and you've got 'Huh.'"

He took another swallow and sat with it a moment. "I'm glad if it gives you some kind of peace. That's something you've had in short supply. So I suppose I'm grateful he's dead."

I didn't know what I'd expected. Some sign, at least, that he gave a shit about what had happened to me. But it had always seemed like he just didn't understand what the big deal was. I wasn't dead. The wounds healed. Why was everyone still making a fuss about it?

"It was good to see you, Dad," I said through gritted teeth. "We should do this again sometime."

"See? Sarcasm. No variety," Dad said. His laugh had a raspy rattle to it. "Is that all you wanted? To give me a hard time and go?"

"Apparently."

"You need a place to stay?"

"I'm good," I told him. I started to leave, stopped. "I . . . I'll come back tomorrow, okay? Before I leave town."

"Don't go out of your way for me," he said. He turned his back on me, shuffling over to one of the leaning piles of food. He started pawing through it. "There's a stack of mail for you by the front door. Get it on your way out. It'd be easier to clean if I didn't have your crap around here, too."

I sighed. "Yeah. I'll do that." I picked my way out of the kitchen. How was I supposed to help someone who didn't want my help? It wasn't like he'd ever done a thing for me, other than not kick me out. I didn't owe him a goddamn thing. Except that he was my dad.

I stood in the doorway, trying to figure out which pile of stuff was supposed to be mine. Finally I spotted it under an unopened Amazon package: a stack of mail two inches deep. Probably a few months' worth.

"Yeah, my mail was definitely the problem. The rest will be a breeze," I muttered. Most of it looked like credit card offers and other junk, but near the bottom of the stack there was one hand-addressed envelope. Probably "fan mail." Someone who'd heard my story on a podcast and wanted to tell me how inspiring I was or explain their pet theories about the case. I stalked out to the car and threw the mail in the passenger seat, and then sat with my head against the wheel, remembering how to breathe again. "Fuck," I said at last, and started the engine.

I held on to my anger all the way back into town.

I still hadn't had anything to eat all day, so I parked myself at the café, with its dubious Wi-Fi connection and endless coffee refills. I found myself a seat in the back, ordered a soup and sandwich, and pulled out my laptop to work on editing last weekend's wedding.

Time fell away from me, as it often did when I got into the rhythm of editing. It was hours later that I remembered to look at the clock—and to straighten my shoulders and stretch my aching back.

I stuffed a twenty in the tip jar on my way out as compensation for camping out for so long and went to get a room at the Chester Motel. It didn't have bedbugs and did have cable, which made it the Chester equivalent of the Four Seasons, at least until you got as far out as the lodge.

I checked my phone when I got into the room in case I had a message from Liv or Cass, but there were just a bunch of texts from Mitch. Wondering where I was. Being pointedly not upset that I'd sneaked out before dawn.

I had *told* him I was leaving for Chester. Just hadn't mentioned when. Plus, we'd broken up. My whereabouts weren't his business anymore.

I deleted the texts and collapsed back on the bed. Without the work to distract me, my mind thrashed its way inevitably back to the things I least wanted to think about. What were we going to do about Persephone?

It was like a bullet left in a body. The flesh had healed around it; digging it out would cause more damage than leaving it. Stahl dying had sparked new interest in our story, but that would be fleeting; the story belonged to the past. This would be different.

I wished I didn't care—that I could be like Liv and want only for Persephone to find her way home.

But why should she be able to leave the woods, when I never had?

---

I woke up an hour later, jolting out of the recursive chase my mind had concocted—monsters in the forest, a trail that looped and twisted and plunged. My mouth was dry, my head fuzzy. I felt like deer jerky that had been in a hot glove box for a week, and my mouth tasted about the same. And of course I hadn't remembered to pack a toothbrush.

I combed my hair into a semblance of respectability and walked the hundred yards to the gas station shop next door to find myself a toothbrush. The inside of the Corner Store looked exactly the same as it had when we were kids, simultaneously overcrowded and understocked all at once, with bumper stickers indicating a less than progressive political stance plastered over every inch of the front counter.

The string of bells over the door jingled as I entered, and Marsha Brassey, who'd gained about fifty years of wrinkles in the past two decades, looked up from her Sudoku and pressed a hand over her heart.

"My goodness, if it isn't Naomi Shaw," she said.

"It's Cunningham now, Marsha," I corrected with strained patience, tired of saying it.

"Oh, that's right. I'm sorry—getting dotty in my old age," Marsha said, flapping a hand helplessly.

"Tell you what, I'll let it slide as long as you never make me pay off my Snickers tab."

She reached over to the candy rack and grabbed a bar to waggle in my direction. "I wouldn't dream of it."

I took it with a smile, like I didn't remember her smacking my backside with a broom for even looking too long at the candy she knew I didn't have the money to buy. Every bad thing that had ever been said about me dissolved like sugar in water when I turned into a miracle. When Chester suddenly decided that after a childhood of being on the outside, I belonged to them.

"What brings you back to town?" Marsha asked as I worked my way down the aisles, grabbing the toiletries I'd left behind.

"Just visiting folks," I said over my shoulder.

"You been up to see your dad yet?" she asked, all sweet like she wasn't just salivating for a bit of gossip.

"That I have, Marsha," I said, bringing my purchases up to the counter. "I'm doing what I can, but you know him."

"Stubborn runs in the family," she said wisely as she rang me up. "Shame to see the place so run-down."

I choked on a laugh. "It was a piece of shit when Grandpa built it, Marsha. I wouldn't waste any grief over it." She tutted.

The bell over the door rang again, and a man in a denim jacket and red flannel shirt stepped in. He was tall and rangy, with hair that fell to his jaw. Sharp features and deep-set eyes gave him a hawkish look.

His eyes caught on mine and widened, and I started to arrange my features in the neutral-but-friendly expression I'd practiced, the one that was the closest to a smile I could manage without unsettling people. And then I recognized him.

"Naomi?" he said. Cody Benham's voice was rougher and deeper than I remembered it, but I couldn't believe I hadn't recognized him the second I saw him.

"Cody," I replied, and the past that had been lapping at my heels like surf on the beach hooked me into its undertow.

Cody and Cass's brother, Oscar, had been best friends. Oscar was the golden boy, Cody the bad influence. Most of the time, he ignored us—our occasional presence the irritating price to pay for Oscar's company. Now and then, though, he'd give us a stick of gum and a "Hey, kid," and he'd seemed so impossibly cool and aloof I'd have done anything to earn those scraps of approval.

Hitting the other side of forty hadn't harmed his good looks, I noted.

"You come back to see Liv and Cass?" he asked.

"Seemed about time," I answered.

"Because of Stahl, right?"

"What about that bastard?" Marsha asked. "What'd he do now?"

"Don't you read the paper? 'That bastard' died," Cody said, hands jammed in his pockets and eyes fixed on me.

"Praise the Lord," Marsha declared. "Congratulations. Or is that not what you say?"

"Under the circumstances, I think congratulations are in order," Cody said, but I could only shake my head, the tiniest of movements. He looked at me steadily, and the genial expression I'd stitched to my face faltered. "Are you free? We could grab a drink, catch up. It's been ages, and honestly, a drink with an old friend is exactly what I need right now."

Old friend? It wasn't how I'd have described it. He was twenty-two the summer he found me in the woods, twice my age, and he'd left town before I graduated high school. But maybe whatever we'd been to each other had turned into friendship in the gap, growing up with or without us.

I shrugged. "I don't have any plans." And being alone with my thoughts hadn't treated me well so far today.

"Try not to sound so enthusiastic," he said with a glint of amusement in his eye. "I promise, I'm much better company than I used to be."

I chuckled obligingly, but I'd always liked Cody's company, despite his indifference to us. Maybe because of it. I remembered slipping out behind the Greens' house to where he was leaning against the fence, smoking. I'd leaned there next to him, and he'd offered me a drag of his cigarette and only laughed a little when it made me immediately start coughing.

I'd been a little in love with Cody Benham even before he saved my life, that day in the woods.

When I remembered anything about the time between the attack and the hospital, it was him—his face above me, the light and shadows flickering across his features as he ran. Most of all I remembered the feeling of his arms. The strength of them.

I finished paying. Cody had just come in for the newspaper, which he tucked under his arm before holding the door open for me. I counted my steps as I moved past him, pressing back firmly against the fear at the sensation of a body that close, behind me where I could sense him but not see him.

Outside I turned casually, like I just wanted to talk to him and not like I was going to have a panic attack if I let someone follow behind me. I walked backward, hand shading my eyes against the sunlight. "So what brings you back into town?"

"My dad's been hassling me to come pick up the crib he built for the new baby. I had a meeting cancel at the last minute, so I thought I'd make the trip and spare myself any more nagging," Cody said.

"New baby? I'm sorry, Cody Benham is a *dad*?" I asked with exaggerated incredulity. "Who'd you dupe into procreating with you?"

He chuckled. "I keep waiting for Gabby to wise up and realize what a reprobate she married, but this is kid number three and it hasn't happened yet, so I'm starting to think I may get away with it."

Three kids? Jesus. When *was* the last time I'd seen Cody? Not since he left Chester, I realized. Fifteen years.

We crossed the street together. The convenient thing about Chester's size was that Main Street—with the gas station, café, bar, and motel—consisted of two blocks. All I'd have to do was amble back to the other side of the road at the end of the night.

It was still early for even the regulars, which meant we could snag the good booth—the one that wasn't under the speaker or the AC that blasted even in the dead of winter. I sat myself down with my back to the door, which wasn't great for the raging PTSD but made it less likely anyone would recognize me from the street. The waitress was a twentysomething white girl who wore her hair in dreads and had a butterfly tattoo, no one I recognized or who recognized me, and the rest of the clientele were only interested in their own bottles.

Once the waitress was gone, the silence turned sludgy as pond scum. Fifteen years was a lot of time, and we hadn't exactly had much in common to begin with, other than one very bad day. "So, Cody Benham. Where have you been hiding yourself?" I asked, before the quiet could get any thicker. "The circus? County lockup? Some internet start-up that sells artisanal mustache wax?"

He chuckled. "Believe it or not, the state legislature. I'm Representative Benham now."

"Huh." I adjusted my weight on the split vinyl seat, patched over with a geological age of duct tape, and propped my elbows on the sticky tabletop. I peered at him, trying to get "state legislator" out of that scruff. "So when did you get respectable?"

"Oh, it's just an act," he said jokingly. "Guess it finally occurred to me that I could stay here or I could do something with my life, but it couldn't be both. So I took off. Got a degree. Met Gabriella."

"That's your wife?" I asked. He nodded.

"Her dad was a state senator, and talking to him, I realized I actually had some opinions to go along with my fancy degree. I ran and for some goddamn reason people voted for me, and here we are."

"You make it sound like you had hardly anything to do with it," I said. Miss Butterfly showed up with our drinks. The bar had started stocking some hipster-approved microbrews to suit the tourists, so I'd indulged in the snootiest-looking IPA on the chalkboard, in honor of Mitch. Cody stuck with a can of Rainier, the ancestors of which had littered the hangout spots of our youth.

"Gotta maintain my local credibility," he said as he poured. "So how shocked are you that I'm all respectable now?"

"A little," I conceded. "I wouldn't think they'd let a guy who got into as much trouble as you did become a politician."

"You know, weirdly, none of our hijinks ever led to official records," Cody said, scratching his chin as if puzzled.

"If you're going to do crime, do it with the mayor's son?" I suggested. Nothing ever seemed to stick to Oscar. He was his father's only son and heir, the town prince. Even Cass worshipped him. And whenever he did piss anyone off, he always managed to charm his way out of it—or his father stepped in.

"Well, I didn't have your poker face, so I didn't have the option of lying my way out," he said.

"You're not still mad that I cleaned you out, are you?" I asked, laughing.

"That was my gas money," he said in mock outrage. I'd forgotten all about that—him teaching me poker in the hospital, until the nurses kicked him out. "Or how about the time you convinced the whole town your dad had cancer, so they'd give you free stuff?"

I winced. "Not my finest hour." I'd kept that ruse up for four months before my dad caught on. But since we were getting free pizza out of it, he let it keep going for another six weeks. I'd been such a wreck in high school. Maybe that was inevitable. Cody had saved me from the woods, but he couldn't save me from myself. I picked at the label on my beer, peeling it from the glass. "I guess being a hero didn't hurt your campaign."

"It came up," Cody said. "But never because I brought it up. I wouldn't use you like that."

"You earned whatever you can get out of it, as far as I'm concerned," I told him quietly. He hadn't just carried me out of the forest. He'd been at the hospital almost as much as my dad, checking up on me. Bringing me presents. Jokingly offering to smuggle me cigarettes. The prickle of tears stung my eyes. I cleared my throat. "So, two kids?"

"Twin boys," he said. "Just turned four. And you? Boyfriend? Husband?" He paused. "Girlfriend?"

"None of the above. Probably," I said.

"Probably?"

I shrugged. "I left on a note of mild ambiguity."

"In my experience? When it comes to relationships, if you could take it or leave it, leaving is always the right choice," Cody said.

"Stop. I cannot handle Cody Benham with words of wisdom," I told him, fending him off with an upheld hand.

"Everything changes," he said.

"Except Chester." But that wasn't true, was it? "Jesus. This place. I swear, every time I come back it's like the ground starts crumbling under my feet. And what's underneath is all the shit I'd rather leave buried."

"I heard about your dad and the house," Cody said.

I groaned. "I don't know what to do. I know I should help, but how am I supposed to do that if he won't let me touch a damn thing?"

"You could get a crew out. There are specialists for this sort of thing," Cody suggested.

"Sounds expensive."

"Got any of that murder money left?"

I snorted at the turn of phrase. "Turned out I wasn't any better at managing it than Dad. Paid my tuition and then spent the rest as fast as I could. I didn't like having it," I admitted. "I'm doing fine, I just don't have a ton of extra cash lying around."

"You could sell the house. The land's got to be worth something."

"I'd have to talk Dad into it."

"He won't have a choice about whether to live there or not if it's condemned," Cody pointed out, but I shook my head.

"Nobody's going to pry him out of there."

"Maybe Cass could help you figure something out," Cody said. "Once she puts her mind to something—"

"She steamrolls over everything in her path to make it happen," I muttered. I stared at my beer, working the last soggy scraps of the label off with my fingernail.

Cody looked surprised. "You two were always thick as thieves. Did something happen after . . . you know."

"No, nothing like that," I assured him. If anything, the attack had made us closer. We might have grown up and grown apart naturally, drifting off into our disparate interests. But after the attack, we lived in one world, and everyone else lived in another. We'd barely spent a day apart until college.

"So you're still close."

"We don't see each other as much as we used to, but yeah. I mean, I was a mess *before* I almost got murdered. I was a disaster after. Still am, in fact. But once Cass sets her mind to something, you can't talk her out of it—and she decided we were best friends when we were five years old. So here we are." Anyone else would have done the smart thing and ditched me a long time ago.

"What about Liv?" he asked.

I dropped my eyes to my bottle. "We don't get to see each other much, but we talk all the time." I didn't mention how many of those calls came at odd hours of the night. Or just how complicated that friendship had become.

My bottle was empty; I'd hardly noticed how fast I was drinking. Cody flagged Butterfly for a replacement. Then his phone rang. "Sorry— I have to take this. It's a work thing," he said. "I'll be right back?"

I waved him off. He walked out past the bathrooms toward the back lot to take the call. I shook my head in wonder. I'd adored Cody, but there was no denying he was the resident bad boy. State representative? Some things did change around here after all.

"Naomi Cunningham?"

I yelped, slopping my beer over my hand. The man standing at the end of the table looked chagrined and took a step back, holding up his hands.

"Didn't mean to startle you," he said.

My heart hammered. I swallowed hard. "You're fine," I said curtly.

With my adrenaline settling, I got a better look at him. He was youngish—early thirties, I guessed, with black hair and a Mediterranean complexion. Italian, maybe. He had the kind of boyish good looks that probably led to a lot of dates and not a lot of being taken seriously, with a wide mouth and big eyes designed to look earnest. He'd called me by my new name, and there were a couple interesting things about that.

"Let me guess. You have a podcast?" I asked.

"How'd you know?"

"You're not a local, and those shoes wouldn't know what a hiking trail was if it bit them," I said. "You called me Naomi *Cunningham* and you recognized me in a dim bar, so that narrows it down to either a casual murder fan or a professional, and I'm giving you the benefit of the doubt. Plus Cassidy warned me."

"Yep, you caught me," he said with a disarming smile. "My name's Ethan Schreiber. I'm working on a podcast about Alan Michael Stahl. Well, not just about him—it's actually about three serial killers from the Pacific Northwest, but Stahl is a big part of it and so obviously you are, too. I was actually planning on getting in touch with you later, but then I spotted you across the room."

"I don't do interviews," I said. I shifted to put my shoulder to him and took a pointed sip of beer.

"That seems to be the theme of the week," Schreiber said. "Cassidy Green said the same thing. Your friend Olivia was a little more forthcoming."

"Olivia talked to you?" I asked, surprised. "What did she say?" If she'd told him about Persephone—

But, no. She wouldn't have. Not until she'd talked to us.

"Oh, I see. You're allowed to ask questions, but I'm not," he said, giving me an exaggeratedly skeptical look. "Tell you what. I'll trade you. An answer for an answer."

"You can't be serious," I said.

He shrugged. "If I don't get anything from you, I'm going to have to restructure the whole episode, and that's going to be a pain in the ass. So I'm willing to be a bit of a dick for a usable statement."

"An admirable dedication to your work," I said dryly, and sighed. "Fine." I needed to know what Olivia had told him. Last week I would have said it was impossible that she would break the silence that had kept Persephone our secret for so long, but now?

Surely I could come up with some pat sound bite for him. Something about being so grateful I'm still alive, how Stahl's death brought up complicated feelings. Lying by omission wasn't *really* lying.

"Excellent." He sat down across from me and pulled a digital recorder out of his pocket. I eyed it suspiciously. "It *is* a podcast," he said. "A traditionally auditory medium."

"Fine," I said again. "When did you talk to Olivia?"

"Yesterday afternoon," he said.

"What did she tell you?"

"Nope, my turn," he said. He turned on the recorder. "Naomi Cunningham, aka Naomi Shaw. You were Alan Michael Stahl's last victim."

"Yes. Now can you answer my question?"

He raised a finger. "That wasn't a question, just a statement. How did you feel when you learned that Stahl had died?"

It was the question I'd expected. "Good." I glanced toward the back door. No sign of Cody returning.

Schreiber raised an eyebrow. "You can't give me a little bit more?"

"It's an answer," I told him.

He scrubbed a hand over his chin. "Look. I know you don't do interviews, and I understand why. When I saw you here I was hoping that face-to-face, I could charm you. Obviously, I was wrong. But I really need this. You and your friends are the heart of this story. You're the part of it that isn't about reveling in evil. If none of you speak up, the story is all about Stahl. The victims get lost. And I don't want that."

"He had other victims," I pointed out. "No one talks about them, you know. Six young women. Six. And few people can even name them—even the people who know every detail of his MO and can recite my entire biography. If you want to do Stahl's victims justice, you should be focusing on the girls who didn't get away."

"Lia Kemp, Tori Martin, Maria Luiselli, Hannah Faber, Ashlynn Raybourn, and Rosario Rivera," Schreiber said, leaning forward intently. "Lia was the youngest. She was sixteen, a runaway. She was a sex worker; Stahl apparently picked her up at a truck stop. No one ever reported her missing, and she wasn't identified for three years after her body was found by hikers. Maria was the oldest—thirty-five. She had three kids. She'd struggled with drug addiction but was clean when it's believed that she met Stahl while hitching home from work. Her shift ended after the buses stopped. She'd walk the four miles or she'd hitch a ride when she was lucky. She knew it was dangerous. She carried a knife in her purse, but it didn't save her. I can keep going."

I sat back in my seat, mouth dry. I hadn't even known all of that. I had never been able to bring myself to read about Stahl. I couldn't even have recited their names like he did. And I'd never heard anyone talk about them like that—like he wasn't just cataloging facts. Like they mattered to him.

"Stahl never faced justice for what he did to those women," Schreiber went on. His voice was rough, and he looked into my eyes as if searching for something. "There wasn't enough evidence to link him to a single one of those murders. Without you, he isn't arrested. He doesn't go to trial. He doesn't spend the rest of his life behind bars. Without you, more girls die. I've done the work, Ms. Cunningham, but without you, there's no ending to this story."

"It doesn't feel like an ending," I said. I stared at the blinking light on the digital recorder, imagining my voice played back. Imagining the people who would hear it, hungry for narrative, the sense of story to make random violence make sense. "You want to know what I feel, hearing he's dead? I feel numb. I feel relieved, because he won't ever get the chance to kill me, like he promised to if he ever got out. And I feel guilty."

"Guilty?" he repeated, surprised.

I shouldn't have told him that. Too late now. "A man died in prison because of my testimony. It's a lot to put on a child. I know he was a horrible person. If anyone deserved it, he did. But it happened because of me, and that's more power than I ever wanted to have. It shouldn't have been up to me."

"Not just you. Cassidy was the one who first identified Stahl, while you were unconscious," he said.

"You really have done your homework." I folded my hands on top of my laptop. I was talking too much. I needed to get my answers and shut him down. "What did Olivia say to you?"

He considered. "Not a lot. She said that she was interested in talking to me, but there were some things that she needed to deal with first. It's funny—she told me something similar, about the victims. That what I was doing was good, because the dead shouldn't be forgotten."

*We owe it to her.* "That's all?"

"Pretty much," he confirmed. "But she wanted to check in with you and Cassidy first—she preferred to have your blessing."

Preferred. Not needed. She was going to tell, with or without us.

*This is a good thing,* I thought. We *should* come clean. With Stahl dead, the only thing keeping us silent was shame and selfishness. Liv was the only one brave enough to admit that.

"Well, then," I said. "We're done. Cheers." I lifted my bottle to him.

"I've got more questions."

"But I don't," I replied with a shrug. "Sorry."

"One more," he pressed. "And then I promise I'll leave you alone."

I sighed and swigged my beer. The hops made my nose itch. "Fine. One more."

Schreiber gave me a considering look, his finger tapping on the table. "Stahl's youngest known victim was sixteen. He targeted women who were alone and lured his victims into his truck under false pretenses. He transported them in his truck to the location where he assaulted and killed them."

"I know all this. I don't want to hear it," I said, my skin crawling, but he didn't stop.

"He sexually assaulted them before stabbing them to death. On four of the bodies there was evidence of restraints being used; decomposition made it impossible to tell in the other two cases."

"What is your point?" I asked, feeling sick. I couldn't hear about the details. I didn't want to imagine what it had been like for those women. There was enough horror in my head already.

"You were eleven years old. You were with friends. You weren't near the road; you were in the forest. You were stabbed, but you weren't assaulted, and you weren't restrained," he said. "There was no physical evidence linking Stahl to the attack. Your testimony, and your friends', was all that the prosecution had to go on."

"Is there a question in all of this?" I asked, keeping my voice steely as fear flashed through me. The questions had been asked a hundred times before, of course, but they were always questions about *Stahl*. Why had he changed his pattern? What had he been doing in Chester?

"Here's my question: Are you sure it was Stahl who attacked you?" he said. His voice was gentle, understanding.

"He was convicted, wasn't he?" I shot back. He was convicted. Liv and Cass had seen him. The police were *sure*.

"That's not an answer."

I sat back, my palms braced against the table. "We're done here."

"I'm not accusing you of anything," Schreiber said. "But these are questions that I need to address."

"I don't know what goes on in the mind of a serial killer," I said. The recording light blinked and blinked. All of this was going to be on the record. I was past caring. "I know what it feels like to have a knife driven into my body. I know what it feels like to struggle for breath because my lung has collapsed and filled up with blood. So I know what those women felt when they were dying. I can't tell you why Stahl changed his pattern or why he was in Chester. But I can tell you that he deserved to rot in prison, and he did, and now the story has a happy ending."

"And yet you feel guilty." He sat back in his seat.

Before I could reply, Cody appeared, approaching from behind Schreiber. "Is there a problem here?" Cody said.

Schreiber turned in his seat, grabbing the recorder as he did. "Just having a chat," he said.

Cody glanced from Schreiber to me. My jaw was clenched, and I felt cold all over. "It's okay," I said, almost a whisper.

"Get up. And get out," Cody growled.

"I—" Schreiber began, but Cody grabbed him by the collar and hauled him up out of his seat. Schreiber scrambled to keep his feet under him and backed away quickly, hands upraised. "I'm going. I'm going."

Cody loomed. He shouldn't have been able to—he was shorter than Schreiber by a good two inches, but he had more bulk, and there was something in the way he carried himself that made it clear he knew how to hold his own in a fight. The same couldn't be said for Schreiber.

"If you change your mind about that interview—" Schreiber started.

"Out," Cody barked, giving him a hard shove, and Schreiber retreated. I shrank down into the booth and didn't relax until I heard the front door slam.

I shut my eyes. *Alan Michael Stahl is an evil man*, I thought, as I'd thought many times before, lying awake and trying not to be. *I did the right thing.*

All this time, I'd been waiting for it to fall apart.

Liv and Cass had been afraid that if people found out about Persephone, they wouldn't believe us about Stahl. They would think that we were liars.

I was afraid they would find out that I *was* one. Because Persephone wasn't the only secret I'd been keeping all this time. I'd lied to the police. I'd lied on the stand. I'd lied to myself, told myself I'd seen Alan Michael Stahl in those woods—and maybe there was even a time I'd believed it.

But the truth was, I hadn't seen him that day.

I hadn't seen anything at all.

Cody slid back into the booth, scowling. "Who the hell was that?"

"Journalist. No big deal," I said. I went to take another drink, but my hand was shaking too much. "I shouldn't have let him start talking. My fault."

"Vultures," Cody muttered. His hand tensed on the table, like he was imagining grabbing hold of Schreiber again. "Are you sure you're okay?"

"I'm sure," I said firmly. I smiled. "But it's good to know that you're still there to rescue me. My hero."

He looked uncomfortable. "It could have been anyone who found you in those woods, Naomi."

"I know. But it wasn't anyone. It was you," I said, tracing random patterns in the pooled condensation on the table with one finger. "And it wasn't just the woods."

He didn't reply. It wasn't something we'd ever talked about. But he reached out and brushed his fingers over my knuckles—a touch with no purpose except perhaps to prove to each of us, *I'm here.* He drew his hand away before it turned into anything more.

"Let's talk about something else," I begged.

"So far I've managed to bring up your newly ex-boyfriend, your strained relationship with your dad, and that time you almost died. Why don't you pick the subject?" he suggested, and I laughed.

Fifteen years was a lot of catching up, as it turned out. I did most of the talking. Cody had always been a reserved guy. Somehow, hearing about my creative disaster of a life didn't send him scrambling for the back exit.

The second beer turned into a rum and Coke, and then another, along with a charcoal slab of a hamburger. I was drunk enough to wonder, as Cody walked me to the motel room after he insisted on paying the bill, if I wanted to invite him inside. He was a good-looking guy, but to me he was still a big brother, a knight in shining armor. Still, I'd made worse decisions. It was kind of my brand.

I turned the key and opened the door a crack, then leaned against the doorframe to look back at him. He was standing close but not too close. I could smell him—too clean to match the local-boy image he was projecting. He smelled like soap and responsible choices. He'd nursed that one beer and then barely had half of his second.

"You can still get outta here, you know," he said. "Leave your past behind you."

"That's just a line from a song, not something people can really do," I told him.

"What song is that?"

"You know, I can't remember," I confessed.

My fingertips grazed the side of his hand, not quite taking it. He looked down at me, a little smile on his lips. I'd slept with a lot of people who shouldn't have slept with me, and not one of them had that look.

"Cody Benham's a dad," I said, shaking my head in wonder.

"It's kind of great," he admitted.

I let my hand drop to my side. "You're not even a little bit tempted, are you?"

"It's not because of the scar," he said quickly.

"Hadn't even crossed my mind," I told him, and it was true.

An alarm on his phone went off. "Gotta call home before Gabby goes to bed," he told me.

"Fuck, you're wholesome." I rocked my weight back, putting distance between us.

"I know. I can't believe it either," he said. He bent and kissed my brow, then straightened up. He was already with his kids; I could see it in his eyes. "I'm heading home first thing tomorrow, but if you need anything before then—or after, for that matter . . ."

"I've got your number," I said, patting the jacket pocket where I'd tucked his business card. "Get out of here, Cody Benham. I'll be fine."

Once Cody took off, I was left with a scratchy motel bed and the unfamiliar sounds of a new place. I hated being alone. I hated being alone at night worst of all. I could never sleep properly without another body near me. Couldn't quiet my thoughts without someone to focus on.

I turned on the TV, hoping it would be enough to distract me. I flipped through a hundred channels that all seemed to be showing *Forensic Files*. Not exactly my idea of relaxing viewing. It wasn't that it made me afraid or reminded me of what had happened to me—it was more that it didn't. I hadn't turned out a tragedy, and it left me feeling like an impostor in the annals of victimhood. I left it on, though, watching the monotonous catalog of violence without taking any of it in.

The show ended—the husband did it, surprise—and another one started up, even grislier. I flipped around, hopping between unfunny sitcoms and a rotating assortment of cop shows, the narratives blending together in a surreal jumble of suspects, motives, and gore.

Then Alan Michael Stahl appeared, glaring from behind a courtroom table and wearing an orange jumpsuit, and I stopped. It was the picture they always used, because you could see the hatred in his eyes. Hatred for everything, but us in particular—we three girls who brought him to ruin.

*Are you sure it was Stahl who attacked you?*

Stahl was already under investigation for the murders when I was attacked. When Cass and Liv gave their descriptions, the detectives realized the connection immediately. I didn't remember how I'd identified him originally. All I remembered was people telling me I *had* identified him. All I had to do was keep agreeing.

I had always told myself that I must have remembered, right after the attack, and been able to identify him; I must have forgotten afterward.

The images of the attack had been lost in the same haze that had stolen most of my memories of the hospital, that had turned the months afterward into a scattered mosaic of moments.

My refusal to do interviews had ensured that I didn't have to deal with the kinds of questions Schreiber was asking. Cassidy had fielded those, and generally people weren't going to ask a preteen if she thought it was weird her best friend hadn't been raped. The defense attorney at the trial had been similarly cautious, feeling gently for gaps in our story—but it wasn't like she could point to the other murders as evidence that Stahl hadn't attacked me, since he claimed to be innocent of those, too.

So the inconsistencies had been glossed over and forgotten. I knew that there were message boards and that sort of thing where people dissected the case in detail, but I never went looking.

". . . never charged with the other murders, but given the strong circumstantial evidence and similarities between the attack on Naomi Shaw and the other victims, those cases are considered closed," the anchorwoman was saying. "In more lighthearted news, tonight we're talking to two local restaurants with a yearly tradition: a battle royale—of pancakes."

I turned it off. Why did people always say it that way? The other murders. They weren't the other murders, because I hadn't been murdered. They were just "the murders." It made me wonder if I'd died and no one had had the heart to tell me.

My phone buzzed. I checked it, hoping for Liv and getting Mitch. The screen was clotted up with notifications. Mitch had called. Seven times. Apparently he'd figured out I was ignoring his texts.

He wasn't a bad guy, Mitch. The trouble was he'd mistaken drama for virtue and suffering for art, and felt impoverished by his own good fortune. I'd known from the start that he'd sought me out because my sad story was written on my face and he was hoping to borrow it, but for a while I hadn't minded. It was as good a way to get laid as any.

But I wouldn't bring him here to see this. To meet the people I grew up with. I wouldn't let him get to know Naomi Shaw, because he couldn't. He'd just turn her into a story that made sense to him.

I'd told him as much, though I might have phrased it less eloquently and with more swearing. If either of us had any self-respect we wouldn't try to come back from the things we'd said to each other.

Self-respect wasn't really something either of us was good at. I could go back. He'd never let me forget it, but he'd let me call a mulligan and retreat into our life of splitting the rent and the groceries and the dinner bill, but not the appetizers because he only ate the mozzarella sticks and they were three dollars cheaper.

I dismissed the notifications and rubbed my eyes. I was sobering up, and that was unacceptable. I lurched over to the mini-fridge, but it was empty. I didn't want to go back to drink alone at the bar. I'd rather drink alone, period. But the Corner Store would still be open.

Marsha was still behind the counter, counting the day's take. I gave her a curt wave and headed for the back. I grabbed the nearest, cheapest bottle of red and ambled up to the counter. She gave it A Look and I bounced one right back at her.

"That stuff is basically cold medicine cut with a little grape juice," she told me.

"That suits the mood I'm in," I replied blithely.

She looked amused. "Can't blame you. But there are better ways to get where you're going," she said. She reached behind the counter, and plunked down a half-full bottle of bourbon. Not bad quality, either.

"Pretty sure you're not allowed to sell the hard stuff, Marsha," I said, feigning shock.

"On the house. Given the circumstances." She pushed it toward me.

It was a Chester kind of gift. So much so I almost laughed. *Here you go, kid, get drunk and puke on some spruces.* I slapped down a twenty.

"I said on the house," she grouched.

I grabbed a Snickers bar. "For the candy. Keep the change." I left before she could object.

I should have gone back to my room. Back to the stiff motel sheets and *Forensic Files* and the faint scent of mold. I got into my car instead. I tried not to think where I was heading, even though I knew before I started the engine. Outside of town the streetlights dropped to an occasional smudge of light. The forest had grown more wild and dense than it had ever been in my childhood. Everywhere else, nature was retreating. But here it was galloping back. From green to brown and back again, like a slow season turning.

I wasn't sure how I knew when to pull off the road, only that this was the place. Twenty years ago, this stretch of road had been blocked by a dozen cars, an ambulance, police, a seething crowd of onlookers. This was where Cody Benham had stumbled out of the woods with a girl in his arms, most of the way to dead.

I parked. I kept the light on in the car, even though it left me blind to the outside. It *felt* safer. I opened the bottle that Marsha had given me and took a swig. I winced. I wasn't much for straight liquor. Wasn't that big on drinking, all things considered, but when the occasion called for it . . .

It had happened right here. Well. Not *right* here. It ended here, though that was the part I remembered least of all. My brief consciousness while Cody was carrying me had failed before we reached the road. I had a memory of the ambulance and the commotion that followed the discovery of my broken little body, but I knew it wasn't real, just an amalgam of all the stories I'd been told.

The reel always ran backward in my mind. Cody's arms, and then the press of the rotting wood against my stomach, and then pulling myself along over evergreen needles and dirt, and then—

I shut my eyes. I wouldn't let myself go back that far. Far enough to feel the first blow of the knife, like a punch to my back—the shallowest blow of all, but enough to send me sprawling. My face pressed against the ground and then I put all my strength into flopping over onto my back, which only meant I could see the knife as it came down. The next blow struck my face, and after that I didn't see much of anything.

I remembered the trees and the pale sky. Cass shouting, Liv

screaming, Cass telling me they'd go get help. Tiny fragments that I couldn't stitch together into a whole, no matter how hard I tried.

I'd never gone back. Occasionally, people had suggested it—a documentary crew, Mitch (he also wanted to film it), a therapist who'd lasted four sessions. I'd always rejected the idea.

I took another swig. It spilled down my chin, spattering my clothes and the seat. I swore and reached over to fumble for the napkins I kept conveniently strewn on the passenger seat, along with whatever else I happened to be holding when I got in the car. The mail I'd grabbed from my dad's house skittered away from my flailing hands. I snagged a napkin and blotted at my shirt, which only left little maggoty shreds of napkin clinging to the fabric. Everything reeked of bourbon now.

I contorted myself to pick up the mail. The hand-addressed letter was on top of the stack. I frowned at it. Almost certainly fan mail. I should just throw it away.

I slid my thumb under the flap. The envelope tore. I fumbled the letter out. It was a single lined page, folded into thirds, the handwriting sloppy.

Ms. Shaw or Cunningham or whatever your name is now—
 I have thought a lot about what I would say to you if I got the chance, but now that I'm actually doing it I have trouble finding the words. You turned my whole reality upside down. I lost all my friends, my house, my life. My dad. The man I thought he was turned out not to be real at all. He wasn't my loving father, he was a monster.
 But the thing is, you lied. My father didn't attack you. You lied on the stand and sent the wrong man to jail. What I want to know is: Why? Were you protecting someone? Are they still out there? Have they hurt other little girls because you covered for them?
 I am trying to understand. I have been trying for years to put together the pieces of my childhood in a way that makes

them make sense, to comprehend what happened to the father I loved. I can't comprehend your part in it.

　　If you're ready to tell the truth, I'd like to hear it.

　　　　　　　　　　　　　　　　　　　　　　　　　　—AJ


I could barely read the words, my hands were trembling so much. AJ. Alan Stahl, Jr.

I'd almost forgotten that Stahl had a son. He'd never been in court. The only image I could summon up was a snapshot, a gangly kid in a striped shirt with Stahl's arm around him. I couldn't remember where I'd seen it.

*He knows.*

A wave of nausea rolled over me. I threw the letter aside, wrenched open the door, and staggered out onto the road. A cold wind sliced past me.

Alan Michael Stahl was an evil man. Liv and Cass had seen him. It was *him*.

Or had they seen someone who looked enough like him that the police could push traumatized children into identifying the wrong person?

The forest stood dark and deep before me. Persephone was in there, somewhere. Because she was why we'd been out there that day, because Stahl was one secret and she was the other, they'd tangled together in my mind. My monster and my goddess, their fingers always catching at my hair, trying to drag me back to that day. I'd always fought that pull.

There was a flashlight in the trunk. I'd gotten it out before I quite knew what I was doing. I stood a moment, flashlight in one hand, bottle in the other, and waited for my better judgment to arrive. There was only the wind, and the distant calling of an owl.

I crossed the road, hopped over the small ditch, and walked straight in among the trees.

I wondered what my therapist would think of me thrashing through the underbrush. Probably not the version of "reintegrating my past selves" that she'd imagined. I should probably call her. That would probably be the smart thing to do.

Thick clouds occluded the stars, leaving my flashlight the only point of light in the gloom. It swept over roots and a thick carpet of evergreen needles, toppled trunks, the occasional swift body of a mouse fleeing my intrusion. Nothing looked familiar. We'd known every twig and rock in this place, but it had grown strange in our absence.

I stopped, trying to orient myself. Where was the trickling creek where we'd scooped up cold water for our potions, the snag we had declared contained the ghost of a witch? Where were the Wolf Hollow, the Dragon Stone? The pond should be close to here, a muddy little patch our imaginations had turned into a lake where we might find a king's sword and a secret destiny.

The shadows seethed. Something rustled to my right. I swung the light toward it but illuminated only a fragment of memory. Liv, her glasses slipping down her nose. Cass with her hands on her hips, chin tilted up in her starting-a-story pose, her golden locks tumbling about her pert little face, every inch the princess she was currently pretending to be.

"I *sensed* something watching me today," she declared. "A most vile spirit. Our enemies are aware of our growing power."

"Enemies?" Liv asked, eyes widening. "What enemies?"

"Wicked beasts who oppose the forces of light!" Cass informed her. "Horrible monsters! We have to keep ourselves safe."

"How?" Liv asked, shivering.

"Warding spells," Cass said, dropping the pose. "We can make magic charms."

"Will that be enough?"

"Of course it will," I murmured. I could picture them perfectly, but I couldn't see myself. Couldn't imagine the version of me before the knife. I remembered what I'd said, though. "We know exactly how to make the charms, right, Cass? And then we'll be safe from the monsters."

Relief in Liv's eyes as I put my arm around her shoulders. The faint flicker of annoyance in Cass's—this was her story, and she wasn't ready to pass it off yet.

I recognized the tree in front of me now. It had gotten taller, but the odd crooked branch was the same, with the little pocket of hollow space where it met the trunk. It was shoulder height to me now, where I'd had to reach up above my line of sight back then.

I took one last swig, then set down the bottle. I wriggled my fingers inside the hollow. It couldn't still be here, could it? But there—something soft. Cloth. Gingerly, I caught it between my index and middle finger and drew it out.

The cloth was a cheap old handkerchief. It had split open, and the contents tumbled out into my palm, worn into obscurity by years of rain and rot. A pair of dice, the spots rubbed away; a wadded brown lump that was completely unrecognizable; a cheap costume jewelry earring. One of our charms, to keep us safe.

We knew it was fantasy, that we were just pretending, but we wished we weren't. We *tried* to believe, filled with the sense that if only we could conquer our doubt, we could make it true. We would find the door in the woods, the world in the back of the wardrobe, the dragon's egg left nestled in the loam.

We knew the world was cruel and dirty and dull, and it was all so brutally unfair that we refused to accept it. There was magic in the world. We only had to find it.

I stumbled past the tree, the bottle forgotten, searching the shadows for familiar landmarks. There'd been that stone where Liv would sit to read while she waited for us. Maybe I could find the tree I'd climbed to reach the abandoned nest high in the branches, getting fifteen feet up before Liv started panicking and made me climb back down—or the overturned shopping cart that roots had grown through, anchoring it eternally in place, which Cass had declared was proof that a dryad walked these woods.

Or the boulder, dropped by some ancient glacier, with the shallow gap beneath its bulk. The gap that three young girls could belly under, into the hollow space behind it. The Grotto, Cass had named it.

But it was all shadow and green now, the magic gone, my memories jumbled and distorted. We'd wandered so deep into these woods. I wouldn't find it, not at night, not drunk. I shut my eyes, and soft rain pattered in the branches above me.

With the sound of the rain and the sough of the wind, I almost didn't hear the footsteps behind me. They didn't register consciously—only in the nestled fold of my brain that stored fear like the broken-off tip of a blade. I came around so fast that I lost my balance. My foot skidded on a patch of wet moss and I went down hard on my ass with a curse. The flashlight spun free of my grip.

A shadow crashed away from me through the trees. I lunged and snatched up the flashlight, swinging it up toward the shadow, but it was too far away and I was too addled and slow. All I caught was the hint of a figure—human. I wasn't alone out here.

Fear raked its teeth across my tender throat and tore my breath away. I floundered, struggling upright. Someone was here. Someone was following me. It was dark and I was alone and no one knew I was here, and these woods had been promised my death and denied it. If I was going to die, the part of me that once yearned for magic insisted, it would be here.

I bolted. I thought I was running for the road, but I couldn't be sure. I couldn't see anything but the ground right in front of me, and the thunder of my heart and my footsteps drowned out any hope of listening for a pursuer.

*Idiot, idiot, idiot,* I berated myself. Branches snagged at my arms. *You're going to die, you're going to die.*

But there was the road, and my car, and the anemic glow of the streetlight. I wrenched open the door and shot inside, slamming it behind me. With the doors locked, I remembered to breathe. I bent over with my fists pressed against my stomach, forcing in one lungful after another.

Had there even been someone else out there? I could have imagined it, couldn't I, that shadow in the trees? My mind was wheeling with memories, with the memory of pain and fear. Who else would be out there in the middle of the night? Why the hell would they run?

So I'd imagined it. I'd gotten drunk, fallen down in the forest, and mistaken a tree for an ax murderer.

I didn't really believe it. But I wanted to, and I tried to, and it was almost the same thing.

A rap on the car window woke me with a jerk. Chief Bishop stood outside, scowling, a navy baseball cap protecting her hair from the steady drizzle. I'd fallen asleep crammed in the driver's-side seat, a dignified line of drool running from the corner of my mouth to my chin. I scraped it off with my sleeve and rolled down the window, squinting in the early morning light.

"Morning," I croaked.

"Looks like you made some less than optimal decisions last night," Bishop said.

"That's an accurate assessment," I acknowledged. My throat felt like sandpaper.

She gave me a skeptical look. "Ms. Shaw, what are you doing out here?"

"You know, it seemed therapeutic last night," I said, not bothering to correct her. I'd always be Naomi Shaw here. "Can't fucking remember why." I rubbed sleep grime from my eyes and blinked a bit. "Are you going to cite me for something?"

"Sheer stupidity?" she suggested.

"What's the fine on that, like fifty bucks?" I asked.

"If I write the Miracle Girl of Chester a ticket, the city council will send me packing," she informed me. "But you are parked practically in the middle of the street just past a blind curve, you stink of booze, and you look like you got in a fight with a tree and lost. I need to know that if I let you drive off, you're not going to wrap yourself around a lamp-post half a mile down the road."

"I'm good," I said. Apart from the splitting headache and the dead-squirrel taste in my mouth. Bishop considered me for a long moment. I squinted at her. "Seriously. Hungover, not still drunk, hand to God."

She sighed. "Find a better place to sleep tonight," she told me, and thumped the roof of my car in farewell. I waited until she'd driven past me to start up the engine.

I managed to get into my room at the motel without anyone seeing me, and by the time I got cleaned up it was a more reasonable hour. My phone was buzzing on the bed. Mitch. I picked it up to reject the call, but then I sighed and answered.

"Hey."

"Naomi. Hi." He sounded startled that I'd actually picked up. I was a bit shocked myself.

"What's up?" I prompted, toweling off my hair with my other hand.

"I just called to say . . . Look, I'm sorry about the way we left things. I get it. I guess things haven't been great for a while now. We've just being going through the motions. Maybe this was inevitable. I just wish it hadn't happened like this."

Shit. Was Mitch breaking up with me?

No, I'd broken up with him. Hadn't I? Yes. Yes, this was definitely my decision. So I shouldn't be upset. I had no right to be upset.

"It's for the best," I offered. "You can do better."

"I don't know about that," he said a forced chuckle. "You and I—"

"I don't really want to hash this out over the phone," I said quickly. The breakup postmortem was my least favorite relationship ritual.

"Right, right. Anyway, I don't know how long you're going to be up there, but you got some mail—bills, looks like a couple checks. I can forward it along to you if you want."

"I'll be back this weekend," I said. "I've got a wedding to shoot on Saturday and an engagement session on Sunday. I'll pick up my mail and some of my stuff."

"You're going to stay out there a while, then?"

I punched the bridge of my nose, squeezing my eyes shut. "I guess. I've got to get my dad's place in order. It's . . ." But Mitch wasn't my boyfriend anymore. He didn't need to know. Didn't *get* to know. "Thanks, Mitch."

"No problem. Happy to help." He sounded strained. I wondered if this conversation would end up in one of his stories, what belabored layers of meaning each word would contain. It would all become a metaphor for the isolation of modern society and the impossibility of relationships, or something.

"I'll talk to you later, Mitch."

"Naomi—"

I pretended I hadn't heard and hung up. I hated breakups. Ambiguous breakups were the worst of all. I preferred the explosive ones, which was why whenever a breakup seemed imminent I had a habit of getting into bed with someone. Lucky thing Cody was taken, or I might've made him the grenade chucked over my shoulder on the way out the door.

I started to toss my phone back onto the bedspread and stopped. The screen showed a missed call and a voicemail—from Liv. I frowned. Liv didn't do voicemail.

I pressed play and put the phone to my ear. At first I thought she must have pocket-dialed me—I heard only rustling and breathing. Then she spoke. Her voice was strained. It sounded almost like it was fading in and out. "Naomi. I have to . . . I'm sorry. I need you to know that. I'm so, so sorry. I love you. I'm so sorry I lied."

The message ended. I fumbled with the phone, calling her back. It rang through to voicemail. "Liv. What's going on? Are you okay? Call me. I'm on my way." I didn't like the way she sounded. The message had come in late last night—around the time I was stumbling drunkenly through the woods.

*I'm so sorry I lied.* Not that *we* had lied. She wasn't talking about Persephone. It was something else.

The last thing she'd said to me was a promise—our promise. To be here in the morning. If that was the lie . . .

She wouldn't have hurt herself. Not again.

Fear seeped into me, slow and cold and unrelenting. "Damn it," I muttered. I called Cass, but she didn't pick up either. "Something's up with Liv. I'm going to her place to check on her. Call me when you get this," I said to her voicemail.

I got dressed hurriedly and hustled out the door. The sun, breaking through the clouds, hit me like it had a personal grudge.

"Morning." Ethan Schreiber was standing a few feet away. He had a coffee cup in one hand, three fingers lifted in a wave.

"Are you stalking me?" I asked him.

"This is the only motel in town," he said, pointing vaguely at the door two down from mine. "Everything all right?"

"Why wouldn't it be?" I asked him.

"You look . . . Never mind," he said, shaking his head. I strode to my car. "Nice to see you again," he called after me. I slammed the door, cutting short his last word, and whipped out of the parking lot. I dialed Liv's number again on the way. Once again, she didn't answer.

The gate was closed and locked. I didn't have the code and I didn't want to panic Liv's parents if it was nothing—it was probably nothing, I told myself, Liv hardly ever remembered to charge her phone, that was all—so I parked and hopped the fence on foot, jogging the rest of the way up toward the house.

I thought of it as Liv's place, but it was her parents' house, of course. They'd lived in the same house, set back among the trees, since they moved to Chester three decades ago. They'd remodeled along the way, expanding the tiny enchanted cottage they'd started with, adding energy-efficient windows and solar panels. Kimiko's kitchen garden was a marvelous sight, bursting with kale and snap peas and pole beans, along with the few tomatoes she always coaxed along in the cool, overcast weather.

I'd lived on a diet of instant noodles, canned chili, and saltines most of the time. Coming over to Liv's place and picking fresh sugar snap peas off the vine had felt like its own kind of magic. Some days when Liv wasn't up for company, Kimiko had let me join her out there, teaching me how to fertilize the plants, how to thin the carrots to give them room to grow. She would let me hold the tender seedlings cupped in my palms as she dug a hole for them, nestling them in where their roots could stretch.

Before you could plant a seedling, she would tell me, you had to harden it. It was used to the indoors, a consistent temperature and moisture and light. Little by little each day you had to set the seedlings outside, sheltered, first for only an hour, then two, slowly introducing them to wind and rain and sun and cold.

She'd said raising kids was a bit like that. You had to harden them, before they were ready to go out safely into the world. If you put them out too soon, all at once, the shock of it would wither them. They would never grow to full bloom.

Kimiko was in the garden now. She was on her knees with a sun hat on, using a little folding knife to deadhead the flowers in the beds at the edges of the garden. Her hair was gray and frizzy and her face lined with delicate wrinkles. The sight of her eased the panic in my chest. If something had happened, she wouldn't be out here, calmly working.

The crunch of my footsteps on the gravel alerted her to my approach, and she looked up with eyes widened in surprise. "Naomi?" she said. "What are you doing in town?"

She could be a bit direct like that, but I'd never minded. "I'm here to see Liv," I said, hands in my jacket pockets to hide their shaking. "She should be expecting me. More or less."

"Oh. I see." She frowned, then stood and waved at me to follow her inside.

There were nearly as many plants inside the Barnes house as outside. Kimiko preferred the garden, but her husband had never met a houseplant he didn't love or a flower pot he didn't want to fill. The house had an exuberant chaos to it—crowded, but nothing like my dad's. Everything had its place here.

"I'm sorry to surprise you," I said as I slipped off my shoes.

"No, don't be sorry," she said. She sounded distracted as she closed the door behind me. She cleaned her pruning knife carefully before folding it shut and setting it on the counter. "Can I make you some coffee while you wait?"

"Wait?" I echoed.

Kimiko wrapped her cardigan around her. "Liv is out. But if she's expecting you I'm sure she'll be back soon."

My breath caught in my throat. "Where is she?" I asked.

"Don't worry. She does this. She likes to go out to the woods to think," she said. There was a weariness in her that I had never seen before. "She was gone until very late last night. She must have left again before I woke up." She caught my look of fear and patted my arm. "She likes to wander. Especially lately. She leaves at all hours. She always comes back. She probably forgot you were meeting."

"It wasn't exactly planned," I admitted. "I just need to talk to her." Fear skittered over my skin. "Kimiko . . . has Liv been taking her meds?" I asked cautiously.

"Yes," Kimiko said firmly. "She's been doing well, Naomi. Very well. Distracted, the last few days."

"Because of Stahl," I said.

She didn't answer, but waved me farther into the house. After the initial hit of the entryway, I was relieved to find that the renovations had rendered the house a stranger to me, no longer the witch's cottage dripping with enchanted plants. The cat sleeping on the back of the couch was orange, not the raggedy black one of my youth.

But the painting on the wall—that I knew. Marcus had painted it. It showed the three of us, sitting on the garden bench with our heads together conspiratorially. He'd given it to Liv for her eleventh birthday, early that summer. He'd painted the faint, barely discernible form of a unicorn in the woods behind us, a dragon winding lazily through the sky.

At eleven, it had been harder to hold on to the magic. We were too aware of how childish and silly the whole thing was. I think all of us sensed that this was the last summer of our fantasy kingdom.

Maybe that was why when Cassidy started the Goddess Game, we'd all thrown ourselves into it so completely. Our last chance to believe. It was different—more sophisticated, in a way. Cassidy had been reading obsessively about Greek myths and had assigned us the "best" goddesses. Hera was a scold and Aphrodite boring, she declared. So I would be Artemis, Liv obviously Athena, and Cassidy would be Hecate, who was the goddess of witchcraft and thus extremely cool. We had begun tentatively, not sure what the rules were, how deep in our pretending we were allowed to go.

Persephone had changed all of that.

"What is it you wanted to talk to Liv about?" Kimiko asked. The edge to her voice suggested that she was more concerned about her daughter than she was letting on.

"Nothing," I said, and flushed. "Sorry, reflex."

"You don't like people getting into your business," she noted. "Me neither. I was always glad Liv wasn't the one with the scars or the one who was good at testifying. The reporters forgot about us pretty fast."

Anyone else would have danced around the subject. "She wanted to talk to me and Cass about something from when we were kids. I don't think I should tell you more than that without her permission," I said.

"Is it about Stahl?" she asked.

"Sort of." It was less an evasion than an inability to answer. It had everything to do with Stahl and nothing.

"When she got the call from that guy at Corrections, she started crying," Kimiko said. Her arms were folded, and she looked out the window as if watching for Liv to come up the driveway. "She got excited. I don't mean happy, I mean in a state of excited agitation."

When we were kids, Cass called it supercharging, when Liv's obsessions reached a fevered high. All her little tics and quirks went into overdrive, and she couldn't stop talking about whatever she was fixated on. She'd start out excited about bees and then she would become apocalyptically concerned with bee parasites reducing populations. She would count every bee she saw, writing the numbers down in a journal, convinced that if she could count every single one it would mean that the bees *weren't* going to die and the world *wasn't* going to starve. She got obsessed with the numbers four and seven. Four was a good omen—much to the chagrin of Kimiko—and seven was a bad one.

Later we'd realize these were the first signs of her illness, which would manifest fully later in life. The meds helped, once they found the right ones. With the meds, she didn't usually get to the last stage, the pernicious magic of ritual and numbers. She'd spin herself up on an idea and spin herself back down again.

"Can I see Liv's room?" I asked. Kimiko's mouth pressed into a thin line. "I'm probably worried over nothing, but I got a weird call from her, and if I can figure out where she is, I'd feel a lot better."

She gestured toward the hall. "Go ahead, then."

I made my way down the hall, past photographs showing Liv at all ages, a jumbled time line. There was no clear demarcation between Before and After. Maybe I detected a hint of hollowness in her eyes, a fear that hadn't been there Before, but it was probably my imagination. The only gap came during the college days, after Liv's big crisis that ended with her back home—for good, as far as anyone could tell.

The lock on Liv's room had been drilled out. I touched the gap in the metal of the knob, remembering that phone call, the worst I'd ever gotten. My turn to sit by a hospital bed, waiting for my friend to wake up—or not.

*I'll be here tomorrow.* I had to believe she wouldn't break that promise.

Her room was meticulously organized. Liv was a collector. Things became sacred to her easily, taking on an almost mystical significance. She displayed her objects carefully, according to her mood and their meanings. A conch shell on her bookshelf, the four arrowheads laid out in a line next to it. Elsewhere was a nautilus fossil, a cross necklace her grandmother had given to her, the plane ticket she'd never used when she was supposed to fly to Japan right before the tsunami but got stomach flu. There was a lot in the room, but everything was cared for and everything had a specific meaning.

Maybe if I had understood them, I could have read the collection of objects like a diary, and they could tell me what I needed to know.

Her laptop was out on her desk. Next to it was a stack of articles and environmental reports. Probably something to do with the work she did for her parents' environmental compliance consulting firm. There was a sticky note on top of the stack with a bunch of numbers and letters jotted down on it—2248DFID, 3376DFWA, 1898DFWA—and a to-do list on a notepad that included "check map ID references" and "pharmacy pickup."

I wasn't sure what I was looking for. Some hint about where she would have gone, or why she would have called suddenly in the middle of the night. What had changed between yesterday morning and last night?

I tapped the touchpad, and a password login popped up. No dice. I tried the drawer. There were pencils, a sketchbook, rubber bands, paper clips, hair ties, three pill organizers—which seemed to indicate that she'd taken all of her pills including last night's, though not this morning's—and loose photographs, snapshots that had been printed at a drugstore.

Most of the photos were of her parents and the cats. Apparently there was a big fluffy gray one in addition to the marmalade gentleman I'd seen on the couch. But there were about a dozen random, poorly framed and badly lit photos of the woods, too.

The sketchbook was full of detailed studies of plants, insects, and birds. She was her parents' daughter, that was for sure. She'd always had her father's love of art, her mother's attention to detail. For a while, she'd had to stop drawing—the antipsychotics she was on made her hands shake too much. That was when we'd almost lost her.

But now she had different meds, a lower dose, and beauty spilled from her again.

I turned the page and froze. This sketch was different. Looser, for one thing, drawn from memory rather than life—at least, I hoped so. It showed the top third or so of a human skeleton. Flowers had been placed in the eye sockets, and around it were arrayed seashells and stones and stranger objects—a set of four jacks, a playing card, a collection of coins.

"Persephone," she had written at the bottom corner of the image, in her tiny, precise writing.

I turned the page. Another grinning skull greeted me. And another, and another, and another—page after page, growing less detailed, more gestural, with each one. Darkness seemed to radiate from the bones until on the last page they were roughly hewn patches of negative space in a field of scribbled pencil lines.

I thought the drawings must have gone back months, but the sketch before the first portrait of Persephone was dated only three days ago. Liv had done all of these since Stahl died. Since she decided to tell us what she'd found.

There was one more thing in the drawer. A small velvet jewelry box. I eased the lid open, praying to find a set of pearl earrings.

It was a bone. The tip of a finger. It might have belonged to any finger, might not have been human at all, except that I knew it was. It was from the right ring finger.

I knew because I'd watched Liv take it.

I looked again at the photographs. They weren't random at all. They were landmarks. The reading rock, the crooked tree, the creek. It was a road map back to Persephone.

I slipped the earring box into my pocket before I left.

L iv's missing," I said when Cass opened the door.

She was wearing a cream silk shell and black slacks, her makeup subdued but precise, and at my greeting she raised her perfectly penciled eyebrows. "Missing? We saw her yesterday."

"And now she's gone. She left the house before dawn and she's not answering her phone."

"That's not exactly unusual for Liv," Cass pointed out. "Come inside, will you? I've been at the lodge since the crack of dawn and I haven't even gotten any coffee yet."

I followed her in. She paced into the kitchen, where she'd been in the middle of making herself a latte. She poured the steamed milk into the mug, her back to me, as she spoke. "Liv hares off sometimes. Especially when things get intense."

"This is different," I said.

"Why?" she asked. She turned, propping her hip against the counter. She blew gently on her coffee and watched me over the rim of the mug. "What makes it different?"

"She left me this message." I held out my phone and played the message for her on speaker. "She said *she* lied. Not us. Just her," I said when it was done.

"What could that mean?" Cass asked. "Did she lie to us yesterday?"

The promise was a private thing. Cass had always been the together one. We were her beloved disasters, but there were things she didn't understand. "We have this thing," I explained reluctantly. "I tell her that I'll be here tomorrow, and she says she will, too. When we're having a hard time. It's a promise. To at least make it one more day."

"I didn't know that." Cass set the mug down carefully, adjusting it by the handle so it sat just so. Her voice was brittle, almost wounded. I wished I knew how to explain that it wasn't a secret we kept from her— not really. It was only that Cass was someone who needed to fix things— and sometimes Liv and I, we just needed to be broken together.

"We've got to find her, Cass. We have to go out there. To the Grotto," I said. She flinched.

"Why? You don't think Liv went back, do you? You don't think— she wouldn't have done something to herself there?" Her voice was frayed at the edges.

"She had a bunch of photos of the woods. Like landmarks, so she could find her way. I think she's been out there more than once," I said. "Have you been back?"

"I tried once," Cassidy said cautiously. "After Amanda was born. I guess—I don't know. I wanted to tell her about it, for some reason."

"You wanted to tell Amanda?" I asked, confused.

Cass flushed. "I wanted to tell Persephone about Amanda," she corrected. "I don't know why, I just did. But I couldn't find it. Her. Everything looked different."

"Then we don't even know if she's still there," I said.

"Of course she's still there. Where the fuck else would she be?" Cassidy snapped.

"Okay," I said, letting her anger slice into me. I could take it, and if I didn't put up a fight it would spend itself sooner. And sure enough, her shoulders slumped, and she put her hands over her face.

"I'm sorry," she said. "This is all so fucked up."

"We have to go make sure Liv isn't there," I said.

"I have a meeting," Cass objected, but her voice was faltering, and she played with her necklace absently. That wasn't a refusal, not from

Cass. When she was saying no, you knew it. It was the yeses that were harder to suss out.

"Surely you have underlings by now," I said, making a joking compliment of it. No demands for Cass. I was starting to remember how this worked.

"Percy," she said, and there was that little nose-scrunch again. "He's like an Energizer Bunny duct-taped to a wolverine. I'm pretty sure he's planning to off me and run the lodge himself." She laughed, but it was a little awkward, like she'd realized halfway through that this probably wasn't the best time to be joking about murder. She cleared her throat. "I'll have him take the meeting. With what I've got on the guy, he can't say no to me." She flashed her teeth, and I managed a smile in return.

And that was that. She'd made her decision, and it was really her idea, not mine at all.

Cass went upstairs to change and call Percy. She returned in more suitable clothes—better suited than my own jeans and sweatshirt, in fact, but I hadn't expected to be doing any hiking when I packed. She made a few attempts at small talk, asking after Mitch and business before we petered out into silence. At least it was only a few minutes' drive to where we were going. I pulled off at the Pond Loop trailhead this time. The trail had been built after I moved away, but if it went to the pond, it would put us close to the Grotto.

"I really don't remember where to go," Cass said nervously.

"We have a map," I reminded her. I took the photos out of my pocket and fanned them, finding one that had a sliver of road. "We just passed this tree. Come on."

We made our way through the woods following Liv's breadcrumbs. They took us along the trail for a few minutes and then off into the unmarked trees. It wasn't long before I realized that not all of the photos led to the Grotto—there were others I recognized from elsewhere in the woods, but we were able to cobble together a path.

The sky was clear, the sun high, but I had brought the flashlight.

If we got where we were going, we would need it. After a while, Cass started breathing heavily.

"I should work out more," she grumbled. "You're still skinny as a stick, I see."

"It's either the fast metabolism or the fact that sitting down to eat makes me nervous for some reason," I said.

"Seriously?" she asked.

I shrugged. "I used to get panic attacks. Still can't stand the smell of peanut butter."

She was silent for a few steps. Finally she said, "I forgot about that. That you were eating your lunch when it happened. I thought I remembered every second of that day." She sounded disturbed.

"It's been a long time," I said. I kept my pace slow, keeping level with her. *Don't let anybody be at your back*, my instincts said. In these woods, I wasn't going to even try to talk my hindbrain out of it.

"I don't want you to think that I've forgotten. Like I don't think about it anymore. About you," she said. "I've done so much therapy, you wouldn't even believe it."

I grunted in amusement. "In a competition of who's had more time getting psychoanalyzed, I do not think you would win, Cassidy Green."

"I'm not saying it's a competition."

"Then you have changed," I replied, flashing her a smile to take the edge off it, and she sighed.

"I was a little shit back then," she said.

"So was I. That's why we got along," I reminded her. I paused. "And it's not like I can blame you."

"What do you mean?" she asked.

I paused. "I know it wasn't easy for you at home. Your parents . . ."

"I'm not about to whine about my rich parents to you," she said. "Even I'm not that clueless."

"At least my dad never hit me," I said quietly. I'd seen her bruises. Always where they wouldn't be noticed. She looked away. "Granted, he was neglectful as fuck and it's a miracle I didn't get carted off by raccoons to raise as their own."

She laughed at that, but quickly fell silent. "It wasn't that bad. Oscar got it way worse, until he got bigger. And when he was around . . ." She didn't finish the thought.

I'd never really understood why Cassidy worshipped her brother so much, but if he was protecting her, that explained it. I'd never known him as a protector. To me, he had been something else entirely.

She was looking at me sidelong. "I know you never liked Oscar."

"I guess," I said dismissively. As if he'd never done anything to me. As if I'd never let him.

There were things I'd never told Cassidy Green. They would only earn her pity—or her hate. I didn't want either.

"The past is the past," she said, like a mantra. She picked up her pace. "All I can do is be a good mom now. Take care of my own, you know? Nothing good comes from digging up old trouble."

"Like Liv wants to."

"You can't tell me you're not worried about what will happen when everything gets dragged into the open," Cass said. "When people start asking questions about what *else* might have been going on."

"You mean about Stahl." I stopped, foot braced against a root.

I could never quite sort out my own memories. I didn't remember deciding to lie about seeing Stahl. I wasn't sure when I had realized—admitted—that it *was* a lie. After the hospital. Before the trial.

There was agony in not knowing the truth of my own recollections. Agony, and hope—because if things were that scattered, maybe I *had* remembered, for a little while.

"You know, don't you?" I asked Cass.

She sighed, tucking her hair behind her ear. "That you never saw him? Yeah. I know."

"How?" I asked. *And who else knew?* I wanted to add, but I restrained myself.

She hesitated. "It's not like I knew for sure. But I know you. I've always been able to tell when you're lying."

"You knew all along," I said, and she nodded, not looking at me. I thought she'd figured it out somewhere along the way. Had she really always known? My stomach clenched, guilt and shame roiling. "Why didn't you say anything?"

She looked at me levelly. "You did what you had to do. It wasn't *our* fault the cops fucked up the identification process. You were making up for *their* mistake. Liv and I saw him. It was the truth. It just wasn't *your* truth."

"My lies sent a man to prison for life."

"And?" she said.

"You don't think that's a problem?" I asked her with a disbelieving laugh.

She crossed her arms. "Naomi. Stop. You're beating yourself up for no reason. We saw him. Liv and I saw Stahl, one hundred percent. I promise. You believe that, don't you? You don't think *we're* lying."

"No, of course not," I said. I opened my mouth, shut it, unable to put it into words. It didn't matter whether I believed them, in a way. It didn't even matter whether Stahl was guilty. A righteous lie was still a lie. A wicked life was still a life. I had destroyed a man, and I couldn't trust my own memories to tell me that I'd done the right thing. I had to take it on faith. I had to trust in what other people had seen.

I'd never been good at trust.

"So why are you so freaked out now? Just because he died?" Cass's lips wrinkled into a frown.

"I got a letter from Stahl's son," I said. "He knows that I lied. He says his father wasn't the one who attacked me. Is there any way—if you were wrong—"

Cass held up a hand. "Hold on. He knows you lied? How?"

"I . . ." The letter hadn't gone into detail, had it? My memory was foggy. "I'm not sure."

"If he *knew* that you'd lied, if he *knew* his dad hadn't done it, don't you think he would have said something? The guy is probably just messed up about his dad dying and lashing out. I think you need to ask yourself why you're so eager to find something that's your fault."

I flinched. She gave me no ground, keeping her gaze locked on mine.

"Bad things happened to you. It doesn't mean you deserved them. You have earned the right to protect yourself. You don't owe the world *anything*. It owes you." She adjusted her jacket. "Let's go."

She stalked off. I followed, half dazed. Guilt and doubt had been my constant companions for decades. I didn't know if I could let them go. Cass didn't understand. She couldn't. She *knew* what she'd seen—she had the certainty of her own memory. And maybe it should feel horrible—the knowledge of what I had caused with my words. That wasn't the kind of weight you should just be able to leave behind. Was it?

"There it is," Cass said at last.

The boulder had been dropped here millennia ago by some glacier and settled into the landscape to stay. Soil had built up above it, letting the forest grow over it, forming a gentle hill. Only the face of the stone was visible, gray and craggy. It reached about a foot above my head. At its base was a seam of shadow. It seemed impossibly small.

I knelt by the seam and bent down, shining the flashlight into the gap. All I could see was dirt and stone; the shape of the boulder obscured the area beyond. "We're going to have to go in," I said.

"Liv's not here. There would have been some sign of her. We should just go," Cass said.

"We have to be sure," I insisted. Liv could be in there. And even if she wasn't, I needed to see. Ever since Liv had spoken the name, Persephone had been haunting my thoughts. Part of me needed to know that she was real—that she wasn't just part of the game we'd played.

Cass didn't budge. I set my jaw. Fine. I dropped to my stomach and carefully wriggled my way under the lip of stone, into the narrow gap beneath. Rock scraped my back. This had been easier at eleven.

The dirt floor sloped away as soon as you were inside. I levered myself down bit by bit and then I was past the lip of stone and the space opened up into a miniature cave, barely three feet tall.

Cass squeezed down behind me after all, and the two of us sat with our backs to the entrance, breathing hard, my flashlight beam fixed on the middle of the chamber. On Persephone.

She was exactly as I'd seen her last. I hadn't been back since that day, but here she was, and the past twenty years collapsed into nothing, into an instant.

She lay curled on her side. Her hands were curved in toward her chest, like she'd been cold, but the skull faced upward—toward the single shaft of light that fell from above, as if in the moments before her death she had turned her face to seek the sun.

Her flesh had long since rotted away, her clothes been reduced to rags. They had clung to her until our clever fingers plucked them away from her arched ribs, from the long, pale bones of her legs. Our whispers still seemed to fill this space, caught echoing between its walls.

Trinkets and treasures lay scattered around her. Our offerings. Beads and coins and jewelry, a crystal ballerina three inches tall, a river stone with a hole worn through it. We'd laid them down around these bones, to worship and to claim her.

"Persephone," I whispered, and the whisper joined the other echoes.

Something touched my hand. I jumped, but it was only Cass. She laced her fingers with mine. "The flowers," she said.

I nodded. There were flowers set in the skull's gaping eye sockets. Lilies. And they were fresh.

The past wasn't the past anymore. It was lying in front of us, and we were eleven years old again, and we were still playing the game.

There'd been a fire at the mill that summer. A faulty bit of wiring had thrown a spark, and with all the sawdust, that was all it took. There wasn't much damage, but it was all anyone was talking about—the what-if of it all. What if Cassidy's dad, Jim, hadn't been working overnight. What if the lone employee working with him hadn't noticed the orange glow across the yard. What if Jim hadn't called it in right away, not bothering to confirm if it was in fact a fire, knowing that flames in this place would spread fast enough that seconds counted.

It would've only hastened the inevitable. The mill would close eight months later. A fire at least would've gotten the Greens a fat insurance payout. But to the three of us, the fire at the mill didn't signify a risk to jobs or money; it was an omen of greater things.

Our games had been fragile in the days since school. We all sensed an ending, and we weren't ready to let go. But it was only after the fire that Cassidy suggested the Goddess Game.

The forces of nature were out of balance, she informed us, having gathered us in our usual clearing in the woods. We had to put them right by performing a series of rituals in the name of the goddesses—otherwise, great calamities would befall us.

"What calamities?" I remembered Liv asking.

"Oh, fires, floods, plagues, the usual," Cassidy said with relish.

"Frogs," I offered helpfully, sullenly standing with my back against a tree. I was angry about something. I was angry most of the time, back then.

Cass picked out our goddesses and assigned us tasks. As Hecate she would design the rituals, of course, and Liv-Athena would do research for us, and as Artemis the huntress I would find things. Magic things. Important things. Whatever my intuition told me the goddesses needed us to find.

We would need to do seven rituals, she'd said. Liv had objected, and I tried to compromise on four—four was better for Liv and her fixation on numbers as omens—but Cassidy insisted. Seven. No arguments. It would be fun, she said. It would be our game for the summer, and we'd take it seriously. She didn't say *one last time*, but we all knew what she meant.

The first few weeks weren't so different than any of our other games. I brought "treasures" from my dad's collections or things I found out in the woods—a few things I stole from people in town. Liv read up on myths, and we rewrote them to suit our own sensibilities. Cass led us through the first "ritual," which involved reciting what she claimed was a genuine prayer to Hecate while walking through the woods in a solemn procession, carrying lit candles.

We almost believed again. We were close. Standing on the edge, wanting to fall forward.

And then there'd been the fight. It wasn't the first, not by a long shot. They started over any little thing. Liv would fret and try to make peace, and Cass and I would rip into each other.

I don't remember what it was even about. I do remember the anger, the thorns of it in my veins, the heat of it in my skin. Cass, blond, beautiful, perfect, stood there with her arms crossed, and I wanted to crack her nose with my fist.

"You're such a stuck-up *bitch* sometimes!" I screamed at her. "You think you can tell everybody what to do!"

"I'd rather be a stuck-up bitch than live in trash," she yelled back, eyes fever bright.

I knew she didn't mean it. She was just trying to get me to break. To hit her, so she could hit me back. There wasn't anyone else to hurt, and we had to hurt something.

Sometimes I gave in to the fight we both wanted. Today I ran. She shouted after me, but I kept going. I had to spend this energy somewhere, and the other option was breaking her pretty face.

"Naomi, stop running! Come back! I'm sorry! I'm so sorry, come back!"

They chased after me. I could hear them crashing through the forest behind me. I leapt over roots and scrambled over logs and ran without paying attention to where I was going. I only wanted to get away.

Hot tears streaked my cheeks. *Trash. You're trash.* My lungs burned. I wasn't Artemis, wasn't a goddess who could endlessly run through the wilds with her sacred deer. But I couldn't stop or turn back, because I couldn't face them.

*Trash.*

Up ahead was a hump in the earth. A boulder, slablike, mostly covered with moss and trees. Only the face of it was bare, so that it formed a small hill, and beneath it was a gap, a hollow space.

Cass and Liv were catching up. Without thinking, I dropped to my belly and skittered under the boulder. I expected a shallow depression maybe big enough to hide in, but to my surprise the ground sloped away beneath me, and I half fell, half lowered myself.

The boulder formed the bulk of the roof of the space, and tree roots and the flow of water had carved the rest. There was a split toward the far side of the chamber, a gap that let in a narrow shaft of light and illuminated the web of tree roots holding up the "ceiling." The chamber—cave—was about three feet tall, maybe five feet across, eight feet long. Enough room for a sitting child. Enough room for the body.

I held my breath. It couldn't be real, I thought—but of course it was. I could have reached out and touched it.

The skeleton lay on its side. Bits of rotten clothing hung from the ribs. All the flesh had been stripped away.

Tentatively I reached out and touched the smooth brow of the skull. My fingers came away gritty. I shuddered.

The skull was cracked on the side of the head. Had that been what killed them?

Liv and Cass were calling. Reluctantly, I turned my back on the body. I pushed myself up the incline and scrambled out from the gap beneath the rock. Liv shrieked as I emerged, caked in dirt, like some primordial beast. Cass babbled apologies, cheeks damp with tears as she grabbed at me, begging forgiveness.

"You need to see this," I said, and she fell silent.

I brought them down into the earth, Liv frightened, Cass curious. We knelt around the skeleton in awed and nervous silence.

"Who is it? What happened to them?" Liv asked.

I almost said then that we needed to get help. It almost happened that way: us running out of the woods, telling the first person we saw that we'd found a body. A story we'd tell the rest of our lives, *the time we found that skeleton in the woods.* Maybe none of the rest of it would have happened. No Stahl, no scars, no shattered lives.

Almost. But then Cass gasped.

"Look," she said.

There, around the skeleton's wrist, was a loop of nylon, threaded through cheap plastic beads with letters stamped on them. It was hard to read in the dim light, the letters mostly worn away. But you could still make it out enough to figure out what it said.

*Persephone.*

"What now?" Cass asked. We'd climbed out of the cave, brushed the dirt from our clothes. The sunlight through the branches cast ragged shadows over our faces. "She isn't here, Naomi. What now?"

Where else would Liv go? She'd gone back to Persephone. The flowers proved that. But Persephone wasn't the only sacred thing in these woods. I pulled the stack of photographs out of my pocket. The path ended here, but the photos kept going.

"What were the other rituals?" I asked.

"What?"

"The Goddess Game. There was the prayer, and the flowers for Persephone, and then—what was next?"

"The burial," Cass said reluctantly.

It rushed back to me. Cass made me sneak into the mill and take some of the burned wood from the fire. I'd gotten caught almost immediately. I could still feel the weight of Big Jim's hand on my shoulder.

"What are you doing, kid?" he'd asked, his voice baritone and unamused. It was late, after sunset. I remembered the glow of the interior light in the second-to-last car in the lot as Natalie Carey got in, giving me just a brief look of sympathy before she started up the engine.

I couldn't remember what lie I'd concocted, only that it made Jim roll his eyes and send me on my way with a charred plank. We'd buried it and consecrated the ground with what Cass claimed was holy water.

I sifted through the photos. There—a circle of stones. We'd put them around the burial site, to mark it. I flipped to the next image. The pond. Water glinted off its surface. "The water was next," I said, and Cass nodded.

"We have to prove our commitment," Cass had said all those years ago. The pond was no more than hip-high almost everywhere, but at the eastern edge was a place where the ground dropped away.

We would stay under as long as we could, Cass had decided. That way the goddesses would know we were dedicated to them. And so we'd slipped beneath the water. I remembered the shocking cold of it, and the silt that made it hard to see and stung my eyes, though I'd forced myself to keep them open so I could watch Cass. So that I could be sure I wouldn't be the first to break the surface. We'd glared at each other, each determined to outlast the other. Cass broke first. I was half a second behind her.

We'd been so busy gulping air into our starved lungs that it took us far too long to realize Liv hadn't come up yet.

How could I have forgotten it? The limp weight of her body as we hauled her out. The way she coughed and gagged and spluttered and finally drew in ragged breaths. How she'd begged us to let her go back, that she needed the goddesses to know that she was committed. That she was *good*. I'd held her, pressed my lips against her forehead, and tasted that silty water on her skin, and I'd promised her she was perfect.

It had been the fourth ritual. Olivia had believed in the power of fours and sevens. She still did.

"I think I know where she is," I said.

"She's fine. She'll come home," Cass said, but she sounded nervous. "Why are you so convinced something is wrong? This is Liv. She wanders off. It's what she does."

My throat constricted. I didn't know how to explain it to her. Liv's call, her absence—they were worrying. But they weren't the only reason that I hadn't been able to get the bitter taste of fear out of my mouth since I left Kimiko.

I should have died that day. I should have died here—almost exactly where we were standing. And ever since, I'd had this feeling like the woods weren't done with us. What had begun that day had gone unfinished. We couldn't escape it forever.

"Where's the pond from here?" I asked.

Cass sighed. "I'm not sure."

"We'll have to backtrack to the trail," I said.

The hike was easier on the way back, following our own path of trampled underbrush, but we still had to stop and reorient ourselves a few times. Back in the nineties it had been basically a straight shot from the road, but with everything so overgrown since then, our path was a winding one.

Liv probably wasn't even at the pond, I thought. She had plenty of places to go when she didn't want to be found. She would call soon enough, and I'd feel foolish, dragging Cass all over like this—brambles in our hair and dirt smudged on our faces like when we were girls.

Cass yelped behind me. I spun in time to see her sprawl to the ground, swearing in a tight voice. I rushed back to her, but she'd already pushed herself up to a sitting position. She groaned.

"I am so out of practice at this," she complained. "I caught my foot on a root or something."

"Are you okay?" I asked.

"I'll be fine," she said, but she was gritting her teeth as she braced herself to get up. I grabbed her elbow and helped haul her upright. "See? All good."

That lasted until she took her first step. Her face went white and she staggered, shifting her weight back to the other foot. "Broken?" I said, thinking rapidly. We weren't too far from the car.

"Not broken. Maybe sprained," she said, then hissed sharply as she tested the ankle again. "It's not too bad."

We were nearly at the pond trail. I glanced north, toward the pond, and then back toward the car. The pond was still a good distance away. "Let's go back to the car," I said.

"And what if Liv is up there and she's spiraling? What if she needs our help?" Cass asked. She tried the ankle again, swore.

"You need to get that ankle elevated and iced before we have to cut you out of your boots," I said. I hesitated. "You said it yourself. Liv does this. She runs off, and she comes back."

"And what if we're wrong?" Cass asked. She gripped my arm for support, her fingers digging in. "You go find Liv. I can drive myself home and get this taken care of before it gets worse, and then you call me and we'll figure out next steps."

"Can you make it?" I asked.

"It's like five hundred feet," she said, rolling her eyes. "I can hop on one foot if I need to."

"You're sure you're going to be all right?" I asked her. I shouldn't abandon her with an injured ankle in the woods. I shouldn't even be considering it. Liv was probably fine, and I was being the worst friend in the world.

But Cass just gave me a wry smile. "It's okay, Naomi. She's always going to be your priority."

I blanched. "That's not it."

Cass gave a one-shouldered shrug, like it didn't matter. "I just wish she could be there for you as much as you are for her," she said. She eased her weight slowly onto her bad ankle, nodded. "Call me as soon as you know anything."

She limped off toward the south, moving at a slow, lurching pace. I stood frozen for a moment. *I should follow her. Get her back to the car, at least.* But with every second that slipped away, the frantic feeling in my chest grew stronger. Cass was right. Liv was always going to be my priority. Because Cass didn't need me, and Liv did. I turned north and started walking.

The Pond Loop trail was indistinct in places, half covered in blackberry brambles. It must not be a very popular hike. I mostly kept my eyes on the ground ahead of me so I wouldn't trip.

"Naomi?"

"Fuck!" I straightened with a jerk. Ethan Schreiber stood ten feet down the path, hands in his pockets.

"Whoa, sorry," he said, taking his hands out so he could hold them up in surrender.

"What the hell are you doing here?" I asked him, my heart still racing.

"I saw your car at the trailhead," he said.

"So that thing you said about not stalking me." I crossed my arms and gave him what I hoped was an unimpressed and not at all rattled look. My heart was hammering in my chest.

He winced. "Okay, now I see where this seems pretty sketchy. I just thought that you and I got off on the wrong foot, and so I had the idea to come talk to you again." He rubbed the back of his head sheepishly. "I thought I could catch up with you, but then I heard voices and I turned around, and that pretty much brings us to when I jumped out of the trees like a madman and startled you. All part of my plan to come across as more normal and approachable and friendly, see."

I sighed. He looked about as scary as a Labrador realizing that no, in fact, you do not want the three-day-old dead bird it has just dropped at your feet. "I'm not going to give you an interview," I said. I started down the trail again, stepping pointedly around him. I assumed he'd take the hint and leave.

Instead, he hurried to catch up with me. "I ambushed you before. It wasn't fair. I thought I could startle you into giving me something, but I can see that wasn't the right approach."

"So you're attempting your dubious charms instead?" I asked.

"They usually work just fine."

"Not on me."

"Apparently. But I'll get there," he said.

"You basically accused me of framing a man for attempted murder," I said. "I don't really see you coming back from that."

"I don't think you framed anyone," Schreiber replied, ducking under a low-hanging branch. "Not intentionally, at least. Tell me—how did you identify Alan Stahl as your attacker? Was it a photo array?"

"I—" I stopped, genuinely unsure of the answer. "What does it matter?" I wasn't going to answer his questions, I reminded myself.

"I've read everything that's publicly available on the case. And some other things that aren't," Schreiber said. "There were massive gaps in your memory. Still are, I'm guessing."

"Trauma does that," I said.

"I'm well aware. I'm not blaming you for it. I just find it interesting that in your police interviews, you could barely even remember what you'd been doing in the woods. What day it was. What the weather was like. But you described Stahl in exacting detail. Down to the birth-mark on his cheek. Every time you were interviewed the description got more detailed." He paused, letting that simmer, then shrugged. "Things took a while to come back to you, I guess."

"Must be." My pulse raced. He didn't know anything. There was nothing to know. Nothing that could be proved.

The trees opened up at the edge of the pond. Frogs creaked and croaked in the water, and insects danced along the surface. The scene had a bedraggled kind of charm to it, but the magic of that summer was long gone.

"Is it at all possible that you were mistaken?" Ethan asked, his voice keeping me brutishly anchored in the present. I wished he would leave—and I was glad he didn't. Time here was slippery. I didn't want to be alone with the past. "Can you see *any* possibility that the man who attacked you wasn't Stahl, but someone else?"

"Will you just let it go? I'm not going to play along with your pet theory," I said.

"Naomi." He grabbed my arm. I snarled, wrenching away from him, and turned with my fingers tightening into fists. But he wasn't looking at me. His gaze shot past me. I started to turn. He reached for me again, as if to stop me, but he couldn't. Nothing could stop this, the moment when endless possibility collapsed into the cruel certainty of fact.

It was her hand I saw first, fingers bent. And then the oil slick of her hair seeping out across the surface of the water, obscuring all but a fractured sliver of her cheek. Then the dark blotch of her torso, loose shirt billowing around her, obscuring the shape of her until my mind refused to see that it was a person at all, was more than this collection of fragments. Shape and shadow jumbled on the surface of the water into something that couldn't be Olivia.

My mind rejected it, but my body knew. I was in motion before my tattered thoughts could stitch themselves together.

Ethan's hand scraped against my arm once more, but I plunged past. I ran straight into the water, thrashing my way through to her. I clawed my way past cattails, feet sinking into silty mud. *Hold on, hold on,* I thought, logic left behind me on the shore. She couldn't be alive and it didn't matter because I had to get to her. I was eleven years old and she was in the water and I couldn't find her, the silt too thick, my hands groping at nothing, nothing, nothing.

And then she was in my arms, and I was dragging her up. And she had coughed and sputtered and fought me, and breathed, and lived. She had lived, and she would live now, if I could only get to her.

Her face was swollen and gray when I turned her over. "It's okay," I murmured inanely. I pulled her against me. Her eyes were shut, her mouth slack. "It's okay. It's okay." I bent over her, my breath knotted in my throat.

*You promised,* I shouted, but the words lodged in silence. *I'm here. You said you would be, too.*

"Naomi. There's nothing you can do. You shouldn't touch the body," Ethan said. He stood in the water beside me, his hand outstretched toward my shoulder, not quite touching me. "We need to call the police."

I shook my head, on my knees in the muck. "I'm not leaving her here." I tried to lift her. She was so thin. Like she was worried that if there were any more of her, she'd only be in the way. But I couldn't get my arms under her, couldn't find my footing. I slipped, struggling under her weight. I couldn't leave her in the water. She was so cold. She hated the cold.

"She's dead, Naomi. She's gone," he said. I shook my head. She couldn't be. She couldn't be, because she'd promised she wouldn't try again. Because she knew I would be there and I would help and we would fix it, together.

But I breathed in the scent of rain and old growth and tipped my head back, let the cold water patter over my eyelids, and I made myself stop. Be still.

*Let go*, I thought.

*Let go*, a girl thought twenty years ago, rain pattering against her cheek, the scent of rotting wood and blood in her nose. *Let go.*

"Breathe," Schreiber said.

"I'm breathing," I told him, though I wasn't sure it was true. I didn't see how it could be. I was supposed to be dead. Olivia was supposed to be alive. I looked at Schreiber. "I'm not leaving her here," I said again, firmly.

He stepped forward, and for a moment I thought he meant to pull me away from her, but instead he slid his arms beneath Olivia's body. "I've got her," he said. He lifted her from me slowly, gently, angling her so that her head rested in the crook of his arm. The tips of her fingers trailed in the water as he waded back to shore, as I followed shuddering in his wake.

He set her down there and placed his coat over her face like a shroud. I sank to my knees beside her. My mind was empty. I couldn't think. Didn't want to.

"I don't have signal here. We have to go back to the trailhead and call the police," Ethan said.

"I'm staying here," I said. I pressed a fist against my stomach.

Ethan nodded. "Okay. I'll be right back. Don't . . . don't go any-where."

There wasn't anywhere for me to go. I was where I was supposed to be: with Olivia. In the woods.

"Why did you do it?" I asked her now. Asked her then, lying in her bed together, the blanket up over our heads as Cass snored on the floor. Silt from the pond still in our hair, the taste of it still on our tongues. "You didn't have to stay under that long."

"Yes I did. The goddesses were watching," Liv said.

"Do you really believe in them?" I asked.

"Don't you?"

"Of course," I said, pretending it was true. "Of course I do."

"I can feel them sometimes," she whispered, and burrowed against me. I put my arms around her, her head tucked under my chin. I held her until she went slack with sleep, but my eyes never closed.

"Of course I believe," I whispered to the dark, but there was no one to answer.

The summer we found Persephone, Dad's drinking spiraled out of control. He'd been seeing a woman, but when she realized he wasn't the fixer-upper she thought, just a money pit, she bailed. Up until then, he'd held down a part-time job tending bar and kept food in the cupboards, but he lost interest in both. I spent most meals with Cass's family or Liv's. Found five dollars tucked in my coat pocket more often than not. Got invited for sleepovers even on school nights. That's how Chester took care of its own: quietly, so you wouldn't seem to be interfering.

The weight of all that pity was almost unbearable, but Liv never once made me feel lesser. We'd been outsiders together. We were all friends, and I'd never have said I loved one more than the other, but I'd harbored the secret truth that Liv was my best friend, the one who understood me.

And now she was dead.

My coffee cup had gone cold in my hand. A fleck of grit floated slowly over its surface, finally clinging to the waxed cardboard rim. I tipped the cup, dislodging the fleck, and watched it drift away again.

"Ms. Cunningham?"

It was the third time Bishop had said it. I looked up through bleary eyes. I sat in a conference room at the Chester police station, a gray blanket wrapped around me, wearing borrowed sweats and a department T-shirt. I wasn't sure how long I'd been there. I couldn't seem to anchor myself in time. I kept slipping back to the pond, to that summer, to a hundred days in between. Anything but now.

"I'm going to ask you a few questions," Bishop said. No *if that's all right* or other niceties that might imply I had a choice.

I nodded like I didn't have anything to hide. Bishop took the next seat over from me, setting a folder on the table in front of her. I stared at it, trying to guess what was inside. Information about me? About Liv?

"When is the last time you spoke to Ms. Barnes?" Bishop asked.

"Yesterday. We met up at Cassidy's house and then I dropped her off at home afterward."

"Did she seem agitated?"

"Did you know Olivia?" I asked, head tilted. Bishop's lips thinned. "Olivia being agitated doesn't mean much. She gets anxious a lot."

"More agitated than usual, then."

Agitated, like she'd ripped open a poorly healed wound we'd been ignoring for twenty years. Agitated, like she was dragging our secrets out into the light. "I'm not sure."

I wanted Bishop to stop talking, but her questions kept coming, relentless, leaving my thoughts no time to find solid ground before they were sent skidding away again.

"Why were you meeting up?"

"Stahl died. We wanted to see each other. You know. Survivors' club." My voice sounded distant. I hadn't made the active choice to lie. It was just habit. Easier than telling the truth. The lies let me stay numb.

"Did Olivia own a gun?" Bishop asked.

That jerked me out of the haze momentarily. "What? No," I said. "She hates guns. They scare her." Growing up in a logging town, you'd have thought she would grow out of it, but she never stopped getting antsy around them.

Bishop made a noise in the back of her throat that I couldn't interpret. "Her father has two guns registered to him. A shotgun and a Ruger SP101 revolver."

"Right," I said. "He bought those for protection when we were kids, but Liv never touched them. Why are you asking about a gun?"

"She was shot," Bishop said without inflection, and there was a strange kindness in that, stripping it down to a simple fact without either gentleness or malice. "The bullet entered the temple and exited on the other side, toward the back of her skull. Her hair might have concealed the wounds," she added, more softly, seeing the confusion in my eyes.

The world shifted around those words, reality reordering itself. I hadn't thought about how she died, only that she was dead. When she had attempted suicide, she had overdosed on pills. Shooting herself was too violent. "Liv wouldn't use a gun. She hated them. She hated blood, she—"

"Do you own a gun, Ms. Cunningham?"

"No," I said. "I mean, yes, I guess."

"You guess? Which is it, yes or no?"

"My boyfriend bought me a gun, but it's registered to him," I said impatiently. Mitch had thought it would help my anxiety. I'd left it in its case. PTSD meant my brain wasn't able to sort out the difference between real threats and imagined ones. I didn't want it making that error while I had a gun in my hand.

"What kind of gun?" Bishop prompted.

"I don't know. It's black. I think it's a nine-millimeter," I said. "I don't know guns. But it's in Seattle. I've never even taken it to a gun range."

"We may need to take a look at it," Bishop said.

"Why?" I asked, baffled. "I told you, it's in Seattle. In the back of my closet."

"What were you doing in the woods last night, Ms. Cunningham?" Bishop asked. I stared at her, uncomprehending. And then I understood, and my breath caught. "What were you doing in the woods?" Bishop repeated.

My mouth was dry. I reached for the cup of water someone had given me along with the coffee, but it was empty. I put my hand around it anyway, tightening my fingers until the plastic bowed. "I didn't hurt Liv," I said hoarsely.

"That's not what I asked you."

"She died last night? There?" It was the only thing that made sense. My breath was thin and sharp and wouldn't fill my lungs all the way. The pond wasn't far from the Grotto. Wasn't far from where I'd been thrashing around drunkenly, chasing after shadows. "I saw someone. In the woods. I thought they were following me."

"You saw someone. A man or a woman?"

"I don't know. A man, I think. It was dark."

"Really." Her skepticism made the word a bludgeon. Anger flared in my chest. The heat of it licked out along my ribs, piercing the cold, muddled haze of grief and shock that had wrapped itself around me. "You're sure you saw someone?"

"Yes, I'm sure," I bit out. But I hadn't been, had I? I'd told myself it was all my imagination.

"Large, small, thin, fat? Could you tell their race, their age?"

"No. They were just a shadow. I saw them moving." It sounded ridiculous. I'd been drunk off my ass, and she knew it.

"And what time was this?"

"I don't know," I admitted.

"I see." Her tone was unsurprised. I set my jaw. "Your best guess."

I tried to track the time line back in my mind, but I didn't remember looking at the clock after dinner with Cody. "After sunset. I had dinner and then I crashed in my motel room for a while and watched TV. I'm not sure for how long."

"What did you watch?" Almost bored. Like it didn't matter.

"*Forensic Files,*" I said. "I watched an episode and channel-surfed for a while. I'm not sure how long. Maybe an hour. I went over to the Corner Store and then drove out. Sat in my car for a while. It couldn't have been much later than ten. So she wasn't out there yet." I sagged, the faintest tremor of relief going through me. If she'd been out there, and I hadn't heard her, hadn't helped her . . .

"What makes you say that?"

"Kimiko heard her coming home early in the morning. Or really late? I'm not sure."

"The gate code to the Barnes residence was entered at 4:47 a.m.," Bishop said. She'd already known. So she was just checking my story. "Did anyone else see you?"

"While I was passed out in my car, you mean? I have no idea," I said, irritated. She was wasting her time.

"Why were you at the pond this morning?"

I was getting a headache. Or maybe I'd had one all along. "I was looking for Liv. I was worried. She'd left me a voicemail that sounded strange. I thought she might try to hurt herself."

"What time did she call you?"

"Ten."

"Around the time you were in the woods."

"Signal is patchy out there. It must have gone straight to voicemail." Or I hadn't noticed it. I'd been too wrapped up in myself, in my memories.

"How were things between you and Olivia?"

"Good," I said tightly.

"You didn't argue with her yesterday?"

"Argue with her? Who told you that?" I asked. It was the wrong response. Bishop's eyes hardened.

"What were you arguing about?" she asked.

"Nothing." Except that we had argued—about Persephone.

Liv had found Persephone, and Cass and I had tried to talk her out of saying anything. I'd been out in the woods that night. Bishop was already looking at me like I was a suspect. Telling her we'd hidden a body for twenty years would hardly make me less suspicious.

"Naomi?" Bishop said. "Is there something you want to tell me?"

I started to open my mouth—and the door opened. Officer Dougherty stepped in and widened his eyes in an expression of exaggerated surprise. "Naomi, honey. You're still here? You ought to be getting some rest, poor thing."

Since the last time I'd seen him, Dougherty had put on some weight around his middle and lost it from his cheeks, which were cadaverously hollow. He sported a gray mustache of the kind that only existed in hipster bars and towns like this.

My memories of the man were hazy. He'd just been a junior member of the department when I was a kid, but he'd risen through the ranks rapidly—not that it was hard when the number of officers in the department was in the single digits. Miller had been grooming him as the next chief for ages, and I still couldn't quite believe the city had brought in an outsider instead. Judging by the looks that passed between Dougherty and Bishop, he couldn't believe it either.

"We're just going over a few details, Officer Dougherty," Bishop said levelly. If Dougherty detected the warning in her voice, he gave no sign.

"You got her statement already, Monica," he said. A tendon in Bishop's jaw twitched. No *Chief* or *Boss* from Dougherty. "And her ride's waiting on her. I think we ought to let the poor girl take off, don't you?"

My ride—he must mean Ethan. Ethan, who'd talked to the police while I shivered in the passenger seat of my car, and insisted they let me have some time and some dry clothes before they asked me any questions. When he'd asked for my keys I'd handed them over without question, and I realized with a start that he still had them.

"I'll let you know when we're finished here," Bishop said to Dougherty.

"Well, that's your call," Dougherty said, nodding. Friendly as anything. Condescending as hell. "Did you know, I've known these girls since they were yea high?" he added, leveling a hand below his hip. His tone was warning, and his message was clear. Bishop was a newcomer. For all my faults, I belonged to Chester. "Damn shame, all of this. But it's pretty clear-cut."

"It is?" I asked. The corner of Bishop's mouth twitched with annoyance.

"It's a tragedy, is what it is," Dougherty said. "Any time someone takes their own life, it's a tragedy."

"You think she killed herself," I said. "Then why—" I cut my eyes to Bishop, who was sitting with her lips pressed together. I looked between them in confusion. "I thought—the questions you were asking—"

"If she shot herself, the gun should be at the scene," Bishop said. "We haven't located it."

"We don't know where exactly she was standing when she died," Dougherty said. "The body would have drifted some. We're checking the bottom of the pond, but it'll take a while."

"In her previous attempt, she overdosed on prescription pills," Bishop said. "Using a gun is a lot more unusual for a woman. Especially one who isn't comfortable around guns."

"A determined person will use whatever they can get their hands on, in my experience," Dougherty said, and that false friendliness was wearing off, revealing the burr of irritation beneath. "And the pills were locked up."

"In the same safe as the gun, which doesn't seem to have been properly secured one way or the other, *Officer* Dougherty," Bishop said. Dougherty lifted his hands as if in surrender, ducking his head.

"So you don't *know* it was suicide," I said. I felt like I was lurching to and fro. I couldn't tell which answer I wanted. Which one would be worse.

"Hon, there was a note," Dougherty said. "Her mother found it about an hour ago." He reached into his pocket and drew out a clear plastic bag. Bishop made an abrupt gesture as if to stop him, fury in her eyes, but I had no attention to spare for their power struggle. A single sheet of white paper was inside, creased at the center like it had been folded. He set it gently onto the table beside me. The letters were shaky, oversized, and slewed across the page so much I barely recognized Liv's handwriting.

I'm sorry. I know that I should be strong, but I can't anymore. I'm tired of feeling like this. I'm tired of lying. I can't keep doing it.

I'm going to be with Persephone now. We never finished. That means this makes seven. It can finally be over. I'm sorry.

Liv

I reached out, my fingers brushing the cool plastic. There was a note. That was that, then. Liv was gone. She'd broken her promise to me. And I'd broken my promise to be there for her when she needed it.

Except this wasn't right. It didn't make sense. She wouldn't have used the gun. And if she was going out to the woods to be with Persephone, why had she been at the pond?

"Who is Persephone?" Bishop asked.

"It was a game we played that summer. The Goddess Game," I said, voice distant. I didn't have to say what summer I meant. Dougherty nodded gravely. *Tell them*, I thought. *Tell them the truth.* But the words wouldn't come. Twenty-two years of silence weren't that easy to break.

"What did Liv lie about, Naomi?" Bishop asked. She gave me a steady look. Not angry, not suspicious. Not content.

"Monica, cut the girl some slack," Dougherty said gruffly. "She probably just meant she was lying about being okay, something like that. We might never know. Let me get Naomi on out of here. Mayor Green wants a word with you anyway."

Bishop's look was brimming with irritation. "You might have started with that," she said, standing. Big Jim didn't like being kept waiting. The Chief served at the pleasure of the city council, which meant at Big Jim's pleasure, and Bishop couldn't afford to be on his bad side. She gave me one last considering look and then waved a hand. "See her out," she said, and stalked from the room.

I stood, leaving the blanket puddled on the chair behind me. My borrowed shoes squeaked on the tile.

"I'm sorry about that," Dougherty said, hand on my shoulder as he shepherded me toward the front lobby. It was all I could do not to shrug it off. "She's not from here, you know how it is. She doesn't know the way things ought to go."

Not from here. Not one of us. That was all that mattered in Chester—who belonged and who didn't. I'd been born here and I still ended up on the wrong side of that equation more often than not.

Ethan Schreiber was waiting in the lobby. He'd had time to change, apparently, because he was wearing fresh, dry clothes. He looked up with an expression of worry as we entered.

"Can I leave you here?" Dougherty asked. *With him* went unspoken. I answered with a nod. Dougherty shifted his weight uncomfortably. "I'm real sorry about Liv. After all you girls have been through . . ."

"Thank you, Officer Dougherty," I managed.

"Call me Bill," he said. I just nodded again and walked toward Ethan, who watched with his hands in his pockets. We didn't say anything as we headed outside. My car was waiting for us in the lot. Ethan pulled my keys out of his pocket.

"What about your car?" I asked him.

He looked at me curiously, and I realized I'd probably asked him the same question already. "An officer is going to bring it by the motel for me," he said. "They gave me a ride back so I could change."

"You didn't have to answer questions?"

"I gave a statement, but I didn't have much to offer," Ethan said. He opened the passenger door for me, and I folded myself into the seat, hands clenched to stop their trembling. I didn't look at him as he started up the engine. "Motel?" he asked. I nodded. He pulled onto the road.

There was a fist around my throat as we cut our way through the dismal strip of downtown. Liv was dead. She'd killed herself, but we'd killed her, too. We hadn't listened to her. We'd wrapped our hands around our secrets like barbed wire, even when they cut into us. Even when there was no goddamn reason not to let go. I was still holding on.

Raw, animal grief consumed me. I bent to it, collapsing in on myself. I couldn't tell if I was crying; I wasn't in my body enough to know. I was in the woods.

"We're here," Ethan said. It took me a moment to remember how to unbuckle myself. When I fumbled with the room key, Ethan took it from me and opened the door, then stepped back to let me pass.

I collapsed onto the bed, my elbows on my knees, and stared at the wall. "This can't be real," I said.

"I wish I could tell you it wasn't," he replied. He shut the door and sat beside me, leaving plenty of room between us.

"You can go," I said.

"I don't have to."

"If you think I'm going to give you a quote, or, or—"

"I'm not trying to get a story out of you right now. I just want to make sure you're all right."

"Why?" I demanded.

"Because I'm a fundamentally decent person, maybe?" he suggested.

"No such thing," I told him. I ran my thumb along the scar on my wrist, back and forth. The one scar on my body that wasn't from the attack. "If I'd answered when she called, I could have talked her down."

"It's not your fault," Ethan said. It was what you were supposed to say, I guess. "She wanted to talk to me. Do you know why?"

"What happened to not trying to get a story out of me?" I asked.

"I'm just trying to understand," he replied, and only then did I notice the way his hands were shaking.

"Are *you* all right?" I asked him.

He gave a choked laugh. "I make a living writing about murders and suicides. I read about all the gory details. Look at crime scene photos."

"It's not the same," I said.

He met my eyes. His breath trembled out of him. I knew that look. Wanting to run without knowing what it was you should be running from. "No. It's not," he agreed. He raised his hand in an odd, abortive gesture, almost like he'd meant to touch my arm. I probably would have bitten a finger off if he tried. "I'm sorry about Olivia. She seemed like a lovely person."

"She was," I said. And then, "She was complicated."

"The best people always are," he replied. He looked away, toward the window. The blinds were shut, casting slashes of shadow across his face. "Is there someone I can call?" he asked.

Cass, I remembered. I'd promised to call her, and I hadn't. She had to know about Liv by now. But I couldn't face her. Anger and guilt tangled inside me. She'd left me on that trail. She'd turned away from me and from Liv, and she hadn't been there when I needed her. When *Liv* needed her.

It was absurd. She'd been hurt. Of course she turned back. But I felt like I had when we fought all those years ago, desperate to hurt each other, desperate for the pain of being hurt.

"No. There's no one," I said. "You can go. I'll be all right."

"I'm two doors down if you change your mind," he said. "Room four."

"Is that some kind of come-on?" I asked him.

"What? No," he said. "Jesus, you really don't have a high opinion of humanity, do you?"

"At least I'm up-front about it," I said with a one-shouldered shrug.

He looked like he wanted to say something more, but he only shook his head. He let himself out and shut the door behind him.

I let gravity pull me down onto the bed, not bothering to take off my shoes, and lay on my side staring at the wall. I felt like I was drifting. It was the same sensation as when I lay against that rotting log, dizzy from the lack of blood, listening to the birds call uncaringly overhead.

It was the feeling of waiting for the world to end.

I must have fallen asleep at some point, because I woke up an hour later, the exhaustion gone and the grief hardened into a knife's edge, sliding across my tender skin. I sat up gingerly.

I needed to do something—staying still was suddenly impossible, nervous energy crackling through me. I needed to talk to Cass. We had to figure out what to do about what Liv had found. And I wanted to be with her. For all the fights and stumbles along the way, she was still one of the two people in the world who knew me best.

The only one now.

When I drove up to Cass's house, she wasn't alone. There was a truck out front, a brand-new monstrosity that could have hauled an elephant trailer. I almost turned around when I saw it, but as I hovered outside the door opened and Cass's mother stepped out, waving to me. I couldn't very well leave now.

I walked up the drive, tumbling backward through time with every step. Meredith Green was a tiny woman, like a twist of wire. Age had distilled her down to her essence, hard and sharp, and what vanity she displayed with her dyed-blond hair and understated makeup had a utility of its own. She was the mayor's wife, and she played the role with efficiency and unwavering dedication.

"Naomi. I'm glad you're here," she said. She took both my hands in hers. She'd always had warm hands, but now they had that papery feel of age. The first time she'd held my hands like this, a soft and inescapable touch, I'd still been in the hospital. The woman who'd sighed like a martyr every time Cass brought me over had called me *sweetheart*, and she had promised that she and her husband would look after me.

"You heard," I said. Of course they had. Jim was the mayor. He'd have known as soon as the police did.

"It's terrible. Marcus and Kimiko must be utterly destroyed. Poor things," she said. She hadn't let me go. I tugged my hands from hers, and she offered no resistance.

"I was hoping to talk to Cass," I said.

"I'm afraid she's not up for visitors," Meredith said. "Maybe later."

"I need to speak with her," I said more firmly.

Her lips pressed into a thin line. "I will not let you drag my daughter into this horror again," she said.

I blinked, taken aback. "I've never dragged Cass into anything," I said.

"It took years for her to recover. Years. And God knows I love that little girl, but if it hadn't been for you—"

"If I hadn't almost been killed, you mean?" I asked.

"Let's not pretend you were some innocent little girl. The things you all got up to in those woods were ungodly. They were perverse," she said. "You invited darkness into your life and you brought Cassidy and Olivia into it, too. And now Olivia has paid the price."

I could have told her that the Goddess Game—that *most* of the games—were Cass's idea, but I knew better. Cassidy Green could do no wrong in the eyes of her parents, and if she did it was someone else's fault.

"Mom? Who's there?" Cass called. She appeared in the hall behind her mother, looking glassy-eyed and disheveled. Her foot was wrapped, and she was limping heavily. She spotted me. For a moment, the world hung on a point of perfect stillness—and then Cassidy gave a gulping cry and rushed forward at a stumbling run, past her mother, and flung her arms around me.

She buried her head against my shoulder and sobbed, and I held her, eyes shut, holding back my own tears.

"I can't believe she's gone," Cass said through racking sobs.

"I know," I whispered. It didn't feel real. Part of me still hoped it wasn't.

"Come inside, both of you," Meredith said, her desire to keep me out slightly less powerful than her desire not to have us make a scene where the whole neighborhood could see us.

Cass grabbed my hand and pulled me through the foyer to the stairs, shuffling along on her bad foot. I cast one last look behind me at Meredith's sour face.

Cass had to take the stairs one at a time, leaning heavily on the rail, and her lips were pale by the time she reached the top. She paused for breath for only a second before waving me forward into the master bedroom and shutting the door behind me.

She stood with her back to me a moment, collecting herself, and when she turned around she was shaky but calm, forcing her words out past tears she was barely holding back. "I'm sorry about Mom," she said. "You know how she can be. She thinks she can micromanage this into being okay."

"She always did have control issues," I said. And Cass wasn't the one who had to apologize.

Cass's room was delicate and feminine, but not in an obvious way—done in soft blues and greens, with gentle lighting and an ornate full-length mirror. There were two pairs of slippers by the bed, and nail polish on the bedside table. I could imagine Amanda and her mother having a girls' night in, dishing secrets.

Not real secrets. Just the fun kind.

I sat down on the end of the bed. Silence settled between us, suffocating. "I'm sorry I didn't call," I said. "I promised to call."

"Don't worry about that right now," Cass said. "You must have been in shock."

"Is your ankle . . ."

"Just a sprain. It's doesn't even hurt that much now. I shouldn't have . . ." She looked away and rubbed tears from her cheek with the heel of her hand. "I should have gone with you. You shouldn't have had to find her alone."

"I wasn't alone," I said dully.

"Who . . . ?"

"Ethan Schreiber was there," I said.

"What? Why?" she asked, alarmed. "Did he have something to do with . . . ?"

"No, he didn't," I said quickly. "He was looking for me, that was all."

"Fuck." Cass sank down, her back against the door, and tucked her arms tight against herself.

"Cass," I said. "We need to decide what to do."

She looked at my blankly. "There's nothing to do. She's dead. We can't help her anymore."

"What to do about Persephone," I said.

Cass's mouth opened slightly, as if she was searching for words she couldn't find. "Naomi, we can't do anything. Not right now, at least. We have to shut up and let this blow over."

"Blow over?" I echoed, incredulous.

She winced. "You know what I mean. We can't let anyone know about Persephone right now."

"Why the hell not? It's what Liv wanted. She wanted Persephone to be found. To have peace. We have to do it for her." I set my jaw, rising to my feet. "We pushed her to this. We were afraid and selfish and we wouldn't listen."

Cass shook her head. "Naomi. It won't bring her back. It'll just cause more hurt."

"What if she didn't?" I asked.

"What do you mean, if she didn't? If she didn't kill herself, she'd still be alive."

"I mean, what if someone else killed her? She was *shot*. She wouldn't have used a gun. And the pond—that was the fourth ritual. Fours are lucky. It always drove Kimiko crazy, remember, because it's an unlucky number in Japan, and—"

"And *what?*"

"And she wouldn't have killed herself there," I said, almost shouting.

"Come on, Naomi. Who would want to kill Liv?" Cass said.

"She was looking for Persephone. Maybe someone didn't want her found."

"Don't," Cass said in a fragile whisper. "Don't turn a tragedy into a conspiracy, Naomi. She was sick. She'd tried before. Please. I'm barely holding it together. Please just leave it alone and let her rest."

"She wouldn't have used a gun," I insisted. My voice sounded strange to my own ears.

"Shit." Cass rubbed the back of her neck. "Who would want to kill her, though? I mean, other than us." She gave a strangled kind of laugh.

"What do you mean, other than us?" I asked.

"Nothing. Just—Liv wanted to tell our big secret, and now she's dead. If it wasn't suicide, and the cops find out the truth . . ." She drew in a long, steadying breath. "But it doesn't matter. Obviously, we didn't do it. And you're right. I'm scared out of my mind, but we don't really have a choice. We have to tell the cops."

I stared at her, my mouth dry. "Do you have an alibi?" I asked.

"Jesus, Naomi." Cass gave me a shocked look.

"I'm serious. Do you have an alibi for around dawn this morning?" I asked her.

"I was at the lodge around five until about twenty minutes before you dropped by," she said.

"Was anyone with you?"

She narrowed her eyes. "Percy was there. Why, do *you* have an alibi?" she tossed back, anger crackling.

"I don't," I said, and swallowed. Her eyes widened. "I was in the woods last night. I was passed out in my car on the side of the road until after dawn. Which Chief Bishop knows. And you're right. Liv didn't have any enemies. But we had a good reason to want her to keep quiet."

"Okay," Cass said slowly. She rose and walked over to the bed. She sat beside me, and we stared ahead, not saying anything for several seconds. When she did speak, her voice was thin. "You wouldn't have killed Liv. They'll see that. Won't they?"

I wished I believed her. But I'd spent a lot of time talking to police, twenty years ago. They'd had the answer they wanted and everything they had done was to make sure reality agreed with it. Once they realized Cass and Liv's descriptions matched Stahl, nothing would have persuaded them that he wasn't their man. And Bishop already had it in her head that I was a suspect.

"What do we do?" Cass asked, sounding lost.

"I think we have to keep quiet for now," I said.

"Are you sure?"

"Just for now," I repeated. "Until we know more about what happened. Can you do that? I'm not asking you to lie to the police, but . . ."

"Keeping quiet isn't the same thing as lying, right?" Cass said. "If you think it's the right call, I won't say anything yet. But are you sure?"

I didn't answer right away.

Maybe Liv had died by suicide—broken by our refusal to listen, by our abandonment of Persephone.

Maybe someone had killed her. And there was only one reason I could think of why someone might want to do that. The same reason that Cass and I would be suspects. Liv had found Persephone, but someone didn't want her found.

"We should figure out what Liv knew," I said. "We should find Persephone ourselves."

"Are you kidding? You just said we needed to lie low," Cass said, looking alarmed.

"It was what she wanted."

Cass gave me a steady look. "Naomi, I know you. And I know when you're about to do something stupid. If you go looking for this girl, someone is going to notice. And all those questions we're trying to avoid? You're going to have to answer them."

"I know, but—"

"For fuck's sake, Naomi, I just lost one of my best friends. I cannot be worried about you, too," Cass said fiercely. She grabbed my hands. "I need you to promise me that you're going to leave this alone until we're sure it's safe. And *then* we will find out what Liv knew. Together. And we will decide what to do about it. *Together.*"

"No, you're right," I said, nodding. It was the only sensible thing.

"Promise me, Naomi. Promise me you aren't going to go chasing ghosts," Cass said.

I hesitated. I couldn't leave it alone. Liv wanted Persephone found. I couldn't bring her back, but I could do that much for her.

But I couldn't do this to Cass. She was already frantic with worry, with grief. She looked ready to crack in two. And she was right—we should at least wait and see how things shook out. Be smart.

I was never the smart one.

"I promise," I lied, guilt slithering under the words. Cass gathered me into a relieved hug, and her tears were damp against my cheek. I surrendered to her embrace.

"It's going to be okay," she said. "We're going to take care of each other."

"Nothing's okay. She's gone," I said, and squeezed my eyes shut.

"I know," she said. She held me tight, and I let her, because she was trying. Even though the last thing I wanted right now was to be touched. "You should stay here. With me. I can make up the guest room."

"No, you don't have to," I said immediately.

"You'd rather be in that ratty motel?" she asked, a wounded edge to her tone.

"I'd rather not run into your mom constantly," I confessed, and she gave a harsh grunt of amusement.

"Makes sense," she acknowledged.

I didn't tell her that she was the one I wanted to avoid. That her touch made me want to flinch away. She was trying to be a good friend. She *was* a good friend. But she wasn't Liv.

That was all I could think about right now. Liv was gone, and Cass was here, and part of me wished it was the other way around.

And I hated myself for it.

I pulled away from her, murmuring my excuses. I was tired, I was drained, I needed to be alone.

I headed down the stairs and out the open front door, pausing for only a moment as the light hit me, and with it the scent of cigarette smoke. I squinted toward the side of the house. Oscar Green was leaning against the fence, a half-spent cigarette dangling from his hand. He'd been sturdy even when he was young. Middle age had given him his father's large build, though he'd kept it from getting quite so well padded. His gray tank top showed off thick, muscular arms, indistinct tattoos twining up them.

He nodded at me in greeting. I couldn't read his expression. I looked quickly away, shame darting through me minnow-quick. *You and me are meant to be*, I thought, the echo of an echo of a memory.

He straightened up like he was coming over to talk to me. I walked briskly to my car, got in, and shut the door behind me. When I looked in the rearview mirror he was standing there in the side yard, smiling a little. He waved as I pulled away, friendly as anything. I kept my eyes on the road and put Oscar Green firmly out of my mind.

Liv had found Persephone. That meant she *could* be found. All I had to do was retrace Liv's path. Find her name. What had happened to her.

And maybe, why someone would kill to keep that a secret.

The trouble with a town as small as Chester was it didn't take long to drive from one end to the other. No time to mull things over in motion. After I left Cass's place I ended up back at the motel by default, pacing back and forth.

I hated police procedurals. I didn't read mysteries. The two episodes of *Forensic Files* I'd watched the day before were the extent of my true-crime education in the last decade. Being part of one of those stories had ruined the rest as far as enjoyment was concerned, and I had no desire to gaze into the maw of human darkness in some quest for understanding. Until now, it hadn't presented a problem.

Which meant I didn't know where to even start piecing together what Liv had found. I was failing her already and I hadn't even gotten started.

I grabbed my phone and plugged in searches. *Missing persons. Identifying a body. Identifying a skeleton.* There was too much and not enough. I had no idea where to begin, and everything I clicked on was either a sad story that had nothing to do with mine or a bunch of basic information anyone who'd ever watched a cop show would know.

Maybe if I was one of those true-crime aficionados who could recite the name of every serial killer since Jack the Ripper, I'd be better off. Mitch's sister was constantly listening to murder podcasts. She'd been nice enough to ask if I minded her listening to the ones about me, and she hadn't asked any intrusive questions afterward, but she was always looking at me weirdly. Somewhere between worship and hunger. Though maybe those were the same thing.

Idly, I typed in "Ethan Schreiber podcast." A handful of podcasts popped up, his name in the credits as a sound editor. I was surprised to see that they weren't anything crime-related at all—one that seemed to be general news, one about pets, and one about UFOs. But on the last one, he was listed as the host. *Aftershocks.* I pulled up the description.

*Aftershocks explores the lasting damage left in the wake of violent crimes. Beginning with the crimes themselves and then moving forward, examining the impact on those left behind—victims, perpetrators, friends, family, and communities forever altered by these unthinkable events.*

There were two seasons. Every crime had several episodes devoted to it, labeled based on who was the focus. *Brenda Martin: The Witness—Brenda Martin: The Family—Brenda Martin: The Killer.* The episodes were substantial, too. They must be in-depth.

I put in earbuds and started one of them mostly at random, skipping past the intro. Ethan's voice, smoothed by the editing, filled my ears.

*Deedee Kent lived a quiet life. That was how nearly everyone described her, from her third-grade teacher to the coworkers who threw her retirement party: quiet. She kept to herself. She didn't have any friends in particular, unless you counted the cats she fed on her back porch. She never married. She'd wave hello to the neighbors, but never stop to chat.*

*It wasn't that she was unfriendly, everyone hastens to add. She was just quiet.*

*Deedee's life didn't seem to leave much of a mark on the world around her. But her death sent out ripples that tore apart a family, changed the trajectory of a life for the better, and permanently altered her community.*

I switched to another episode, and another. *Anabelle Gross was walking home from her computer class—Daniela Arroyo had just graduated high school—found his body three days later—missing poster still hanging in the window—every year on her birthday—*

The stories blended into one another as I switched randomly between episodes, listening to only snatches of each before my stomach turned.

Children. Old women. Young men. And the only thing they had in common—*we* had in common—was that someone had come for them. To kill them—but that word wasn't sufficient, was it?

To annihilate them. To turn everything they were into what was done to them. Into the pain and the fear and the ragged, gaping hole that was left when they were gone.

I turned it off and threw the phone onto the bed, tasting something sour. It was endless. Death and loss and violence. I didn't want to hear about people shot or beaten or strangled to death. I didn't want to imagine them dying, alone and afraid. Because they were all alone, even when they weren't.

Everyone dies alone.

So had Liv. So had Persephone. Both of them, alone in the woods. Like I had been, bleeding, crawling toward safety that didn't exist.

I'd never really escaped. None of us had. We tried to find our way out, but it drew us back in. We'd all rot among the roots and stones eventually.

I rubbed at my arms, fighting a chill that seemed to radiate from my core. My nerves prickled, an unformed sense of dread and danger growing steadily as my damaged psyche translated my anxiety straight into panic. I clenched and unclenched my hands, trying to focus on the physical sensation.

"You are safe," I told myself, monotone. "You are here. You aren't in the woods."

*Yes, you are,* my whole body insisted, and I dug my nails hard against the scar on my wrist. Like I could slide them under its edge and pull that seam of flesh open again.

A casual knock on the door brought me whirling around. It was a solid five seconds before I processed what I was supposed to do and went to answer it.

I opened the door to discover Ethan Schreiber in a cozy brown sweater, a white paper bag flecked with grease in one hand and a cardboard tray with two foam cups in the other. I stared, unable to interpret the scene or comprehend how he had transformed from a voice in my ear talking about Deedee Kent to the man standing in front of me.

He held out the bag. "You strike me as someone who needs to be reminded to eat," he said. The scent of diner burger and French fries oozed from the bag. My stomach growled.

"You brought me a burger," I said blankly.

"And a milkshake," he confirmed. He smiled—the kind of close-lipped smile you gave an animal you were hoping wouldn't maul you.

"Thanks," I said, and stuck out a hand.

He pulled the bag back out of reach. "It comes with company."

I folded my arms, irritated. Irritated was better than panicked. I held on to it. "That's blackmail."

"I think it's closer to bribery," he replied. "No interview, promise."

"What, you just want to spend time with me?" It was supposed to sound biting. It came out pitiable.

"I want to make sure you're all right," he said. He had a face made for sincerity. He was like a puppy pawing at your arm to comfort you, with those big brown eyes. "But if you really don't want company, I'll leave this with you and go."

My gut tightened. I didn't want Ethan Schreiber here. I wanted to be alone even less. This is how I ended up with guys like Mitch, I thought. Even the terrible ones were better company than my own mind.

I sighed, dropping my hand from the door and turning away. It took him a few seconds to catch on and follow me inside.

He set the food out on the tiny table in the corner. I really was starving. I unwrapped the grease bomb of a burger and wolfed it down. Ethan approached his more strategically, watching me with something between horror and admiration. I sucked a stray glob of ketchup from my thumb and moved on to the fries at a more sedate pace.

"How are you holding up?" he asked.

"I hate that question slightly less than I hate being asked if I'm okay," I told him.

"You don't like answering questions at all, do you?" He quirked an eyebrow at me.

"That's another question," I pointed out. I took the lid off the milkshake so I could attack it with a spoon.

"I surrender," he said. He threw up his hands. "I'm sorry I barged in here."

"No, it's fine," I said quickly. Alone, my thoughts had scrabbled through my skull like panicked rats. With him here, they'd settled to faint, anxious scurrying. "I'm not . . . good at being alone," I confessed.

He gave me a sidelong look, considering. "I wouldn't have guessed that. You have a loner vibe."

"No, I have an asshole vibe. Which just means that I end up spending all my time with other assholes," I said.

"Does that include me?"

I shrugged. "Haven't decided."

He watched me as I skinned a spoonful off the top of the milkshake. The pause had a tender quality I knew all too well—that moment where you were trying to decide whether to address the obvious subject or skirt around it. He was going to ask me about Liv. His lips parted, the words starting to form.

"Maybe you can help me with something," I said quickly, groping for a distraction.

"What sort of something?" he asked.

I shifted in my seat. Ethan Schreiber, it occurred to me, was exactly the person to ask about how to track down a missing woman. If I could do it without revealing too much. "I'm working on this project," I said. "Just a personal thing. And I'm trying to do some research, but I don't really know how to start."

"I am good at research," he conceded.

"I know," I said. He gave me a curious look. "I sort of looked up your podcast. I only listened to a minute of it, but it seemed like it was . . . good."

"Not our best review ever, but I'll take it," Ethan said.

"So that's what you're working on here? An episode of *Aftershocks* about Stahl?" I said. I wondered what the episode titles would be. *The Survivor. The Families. The Son.*

"No. This is a new project. It's still in development. I haven't quite found the right format yet." He considered me, like he could tell I was stalling. I didn't know how to ask what I needed to without raising suspicion. "What is it I can help you with, Naomi?"

No more stalling, then. "Right. So. If you were trying to find a missing person, how would you start?" I asked in a rush.

He stared at me for a beat. "Does this have something to do with Liv?"

"Liv isn't missing, is she?" I said sharply.

"Okay," he said, drawing out the word. "Then why are you asking about missing persons?"

"I told you. It's personal," I said.

He rubbed a hand over his head. "Um. Okay. Am I law enforcement or a civilian?" he asked.

"Civilian." I snagged a French fry and dragged it through the last smudges of ketchup.

"If I was a PI or something, I'd start by talking to family, friends, roommates . . ."

I shook my head. "No, not that kind of missing. You know someone is missing, but you don't know who they are."

"So I'm trying to identify a Jane Doe and hopefully match them up with a missing-person report?" he asked. He looked at me curiously. "You really aren't going to tell me what this is about?"

"I wasn't planning to, no."

He rested his palm on the table, one finger tapping an idle rhythm. "There's a theory," he said. "It's pretty popular in certain true-crime-fan circles. Alan Stahl was active for five years. His attacks all took place in the summer, one or two each year. Except for one year. People call it the 'quiet summer.' But there are some people who think that he didn't take the year off—that we just haven't found the victim or victims. So you have two camps—the quiet-summer theory and the missing-summer theory."

He thought I was looking into Stahl. I almost objected, but then I glanced away, as if he'd found me out. It was a safer explanation than the truth. "It's been bothering me, what you said about the profile not fitting," I said. That much wasn't a lie. "I thought that maybe if there were other victims that had been missed, there would be some connection to explain why he targeted me."

"Naomi, your friend just died. Is this really the time to be worrying about that?" he asked.

"I need to focus on something," I said, and my voice broke. It was true. Not for the reasons I was implying, but true all the same.

"A lot of people have spent a lot of time trawling through missing-persons reports to try to match them up to the quiet summer. There's too little to go on. Too many missing girls," he said.

"Humor me," I told him.

He sighed. "You don't have a body or a missing person, you've got an MO and a hunch. Which makes this basically impossible. You need to find a report of a murder or a missing person that matches the MO and go from there. It's a huge task. You could start by looking at the forums where people discuss Stahl and the quiet summer. They'll have done a lot of the work already. Or you could look at the Doe Network."

"What's that?" I asked.

"Here, I'll show you." He pulled out his phone and tapped something in, then handed it to me. It was a simple website with the banner "International Center for Unidentified and Missing Persons." "It's a database of reports on unidentified bodies and missing persons. You can search by gender, location, date. . . . It's got the advantage of being a lot better organized and centralized than casual message boards."

I tapped through the menus until I found missing women in Washington state. It loaded slowly—dozens and then hundreds of missing women reduced to tiny thumbnails of smiling faces. I made a noise in the back of my throat, guttural.

"It's kind of overwhelming," Ethan said.

There were numbers under each photograph. 1292DFWA. 2546DFVA. "What do these mean?" I asked, my heart pounding. I'd seen those numbers before.

"Case numbers," Ethan said. "The DF means 'disappeared female' and then there's a state code, if I remember correctly. I'm not sure about the numbering system."

There had been three numbers on the sticky note in Liv's room. She'd been looking at these same photographs. Persephone was one of these faces.

"You know," Ethan said carefully, "there's another piece to the missing-summer theory."

I looked up from the sea of photographs. He was leaning forward, elbows on his knees, gaze fixed on my face.

"Stahl dumped the first couple bodies in places where they were found quickly, but after that he started hiding them," he said. "That's part of why the six-victim number is almost certainly incomplete. Part of the evidence against him was that he was seen in the woods half a mile from the third victim's body, a few days before she was found. *Months* after her death. Which suggests that he was going back to visit the bodies. Probably a way of reliving the kills."

I shuddered. "As if he wasn't awful enough already."

"The thing is, nothing about your attack makes sense as part of his pattern. Unless—"

My skin prickled as I realized what he was talking about. "Unless I wasn't a target," I said. "I was a witness. He wasn't there for me at all."

"He was there to visit a body," Ethan said.

Not just *a* body.

Persephone.

From the moment I saw the numbers on Ethan's screen, I knew I had to go back to Liv's room. And from that moment, I constructed reasons I couldn't. The police were there. Marcus and Kimiko wouldn't want to be disturbed. The cops had probably cleared out everything anyway.

Liv had found her. I could do the same. I didn't need to go back to that place—go back to where Liv wasn't anymore. Face her parents.

Lie to them.

Keeping secrets from the police was one thing. But the idea of looking Kimiko in the eye and keeping silent about the thing that might explain what had happened to Liv . . .

I couldn't hurt them like that, I told myself, and what I really meant was that I couldn't bear the guilt.

For the next several days, I dug through missing-persons reports, checking for anything that might connect them to Chester or Stahl. I watched endless hours of TV as I skimmed the surface of a hundred tragedies, surfacing only to steal a few minutes of restless sleep, to shower.

And to eat, which I only remembered to do because Ethan kept turning up at my door. Sometimes I shut the door on him. A few times I let him in, and we sat together while we ate. We didn't really talk—he managed to restrain himself from asking questions, somehow, and when he did speak it was to update me about what he knew. They'd searched the lake but not turned up the gun. The Barneses' revolver was indeed missing, though, and probably lost in the silt among the abandoned bike wheels and random bits of junk that made metal detectors useless. Liv's body had been shipped off so that a proper autopsy could be conducted, but no one was expecting to find anything but the obvious.

Even when we sat in silence, those few minutes that punctuated the day were easier than the hours that stretched on alone. I found myself listening to *Aftershocks*, scrubbing past the descriptions of the crimes—which were mercifully brief—and listening to Ethan unfold the stories of what came after. It was his sincerity that sold it, I thought. During the interviews I could imagine those sincere eyes of his, inviting everyone from grieving mothers to remorseful killers to bare their souls for him.

He was good at his job. It was almost disappointing.

By the end of the week I was forced to admit that Ethan had been right. The task was too immense for me to figure out on my own with only the Doe Network profiles to go on. But Liv had known. Liv had found her.

I knew what I had to do, but I wasn't looking forward to it.

I got myself cleaned up most of the way to respectable, even remembering to dab concealer over the dark circles under my eyes. My hair was getting shaggy at the back, but I finger-combed it into something resembling order and headed outside, my gait stiff.

As I unlocked the car I glanced across the street and paused, faint unease scratching at the back of my mind. There was a black Toyota Camry parked across the street. It had been there yesterday, too. And the day before.

It was just a car. Nothing weird.

I started up my engine. In the rearview mirror, I watched as a man crossed the parking lot from the small park near the Corner Store, where there were a few benches and picnic tables. All of which had a clear view of the motel.

I couldn't make out much in the mirror. He was white, midthirties, with medium-brown hair cut a bit long and mirrored sunglasses. I'd seen him before, hadn't I? The last few days, at the diner and the gas station. He'd been hanging around.

The image of the boy in the striped shirt popped into my mind again. AJ Stahl.

As I pulled out, he started up his car. I watched in the mirror as he turned out of the parking lot—following right behind me. My heart hammered. I reached for my phone, but stopped. Who would I call? What would I say that wouldn't sound crazy?

Then, a minute out from the Barnes house, the Camry slowed and turned, pulling off to a trailhead. I let out a breath, sinking back against the seat.

*You're being paranoid*, I scolded myself. I kept my eyes on the rearview, but the Camry never reappeared.

The gate to the Barnes house was open. When I pulled up in front of the house, there was a casserole sitting on the front porch, covered in foil. It didn't seem right to step over it, so I picked it up and rang the bell. It took a couple minutes for Marcus Barnes to appear. He was a tall, solid man, but he seemed smaller under the weight of his grief. He looked dully down at the dish in my hands.

"You too?" he asked.

"It was on the porch," I said apologetically.

Marcus Barnes was an unlikely man to have married Kimiko, to have fathered Liv. The two women were both quicksilver in their own way, and he was solid as the wooden beams of his house, but maybe that was why it all worked.

"You might as well bring it in," he said. He turned and walked inside and I followed, still holding the casserole.

Marcus went into the kitchen, which was cluttered with more foil-covered dishes. That probably meant the freezer was already full. I remembered this part. I'd been pulling potpies and macaroni casserole out of the freezer a year after the attack. I set the latest offering down on a clear patch of counter.

"It's kind of a mess," Marcus said. He was wearing pajama pants and an ancient Nirvana T-shirt. He looked like he hadn't slept in a week.

"I can't imagine what you're going through right now," I said.

"Third time's the charm, right?" he asked, voice rough.

"What?" I asked, uncomprehending.

"The first two times I got a call like that, it turned out she was still alive," he said. His gaze was fixed on a point around my elbow. "First the woods and then the attempt. I think part of me has always known that everything since that summer was borrowed time."

I didn't know what to say. I didn't know if there were any words in the world that would make even the smallest difference, and if there had been, my own grief drowned them out.

"Where's Kimiko?" I asked.

"Sleeping," he said. "Chief Bishop was just here. Asking again if there was anyone who might want to hurt Olivia. Covering their bases, she said. I didn't know what to tell her."

"Liv didn't have enemies," I said.

His eyes flicked to my face and grew sharper. "Have they talked to you yet?"

"Yes. After I found her."

"You found her?" he asked, voice hoarse. "They didn't tell me that." He sounded angry, and I couldn't help but feel the anger was for me. As if by finding her, I'd made it all true.

"I'm so sorry, Mr. Barnes."

He looked away, and by the tension in his face I could tell he was trying not to cry. "She never forgave herself, you know. For what happened."

My brow creased. "When we were kids? There was nothing she could have done," I said, shaking my head. "If they'd tried to stop Stahl he would have killed them."

It was Persephone who had saved them. They'd been down there with her while I sat stewing over some remark Cass had made. Stahl hadn't seen them. Sometimes I thought I remembered lying under the overhang with them. I could smell the dirt, see Cass's hand pressed over Liv's mouth. Sometimes it was just as vivid as my real memories, and I had to remind myself that it wasn't possible.

They'd hid, watching Stahl kill me. Only after he left did they stumble out to help me. Cass tried to find my pulse, but between the shock and adrenaline and the fact that she didn't really know what she was doing, she couldn't find it. I still remembered Liv promising they were going to get help, Cass telling her it was too late, they just had to run. I couldn't move or respond, but I could hear her.

They thought I was dead. It wasn't their fault that I wasn't.

"She hated that she left you for dead," he said. "Sometimes I think she would have moved on if you *had* died, but having you around meant she never could. She always had to remember that day."

I kept my mouth shut. It was more or less the same thing Cass's mom had said, only dressed up nicer. If it weren't for me, their daughters would have been normal. Fine. But when that knife went into my body, it was their good girls who were truly wounded, and their wounds that mattered.

"She was doing so well," Marcus said. "I don't understand what happened."

"I wish . . ." I trailed off. I wished I had listened to her about Persephone. I wished I hadn't let her leave the car. I wished I'd gone with her. I wished I hadn't been passed out in my car on the side of the road while she was in the woods, while she was—

"She told me you had a fight that day," Marcus said. His eyes were on me now, sharp and focused. My mouth went dry. Marcus must have been the one to tell the police that we'd argued.

"I wouldn't call it a fight," I said. I chose my words carefully. "We were all feeling pretty raw. Liv wanted to talk about things, but Cass and I weren't up for it." I felt bad pulling Cass's name in, using her as a shield—the Good Friend. The stable one.

Marcus considered me for a long moment. Then his shoulders slumped, his weariness settling more heavily over him. "Is there something you need from us, Naomi?" he asked.

I wished I could say no. It was wrong asking anything of them right now. "I saw something earlier, in Liv's room. I need to look at it again," I said reluctantly.

He shook his head. "If there was anything important in her room, the police have it. And if you know something, you should talk to them." His look had a challenge buried in it.

"If I could look anyway—"

"You should go," he said firmly.

"Marcus." Kimiko appeared in the hallway, wearing a terrycloth robe and slippers. Her eyes were red from crying, but her face was hard now, closed off. She said something sharp and short in Japanese, which Marcus answered with a grunt before turning away. She looked at me. "Take off your shoes," she said, and walked away down the hall.

I decided that was the only invitation I was going to get. I slipped off my shoes and followed her. She walked into the middle of Liv's room. Half emptied, it had a look of ragged chaos that all her clutter never created. Its order had been disrupted and it hit me in the gut all over again—Liv was gone.

"Go ahead," Kimiko said. It was clear that this time, she wouldn't be leaving me alone to my search.

I went to the desk again, but of course her computer and all her notebooks and notes had been taken. The drawer was empty. They had the sketchbook. What would it mean to them? Would they realize Persephone hadn't simply sprung from her imagination?

"What is it you're looking for?" Kimiko asked.

I hesitated—could I chance telling her? It was worth the risk, I decided. "It was a set of numbers and letters. Four numbers followed by four letters. She had them written down on a sticky note."

She nodded and walked out of the room. I stared after her, uncertain if I should follow, but a minute later she returned with a crumpled envelope. "She left this in the recycling," she said. "She was always taking notes on whatever was nearby."

There were more numbers on this one, in an exacting column. Two dozen. It must have been before she narrowed it down. The state codes were from all over the place—as far as Oklahoma. If she'd eliminated everything but Washington and Idaho, I had eleven entries to work with. That was more manageable. "Thank you," I said.

"What do they mean?" she asked. When I didn't answer right away, she crossed her arms. "Did someone kill my daughter because of those numbers?"

"The police say it was suicide."

"Do you believe that?" she asked bluntly.

"No," I said, realizing as I said it just how certain I was. "I don't know who would want to hurt her. But I know she found something before she died. A—a secret. She wanted to tell me, but she didn't get the chance. I need to know what it is."

"You should tell the police," Kimiko said.

I looked down at the numbers in my hand. All the logic and sense in the world said I should call Bishop right now and tell her everything, even if that made me a suspect. But letting go of these secrets felt like letting Liv go. Letting go of the last thing I had of her that was ours alone. Hers and mine and Cass's. One last bond. "I can't," I said helplessly.

The familiar shame of the lie shivered with new hope. If one of these numbers belonged to Stahl's missing victim, then I'd told the truth, even if I hadn't known it. It would be proof that it was him, and that I hadn't gotten the wrong man arrested.

Kimiko sighed. "You were a good friend to her. But she's gone. You take care of yourself first. The dead don't need our help."

"I need to do this," I said.

Kimiko only nodded. When I walked out she stayed, running her fingertips over the empty space where Olivia's things had been, as if beginning to map the shape of her absence.

It was quick work to match the case numbers with names, but from there my progress ground to a halt. The women in the missing-persons listings ranged in age from eighteen to forty-six. There were blondes and brunettes, white, Black, and Latina. None were named Persephone, but I hadn't expected they would be. Any of these women could have been Persephone—or none of them.

Except that Liv had been sure.

The dates for their disappearances covered a range of almost a decade. If I looked only at that "quiet summer," two years before the attack, there were four possibilities, but I couldn't assume that Persephone was Stahl's victim. Or, if she was, that he'd killed her that summer. No one knew how many unknown victims might be out there or when he might have killed them.

I started searching for the names with various combinations of keywords. Most of them had doppelgängers on Facebook and the like, cluttering up the results. Here and there I found articles or posts about the women I was looking for and scoured them for any information that might be relevant. April Kyle was from Spokane and liked the outdoors; she'd run off with an older boyfriend. Marjorie Campion had three children and a dog and was a known drug addict. There were women who seemed made to disappear into the cracks and those whose vanishing had turned communities upside down, and all of them were just as thoroughly gone.

I bookmarked another article and flipped to the next tab I had open, a forum post from a girl trying to find information about a missing aunt. I rubbed my eyes and checked the name—they were all blurring together. Jessi Walker. Nineteen when she disappeared, though her family didn't ever file an official missing-person report, because she'd packed her bags. A few weeks passed before they realized she was gone for good. The niece writing the post got a Christmas card and a birthday card from Jessi, and then she went silent. They'd been close and the niece was certain that something had happened to her.

Jessi Walker's niece wasn't sure when she'd actually gone missing. Sometime after April, two years before my attack. I'd looked up how long it would take for a body to become a skeleton, and my best guess was that it would have happened within a year or two of lying in the Grotto, so that matched. And that was the "quiet summer."

It was all just guesswork. How had Liv figured this out?

I started to bookmark the page and close it out, and then I froze. I hadn't looked at the username the niece had created to post on the message board.

*Persephone McAllister.*

The name on the dead woman's bracelet wasn't hers. It was her niece's. A remembrance of the girl she left behind but never forgot.

I pulled up the case entry again, heart beating fast and hard. The attached photo showed a young woman in a cotton sundress, smirking a little at the camera. She had brown, wavy hair and a slender build—Stahl's type. The look in her eye hinted at an urge to wander, a restlessness that had wound its brambles around my own heart.

It was her. It was Persephone.

"Found you," I whispered. She smiled that coy little smile at me, her weight balanced on her back foot, entirely aware of the camera. I almost felt like I recognized her. Like if I passed her in the street, I would have waved. I'd been nine years old when she left home, and she was nineteen—a decade older, not someone I would have spent any time with.

A decade younger than I was now. Had Stahl offered her a ride?

Had he dragged her into the woods, hidden her away where no one could find her?

I shuddered. I understood what Cass meant, now, when she said she wanted to tell Persephone that she'd had a daughter. *He's dead*, I wanted to whisper to those bones.

I'd found Persephone, just as Liv had, and this must be how Liv had felt, too, like she had searched the underworld for her ghost and sighted her at last. Jessi wasn't Persephone but Eurydice, and Liv was Orpheus, guiding her back toward the surface only to—foolishly, inevitably— look back as she had been forbidden to do, and now both of them were lost below.

Or had Orpheus been lost with his bride? I couldn't remember any-more. We'd known all the stories by heart back then, small-town girls who could recite the names of all nine Muses and the lineage of ancient heroes, but that was a long time ago.

I rubbed my hands over my arms, suddenly cold. Her name was Jessi. She wasn't Persephone at all. Inexplicable grief passed over me like a shadow—mourning for the thing we'd imagined her to be. She hadn't been our talisman, our goddess, our protector. She had been a girl, so much younger than I was now, who died in the forest and was lost. Who was missed. Who was mourned.

My first instinct was to call Liv. My second was to call Cass. But Liv was gone, and Cass—I'd told her I wouldn't go looking. I'd broken my promise.

My fingernails dug at the scar on my wrist. *Persephone, Persephone,* I thought, and the voice in my mind was the voice of my childhood self—and Cass's and Liv's, too, echoing together in that tiny space with our hands clasped in a ring.

*Speak to us, Goddesses. Tell us what to do. How to please you.* Hecate, Artemis, Athena, Persephone. The air thrumming with the power of our belief, our wanting to believe. *You go first,* Cass had told Liv, handing her the knife. We would each cut ourselves, just enough for a few drops of blood. The fifth ritual. But Liv's hand shook, and I took it from her. *I'll do it.*

I'd cut too deep, the knife skating up the side of my wrist with startling speed. It was just supposed to be a few drops. Liv had screamed. I'd started panicking.

Cass, though, stayed calm. She wrapped her jacket around it tight and we ran to my house, where we could be sure no one would be paying attention. Cass cleaned it with hydrogen peroxide, then sewed it up with a needle and fishing line while I bit down on a dishrag. Liv hovered on the other side of the room, hands pressed over her ears, trying not to retch. She hated blood.

Cass bandaged it up, and I'd hidden it under my sleeve while it healed. At first Cass had said she and Liv would do their cuts later, but eventually she declared that my sacrifice was enough to complete the ritual.

Part of me had wondered, later, if that was where things had gone wrong. We owed the Goddesses our blood, and if we didn't give it willingly, they would claim it.

But there had been no Goddesses. No Persephone. Only a girl, long lost.

I shut the computer and its image of Jessi Walker. I jolted out of my chair. My fingers skimmed over my skin, bumping over scar tissue, a half-conscious inventory of old wounds. I combed my hand through my hair, pulling hard enough to hurt, and there was relief in the pain. It was simple. Stimulus and response, a clarity of causation that was better than the mire of my mind.

I gulped down a breath. This was the point at which I should call someone, but I had no one to call. My therapist, I supposed, but I hadn't talked to her since Stahl died, and the idea of explaining everything made me feel ill. I wanted Liv.

I pressed the heels of my hands to my eyes. I couldn't breathe.

I dropped my hands and strode to the door, my thoughts half-formed and wild. I walked the few steps to room 4 and knocked before I could think better of it.

Ethan answered the door, looking concerned. "Naomi. Are you okay? What's up?" He'd lost the cozy sweater he usually wore and was down to an undershirt and jeans. The sweater had hidden a surprisingly muscular build and a tattoo on his left shoulder—a solid black ring about four inches across. He rubbed a thumb across it absently as he spoke.

"Can I come in?" I asked.

He glanced behind him. "Uh. Sure," he said. He opened the door farther and stepped backward, letting me enter without putting my back to him. I shut the door behind me and stood there, fingers resting against the cold door.

His dirty clothes were heaped in an open suitcase at the end of the bed. Recording equipment was stored more neatly by the desk, and his laptop was open, with sound-editing software up and running. I wondered if he was editing my "interview." I walked over, trying to decode the tangle of sound waves and icons.

"Naomi?" His fingers brushed my elbow. I dragged my eyes back to his face. "What's going on?"

"I don't want to be alone," I said. His fingertips were still on my elbow, barely touching me, like he was afraid of what would happen if he made real contact. Or if he let go.

"Do you want to talk?" he asked.

Did I? I needed to tell someone. I needed to speak the words to ease the aching pressure in my chest, but I had no one to tell.

"Tell me what's happening," he said. His voice was so painfully gentle, so kind. His touch as tender as he'd been when he lifted Liv from the water.

"I can't," I said. I stepped toward him.

Some people reach for a bottle. I have never been able to silence my thoughts with alcohol. It only ever blunts my defenses, lets loose all the creeping things in the corners of my mind. I've found other ways to cope. I stepped into him and he let out a startled breath, eyes widening. I rested a hand on his chest. His heart beat rapidly under my palm, and I thought of the rush of blood, of how easily it escapes the skin.

"Naomi," he said.

"Ethan," I replied. I leaned into him, almost touching, not quite. A gap that was easy to close, if he wanted to.

He wanted to. But he didn't. His hand skimmed up my arm, over my shoulder, until his fingers rested at the back of my neck. "What are you doing?" he asked me.

"I told you. I don't want to be alone." I didn't want to be alone, and he was beautiful, and he was alive, and he had been kind to me, and that was more reason than I'd ever needed.

"I don't want to take advantage of you," he said, voice rough.

"I'm not the one being taken advantage of here," I assured him. My fingers slipped under the hem of his shirt, fingernails nicking skin, and he took a sharp breath. "Tell me to leave, and I will."

"I don't want you to leave," he said softly.

"Good."

He kissed me, his kiss as hungry as mine, and we tumbled toward oblivion.

We lay with the motel sheets tangled under us, breath still quick, pulses settling. Ethan's hand rested on my thigh. I rolled away, sitting up at the edge of the bed and snatching my clothes from where they'd fallen.

"In a hurry to leave?" Ethan asked, and I could hear him trying to figure out if he should be hurt.

I pulled my shirt over my head and looked back at him. He didn't have a single scar on his body. Just that tattoo and a look in his eyes I couldn't quite read. "Should I be?" Most people were happy when I didn't try to stick around. Most of them could tell I was more trouble than I was worth.

He didn't answer at first. He sat up and pulled on his pants. "Why did you come over here?"

"I told you. I didn't want to be alone," I said. I stood, crossing my arms against a chill.

"And now? Do you want to be alone?" He turned, half facing me.

"No," I said. One word and still my voice cracked it down the middle. I rubbed my upper arms. I couldn't seem to get warm.

"I can help you, you know. If you're looking into Stahl, I mean. I've done a lot of research into the quiet summer already. If you're trying to find a missing victim—"

"I found her," I said, cutting him off. He looked startled.

"How? The number of women that go missing every year—even

just narrowing it down to a few possibilities is next to impossible. And without a body, there's no way to be sure it's one of Stahl's victims."

I drew aside the curtain, looking out at the nearly empty lot. I should leave. I'd gotten what I came for, and I had no reason to rely on Ethan Schreiber for more than that.

I watched him approach in the reflection in the window, quelling the little shiver of fear at the sensation of someone at my back. I closed my eyes. His palms ghosted over my shoulders. His lips brushed against my hair, not quite a kiss. It was as if he was afraid that if he actually touched me, I would vanish.

"Whatever you're doing, whatever you're holding on to, you don't have to do it alone," he told me.

I'd come to Ethan's door to make a mistake. It was what I always did. If I knew what mistake I was making, I wouldn't be surprised when it hurt me. I'd needed this. Needed him.

Maybe I still did.

"I have to know that if I tell you, it's going to stay between us," I said. "At least for now. Until I know all of it."

"All right," he said easily.

I met his eyes in the reflection. "You can't just say that. You have to mean it."

"I do," he promised.

"This isn't a story. It's my life."

"I don't care about the story," he said. I made a skeptical noise. "Naomi, when you are ready to tell your story, I'd like to help. But that's never really been why I came here. I wanted to know the truth for myself."

I nodded slowly. I believed him, or I wanted to believe him, and the difference was so small it didn't matter.

"You said that the only way the attack made sense was if there was a body in the woods," I said. I watched his reflection, the image of him as half real as his touch. "There was. That's why we were there, too. We found her that summer, and we never told anyone. But Liv found out who she was. That's why she asked me to come. Liv knew who she was, and now I do, too."

I turned toward him. It was easy to tell Ethan secrets. I understood now what he meant about people talking to him. There was no judgment in his eyes. "Tell me what happened," he said. And for the first time since that summer, I found myself telling the truth.

---

When I was eleven years old, I believed in magic.

The meaning of belief has changed over the ages. We tend to think of it as a matter of fact. *I believe this thing is true; I hold it to be factual.* But once, it meant something different, a meaning that lingers when we say *I believe in you.* It is not a statement of factual existence, but one of faith and loyalty. To believe is to hold dear, to cherish, to claim as a truth more fundamental than fact.

I believed in magic. We all did.

When we saw the beads that spelled out Persephone's name, it was a sign. There were seven rituals to perform for the Goddess Game, and now we knew they came from her, that they were *for* her. None of us even suggested telling our parents or the police. They belonged to that other world; Persephone belonged to ours.

We made her offerings and whispered secrets to her bones. We never told. And then came the end of the summer and the attack, and the chance to say something slipped further and further away with each passing hour, each day, until it had gone from secret to lie, and we were trapped in it.

"You have to understand," I said, standing with my back to the wall, my arms folded. "Everyone kept telling us how important it was that we be believed. That our testimony was found *reliable.* They told us that it was up to us to keep Stahl from killing more women. If they'd known about Persephone—"

"The defense would have shredded your credibility," Ethan said. He sat on the end of the motel bed, his elbows resting on his knees. "So you kept her hidden."

"We were kids," I said. "We were stupid."

"You went through something no child should have to experience. Whatever you had to do to survive was justified," Ethan said.

"Even lie about what happened that day?" I said quietly. He gave me a sharp look.

"You're not talking about the body now."

I shook my head. I sat next to him. "I was eating my lunch. The first blow came from behind me. I fell. I managed to turn over, but I could barely move. All I remember is the trees. And the knife," I said. I stared at the painting on the opposite wall, a landscape of a lake, the colors muddy and off-putting. "I never saw his face. But Cass and Liv saw, and they were sure, and the police wanted me to be, too. So I said it was him. I said I was sure."

Ethan didn't look the least bit surprised. "They needed to put him away. It would be a shock if they managed *not* to influence you. Given the condition you were in, it wouldn't have been hard to get you to ID Stahl. Even to convince you that you had seen him."

"For a long time, I told myself that I must have," I said. I pushed off the bed, started pacing. "I let myself believe it. I had to. If I said I was wrong, that it wasn't him, everyone would have hated me. I was an idiot. I was a coward. I—"

"Slow down, Naomi," Ethan said. I stopped in my circuit. He stood, but kept his distance. "Let's take this one thing at a time. Start with Persephone. Who is she?"

"Her name is Jessi Walker." I pulled up the file on my phone and showed him. He read through it with a faint frown.

"She fits the type," he said, more to himself than me.

"So she could be another victim."

"Maybe." He handed me back my phone. "There's a trap that investigations tend to fall into. They get tunnel vision. They ram the evidence into place around a single theory, instead of staying open to the possibilities. We have a theory: Stahl killed Jessi Walker. But the only thing we know for sure is that Jessi Walker died. It might have been misadventure, not murder."

"But it makes sense. It explains why Stahl was in the woods. It means—"

"It means that the right person got locked up for attacking you. It absolves you," Ethan said. If he'd said it gently, tenderly, I think I would have hated him for it. But there was no forgiveness in his voice, just cold truth. "You need to decide if you're trying to find out what really happened, or if you're trying to prove you didn't do anything wrong."

I looked away. "I never wanted to know too much about Stahl—the things he did. I've always just accepted that he killed all those women." I'd never thought about his son, either—the damage done to him. The life he must have lived. I swallowed against a hard lump in my throat. "I didn't want to think about what it would mean if everyone was wrong, and I sent an innocent man to prison," I said.

"You didn't," Ethan said sharply, and I glanced at him in surprise. "That is one thing you do not need to feel guilty about."

"They didn't have enough evidence to convict him."

"That doesn't mean they didn't have enough to know it was him. Don't waste any energy fretting over Stahl. He's dead and the world's a better place without him."

His certainty would have been comforting, if I was capable of being comforted. But I was thinking of the letter now. "Even if that's true, if Stahl didn't attack me, it means that whoever did got away with it. Maybe even did it again." *To a girl who wasn't as fortunate as me*, I didn't add.

Ethan rubbed a hand over his chin. "For now, let's focus on Jessi. It's been a long time, and Stahl sometimes drove with his victims for hours before he turned on them. She might have been from just about anywhere. We need to find out where she was before she disappeared."

The *we* was more comforting than it should have been. "I think I recognize her," I said. It had been bothering me since I saw the picture, that lingering sense of familiarity. "I can't tell if it's her that I recognize, or just the type, but there's something there. And I never left Chester back then, so if I do recognize her, she was here."

"Who'd remember her, around here?" he asked.

I sighed, realizing the obvious next step. "My dad might know," I said. "And he won't spread our business around town like just about anyone else would."

"Then let's start there."

"You're in for a treat. But we'd better wait until morning. This time of night, he'll be past making sense," I said. I shrugged into my sweatshirt and stood with my hands in my pockets.

"You can stay, if you want," Ethan said. I gave him a skeptical look. "I'm a night owl. I'm just going to sit up catching up on editing. You could get some sleep with another body in the room."

"That would be good," I admitted. "I can sleep alone, I just . . ."

"Don't get any rest doing it?" he asked. I nodded. It wouldn't matter that I didn't know him. Didn't have any particular reason to consider him safe. I'd gone home with strangers for the chance to get a solid night's sleep. At least I'd had a real conversation with Ethan. "I'm the same. Not the part about needing someone there, but sleep not being a friend when it does arrive."

"Thus the night-owl habit."

"And the borderline criminal amount of coffee I drink," he confirmed. "Go ahead and get some rest."

I made Ethan promise to wake me up when he needed the bed and then I took him up on the offer. With the sound of him clicking the keys and shifting in his seat, the constant tension in the back of my mind eased just a fraction. Enough for the exhaustion to come roaring in.

Sleep claimed me, and for once, I didn't dream.

———————

I woke with light hitting my eyes, still in the bed. I propped myself up on my elbow and found Ethan, asleep with his head on the desk, cradled in one arm. I shook my head at him and crept over to my shoes, pilfering his room key as I went.

Fifteen minutes later I was back with coffee and he was sitting up, rubbing sleep from his eyes.

"I hope you like your coffee black and terrible," I told him.

"Wouldn't have it any other way," he said.

"You should have woken me up," I admonished, handing him a cup. He popped the top off to blow on it, steam coiling around his face.

"You needed the sleep more than I did." He looked good rumpled. It made him look less earnest. I reached over and combed his hair back with my fingers, and he startled slightly at the touch.

I swayed back a step, keeping my expression casual. "I'm going to go shower and change. Meet you back here?"

"I'll try to be presentable by then," he said by way of confirmation.

At the door I paused and looked back. Ethan sat with his spine like a comma, hunched over his coffee, the blur of sleep still in his eyes.

"Thank you," I said, and left before he could respond.

———

We drove up to the house around noon. When Ethan stepped inside, he went stock-still. I slid in behind him but didn't shut the door. Being closed into that tiny space with another human being would have been too much—tipping Ethan from comfort to threat in the careful calculus of my brain. One of us would have ended up bleeding.

"This is . . ." Ethan said. I didn't meet his eyes. I hadn't warned him. It wasn't that I was ashamed. More like I needed to see his shock to prove that it really *was* that bad. "Was it like this growing up?"

"You could still get around," I said. I pointed at a stack composed of a broken file cabinet, an Easter basket, and assorted bulging bags. "There was a clear patch there where I played when I was a kid."

"Naomi?" Dad called from somewhere in the back of the house. "That you?"

"Yeah, it's me," I answered. "Can I come in and talk to you?"

"No, I'll come to you," he hollered. Plastic bags rustled and things slipped and thunked, and then he appeared, climbing over drifts of junk with a spidery walk. He saw Ethan and scowled. "Who's the pretty boy?" he asked.

"I'm hoping to ask you a couple questions," Ethan said, and introduced himself with a polished spiel. We'd decided on the way over to let him take the lead, make like this was all a project of his. It was easier to explain than my own interest.

"What kind of questions?" Dad asked. He was looking at me. Wondering why I'd brought this into his house.

"Do you remember a girl named Jessi Walker? It's possible she was going by a different name," Ethan said. He held out his phone with the photo of Jessi pulled up.

Dad stared down at it long enough that I knew he'd recognized her. "Why are you asking about this girl?" he asked. He didn't take his eyes off her picture. The phone screen idled, turned off.

"She apparently went missing around here in the time frame that Stahl was killing. I've been trying to identify potential unknown victims."

"Jessi with an *i*," Dad said musingly. "I knew her, but Alan Stahl didn't kill her. She just left town. You knew her, too." He nodded his chin at me.

"I thought I recognized her," I said. "But I don't remember why."

"She worked at the Chester Diner. Waitress. She always made sure they gave you an extra pancake. Said you reminded her of her niece," Dad said. I tried to reach back to the memory, but everything before eleven was ragged at the edges.

"You said she left town. Do you know where she went?" Ethan asked.

"No, I don't. I know she said she was leaving and then she was gone. She was a waitress. We didn't pour our hearts out to each other," Dad replied. "You think she got killed?"

"She was reported missing. She hasn't been seen since," Ethan said smoothly. "Is there anyone else who might have known her better? Known where she was going, maybe?"

"Eh. She was a kid. I didn't socialize with her," Dad said. "And it was a long time ago."

"Do you have any idea who she might have hung around with?" I pressed. "Come on, Dad. It's important."

"Why?" he asked. "He's nosy, that's why he gives a shit, but you?"

"I'm just helping out," I said, setting my jaw.

He grunted. Looked at Ethan. "You sleep with her yet?"

Ethan's face reddened. "That's not—"

"Leave him alone, Dad," I said warningly.

"Don't go thinking it makes you special if she does. It's like a hand-shake with this girl," Dad said.

"For fuck's sake, Dad—"

He gave an exaggerated shrug. "Nothing wrong with it. Just think the boy ought to know what he's getting into."

"All right. We're leaving," I said, turning. At least we'd confirmed that Jessi had been in Chester.

"Oscar Green," Dad said. My head whipped back toward him. "She hung around with Oscar Green. That's all I remember."

"Thank you," Ethan said quickly. He touched my shoulder with the very tips of his fingers, propelling me toward the door. I let him, stalking forward and not stopping until I heard the door shut behind me. Then I turned on Ethan, clamping my teeth down over anger that wasn't meant for him.

"I should just burn that fucking house down to the ground and be done with it," I growled.

"I take it you and your dad don't really get along," Ethan said mildly.

I laughed. "You could say that."

"Cassidy's book wasn't very flattering in its portrayal of him," he noted.

"He was pissed about that, but he got a big enough cut of the money that he didn't say anything," I said.

"The Greens split the royalties?" Ethan asked, sounding a bit surprised. "Even though you didn't cooperate?"

"I think they felt guilty about profiting off the whole thing," I said. "Or maybe it was just preemptive defense against bad publicity, making it all about the girl who *didn't* get stabbed."

"Cassidy did seem to be the one who came out of the experience relatively unscathed," Ethan said.

"It looks that way, doesn't it?" I asked. "But she was just as damaged as me and Liv. She's better at hiding it, but it's there."

"How well do you know her brother?" Ethan asked.

"Oscar." His name was like a bit of gristle between my teeth. "He's an asshole."

"Sounds like there's a story or two behind that assessment."

I didn't answer. Remembered T-shirt fabric rucking up against my ribs, fingertips digging into my skin.

"Is he in town? Should we talk to him?" Ethan asked.

I hesitated. "Look—I'm tired, Ethan. Can we just pause for a second?" It was too much. The house. Dad. Persephone, transformed from an immortal goddess into a girl with bad taste in friends. A girl who had existed in the realm of memories I would give anything to excise. The version of my childhood that wasn't full of dragons and potions and fairy circles. The one that was cruel and ugly and mundane.

"Yeah. Sorry. We can head back," Ethan said. I nodded, relieved. He didn't move right away, his dark eyes searching mine. I tugged my gaze away, marched to the car.

There were things Ethan didn't need to know about me. I was more than what Alan Stahl had done, but that didn't mean that all of the rest was free of shadows.

So Oscar Green's an asshole," Ethan said as we drove. "That doesn't say great things about Jessi."

"He's the mayor's son. He's always had plenty of friends," I said, watching the trees slide by. "He's charming when he wants to be. Plus, he's good-looking." *You and me are meant to be,* a voice crooned in my memory. I shoved it away.

"A fellow pretty boy?" Ethan said, trying too hard for humor.

"Too rough around the edges to be pretty," I said. "Plus he's big enough to break a skinny guy like you in half without trying."

Ethan chuckled, accepting the gentle ribbing. "Unfortunately, I can't see how to get around talking to him. If we're going to prove that Stahl killed Jessi, we need to know when exactly she disappeared. We may be able to match it up to Stahl's movements."

"Even this long after the fact?" I asked.

"A lot of his trips are in the old case files. The detectives did a fairly thorough job mapping out his movements to try to connect him to the other murders."

"Not the 'other' murders, just the murders. I'm an almost," I said with a curl of a smile, no humor in it.

"There is something else we need to consider," Ethan said, with the kind of care that suggested he wasn't sure how I was going to react. "If Jessi isn't one of Stahl's victims, it might be a good idea to be careful who we talk to."

I frowned. "Why?"

"Because it's possible—maybe even probable—that her death was an accident. But if it wasn't an accident, and it wasn't Stahl, someone else killed her. And they might not be happy about us digging around."

I pressed my knuckles against my lips. "Liv found her, and now she's dead. If it wasn't suicide . . ."

"Someone might have killed her to keep her from revealing what she'd learned. And that means that you and I need to be careful," Ethan said grimly.

I didn't know which answer I needed more. If Stahl had killed Jessi, we'd been right, and it had been him out there that day. But that meant there was no reason for anyone to want to hurt Liv, except Liv herself.

If Stahl hadn't killed Jessi, maybe whoever did had gone after Liv to silence her. She hadn't hurt herself after all.

Or I was wrong about everything. Stahl had nothing to do with me. Jessi's death was a random accident. And Liv's death was exactly what it looked like.

No matter what the answer was, I had failed her. I hadn't been able to save her.

We pulled in to the motel. Ethan got out of the car and stretched, his shirt riding up to bare a strip of skin. "Is there anyone else from that crowd who's still around? Someone else who might have known Jessi?" he asked.

"Oscar mostly hung around with Russell Burke," I said.

"Where's he?"

"Dead."

"He probably won't be able to help us, then. Who else?" Ethan asked, squinting in the sunlight.

"Cody Benham," I said reluctantly.

"The guy who saved you?" Ethan's eyebrows raised.

"More than once," I said, half to myself. "He and Oscar used to be friends."

"But not anymore?"

"Not anymore," I confirmed. I could pinpoint the end of that friendship to the minute. The smell of gasoline and asphalt in the air, fingertips bruising my ribs.

"Do you have his number?" Ethan asked. "Would he talk to you?"

"Yes. To both," I said. Cody had his job. A pregnant wife. He'd gotten out of Chester in a way few of us ever managed, and I didn't want to drag him back into this.

"You don't have to do this," Ethan said, seeing my expression. "You could walk away. Or tell the police what you know, and let them handle it."

I shook my head. I had to finish the work Liv had started. "I'm not going to stop now," I said. "I'll call him."

----

Cody picked up right away. "I was so sorry to hear about Olivia," he said as soon as I told him who it was. "Are you back in Seattle yet?"

"No, I'm staying in Chester for a while," I said. I sat in my motel room, alone, too conscious of Ethan's presence two rooms away. "I've got to head back to Seattle for the weekend for work, but otherwise I'm planning to stick around. Until the funeral, at least."

"Have they set a date?"

"They're still waiting for the body to be released," I said.

"I see." He paused. "I didn't know Olivia very well. She didn't talk to me like you did."

"I don't remember talking to you. I remember *trying* to talk and stammering a lot," I admitted. He gave a low chuckle.

"You were a sweet kid. Too smart for your own good. All three of you, really, each in your own way."

There was an intimacy to talking like this, just Cody's voice and mine, like the world had narrowed down to the reality we shared. Those brief moments where our lives had intersected, which it seemed like no one else would really understand.

I didn't want to break that sense of shared reality, but I had to. "Cody, I'm hoping you can help me with something."

"Anything you need," he said immediately.

"Did you know a girl named Jessi Walker?" I asked. There was silence on the other end of the line. "I think she was friends with Oscar."

"Yeah," Cody said finally. "I know Jessi. Knew her, I guess. I haven't seen her since— God. Must be almost twenty-five years. Why are you asking about Jessi?"

"There's a chance she might have been one of Stahl's victims," I said.

"Jessi's not dead," he said. "Is she?" Uncertainty made his voice crack.

"She was reported missing. After she left town no one ever saw her again," I told him. "My dad said she hung around with Oscar, and I figured if she spent time with Oscar, she must've spent time with you."

"We were friends," he said, sounding disturbed.

"What can you tell me about her?"

"I'm not sure. I don't think she ever talked about herself much. I got the sense she came from a bad background. She hitched into town and charmed Marsha into offering her a shift. Inside a week she had a second job at the diner and she was even helping out in the office at the mill on the weekends, which is where Oscar and I met her. She was—the word that springs to mind is *vibrant*. Funny and brash. She had these moments of sweetness, too. You really think she's dead?"

"Yes. I do." I didn't say how I knew. Let him think it was instinct.

He let out a long breath. "Jesus. We all assumed she just left. She always said she wasn't going to stay long. She hitchhiked sometimes, I know that."

"Did you see her the day she left town?" I asked.

"No. I was pissed, actually. I knew she was leaving but she didn't say when, and she didn't say goodbye. Just took off."

"Do you know anyone who might have?"

He paused. "Oscar," he said.

"Yeah, I was kind of afraid that was what you were going to say," I said, rubbing my eyes. "What was their relationship like?"

"In one word? Messy," he said. "Oscar was always magnetic to women in a way I didn't understand. He had this way of making you work hard to impress him, so that when he did throw a scrap of approval your way it was addictive. The more he ignored girls, the more they seemed to fling themselves at him."

"And Jessi was like that?"

He grunted. "The opposite. She was the one who wasn't impressed. And he was the one who got obsessed. I never saw Oscar fall for someone until Jessi. Or after, either."

"Were they ever actually together?" I asked, trying to imagine Oscar in love. But then, I'd never known the side of him that he showed everyone else. From the beginning, he'd taken one look at me and realized there was no need to charm me. I was no one. I was alone. He didn't need to bother with masks.

"I wouldn't say together, exactly. Sex, yes; relationship, not so much. But something was going on there," Cody told me. "Things changed between them all of a sudden a little while before she left, but Oscar didn't talk about it. And we weren't exactly the kind of guys who had a lot of heart-to-hearts about our love lives."

"Right," I said. I scratched at an itch on my jaw. I'd been hoping Cody would tell me that Oscar barely knew Jessi. That there was no reason to talk to him. But it sounded like he was right in the middle of everything. "Do you remember when she actually left town?" I asked Cody.

"I don't remember exactly. Late August, I think? Definitely the end of the summer. She was only in town three months or so."

"Thank you. That helps," I said. It was a start, at least.

"You really think Stahl might have killed her?"

"I'm not sure," I said. "But it looks like a possibility."

He was silent for a moment. Then he asked, "Are you all right, Naomi?"

I started to answer automatically. But in this tiny slice of shared reality, I didn't want to lie to him. "I keep feeling like I'm going to wake up and realize you never found me," I said.

"I have that nightmare, too," he said. "But I did find you. You're alive, and you're safe, and you don't need to go chasing Stahl's ghost. Focus on living."

"Thanks, Cody," I said.

"Take care of yourself, Naomi."

We said our goodbyes. I hung up and sat with the phone cradled in my lap, letting my awareness seep slowly outward again.

A few minutes later, I walked to Ethan's door. He opened it before I even knocked and beckoned me in.

"Get anything?" he asked. He had files pulled up on his computer—notes on Stahl, it looked like, and a map of the peninsula with dates and names scrawled on it—possible missing victims, maybe.

"A bit," I said. "He didn't know she was missing. He said she took off suddenly, but it wasn't surprising."

"And when was that?"

"Late August," I said.

He frowned. "You're sure?"

"He was pretty sure. Why?"

He sighed and ran a hand through his hair. "Because if Jessi Walker was alive and well in August, there's no way Stahl killed her. His mother had a stroke in late July. He spent two months on the East Coast to help her while she recovered."

"That can't be right," I said. "Maybe Cody got the dates wrong."

"Or Stahl had nothing to do with Jessi's death," Ethan said.

I sat heavily on the bed, cupping my head in my hands. If Stahl hadn't killed Jessi, he wouldn't have gone out to the woods to visit the body. He would have had no reason at all to be in Chester, to be off the trail and happen to stumble into me. And no reason to kill a random little girl eating a peanut butter sandwich who hadn't even seen him.

"They saw him," I whispered. "Liv and Cass."

"They saw someone," Ethan said gently. "Eyewitness testimony is unreliable even with adults."

"Then Stahl didn't attack me," I said leadenly. They'd been wrong and I'd lied, and the wrong man had gone to prison because of us. Because of *me*.

"We don't know that. It doesn't prove anything either way," Ethan said, but I could see in his eyes that he was certain now.

I stared at him. "That's what you thought all along, isn't it? You never really thought it was Stahl."

"I thought it was a possibility," he hedged. "But it didn't seem likely. The way you described the cave, you had trouble getting into it. Stahl was a big guy. He could have shoved the body in there, but he'd have trouble accessing it later. He'd want someplace he could get into and out of easily."

"Then why go along with the whole theory? Why even tell me about the quiet summer?"

"Because you wanted it to be true. I thought it would help you open up and talk to me. And then it let you accept my help. And like I said—I didn't think it was impossible that it was true. I was hoping it would be. You'd have your answers."

"Fuck." I lay down on the bed, staring at the ceiling. I should have been angry. I just felt wrung out—and oddly relieved. I hadn't really understood why Ethan was helping me. Now I was starting to. "Are you going to turn this into a podcast?"

He sat down next to me, his weight making the bed sink. "This is all a bit beyond the scope of the project I pitched," he admitted. I snorted. "I told you. I won't use anything without your permission."

"But you'd like to."

"I'd be an idiot not to," he said.

"You are kind of an idiot, though," I said. "Otherwise you wouldn't be looking at me like that."

"Like what?"

"Like you expect something more than what my daddy says I am," I told him. I wrapped the edge of Ethan's shirt around my fist, the shape of my knuckles distinct under the thin fabric. I pulled him toward me and he leaned forward, bracing himself with a hand beside my head as he looked down at me.

"What your dad said—" he began.

"It's true. More or less. I'm a disaster. And a liar. And apparently, I sent the wrong man to prison."

He didn't tell me it wasn't true. He didn't tell me it wasn't my fault. "Someone killed Jessi. Someone killed Liv."

"Or Jessi fell and hit her head, and Liv killed herself," I said. And I was the only villain in the story after all. The girl who lied.

He splayed his hand over my chest, as if to feel my heartbeat, and his fingertip grazed the edge of the ridged scar beside my sternum. The one that had come the closest to killing me.

"Someone did this to you," he said. "Maybe we were wrong about it being Stahl, but right about the reason. The man who killed Jessi saw you. He tried to kill you. Silence you. And when Liv put the pieces together, he silenced her, too. You caught the wrong monster twenty years ago. That means there's another one still out there. And you're going to find him."

"I like the girl you think I am," I said. I rubbed the cuff of his T-shirt sleeve idly between my fingers. "If you were smart, you'd get far, far away from me."

"I'm not going anywhere," he said. He kissed me, softly, and I shut my eyes and told myself that my father was right and none of it meant anything at all.

Ethan passed out sometime around two p.m. I got dressed quietly so I wouldn't wake him up. There was no chance of me getting any sleep. My thoughts were caught in an endless loop, cycling between Jessi and Liv and that summer twenty-two years ago. I was ready to accept that Stahl hadn't been the one who attacked me. He wasn't the thread connecting the three of us.

Except that Liv and Cass had seen him.

Unless they hadn't.

There was only one person left who could tell me exactly what they'd seen.

At two o'clock on a Friday, Cass would be at the lodge. The sensible thing would be to call or to go by her house later, but instead I drove out of town, along the winding road that led farther into the moss-draped trees. You came upon the lodge suddenly—rounding a thickly wooded turn to discover it right in front of you, nestled against a backdrop of a hundred shades of green and brown. When we were kids it was a single building, sagging and waterlogged, with scratchy sheets and stained carpeting. It had closed completely the year before Cass bought it.

Two years after that, she'd transformed it. Huge, rough wooden beams supported the roof, artfully primitive, while the all-glass front entrance added an elegant modern touch. Inside, works by local Native artists decorated the lobby, and the front desk sold tiny packets of salted caramel popcorn for four bucks a pop.

"Can I help you?" chirped a tiny brunette from behind the counter, her cheeks rounding with her perfect customer-service smile.

"I'm looking for—" I started, but I didn't get any further.

"Naomi! What are you doing here? Is something wrong?" Cass asked, striding across the lobby. Belatedly, I realized that I hadn't changed or brushed my hair, and I probably looked terrible.

"I just need to talk to you," I said. Cass's eyes darted past me. Her expression was tight with discomfort. This was her space, and I was intruding on it. Causing chaos. But she only waved a beckoning hand and marched down the hall. I trailed behind as she made her way to one of the conference rooms on the ground floor and opened it with a keycard. As soon as we were both inside, she shut it and turned to me, spots of pink high on her cheeks.

"You've been avoiding me," she said.

I winced. I couldn't say anything in my defense, because she was right. "I'm sorry." It was utterly inadequate. One of her friends had died, and the other disappeared on her.

Her lips thinned. "It's fine. What do you need?" she asked, her voice strained.

I tensed. Maybe coming here had been a bad idea. But it was too late now. "I need to know exactly what you saw the day I was attacked," I said.

She let out a groan, covering her face with one hand. "Naomi. You have to let this go."

"It's not that I don't believe you," I told her pleadingly. "I just need to hear it—from you, I mean. I don't remember. I need you to do it for me." *Tell me I didn't do anything wrong.*

She looked at me for a long moment. Then she reached out and took my hand, drawing me gently over to one of the long tables and ushering me into a chair. We sat across the corner of the table from one another, and Cass kept her hand over mine.

"I'm going to tell you this once," she said. "And then you are going to stop torturing yourself, okay?" At my nod, she took a deep breath. "Liv and I were down in the Grotto. We heard you scream, and we started to climb out to see what was wrong. That was when I saw the man. He was standing over you. He had a knife in his hand. You were on your stomach, and you were kind of . . . flopping around."

She swallowed, looking queasy. My heart beat fast in my chest. I hadn't actually heard Cass testify; my testimony had been last, and I hadn't been allowed to listen to the others. Hearing it now, my heart ached for the little girls we'd been.

"You managed to roll over. He dropped down on one knee and the knife came down again, and it—I think that was the one that got your face."

I touched a finger to the scar automatically. That blow had been one of the hardest, but it was at an angle, laying open the flesh from the hinge of my jaw almost to the corner of my mouth.

"Liv tried to climb out. She shouted for you, but I grabbed her and put my hand over her mouth. He was so focused he didn't hear—and you were screaming, too. I had to wrap my whole body around her to keep her there. His hand kept coming up and going down again. Over and over." She looked to the side, taking short, sharp breaths. "Then he just . . . stopped. He said something, I think, but I couldn't tell what. He walked away."

I pictured the scene. The spot where I'd sat. The Grotto. I frowned. "I was pretty far from the boulder," I said.

Cass's head tilted. "I guess."

"And he had his back to you."

Her brow furrowed. "Not completely. I could see the side of his face."

The side of his face, from what, fifty feet away? Sixty? More? "Do you remember exactly what you told the cops? The description you gave?"

"Not *exactly*," she said. "I would have told them he was big. Short, brown hair. White. No beard—I remember they asked about the beard, and I was sure he didn't have one. But when Dougherty showed me the photo of Stahl, it looked just like him."

"Wait. Dougherty showed you a picture of Stahl? When, at the hospital?" I asked.

She shook her head. "No, it was before the ambulance even got there."

On the side of the road. Before they even knew I was still alive. "Cass, I thought you gave the description to Chief Miller."

"I did," Cass said slowly, a line appearing between her eyebrows in faint confusion. "He's the one who asked me about the beard, so yeah, he's the one I gave the description to."

"But Miller got there after the ambulance," I said. You couldn't live in Chester without knowing every step of that story. From Leo Cortland on down, everyone wanted you to know exactly where they'd been that day. And Miller always talked about rolling up to a scene already swarming with sirens and two little girls shivering in the back of an ambulance. "So Dougherty showed you the photo before you gave your description."

She wetted her lips. "Maybe. No. I told him—I told him there was a man, a big man. I told him about the brown hair."

"And the beard?"

She shook her head. "I don't know."

"*Was* it Stahl you saw?" I pressed.

"How am I supposed to answer that? I told them what I saw then. Now all I see when I think about his face is Stahl in the courtroom, glaring at us like he wanted to slit our throats."

I felt numb. There'd never been any chance of a genuine identification. Cass and Olivia might have seen anyone out there, but Dougherty shoving that photo in their faces while they were traumatized and panicking? Of course they'd thought it was Stahl. His face could have imprinted itself over any genuine memories.

The truth had been trampled over before I ever woke up.

"What's going on, Naomi?" Cass asked. There was an edge of fear in her voice.

I sat back in my chair. I felt that sense of vertigo again—teetering on the edge of a fall. "It's nothing," I said. "Don't worry about it."

She gave me a tired smile. "There's no chance of that, Naomi. I always worry about you."

Back at the motel, I stood under the anemic shower, heat turned hot enough to blister. The last shreds of hope I'd had that Stahl was my monster after all had been torn away with Cass's story. My lie had haunted me all this time, but I'd had Liv and Cass as witnesses to the truth. I'd always been able to hold on to that, and believe that no matter what I'd done, the outcome had been . . . if not *just*, then *correct*.

But now that was gone. It wasn't just Cass's testimony that had been contaminated—her memories couldn't be trusted, either, any more than mine could. We'd ruled out any reason for Stahl to be there. And then there was the fact that his son seemed to have proof he hadn't been. Or if not proof, something that made him certain.

His son. God. I'd been doing my best not to think about him. I could believe Stahl was a wicked man, whether he was in those woods or not. But his son had done nothing to me, and I'd torn his life to tatters.

I shut off the water and toweled myself off, and didn't feel clean at all.

I'd kept the letter. Maybe I should have gotten rid of it. Burned it, shredded it. But I'd left it in the bottom of my bag instead, and after I'd pulled on fresh clothes I pulled it out. It was covered in muddy shoe prints, the text nearly illegible, but I didn't need to read it to know what it said. The words had seared themselves in my mind.

*I am trying to understand.*

If Ethan was right, Stahl was a murderer. He'd died where he belonged, and whatever my sins, I hadn't caged an innocent man.

But was he right?

I'd worked hard to avoid learning too much about Stahl's crimes, my stubborn way of retaining control—some sense of identity beyond what he'd done to me. Now I pulled up article after article, waded through forum threads and blogs with black backgrounds and neon text. I stared at photographs of dead and mutilated women, their swollen faces, the wounds that, unlike mine, had never closed. I examined time lines and transcripts, and piece by piece I mapped the holes that had been there all along, that people before me had found and argued over. Holes that hadn't mattered, because Stahl wasn't in prison because of these dead, discarded women. He was there because of me.

I found myself staring at a photograph of a single-story home. The photo was black-and-white, pulled from a newspaper. Uniformed police officers trooped in and out of the front door, carrying boxes, while a woman and a boy—twelve, maybe thirteen—stood off to the side, watching. Her hand was on his shoulder; he stared at the camera. The low quality made his face indistinct, but those eyes seemed to bore through me.

"Police raid Stahl's home while his wife and son look on," the caption read. So that was AJ Stahl, watching his world fall apart. I'd done that.

He had to hate me. He must want more than anything to see me hurt the way he hurt. And maybe not just me. I'd been the one to point my finger at Alan Stahl in that courtroom, but Liv and Cass had been part of it, too. If his father wasn't a killer after all, if he'd been innocent, AJ would hate all of us for what we did to him.

I hammered on Ethan's door, the letter clutched in my hand. He answered, tousle-haired and startled. He looked down at the letter, then back at me. "Naomi—" he started.

"Why did police think that Stahl was the Quinault Killer?" I asked.

He frowned at me, then started listing off facts. "He was known to be in the area of four of the attacks. He went on long camping trips every summer coinciding with the killings, and—"

"So it could have been a coincidence?" I asked. He sighed and motioned me inside. I stalked past him, still clutching the letter.

"There were also witnesses who saw him near one of the dumping grounds and talking to Hannah Faber at a gas station."

"Him, or someone matching his general description? White guy, brown hair, stocky build, average height. Not exactly distinct," I said. No better than the description Cass had given. A description that could have led to anyone. I gripped the paper tight. My hand was shaking. "They told me he killed those women. They told me they were *sure*. There was no way they were wrong."

"The police?"

"Everyone," I said, voice raw as I paced back and forth in the tight space. "Miller and Dougherty. The detectives. The lawyers. They told me it was him, and I could stop him. But this is all they had?"

"That, and a profile that matched. He was cagey in interviews. They found blood in his truck, but there was a lab screw-up and it got contaminated," Ethan said.

"There were other suspects."

He grimaced. "Not good ones."

"I was looking at this message board, and they were saying that this other guy, Franklin Church—"

Ethan shook his head. "Church didn't have the smarts or discipline for these murders. He was on his way to being a spree killer when he was arrested; he wouldn't have gone a full year between killings. I've looked into all of this, Naomi. It was Stahl. He might not have attacked you, but he was a killer."

"I don't know why I always assumed that there was better proof," I said. "I told myself they had something that wasn't admissible in court, some technicality. But it was all just a big guess? I put a man in prison because of coincidence and gut instinct?"

"You really didn't know any of this?"

"I couldn't," I told him. There were just things that needed to be true for the world to hold together. So you didn't look too closely. But now I had, and I could see the cracks running through the foundation of everything I'd believed. "I ruined this man's life. Destroyed his family's lives," I said.

I held the letter out. Ethan took it gingerly, brushing away flakes of dried mud. He stared at it, not moving, his eyes tracking slowly over the near-illegible words.

"It's from Stahl's son," I said. "If he blames us for his dad dying, he'd be furious, wouldn't he? He'd want revenge. He could have come after Liv, and—"

"Whoa," Ethan said, looking up sharply. "Naomi. First off, you didn't kill Alan Stahl, cancer did. And second, there's no threat in this letter. Nothing to suggest wanting to do you harm."

"Wouldn't you want to hurt the person who ruined your life?" I asked. He didn't answer. I turned away.

"Naomi, wait."

"I've got to take off," I said, a bitter taste in my mouth. "I've got a wedding to shoot tomorrow."

"What about Persephone?"

"I'll be back Monday. I just— I have to go," I said. I had to run. If I could outpace this, I wouldn't have to feel it. This wretched, heartsick pulse running from the pit of my stomach to the base of my skull.

I'd wanted to find answers. Instead, I'd been undoing them.

I wanted Ethan to stop me. But he said nothing, and I walked away, my guilt between my teeth like old leather.

I threw my things into the back of the car and took off. I meant to drive straight out of town, but near the trailhead I slowed. Pulled over. I sat in the car, my gut twisted in a knot, my thoughts filled with the faces of dead girls.

Everything that had been certain in my life was shifting. Olivia was just one more in a litany of names, women who'd never known justice. I got out of the car and walked slowly toward the trail. The sounds of the forest folded over me.

I thought I was walking toward the pond, but I turned away from the trail. Some part of me was searching for Liv, and she wasn't there. Not really. She never had been.

The shadows of the Grotto welcomed me in. I knelt in the black dirt beside Persephone's bones and lifted the bruised and rotting petals from her eyes. I brushed smooth the dirt around her skull and straightened the charms around her, and the ghosts of girls long gone whispered in the hollow space around me.

"I like it here," Liv said to me in my memory. It was August, hot and dry. Her skin was tanned, mine red and rough with my ever-present sunburn. "It's quiet. Easier to think." She nestled coreopsis blooms into Persephone's eyes, adjusting them just so. The scent of cut stems was sharp and green.

"I like it, too," I said, for the sake of agreeing. Grabbing at every little connection I could claim.

"You should tell Cassidy what happened," Liv said quietly, rearranging the stones beside Persephone's clavicle into some arcane order.

"Nothing happened." I pulled up a weed struggling to grow in the thin seam of light that infiltrated the Grotto. Its roots ripped free reluctantly. "Oscar's a jerk. Whatever."

"If Cody hadn't been there—"

"But he was. And it's fine." Even in the forest, I couldn't stop smelling gasoline. Hearing the crunch of a burst bottle under my heel. "Let it go."

"If something happened to me, you wouldn't let it go," Liv had said. She brushed the back of my hand, then laced her fingers with mine. Her dark hair blended with the shadows, her lips a perfect red.

"Never," I promised her.

In the present, alone, I ran my fingertip along the arched brow of bone. "I'm sorry," I whispered to whatever ghosts would listen. "All I've done is make things worse. I don't know what to do."

I waited—for an answer, for courage, for something I couldn't name. But there was only the endless tangle of uncertainty and the thorns it had left under my skin already.

And then a harsh, inorganic buzzing in my pocket. I pulled my phone out, surprised I had signal enough for a call to come through. The screen showed a single bar of signal and the Chester PD on the caller ID.

I put the phone to my ear. "Hello?"

"Naomi, hon. It's Bill." Dougherty's voice was garbled from the poor signal. "How are you holding up?"

I stared at the dead girl's bones as I answered. "I'm fine." More than anything, I felt numb.

"That's good, that's good," he said, with more enthusiasm than my tepid response warranted. "I probably shouldn't be calling you, Naomi. I don't exactly have the go-ahead from the new boss. But I thought you ought to know, we found the gun."

The words didn't register at first. The gun. The weapon that had killed Liv. "Where?" I managed.

"In the pond, like we expected. Just took us a while to sift through all the junk in there," he said. "Look, I know Bishop has been hassling you. You know how it is, new to town, gotta prove herself. Jim's told her to simmer down, though, now that we've got the weapon."

"Was it Marcus Barnes's gun?" I asked.

"Sure was."

"And you're sure that . . . You're sure that's the gun that killed her." I swallowed hard.

"Well, we don't have the bullet, so we can't match the ballistics. But there's no other reason for that gun to be in that pond, is there?" He cleared his throat. "I imagine it's a relief for everyone, to have things wrapped up."

"You're putting it down as a suicide, then."

"Seems pretty clear, doesn't it?"

I hadn't thought Liv had killed herself—but I'd been wrong about everything so far. Maybe I was wrong about this, too.

My fingertips found the spiderweb cracks in Persephone's skull, tightening in toward a center where one fragment had long since fallen away, leaving a ragged black gap.

*No.*

Liv wouldn't have shot herself, and she hadn't been suicidal. She'd been disappointed, but she wouldn't have given up that easily. Not when she had something that she cared so much about and was so close to seeing through.

Not when she'd promised me.

Dougherty was talking about Bishop again. About how she wouldn't have any choice now but to admit it was suicide and move on. His voice dipped in and out. "So I don't think she'll be bothering you again," he said. "And if she does, you let me know and I'll talk to Mayor Green about it. Make sure she understands."

"Thank you," I bit out, because it was what he wanted to hear. Bishop saw it. She knew Liv hadn't hurt herself, but would that matter? If Mayor Green told her to drop it, she'd be risking her job to do anything else.

"It's no problem, hon," Dougherty said. "Hey, you made my career. I kind of owe you, I figure."

"Made your career," I repeated dully. The words didn't make sense. And then they snapped into focus. "You mean because you were the one who got Stahl."

He made a demurring sound. "I wouldn't say I got him, just put the pieces together. My brother-in-law knew a guy working on the case, and he told me all about the guy they were looking at. I'd been carrying his photo around just in case I spotted him. Figured it was only a matter of time before he came hunting around here. As soon as those girls told me what had happened, it clicked."

Silence stretched. I heard him shift, chair creaking, like he was expecting me to chime in with a bit of praise and was slowly realizing it wouldn't come. He had no idea what he'd done. The error he'd set in motion.

And now he was doing it all over again. He'd known from the start it was suicide, like he'd known from the start it was Stahl. He was never going to look for another answer or consider that he could be wrong.

"Look, I—" he started. Then nothing. I kept the phone to my ear, waiting for him to finish, for several seconds before I realized the signal had finally dipped to zero.

The walls of the cave were close around me, and I couldn't tell if it felt like threat or comfort. I clawed myself free, fleeing both, and staggered through the woods. The trees blurred around me as I made my way toward the road, my thoughts an endless inventory of ghosts.

I drove straight out of Chester, anger a sharp pain behind my sternum. Around Sequim, I pulled off at a rest stop to stretch my legs. A family with a little fluffy dog was playing on the grass nearby. Their car was piled with camping gear, tents and sleeping bags strapped to the roof. I sat at a picnic table, watching the dog chase a ball back and forth.

I'd only gone camping once as a kid. It was the year before that summer. Cass hated camping, so Liv and I spent a week in the woods with Marcus and Kimiko, just the two of us. We shared a tent and stayed up late into the right, whispering. I would sneak my hand out from my sleeping bag, and she would find it, and we would let our fingers slide over each other, lacing and unlacing.

I remembered the feeling in the pit of my stomach as we lay in the tent, an excruciating longing. It would be years later and far away that I'd finally recognize what it meant—that I had been more than a little in love with Olivia. *Gay* was just a synonym for *stupid* when we were growing up in Chester. *Bisexual* was a punch line to a dirty joke. I'd been well into college before I realized I was attracted to women. And by then, even if Liv had felt the same way, things were too complicated, Liv's stability too precarious.

I had wanted that trip to last forever. We were supposed to go again the next year, just the two of us. But the day before we were going to leave, Cass took a fall on her bike and sliced up her calf on the chain. We stayed to keep her company while she recovered, instead. The Barneses talked about rescheduling, but then the mill burned and the Goddess Game began, and the camping trip was forgotten.

A trucker had pulled in right after me, and as he exited the restroom he headed toward me, making the kind of eye contact that could go one of two ways—either he wanted me off-balance or he wanted to make sure I knew he wasn't trying anything funny. He was a big-set guy with thick hands and hairy knuckles, and I decided to be contrary and assume the best.

"Afternoon," I said, giving him a nod.

"Sorry to bother you, miss," he said. "I've been heading in the same direction as you for a bit now, and I thought you should know there's somebody following you."

"I'm sorry, what?" I said, my intentional calm dissolving. "What makes you think that?"

"There's a black Toyota Camry that's been dogging you. Staying in your lane, making sure you don't get more than a couple cars ahead. I thought you must be traveling together, but then when you pulled off here, he parked on the shoulder just up ahead. Figured I should let you know."

"I appreciate it," I said, trying not to sound queasy. He could be wrong. Paranoid and bored after a long stretch on the road.

Except he'd said it was a black Toyota Camry. Like the one I'd seen in Chester, too many times to quite dismiss as a trick of my imagination.

"Want me to follow you out, keep an eye on you?" he asked, adjusting his baseball cap over a thick mop of black hair.

I shook my head. "I can look out for myself," I said.

"I don't mean to be rude or sexist or anything," he said, and I gave him a twisted-up smile. His eyes tracked predictably to my scar, and I could see the question in his eyes.

"You should see the other guy," I said.

"Oh yeah?" he said. "He missing an ear?"

"He's dead, actually," I replied, deadpan. He stared at me a beat, then decided I was joking, and chuckled.

"You be careful," he told me.

"Sure thing," I replied with false cheer, and gave him a wave as I headed back to my car.

I pulled out, my nerves jangling. I'd hoped the trucker was wrong, but there was the black Toyota, waiting on the shoulder. I drove past it and hoped against hope that it would stay put. No such luck. When I was a decent distance ahead, it pulled back onto the freeway.

Over the next few miles I tried switching lanes randomly, moving into exit lanes and back out again. He didn't always stay in my lane, and sometimes he dropped back, but any time it looked like I might be taking an exit he was there right behind me. The windows of the car were tinted. I couldn't make out anything about him other than a vague silhouette. It might not even have been a man, much less the one I'd seen in Chester.

I memorized the license plate, wishing I'd thought to back in town so I could be sure it was the same car, and tried to tell myself there was nothing he could do to me on the road. When we pulled into the ferry terminal, he was two cars behind me. I shut off my engine.

The ferry was chugging toward us, but still at a good distance. It would be fifteen minutes before it reached the dock, and my stalker was just sitting back there, watching me. I was boxed in, cars to my left and right. On the ferry it would be worse, surrounded by water so I couldn't even run.

I couldn't sit here and wait for something to happen. I already felt like I was crawling out of my own skin. I unbuckled my seatbelt and threw open my door, striding down the line of cars to the black Toyota. I rapped on the window, glaring in at the indistinct figure in the driver's seat. They shifted but didn't roll down the window, so I knocked on it again.

"I know you're following me," I said. I was drawing attention, now, heads swiveling toward me, cell phones emerging as the onlookers sensed a video opportunity. "Roll down the window. Who the hell are you? What do you want?"

"Ma'am, is there a problem here?"

A security officer stood nearby, his hand resting oh-so-casually at his belt next to his Taser. He was a young Latino man, with a long face and intense eyes. I was keenly aware of how this must look. Like I was out of my mind, the classic white woman on a tear because the world hadn't lined up just so to cater to her.

"This car has been following me," I said, as calmly as I could, but my voice shook. So did my hands. I balled them into fists and then forced them to relax. *Don't look crazy. Do not be the psycho lady. Do not ruin this nice security officer's day with your bullshit.*

"I'm sure they're just going the same way," the security officer said soothingly. "Please return to your vehicle."

"They were following me," I insisted. *My best friend was murdered, and her killer might be after me, too,* I thought, and stifled a bray of frantic laughter at the thought of having to explain *that.*

"Ma'am, get back in your vehicle and I'll speak to the driver and work this out," the security officer said. God, he was young. Could he even drink yet? But he was good at this, the soothing tone, the steady hand held up just in case I got it in my mind to move toward him.

"Fine," I said. I'd already drawn too much attention. I retreated, but I didn't get inside my car, just stood outside the open door.

The security officer tapped on the window of the Camry. Instead of rolling it down, the driver opened the door, which blocked my line of sight. The driver shifted in his seat to talk to the security officer, putting one foot on the ground. A man's shoe. I caught a glimpse of medium-brown hair, no gray in it—but then the foot was retreating, the door closing. It might have been the man from Chester. It might not.

The security officer walked back my way with that *Here we go* gait of somebody not sure of their reception. There were still a few phones pointed in my direction. I couldn't give them a show. It would take about thirty seconds to identify me if I did something wild enough to end up on the internet and then all my attempts at a thin façade of anonymity would be out the fucking window.

"The gentleman in the other car says he isn't following you. You're just heading in the same direction," the security officer said. "He's sorry about the misunderstanding. Do you think we can all move on?"

"He *was* following me," I said, keeping my voice low. The family in the minivan next to me had rolled down their windows and were watching without an ounce of shame. "Every time I switched lanes, he was right behind me. He waited past a rest stop for me. I'm not imagining this."

"I can see that you're very concerned, but I spoke with the gentleman and he's quite insistent that he has no idea who you are and has no reason to be following you," the security officer said. "What we can do if you're still worried is have you pull out of line after things clear out, and you can wait for the next ferry. He can go on ahead, and that way you can be sure that he isn't following you."

He didn't suggest that "the gentleman" be the one to wait, I noted. It was clear who was the suspicious one in this situation. "Did he give you his name?" I asked.

"Ma'am, I think it's best if you wait in your vehicle."

So I wasn't even going to get that. "Okay," I said. Surrender was easier. I slid back into my seat, closed the door. Locked them. People were still staring, but soon they lost interest. I fidgeted. The ferry drew closer, and I watched the Camry in my mirror. Predictably, nothing happened.

Nothing happened, and I was stuck, and I was going to start tearing my hair out in a minute. I grabbed for my phone, pulled up my recent calls. Mitch was at the top—I'd called to let him know I'd be dropping by to grab my gear. Ethan's number was right below, and after a moment's hesitation I stabbed at it.

It rang long enough that I imagined he was deciding whether or not to answer, but finally he picked up. "Naomi. Have you made it home yet?" His voice was devoid of inflection.

"I'm waiting for the ferry," I said. Silence. "I'm sorry about earlier. About freaking out."

"I don't blame you at all for freaking out. It's a lot to take in."

"I shouldn't be taking it in. I should have faced this a long time ago."

I watched the ferry pulling ponderously up to the dock. They still had to unload. The Camry lurked in the rearview mirror. "What do you know about Stahl's son?" I asked.

"Is this about the letter again?" Ethan asked.

I chewed my thumbnail. "He knows I lied. What if he doesn't just blame me? If he thought that Liv—"

"I don't know, Naomi. It's a big leap from wanting to know the truth to killing someone," Ethan pointed out.

"If his father was violent, wouldn't he be predisposed to violence, too?"

"And you're just like your father."

I grunted, conceding the point. Except that I was, more than I liked to admit. Terrible at relationships. Self-destructive coping habits— mine just involved emotionally damaged men instead of a bottle, except for the times it involved both. Who knew what version of his vices Alan Stahl had left his son. "Still. Who is this guy?"

Ethan sighed. "His son's name was Alan Stahl, Jr. He was twelve years old when his father was arrested. Because he was so young, he wasn't even named in most of the contemporaneous news coverage. He's never spoken publicly about his father."

"Do you know where he's living? What he does?" I asked. The man following me was the right age, but so were a lot of people.

"No," Ethan said. "I don't."

"So you'll hassle me for an interview, but not him?" I asked, needling him a bit. Cars continued to trundle past. Not long now. If I could just stay on the phone with Ethan, I could keep my heartbeat from racing, my adrenaline from spiking. I could keep from just ramming my way through this line of cars to get out, to get *free*, and damn the consequences.

"I can only hassle the people I can find," Ethan said. "You sound . . . I don't know. Are you okay?"

"Just feeling a bit on edge," I said with a manic lilt. "Have you ever thought about how ferries are basically just big floating prisons, and if anything went wrong you're basically fucked?"

"I'm pretty sure they have lifeboats on ferries. And very strict safety codes. Is something else going on?"

"Don't overreact," I said. "But I sort of think someone's following me."

"Following you? Who?"

"I'm not sure. Youngish guy, I think, brown hair, but that's all I could see. If I give you the license plate number, could you figure out who owns it?" I didn't tell him I thought it might be AJ. He already thought I was paranoid.

"Not by myself, but there are plenty of services online," he replied. "I'll see what I can do."

I read the number out to him, and he took it down.

"Are you safe right now?" Ethan asked.

"I think so. I'm going to pull out of line when they load. He'll have to get on the ferry."

"Do you want me to stay on the phone?"

"No, that's okay. It looks like they're loading now," I told him. "Thanks, though. Thanks for not acting like I'm crazy."

"Will you call me when you get home? Or text. Just let me know you made it safe."

"You're sweet," I told him.

"Is that a good thing?"

"I think so," I allowed. "But don't let that go to your head."

"I wouldn't dream of it."

I hung up. The first line was moving now, and with each second that I got closer to being able to move, my body got tenser. Finally the lane beside me cleared, and the security officer waved me off to the side. I peeled off, then paused, watching until the Camry drove onto the ferry.

There. He was gone. And I was left idling in the parking lot, feeling like a paranoid fool.

I couldn't get on that ferry. I'd started to think of it as a prison and now I couldn't stop. I pulled up the map on my phone. The drive wasn't that much longer than waiting for the next ferry, I told myself. It was a perfectly reasonable thing to do.

As lies went, it was weak, but I sped away from the terminal.

I pulled up to the apartment late. I winced as I spotted Mitch's car in his spot. He'd said he wouldn't be in, but that was before I decided on my detour. I braced myself as I unlocked the door. He was on the couch, a beer on the side table next to him and his laptop open to a blank page.

"Hey," he said, sounding surprised as if he hadn't known perfectly well I was coming by.

"Hello, Mitch," I said. I dragged my bangs back from my eyes. "I'll just grab my stuff and get out of here."

"You're not staying?" he asked.

"No," I said slowly. "I was just going to get a hotel room."

He set his laptop aside and stood, tucking his hands in his pockets in a way that made him seem smaller, more vulnerable. "You should stay. It's your apartment, too."

"Not really," I said. I'd never been on the lease. Hadn't picked it. Hated the neighborhood and the color of the curtains.

"I'm not trying to get back together," he said, which did not allay my suspicions. His apparent earlier surrender aside, breaking up with Mitch was going to be like trying to pry an octopus off your leg. "I can sleep on the couch. It just seems silly, you getting a hotel room when your bed is right there. And free."

He had a point. The motel in Chester wasn't expensive, but it was chewing its way through my savings at a steady pace. Though at least the motel didn't come with strings. Or tentacles. "Mitch, I'm exhausted. I just want to sleep. If you're serious, I'll take you up on it, but it doesn't mean—"

"I know, I know," he said, holding up his hands as if to ward off the accusation.

"Thanks," I said, still not quite believing him. We stood for an awkward second, and then I headed down the hall. I shut the door behind me and stood in the familiar room, feeling adrift. This had stopped being home the moment I left for Chester, and being back in it unsettled me. Like I was an intruder, and I was going to get caught.

I changed out of my car-stale clothes into a tank top and sweats. Despite what I'd told Mitch, I wasn't quite ready to sleep yet. I propped my laptop up on the bed and plugged "Alan Stahl son" into the search engine. A few articles and associated images popped up right away. The photo from the article I'd seen earlier of the police raid was the clearest picture of him.

Ethan was right—there was next to nothing about the guy. I had a notion kicking around in my head that I'd known a few things about him. The phrase *muddy soccer uniform* kept popping into my mind, but I couldn't find it anywhere in the scant information available. And it wasn't like I was an avid reader of Stahl articles.

But I had read Cass's book. I shut the laptop and went over to the bookshelf. I hadn't wanted anything to do with the thing, but Mitch kept a copy. Claimed that it gave him a glimpse into my "shrouded psyche," whatever the fuck he thought that meant.

There wasn't much of me in these pages. Cass's picture of that summer, as relayed by the author, Rachel Devereaux, was sun-drenched and flawless. Its version of the Goddess Game was a twinkling bit of fantasy, the kind of magic with no bite to it. It had none of the desperation that had suffused those months.

Things had been changing. Where I'd had two worlds, one cruel and one fantastical, I was about to have only one. I remembered it as a period of stomach-churning dread, but in Cass's words it was a time of delight and whimsy.

The "Cass" sections were interwoven with straight reporting. The index pointed me toward a few small excerpts from these. Alan Junior's birth, mentions of him in the context of the marriage. Nothing much about him as a person, though you got the sense that the author was doing her best to conjure up a personality behind the name. The closest she got was in a passage about his bedroom, glimpsed only in one photo among many in the police files. That was the one I remembered:

> Trophies and ribbons crowd one small shelf. Second- and third-place wins in soccer tournaments and track events, not one blue ribbon among them. The muddy soccer uniform draped over the side of a hamper suggests a boy still trying to earn that first-place ribbon, that trophy—still trying to impress a distant and indifferent father.

Or it suggested he was a decent but not great athlete who hadn't done his laundry. The passage was illustrated with the photo I remembered—a nine- or ten-year-old AJ with his father. Lightly curling brown hair and a tentative smile. He was a wisp next to his broad-shouldered father. He looked like a normal kid—a nice kid. But Stahl looked nice, too. If I'd seen the photo without knowing who he was, I might have said he had kind eyes. The same eyes that seemed to radiate pure evil in the photos from the trial.

The answers I wanted weren't here. There was no wicked version of the boy, no mini Psycho Stahl, to conjure from such scant details. If he was a monster like his father, the proof wasn't in these pages. I flipped idly through the book, recognizing passages here and there. I'd read the book in a rage, searching for tiny factual details that weren't quite right so that I could discount the rest. The parts that called my father a drunk, a man who couldn't protect his daughter. That cast me as the helpless victim of life and circumstance and Stahl, reduced to what was done to me. As for the other "characters" Devereaux constructed . . .

Cody's name caught my eye.

Cody Benham, the best friend of Cassidy's brother, Oscar, is an unlikely figure to become the shining white knight of the story. Frequent run-ins made him a common subject among the local police, and Chief Miller described him as a hot temper in search of a brawl.

She'd somehow neglected to mention that all of Cody's youthful indiscretions had occurred with Oscar's willing participation—and instigation. And that the closest Cody had come to actually getting charged was . . . well. It was because of me, and it had ended their friendship. An act that I hadn't honored, in the end. Cody had tried to save me from Oscar, and I'd thrown that away, like I threw everything away.

My eyes skipped over the page.

Oscar Green, Cassidy's protective older brother, is a muscular young man, with long lashes and a slow way of speaking. He oozes that kind of backwoods charm, a lumberjack with a Shakespearean vocabulary.

"Oh, fuck off," I said. I wondered if he'd gotten her into bed. Probably. He'd nail anything with a heartbeat, and as Cody had said, entirely too many women found his brand of *I don't give a fuck about anything, including you* alluring. Not that I could exactly throw stones.

I shut my eyes. I didn't want to think about Oscar, but his name kept coming up. That was the way with Oscar. I tried to stay away from him and it never worked.

*You and me were meant to be.* Memory stirred under my fingertips.

The bedroom door opened. I looked up blearily as Mitch entered, carrying two glasses of bourbon. "I thought you'd still be up," he said. He held the drink out. I didn't move. "It's just booze, not betrothal," he joked. I set the book aside and took the drink, and he used the motion of handing it to me to sidle closer and sit down on the bed beside me, not quite touching me.

The cold glass nestled against my palm, but I didn't take a sip yet. I studied Mitch instead. Everyone I'd ever been with, I'd been trying to be a particular version of myself. With Mitch, I was an artist who could make some meaning out of her damage. She'd come from the forest, but she didn't belong to it anymore. She was a daydream I'd had, that I'd lived in for a while.

I wondered who I was trying to be with Ethan. But the past few days, I hadn't had the option of being anyone but myself. Everything that had happened had stripped me down to the bone.

"How was it? Going back home?" Mitch asked. He swirled his drink, ice cubes clinking against the glass. "How's Olivia?"

He didn't know. Of course he didn't know—I hadn't told him. But it seemed impossible. The world had changed. He should have noticed.

"Olivia is dead," I said.

Mitch's face contorted, passing through shock and confusion and anger and then settling into baffled horror. "I'm so sorry," he said. The right words, the wrong expression. He reached out, put a hand on my knee. "My God. What happened?"

I couldn't. I couldn't go through it all over again. I shook my head, and he stroked his thumb across my kneecap.

"You don't have to tell me," he said. "Not now. I'm just so sorry."

"Thank you," I said. "I just . . ."

He leaned forward, closing the gap between us. I knew what he was doing, but I didn't say anything, didn't stop him, just froze as his lips met mine. His kiss was deep and tender and ardent. I knew the scent of him, his aftershave and expensive lotion, knew his touch, but like the apartment they had become alien.

His lips moved to the hinge of my jaw, my neck, my collarbone. He took my drink from me, setting it on the bedside table, and guided me gently down onto the bed. He kissed my neck and I stared at the unblemished ceiling.

"It's okay," he murmured against my skin. His thumb trailed over my hipbone. "You're all right." His hand slid up under my shirt, bunching up the fabric.

*You and me are meant to be.*

I shut my eyes, shuddering. I hadn't thought of those words, that voice, in years, but now they were like the silt at the bottom of the pond, refusing to scrub free. Mitch's hand slid under the waistband of my pants. "Stop," I whispered. He didn't hear me. "Mitch, stop." I caught his wrist. His fingers stilled and he looked at me with soulful concern.

"Let me make you feel better," he said, low and sincere. "I love you, Naomi."

I swallowed. *You and me, you and me, you and me.* Hand under my T-shirt. A cheap blanket beneath me, an unbearable sense of weight. "I slept with someone," I said.

"What?" Mitch pulled his hand out of my pants. His hair fell over his eyes as he hovered over me, his thigh against mine.

"Exactly what I said. I had sex," I said. I needed him to stop touching me. I pushed him off, and he sprang away like I'd sprouted thorns. I yanked my shirt down where it had ridden up and smoothed my hair back into order.

"We've been broken up for *days*, and you fucked someone else?" Mitch asked, incredulous.

"Yeah, well. It's what I do, apparently," I said.

"Who?" he demanded.

"No one you know." I grabbed my bourbon and took a few swallows. My head was ringing, my shoulders tensing as memories snarled together. *Cheap blanket against my bare shoulders—no, a concrete wall. Hole in the roof the size of a fist, leaves shivering just beyond. The smell of the forest. The smell of gasoline.*

Of all the shit in my life, I'd thought I was over this part, but apparently I wasn't.

Mitch's fly hung open. I hadn't noticed him undoing it. Everything was weirdly blurry around the edges. My hand shook. "I don't get a name, at least?" he asked, affronted.

"Oscar," I said, not thinking, not thinking about *now* at least, and then I shook my head. "No, it wasn't, it—"

"You don't even remember his name?" he asked with sneering contempt.

"Get out," I said, not looking at him.

"It's my apartment. This is my bed."

"Then I'll go." I stood.

He shook his head viciously. "Forget it. You can stay here tonight. But after that I want you out of here." He strode out, slamming the bedroom door behind him. A moment later I heard the front door follow suit. Probably going out to drive around angrily. I sank back onto the bed, head dropping into my hands.

What the hell just happened? I should have just fucked him so he could feel like he was helping.

But when he'd touched me, all I could feel was Oscar's hands. Oscar hadn't smelled of aftershave and lotion; he'd had that cut-wood scent of the mill, machine oil, sweat. He'd laid down the ratty blanket like it was the most noble thing anyone had ever done for a girl, and right before he thrust inside me he told me, *Don't worry, it's supposed to hurt.*

I threw back the rest of the bourbon, feeling it scorch down my throat. Why had I said *Oscar*? That was years ago. And it was yesterday.

*The flesh does not acknowledge linear time*, a therapist had once told me. The past is written alongside the present on our skins. I told him he should have written poetry instead of prescriptions. He accused me of deflecting insight with sarcasm.

He was the one who'd told me that it was a mistake to order my life into Before and After, as if the attack was the root of every bad thing that had happened since, as if my life had been utterly reordered by the cataclysm that found me. And he was right. Oscar was Before, and he was After, and he was, whether I liked it or not, *Now*.

Oscar had known Jessi Walker. And she was the one solid piece of all of this I still had. She was what Liv had been chasing. The reason we'd been in the woods.

Sometimes it seemed like the only thing I'd ever been good at was surviving being broken. I didn't know how to be whole. So any time I felt like I was healing, I found a way to break myself again.

Stahl was the worst monster from my childhood. Oscar had been the first. But I hadn't run from him. Years after the woods—after all of it—I'd gone back, again and again, until there was nothing left that he could take from me.

Until I had run out of ways to break myself apart.

Saturday's bride was a hugger. And a crier. She had shock-blue hair, combat boots under her poofy princess dress, and a Rebel Alliance tattoo on her shoulder. For a few hours, I lost myself in the work, capturing the moments of heady bliss and wild energy and the soft, tender seconds in between—the groom's grandmother sitting at the edge of the dance floor with her eyes full of pride, the flower girl twirling slowly to watch her skirt billow out, the moment the bride leaned her head briefly on her father's shoulder in a moment of rest.

We made our lives of rites and rituals, and this one was bright with joy and meaning. I stood on the edge of it, a witness but not a participant. More than ever I felt the wall between me and the images I took.

At the end of the day I packed up my gear and headed to a hotel I couldn't really afford. I still had the engagement shoot tomorrow, or I would have just headed back to Chester. For all the crowds around me, I'd felt isolated all day, exposed. At least I had work that I could focus on.

At the desk in the hotel room, I pulled up a few shots I'd already identified, doing the most basic of touch-ups on them before zipping off a few web-sized JPEGs to the bride. *Just a preview!!! I thought you might like to share these. CONGRATULATIONS!!!*

I was uncomfortable with exclamation points, but one had to make certain sacrifices to work in the wedding industry.

My stomach growled. I'd snagged a couple appetizers at the wedding, but otherwise I hadn't eaten. I was only a few blocks away from one of my favorite Thai places, and suddenly I could think of nothing else. I sent another couple of quick emails—telling my engaged couple I was looking forward to seeing them tomorrow, confirming dates for a spring wedding—and headed out.

Forty minutes later, sated with noodles and curry, I felt a bit more human and a bit less panicked. It was harder to be scared on a full stomach. Carrying my leftovers in one hand, I walked back to my room. Ethan called just as I was making my way down the hallway.

"I've got good news and bad news," he said when I answered.

"Bad news first. Always."

"The car following you was a rental, and I've got no way to find out who rented it."

"Shit. What's the good news?"

"That's also the good news. That I found the car," Ethan said sheepishly. "I was planning to do that in the other order."

"Can't you, like, call and pretend they rear-ended you or something? Or hack into their database? Rappel down through their skylight?"

"Naomi, I make a podcast," Ethan said.

"You could have skills. I don't know. Hold on, I'm getting a text." I juggled my keycard as I checked. Tomorrow's couple wanted to know if I could be there at eleven instead of noon. No problem—that would give me more time to get back to Chester afterward. "I've got to answer this. I'll call you back in just a sec, okay?" I shouldered the door open and stepped into the room.

"I'm not going anywhere. Talk to you later."

I hung up and shut the door behind me with my foot, then typed out a reply as I moved farther into the room.

The shadow was in my peripheral vision. I didn't notice it until it moved—and in the same instant I realized it was a man, lunging toward me. A man with brown hair and a cold look in his eyes.

Pure white panic flashed through me. He was in my room. He was going to kill me.

I struck out in blind fear, swinging with the hand holding my phone. It clipped him in the temple, and with a yell I drew my arm back to hit him again. Swearing, he grabbed the phone from my hand, tearing it out of my grip, but I didn't stop, clawing at his face. I wouldn't go without a fight, not this time.

His hand closed around my wrist. He yanked hard, spinning me half around, then shoved me hard in the back. I hit the wall face-first and rebounded with a cry of pain. I sprawled backward, my hip and ribs catching the hard bed frame on my way down, and I lay in a heap on the floor, my vision blurry.

I stared up at him, blinking to try to clear my vision, waiting for him to attack me again—but he only bent, grabbed my phone from where it had fallen, and ran out the door.

The door slammed shut. The pain in my ribs throbbed with my frantic heartbeat, but I sucked down a breath and then another.

He hadn't killed me. I was alive.

Every part of me hurt. I dragged myself up holding on to the end of the bed. I tasted blood and realized that my nose was bleeding. The closet mirrors showed a wild-eyed woman, red smeared over lips and cheeks and chin.

I tried to get my feet under me, but standing up made the room spin. I crabbed my way over to the bedside table and fumbled for the room phone. And then I stopped.

Who was I going to call? The police?

Yes. Obviously. That was the sensible thing. And then I'd explain to them about the man, about the Camry, about Chester. Persephone, Liv, Stahl—they were all tangled up in this, and if I gave the police the end of that thread they would follow it.

*This is stupid. Call the cops.*

Because that had worked out so well before. The cops were at least half the reason I'd ended up on that witness stand, testifying against the wrong man. They'd wanted Stahl, and they'd used me to get him.

I gathered up my things in a rush, clawing everything into my suit-case and barely getting it closed before I hurried out the door. Moving at a shuffling run, I made it down the back staircase and to my car without running into anyone. I sat behind the wheel, taking gulping, painful breaths, and watched pedestrians wander by, unconcerned.

I leaned my head against the wheel and sobbed.

**M**y ribs and hips were bruised, but nothing was broken, I decided. Not even my nose, though by the time I hit Tacoma it had swollen up and was bruising fast. There was a hard-edged bruise on my ribs, though, and a splotch on my hip from where I'd fallen, and my arm was red where he'd grabbed it. But I didn't have a concussion or any broken bones, so I was lucky.

I was lucky he'd left without doing worse.

I'd filled up on gas before the wedding. I drove straight through to Chester, and even taking the long way around the Sound to avoid the ferry, I didn't stop once. I kept watching for a black Camry in my rearview, and a couple times I pulled off at weird spots to make sure no other cars were following me either. When I got to the Chester motel well after nightfall I was alone, as far as I could tell.

I went straight to Ethan's room. I hadn't called him—without my phone, I didn't even have his number—and he greeted me with surprise and alarm.

"Naomi! I've been trying to call you— What the hell happened to your face?" he asked.

"My face isn't even the worst part," I told him, sounding like I had a head cold. I pushed in past him, shut the door, and engaged the chain. "I couldn't call you because my phone got stolen. By the guy who did this." I gestured at my face. Scar or no scar, I liked my face. It had severe angles that intimidated people, an effect that the scar actually helped but which the puffy, purplish state of my nose completely ruined.

"What guy? What happened?" Ethan asked. "When was this?"

"A few hours ago." I went through the sequence of events—the Camry, getting back to the hotel, the intruder. When I got to how I'd decided not to call the police, he sank down on the bed, elbows on his knees and hands laced behind his head.

"Naomi. You *have* to tell the cops. Call Bishop. Let her know—"

"No. I know it's the smart thing. I know it's the logical thing and probably the moral thing, but no. I can't. And you can't. Please. There's too much at stake. Too much that could go wrong."

"You can't keep it quiet forever."

"But I can until I have the answers," I said. "I swear to God, Ethan, as soon as I know who's responsible for all of this, I'll hand everything we have over to the police. But I don't trust them. They got the wrong man before. And Liv died."

"You don't know if Liv's death is connected."

"How could it not be?" I paced. He watched me, eyes dark with concern. "Either the person who attacked me is trying to cover his tracks, or dear AJ is out for revenge."

"You're jumping to conclusions. You have no reason to think Stahl's son is after you."

"That letter—"

"There's a big difference between wanting answers and wanting revenge," Ethan pointed out. "There aren't any threats in that letter. Only questions."

"I ruined his life."

"Having a serial killer for a father ruined his life," Ethan replied.

"Except he wasn't a serial killer, was he?"

"Don't go down that road. Stahl murdered those women."

"You can't be sure of that. No one can except Stahl, and he's dead."

"I'm sure," Ethan insisted. "And even if he wasn't, none of this is your fault. You were a child. Nobody protected you. Not the way they should have."

"Do you believe that? Or do you just want to?"

He guided me toward him, more invitation than insistence. "You need to slow down, Naomi. You need to rest."

I let him gather me in, his hands shifting to my waist. I leaned my brow against his, letting out a long, shuddering breath. "You keep saying that. But I don't think I know how to rest," I said.

"I knew that about you the moment we met," he said. "We aren't going to get anywhere spinning wild theories. We need to start at the beginning. Go back to the attack."

"But the attack wasn't the beginning," I said. "Persephone was the beginning."

He nodded. "We found her. Now it's time to find out what happened to her. And we will. But first, sleep. You'll be safe. I'll be here." He brushed my hair back from my forehead, the motion delicate. I didn't want to like Ethan Schreiber. I didn't want to trust him. But I needed to.

Sometimes, surrender was the kindest thing of all.

---

I dreamed I was in my father's house. I was a child, and something was hunting me. I could hear it breathing behind me. I ran through winding corridors of bulging bags and mildew-rimed boxes, trying to find the door, but they went on and on and on, and the corridors became paths among the trees. I slid beneath the lip of the boulder and tumbled into Persephone's bony arms, and they wrapped around me tighter and tighter as the wolves outside howled in hunger.

And then I woke, shuddering out of the dream. It took me a moment to remember why I was in Ethan's room. He was at the desk with his laptop open. No, with *my* laptop open.

"What are you doing?" I demanded, thrashing my way free of the blankets.

He looked up with a hint of guilt. "I'm tracking your phone. I didn't want to wake you."

"Oh." I should have thought of that. Blame it on the head trauma.

I wrapped the coverlet around me and stood next to him. He had the Track My Phone page open, but all it showed was a last location—the hotel.

"He must have turned it off. But if he switches it back on, we'll know where," Ethan said.

"How did you log in?" I asked. I was hardly a security whiz, but I did have everything password protected.

"Your password for the phone was stored on your browser," he said. "I guessed your laptop password. Took me a few tries, and I locked myself out twice, but I got it. Artemis—that was your goddess, right?"

"Cass picked it," I said. "Probably not the most secure."

"It is in the book," he acknowledged. "I would have just asked you, but—"

"But you didn't want to wake me up," I said. It made sense, but it still made me feel uneasy. An intruder had rifled through my files, and the fact that he was a friend didn't make it less unsettling. He'd brought all my luggage in, too, leaving it by the wall. I should be grateful for that, too—I shouldn't have left my expensive gear out in the car overnight. I should be. I wasn't.

"I've been thinking about what we know, and what we don't," Ethan said. "I still think that the most useful thing to pursue is Persephone— Jessi Walker."

"What about Junior?" I asked, shaking off my unease. He was just trying to help.

He sighed. "I can keep looking, but he's done a pretty thorough job of vanishing," Ethan said.

"If I could just see a picture of him, I'd know if it was him," I said.

"I'll see what I can do," he assured me. "In the meantime, I think we need to make a rule. No going anywhere alone. He could have killed you."

"He didn't, though," I said. I wasn't sure what that meant. Did it mean he hadn't killed Liv? Or was it just because I'd caught him by surprise? Ethan was right. We didn't know how to find answers about my mystery man, not yet. The questions we knew how to ask were about Jessi. Although I did have one lead.

Oscar.

But talking to Oscar would mean Ethan finding out about the worst decision I'd ever made. It would change things. The disgust I felt at myself—he'd feel that, too.

"You should get yourself cleaned up," Ethan was saying. "You look—"

I held up a warning finger. "If you ever want me to ill-advisedly hop into bed with you again, you will stop talking," I said.

"Stunning. Truly stunning," he course-corrected. I rolled my eyes.

"Very convincing."

I commandeered the laptop long enough to email my engagement-shoot clients, letting them know I'd had a family emergency and had to reschedule. Then I showered, cleaning tenderly around my various injuries. I was moving like a geriatric patient, shuffling and hunching, and the hot water did little to ease my tightly wound muscles, but I at least looked less like an accident victim by the time I emerged from the shower. As I dried off, Ethan's muffled voice filtered in. He was talking to someone.

". . . longer than I expected. No, nothing's wrong. I'm just doing some research." Who was he talking to? "No, you don't want to know, because it always upsets you. No. No. Yes. Mom—"

I relaxed a bit and then scolded myself. Who did I *think* he would be talking to? My initial reaction had been suspicion, but that didn't make any sense. If he was talking to someone nefarious he wouldn't take the call while I was a cheap hollow-core door away.

I stepped out, drying my hair, and he gave me an apologetic look as he continued talking. "It's my job. I like it. I know you don't get it, but I really don't want to have this conversation with you right now. I prom-ise you I am fine. I'll come visit soon. Okay. Give my love to George and the girls. Love you, Mom. Bye." He hung up and sagged.

"Let me guess. Your mother is horrified by the fact that you spend all your time researching gruesome murders?"

"Pretty much," Ethan said. "Her husband doesn't help. He thinks it's a sign of fundamental amorality or something. A small price to pay for her having a decent guy in her life."

"Being worried about you means she cares, at least," I said. I finger-combed my damp hair into a semblance of proper order.

"Do you ever talk to your mom?"

"Once a year on her birthday," I replied. "She swooped in to play Good Mother for a few weeks after the attack, but it didn't last long. We get along better at a distance anyway. She just was never meant to be a parent. What about your dad? You close with him?"

"He died," Ethan said plainly.

"I'm sorry," I said, blanching.

"Don't be. It was a long time ago," he replied, seemingly unbothered. "I could use some breakfast. Can I get you anything?"

"Eight gallons of coffee and something loaded with carbs," I said. "And I should probably go check in again."

"Or you could stay here," Ethan said mildly.

"I don't think we're ready for cohabitation," I told him.

"It's not that," he said. "You were attacked. I know I'm going to feel a lot better if you're not alone."

"I don't—" I hesitated. "I don't know what this is, between us."

"It doesn't have to be anything. Let's start with breakfast, and go from there."

He kissed my forehead before I left—just about the only part of me that didn't hurt. I tried to pace, but my bruised ribs wouldn't let me, so I curled up in the chair in front of the laptop instead, poking my way through what little information there was on AJ Stahl again. I tried to make those old photos match the guy who'd jumped me, but it had been too long. He could have grown up into anyone.

I'd left the phone tracker open on the side of the screen. Suddenly the little dot vanished, the map reloading to a new location. Just as abruptly, it pinged "signal lost." Someone had turned on the phone and then turned it off. But I'd had it for a brief second. I had an address.

I copied the address, heart hammering, and plugged it into the search. A nail salon in Redmond? Wait—it was one unit of the building. I checked the other businesses. A dog grooming place—probably not sinister—a pho joint, a board-game shop, and something called Jessup Consulting.

"Vague. Not at all suspicious," I muttered. I pulled up their website. The web design was definitely criminal, with retina-searing colors and a stock photo of a comically serious-looking dude with a wired earpiece and a sharp suit. The header told me they provided security and investigation services.

The guy in my hotel room was a PI?

A personal grudge was one thing. Hiring people to come after me—that was something else.

Twenty minutes later, Ethan arrived with takeout to find me lost in a flurry of open tabs and scribbled notes. I'd tracked down the name of the owner of the company, Terry Jessup, and from there found a half dozen current and former employees. None of them were my guy. Jessup Consulting came up as a minor note in a few articles, but nothing relevant—work for corporations and small companies, mostly. Nothing that stank of "violent personal vendetta."

"Why would this guy attack you?" Ethan asked. "It doesn't exactly sound like normal PI work."

I frowned. Ethan was right. At a glance, Jessup Consulting didn't seem like thugs for hire. And why attack me? He hadn't killed me, and he could have. So rough me up? Why?

Except that he hadn't attacked me, had he? Not exactly. He'd lunged for me.

Or he'd lunged for the door.

I'd surprised him in my room, and he'd tried to get out. And I'd gone completely psycho, trying to brain him with an iPhone. I rubbed my forehead with the tips of my fingers. "I went after him. He was just trying to stop me," I realized, and almost laughed. He hadn't been trying to kill me at all.

"He still broke into your room," Ethan pointed out. "If he wasn't after you, what was he after?"

"All he got was my phone, as far as I know. And there's nothing incriminating on that," I said. You couldn't be friends with Liv and not have a little of her paranoia rub off on you. Sensitive stuff did not belong on the cloud.

"Is there anything else they could have taken?" he asked.

"I checked all my gear. It's still here," I said. Unless. I walked painfully over to my roller bag and unzipped it. My cameras were there— but I popped one open and sure enough, the data card was gone. "Fuck. Oh, *fuck.*"

"Was there something important on the drives?" Ethan asked.

"Yeah, an entire wedding," I said. "*Shit.* I hadn't uploaded everything yet! Goddammit. I always upload everything right away, but I was starving and then *he* was in the room."

"You're missing wedding photos," Ethan repeated, carefully neutral.

"They're important," I insisted.

"Of course. But they aren't going to get you killed or arrested, so I'm going to call this a win," Ethan said. "Jessup Consulting will have them. We can get them back. Especially if they don't want to get reported to the police for having an employee assault you."

"Okay." I took a breath, released it. Calm. I could do calm.

"Sit. Eat. Relax. I'll see if I can turn up anything more," he said. He eyed the tabs in the browser skeptically. "Do you ever close tabs?"

"I might need them later."

"One of them is playing 'Old Town Road.'"

"I usually just mute the computer when that happens," I said. "Easier than finding it."

He sighed and sat down to work.

After I'd eaten, with Ethan still rooting unsuccessfully around the internet for signs of my assailant, I went on a pilgrimage to the ice machine. When I stepped back out of the alcove, bucket of ice in hand, I found Chief Bishop waiting for me.

"Jesus Christ," she said as soon as she saw me. "Who the hell did that to you?"

"There was a scuffle over the bouquet, and I caught an elbow," I said. She blinked at me. "I'm a wedding photographer. Sorry, bad joke. I got mugged." Close enough.

"Here?" she asked in disbelief.

"I was back in Seattle shooting a wedding."

"You didn't mention you were leaving town," she said, hand on her hip. She'd parked her car slantwise across two spots, right next to mine.

"I didn't realize I had to check in with you about it," I replied.

She frowned at me. "Olivia's death has been ruled a suicide. We've released the body. The funeral is on Tuesday," she said.

My balance faltered. I managed not to stumble, but only just. It was official, then.

"I think it's a mistake," she added flatly.

"You think Liv was murdered?" I asked. She nodded. "Then why—"

"I've been in this town six months. I'm new, I'm not from here, and my job exists up until the exact moment that Jim Green tells the city council to get rid of me," she said, voice thick with discontent. "He made it very clear that it was time to *move on*. But I don't buy it. That girl killing herself that way, when she was terrified of guns and blood and everybody in her life, you included, was watching her like a hawk for the slightest hint of suicidal ideation? Yes, I think she was murdered. But if I don't sign that paperwork, I don't have a job and can't do anything about it. So here we are."

I tried to take a full breath to steady myself; pain lanced through my ribs. "I think you're right," I said.

She tapped her fingers against her belt. "We checked that pond three times. We'd just about given up. But Dougherty absolutely insists it's there, so I drag my ass out in waders one last time, and miraculously, we find it. Maybe we missed it. But I don't think so."

"You think someone dumped it in the pond after you'd already searched it. Someone like me?" I tried to look composed and confident, but it was hard with a bruised face and an ice bucket dangling from one hand.

"You're hiding something," Bishop said. "That makes me uneasy."

"Everyone's hiding something," I said softly. "I need to go ice my face. Unless you actually need me—"

"Actually, I'd like you to come down to the station. That's why I stopped. We've been trying to call you."

"My phone was stolen. Mugged, remember?" I said.

She grunted, unimpressed with my excuse. "We've got a couple of loose ends that need tying up. For the paperwork, you understand."

"Fine," I said, waving a hand. "When?"

"Tomorrow. Ten o'clock," Bishop replied.

"Fine," I repeated. I just wanted out of this conversation. Bishop gave me one last level look before she headed back to her car.

I turned to find Ethan standing at the open door. "What was that about?" he asked as I slid past him.

"She's just doing her job," I said. Better than anyone else in this town. "I'm supposed to go to the station tomorrow."

"Not looking like that," Ethan said. I dumped a handful of ice into a plastic bag and pressed it against the bridge of my nose. "You don't want to walk through town that bruised up. You're going to get the kind of questions you don't want to have to answer, and not just from Bishop."

"I've only got the one face, Ethan."

He made an amused sound. "Don't worry about it. We'll figure something out," he said.

I shifted the ice so I could look at him better.

"What?" he asked, seeing my look.

"Nothing. Just thinking about what a nice guy you are," I said. He gave me a puzzled smile and turned to the computer. I watched him work, a strange mix of pleasure and anxiety needling at me.

Everyone was hiding something, and I didn't know yet what Ethan was hiding. The thing was, I liked Ethan. A lot. I might even have said I was falling for him, if there was room in my body for those feelings right now. But I wouldn't feel safe feeling anything for him until I knew what was wrong with him.

What would make him stick around with someone as broken as me.

––––––––––––––––––

In the morning I woke to find Ethan gone. In an hour I was supposed to be at the police department. I showered and dressed and looked at myself skeptically in the mirror. The swelling had gone down, but my nose was a godawful shade of greenish-purple that streaked into the bags under my eyes. I dumped out my makeup bag. I had a small tube of concealer, mascara, eyeliner, and a basic nude lipstick.

The door opened. Ethan entered, carrying yet another bag of take-out from the diner and a shopping bag. "I picked up some supplies," he said.

"What kind of supplies?" I asked suspiciously. He emptied the shopping bag on the bed, and a dizzying array of makeup spilled out.

"I had to get a few shades because I wasn't sure about the best match," he said. He peered at me, then grabbed a handful of products and came over. "This one looks closest," he said, holding the tube up to my cheek.

"Thanks," I said. I looked down. He'd gotten me liquid concealer and concealer in stick form and a yellow-tinted "color-correcting" concealer and a powder and I stared at them without comprehension.

"Here," Ethan said, seeing how lost I was. "Let me."

He opened up one product after another, layering them on, dabbing with gentle touches of a makeup sponge so he wouldn't hurt me. Slowly, the bruises vanished and the makeup blended in with the rest of my skin.

"I have to do your whole face or it'll be obvious you just used concealer on one spot," he said.

"Don't cover up the scar," I said quickly.

"You never hide it, do you?" he asked.

"I don't let myself." I held still, watching his face as he worked. "You're good at this."

"I used to help my mom," he said.

"Your dad?"

He grunted. "My dad treated my mom like a queen. After we lost him, it was like she was punishing herself by dating assholes. It took her a long time to crawl back out of that hole. As soon as I turned eighteen I left. I couldn't stick around and watch her repeat the same mistakes over and over again. We didn't talk for a good five years. But then she met George."

"You don't talk about yourself a lot, do you?" I asked.

"What makes you say that?"

"You just seem uncomfortable. Like you haven't practiced enough for it not to hurt when you explained it," I said.

"I'm more used to talking about other people's pain, I guess," he said. "You're all set."

I looked in the mirror. You could tell I was wearing makeup—no one's skin was that consistent—but the bruise was invisible. "You're a magician."

"Ta-da," he declared, waving his hands.

"And kind of a hokey one at that," I added. He chuckled. "I guess it's time to face the music."

He drove me, since lifting my arms to hold the steering wheel made my ribs ache. We walked into the police station together and the woman behind the front desk gave us an appraising look. I'd known her name once, but it escaped me now.

"You can come right on back, dear," she told me. "You can wait there." She jabbed her pen at the chairs along the wall, pinning Ethan with her gaze.

She showed me back down a hallway and into a conference room. "It'll be just a minute," she said, and disappeared. I eased myself into a chair. Sitting down and standing up were the hardest on my ribs, and I didn't want to have to do either in front of people.

It was less than a minute before the door opened. It wasn't Bishop who entered but Officer Dougherty, along with a man in a gray suit I didn't recognize. "Naomi. It's good of you to come down and help us out."

"With the paperwork," I said, half a question.

Dougherty cleared his throat. "Well, thing is, we were hoping you'd also help out with some information. To be clear, there's no legal requirement for you to do so," Dougherty said. "But Mon—Chief Bishop—that is—"

The man in the suit gave a professional, detached sort of smile. "Chief Bishop is indulging me," he said. He stepped forward, putting out his hand. "Nice to meet you, Ms. Cunningham. I'm Sunil Sawant."

"Are you with the county sheriff?" I asked, hazarding a guess.

"No. I'm actually with the FBI. Here from the Seattle field office," he replied. I froze, staring. He walked over and took the seat next to me, swiveling to face me but leaving a good distance between us. Close but not intimidating. Not intimate. "Monica and I go back a ways, and I asked her to let me come on out here."

"I thought Liv's death was ruled a suicide," I said. "How does that involve the FBI?"

"It's a matter of personal interest, not really official. Just a casual conversation," Sawant said. His tone, his body language—everything was friendly and relaxed, but I felt myself tensing. Dougherty stood behind him, hands on his hips. If his mustache was a little bit longer he'd be chewing on it. He looked like he wanted to throw the guy out, but he couldn't—not if Sawant was Bishop's guest.

Sawant could ask the questions Bishop couldn't, not without risking her job. He could push, and she could claim ignorance.

"So . . ." I trailed off. Let him think I couldn't think of a single thing that might interest the FBI, as opposed to approximately ten thousand.

"You told Chief Bishop that you were in town to see Olivia. Is that right?" he asked.

"That's right," I replied. "She asked me to come visit."

"And this was prompted by Stahl's death."

"More or less," I said. "All three of us met up. Me, Olivia, and Cass. Cassidy Green."

"Yes. I know the case quite well," Sawant said. The corners of his eyes creased in something like a smile. "You three were instrumental in putting him away."

"That's what everyone tells me," I replied. He didn't strike me as one of my fan club.

"You don't agree?"

"I don't really like to think about it," I said.

"Ms. Cunningham, I saw Liv's note. Like I said, I'm very familiar with the Stahl case," Sawant said. "I've been fascinated by it since my first criminology course in undergrad. When I joined the Bureau and got access to those files it was like being a kid in a candy store. You know what struck me? The bits and pieces that were missing. Especially around the interviews with you three girls."

"Missing," I echoed. "What sorts of things?"

"There are minor inconsistencies and omissions regarding when the identification was made, in Cassidy's and Olivia's cases. And in your case, there are some conflicting reports about who was in the room. And who had spoken to you beforehand. Is it possible that someone told you about Stahl before you identified him to police?"

I swallowed. My first instinct was to lie. It was easier to keep a secret than end it. "It's possible," I said instead. "But I wouldn't be able to tell you for sure. I only remember bits and pieces from the hospital, and it's all jumbled."

"You were unable to describe any details of the attack, but you identified Stahl immediately."

"I told you. I don't remember any of it," I said. "I would answer you if I could, but I really have no idea what I said." Over Sawant's shoulder, Dougherty's face was pinched.

"And what about the attack? Do you remember that? Do you remember seeing Stahl?" he asked, leaning forward.

"No," I said. He stared at me, like he hadn't been expecting that answer and had no idea where to go. "Any memories I have are too conflated with things I've learned or seen or been told. If you asked me to testify today, I couldn't. As for what I said back then—it was a very long time ago, and I've worked very hard to forget as much as I could. You probably have a clearer idea of what happened than I do, if you've read the files."

Dougherty looked uncomfortable. Sawant shifted. He glanced down at the pad of paper he'd brought with him, jotted down a note I couldn't read, and looked up again. "In Olivia's suicide note, she said that she was tired of lying. What was she lying about?"

I hesitated. This part of the truth didn't just belong to me. I'd promised Cass. "It could have been a number of things. Or nothing at all," I said. "Reality and Liv didn't always get along." I regretted the words as soon as I'd said them. She deserved better than that from me.

"You're saying what she wrote in that letter was, what—a hallucination?"

"Technically, that would be a delusion." I looked him dead in the eye. "I don't know what Liv was referring to in that letter. I know that she was struggling, and that she often hid the extent of that struggle from us."

"So you didn't know she was suicidal."

"She wasn't," I said, sounding more stubborn than sure.

"She killed herself. That's the definition of suicidal, isn't it?" Sawant asked. "Unless you don't think it was a suicide."

"It's easy to assume that because Liv was ill, she killed herself," I said slowly. "It's the obvious answer. But after last time, we all got really familiar with the warning signs. Liv didn't feel hopeless. She was engaged. She was making plans. And—" I hesitated. "She promised."

"She promised," he repeated, skeptical.

"It was something we did. We would promise each other to still be here in the morning."

"It wasn't just her making the promise, then?" Sawant said.

I curled my hands in my lap. "It was something both of us needed. And it's not a promise she would have broken."

"She left a note."

That was the part I couldn't explain and couldn't understand. "Maybe it wasn't a suicide note. Maybe she meant . . ." I trailed off. I couldn't think of a way to interpret those words as anything else. "She wouldn't have done it."

"I am, in fact, inclined to agree with you," Sawant said. Relief ran like cold water over my skin. "I think it's clear that someone murdered Olivia Barnes. And I think it's because she was done covering up an old lie. A lie about what happened in those woods twenty-two years ago."

He let that hang. Persephone's name was lodged in my throat. I'd promised Cass. But we were long past promises.

"What is your relationship with Oscar Green?" Sawant asked, cutting me off before I could speak.

I frowned. That was not the direction I'd expected him to take. "I don't have one," I said.

"You were romantically involved, though."

"Who the fuck told you that?" I asked, anger lancing through the words. Sawant sat back a little like he'd hit on something significant.

"You and Oscar Green have had a romantic relationship in the past, have you not?" he pressed.

"No, it's not—we're not—" *Romantic* had never factored into it. *Relationship* was laughable.

Sawant kept going. "Not back then, of course—you were only eleven. But your best friend's big brother? Handsome guy, popular, cool as can be? It would be surprising if you didn't have a little crush."

I choked on a laugh. "You have no idea what you're talking about," I said. *You and me—*

"Oscar has quite the record. Nothing at all in his juvenile record and then he moves away from Chester for a few years and boom. Assault, disorderly conduct, assault."

"That's Oscar for you," I said. The idiot should have realized he couldn't get away with half the shit he did once he wasn't in Chester with a mayor for a dad.

"I got to thinking. If it *wasn't* Stahl who attacked you, why would you say that it was? Unless you were covering for someone. Like the mayor's son."

"Why would Oscar try to kill me?" I asked, shaking my head.

"Maybe you knew something that could derail his privileged little life," Sawant suggested. "Something he'd done."

*Bones in the woods,* I thought. *She used to hang around with Oscar Green.* "I can't imagine what that would be. And to be clear: I wouldn't cover up *littering* for Oscar Green. I sure as shit wouldn't fail to mention he'd stabbed me." *But would Cass?* I wondered, and hated myself immediately for thinking it.

"Interesting. Because I've heard some things about the two of you that might cast doubt on that," Sawant said. "Lies have a way of rippling out. Sometimes the consequences arrive years later. Liv wanted to tell the truth. Did you want that, Naomi?"

The truth.

I could have told him everything. I could have made Agent Sawant my savior, my way out—hand over everything I knew, everything I'd done, and trust him to put the pieces together. It was the smart thing to do. The right thing to do.

And I couldn't. I'd held on too long and too tightly. The truth belonged to me, and I would be the one to find it. *To find her*, I thought, and I wasn't sure if I meant Liv or Persephone, or why it still felt like they were lost.

"I'm done having you call me a liar," I said. I stood abruptly, powering through the burst of pain. "We're finished."

"Naomi—"

"The lady said she's finished," Dougherty said. He put a hand on my shoulder as I walked past Sawant and ushered me out into the hall.

I glanced behind me. Sawant turned in the chair, relaxed with one elbow on the table, watching me with sharp eyes. He wasn't fooled.

But was he right?

I couldn't avoid Oscar any longer.

I'm sorry about that. I don't know what Bishop is thinking, letting him spring all that on you," Dougherty said once we were safely out of earshot.

Past him, down the hall, Bishop herself stood in her office doorway, watching us. She'd stayed out of the room. Left herself room to claim she had nothing to do with it, if the wrong people got pissed. She straightened up and walked toward us.

"Bunch of nonsense, really. Oscar's rough around the edges, but he's a good kid," Dougherty said, just as she got to us.

That "kid" was forty. "Can I go now?" I asked Bishop. Dougherty half-turned, as if just realizing she was there.

"We really can't keep you," he said.

Bishop's cheek twitched like she was trying not to scowl at him. "No, we can't," she agreed.

"Okay, then," I said. I headed down the hall, shoulders tensed and ribs twinging, leaving them to their little power struggle.

The problem wasn't that Sawant had been off base. The problem was that he was *almost* right about so many things. No, I wouldn't have covered up for Oscar. But there were plenty of people who would. Who might have seen Dougherty's eagerness about Stahl as an opportunity to shift the blame.

Like Cass.

Cass and Oscar had always been close. He had no time for Liv or me, but whenever Cass wanted a turn with the Nintendo or a lift into town he'd always oblige her. And she thought the world of him. She'd never seen the other side of him—the one he saved for people like me, who couldn't complain. I'd never told her. I was too afraid to find out who her loyalty really belonged to.

And it wouldn't have been the first time she covered for him, either. As far as their parents were concerned, Oscar could do no wrong—the trouble he got into was never his fault. I remembered vividly the night Chief Miller came by the Greens' house, asking where Oscar had been the night before. Big Jim looked over at Cass and said Oscar had been home watching her, and she'd chimed in to confirm it, her eyes wide and sincere. Except Cass and I had been together that night, and Oscar certainly hadn't been there.

But that was some vandalism charge. This was attempted murder. Would Cass have gone that far for her brother? And made Liv go along, too?

Lost in thought, I stepped out into the main lobby and halted, surprised. Cody Benham was standing by the front desk, chatting amiably with the secretary, who was beaming at him. When he saw me he straightened up, murmured something, and tapped the desk in a kind of casual goodbye. He strolled over to me with a quizzical look.

"Naomi. Is everything okay?" he asked.

Ethan, sitting in one of the chairs out front, looked up from his phone and got to his feet. I shrugged at Cody. "I think so. I was just leaving. What are you doing back in town?"

"I'm here for the funeral. Bishop said she needed to talk to me, so I agreed to come down a day early. You?"

"Pretty much the same," I said.

"What did she want to know?" he asked.

"It wasn't her asking questions. There's some guy from the FBI. Agent Sawant."

Ethan stood an awkward distance back. At this, his brows raised. "The FBI is interested in Liv's death?"

"More interested in the possible connection to the Stahl case," I said. Ethan's expression grew worried. Cody just looked more confused.

"What connection could there possibly be?" Cody said.

"I'm sure he'll tell you," I said. I paused. "He's asking about Oscar."

Cody sighed. "That explains why he thinks I have anything relevant to add. In a town this size you don't exactly have a lot of choices for friends your age. Even so, I can't believe I did such a colossally shitty job of choosing mine."

"You used to hang out quite a bit, didn't you?" Ethan asked.

Cody rounded on him, a dangerous glint in his eye. "I think you've harassed Naomi enough already, don't you?"

"Cody." I touched his arm. "It's okay. Ethan's . . . I'm helping him out. With his podcast."

"We got off on the wrong foot," Ethan said. "Entirely my fault. I promise you I'm not pushing Naomi into anything she doesn't want to do."

"And I promise I'm perfectly capable of telling him off if he does," I added, lest this turn any more paternalistic than it already was. Having two guys square off with each other in the name of my honor should have been flattering, but it turned out to just be irritating.

"All right, then," Cody said, but the suspicious look in his eyes didn't fade.

There was something weird happening between the two of them, and I didn't have the energy to unpack it. "We should get going," I told Ethan.

"Right. Lots of work to do," he agreed.

"Can I have a quick word with you, Naomi?" Cody asked.

"Of course. Ethan, could you—"

"I'll wait in the car," Ethan suggested. He touched my elbow in a gesture that might have been comforting and supportive, or might have just been a way of yelling *WE HAVE SEX* at Cody. As I was working on myself as a person, I decided to believe the former.

Cody's hand on my arm, ushering me farther from the front desk and the obviously eavesdropping receptionist, was definitely of the protective sort. "Do you know what you're doing there?" he asked.

"A six-foot-two podcaster," I said, deadpan. Cody grimaced at the attempt at humor. "I know what I'm doing. He's a good guy."

"What do you know about him?" Cody pressed.

"Plenty," I said, defensive.

"I've heard from other people around town. They don't like the kind of questions he's been asking."

"Please. This town will gossip to anyone with a pencil and a notepad," I said dismissively.

"Just be careful, Naomi. Keep in mind that his interests and yours may not be the same thing."

"I'm all grown up, Cody. I don't need a white knight to rescue me from ogres anymore," I reminded him. I stood on my toes and pecked his cheek, then started to turn away. He caught my sleeve, arresting my movement.

"What happened to your face?" he asked, voice rough and low.

"Nothing."

"It's bruised," he said.

"I fell and smashed it," I told him, not mentioning the guy who had helped me along. "Don't walk in heels with your hands full. Pro tip." He didn't let go. "Cody. It's fine. And it wasn't Ethan, if that's what you're thinking. Trust me, if a guy raises a hand to me—"

"You let me know, and I'll take care of it," Cody said.

"Yeah. I remember," I replied. "I gotta go, Cody. I appreciate the concern."

Dougherty cleared his throat. Cody glanced over at him. "Look, Naomi. Don't talk to Sawant or Bishop or anyone else again without a lawyer, okay?"

"I didn't do anything," I said.

"All the more reason to make sure you cover your ass. Trust me. Get a lawyer."

"I wouldn't know where to start," I confessed.

"I can get you some names. Give me a call later, okay? And don't worry about the cost. I'll make sure it's covered."

"I think I preferred it when your version of protecting me was punching people out," I said. He gave me a look. "Okay, okay. I'll call you. Now get back there before Dougherty starts tapping his foot."

I waved him off. He followed Dougherty into the back hall and out of sight. I headed out to the parking lot. Ethan was leaning against the hood of the car, hands in his pockets.

"Everything okay?" he asked. I just gave him a little shake of the head and got into the passenger seat. Cody's words had settled into my skin. I didn't know much about Ethan. And I was trusting him with everything.

I filled him in about the conversation with Sawant as we drove, trying not to let myself get emotional about any of it. "Doesn't sound like he has anything solid," Ethan commented when I was done.

"Doesn't seem that way, no," I agreed.

"What did Benham want to talk about?" Ethan asked.

"He's just looking out for me."

"You two are still close?"

"Not close. Haven't seen him in ages. But there are some things that don't go away," I said. I leaned my head back against the headrest. "He can be a bit overprotective. Although to be fair to him, there was a time when there was no 'over' about it."

"You mean him finding you. Carrying you out of the woods."

"That. And before." He didn't ask; just waited. I trailed a fingertip down the cool glass of the window. But that story didn't belong to him. I'd given him enough of me for now, and eventually the silence settled into an answer.

The summer of the Goddess Game, Oscar had been home from state college, and so had Cody. They were both working for Cass's dad at the mill, like they did every summer. Cody had always done the bare minimum, working mostly to spend time with Oscar and have money for cigarettes. Oscar threw himself into the work. He'd get the company one way or another, eventually, but you could tell he meant to earn it. Or at least look like he did. But at some point, that changed. Oscar stopped showing up for work or showed up drunk half the time. Cody started getting more serious—like he'd suddenly realized he didn't have family money to fall back on like Oscar did.

I'd avoided Oscar for the most part. Not out of any fear, just because a kid can tell when a grown-up doesn't like them. The contempt some adults have for children is a frightening thing to be aware of as a kid. But that year, contempt turned to cruelty.

Puberty had started to encroach that summer, and I wasn't about to ask my dad to buy me a training bra, so I wore bulky sweaters and loose T-shirts most of the time. Oscar noticed—not out of desire, but because he had a new stick to jab in my side when he felt bored.

"What are you smuggling under there? Apples?"

"Looks more like a couple of cherry pits."

"Did a bee sting you?"

"Ooh, little Naomi's a *woman* now. You bleeding yet?"

If Cody was there, he'd jostle Oscar's shoulder. "Shut up, man. She's just a kid. Jesus."

Dad told me to laugh it off. Think of something clever to say in return. Cass told me to ignore it, that he didn't mean anything by it. Anyone else who overheard tended to chuckle—*That Oscar, such a rascal, but such a good boy at heart.* Cody was the only one who ever acted like it was Oscar who ought to change his behavior.

I put my head down and ignored him. Day after day. Until *that* day. Sweat sticking my shirt to my back under the sweatshirt I wore to try to hide the slight swell of my breasts.

I had Persephone's knucklebone in my pocket like a talisman and Cass's instructions on my mind. "Today, we must make an offering of a particular sort. Something taken, not given. Something of value. That means it has to cost money, but you can't pay for it." Eyes sparking with mischief. "Go forth, Artemis. Fetch the offering for the Queen."

I'd stolen about a hundred Snickers bars from Marsha, but perishables were a no-go. We'd decided that after the initial offerings of bread and milk made the Grotto smell like, as Cass said, "a football player's ass crack."

So it had to be something else. Something with *meaning*. Marsha kept a little rack of cheap bracelet charms by the register. I nipped in, paid for the Snickers for once, and pocketed a silver dolphin the size of my pinky nail. Even then I was good at lying. I spent forever counting out coins and shuffled off like I was embarrassed to have to scrounge for the last five cents, and Marsha was so exasperated she never noticed what I'd taken.

I came around the side of the building, away from the road—the fastest way back to the trail that would get me close to Persephone—and Oscar was there. He had a cigarette pinched between his fingers, the glowing end ready to kiss his fingertips if he took another drag. He flicked it onto the ground and looked at me with hooded, lazy eyes.

"Got milk?" he asked, and laughed at his own shitty joke. I started past him. "Come on, little girl. I didn't mean anything by it."

"Fuck off, Oscar," I said. It was maybe the first time I'd spoken to him in more than a mumble, and it came out feral.

"Pussycat's got claws," he said with a chuckle. He ambled toward me, hands in his pockets. "You want to bite and scratch, is that it? Grrr." He swiped at me with a lopsided grin. I danced away.

"Leave me alone." Still trying to sound fierce. Still failing.

"Come on," he said again. He grabbed my wrist, spun me around like we were dancing. Like we were playing. "You know when a guy is mean to you, it just means he likes you."

"You don't like me," I told him, knocked off-balance in more ways than one.

"Maybe I do. Maybe I don't. Want to find out?" He tugged me in closer. I could smell the booze on his breath. It was eleven in the morning and he smelled like liquor. I knew the smell, and I knew the way it made my dad, maudlin but harmless. I didn't think Oscar was the same kind of drunk.

"Just let me go," I said, barely a squeak. It only made him laugh again. He swung me around, one hand on my waist, and then my back was up against the wall of the convenience store. The scents of malt liquor and tobacco and gasoline mixed together. I felt sick.

"We are destined to be together, did you know that?" Oscar asked. His head tilted, a sly smile playing over his lips. I looked at him in mute incomprehension. "Oscar the Grouch loves trash, see? I'm Oscar, you're trash. You and me were meant to be." He said the last sentence in a crooning song, a leer on his lips.

"You wish," I bit out. Stupid thing to say. He just grinned wider.

"You mean *you* wish, don't you?" he said. His hand snaked up under my sweatshirt, scrunched up the fabric of my T-shirt. "Do you even really have anything under there?"

His questing fingers dug into my ribs. I didn't move. Didn't fight back, didn't scream. I'd tried to be Artemis, the fearsome huntress, since the summer began, but there was none of her in me now. Only the quailing fawn before the hunting dog's snapping teeth. I froze, not fear but numb surrender washing through me.

And then Oscar was hauled backward. "What the fuck are you doing?" Cody demanded, yanking Oscar off me.

"Just kidding around," Oscar said, laughing, hands held up in surrender.

"She's eleven years old!" Cody shouted. His face was red with anger. He shoved Oscar hard in the chest, knocking him back a step, and moved up to match. "What are you, a fucking pedophile?"

"I wasn't going to do anything. Fuck! Relax, Benham," Oscar said. "Not like she has enough under there to actually cop a feel."

Cody swung. Oscar didn't even put up his hands, like he couldn't believe Cody was going to do it. Cody's fist connected with his jaw, and Oscar reeled, blood bursting from his split lip. He gave Cody a level look, one hand up. A look like Cody had made his point.

But he wasn't done. "Do not. Fucking. Touch her," Cody said, and then he was on Oscar again. This time Oscar tried to fend him off, swing back, but Cody had been in just as many fights as he had. Was just as big as he was. And the fury in his eyes was like a wildfire. He slammed Oscar against the wall. "You piece of shit—"

Fists thudded dully against ribs. Oscar wheeled away. Cody caught him by the collar and swung him around, throwing him to the ground, and then it was his boots connecting with Oscar's torso.

"Go near her again and I will kill you," Cody said, ragged but calm. He looked at me, eyes still burning. Oscar groaned, clutching his stomach. "Get out of here, kid."

I ran. I didn't look back. I ran to the trees and down the trail, in among the forest paths that still felt like safety. I ran until my breath was a sharp wheeze and a knife's point of pain was lodged behind my lung and then I stumbled to a stop, braced against a tree trunk.

*You and me were meant to be.* Because I was trash.

I'd never forgotten it. I'd never entirely stopped believing it. And that day in the shed when I was newly fifteen and trying to discover what kind of oblivion might suit me, he'd whispered it again, and I'd said nothing. Nothing at all.

We pulled up in front of the motel, and Ethan sat tapping his thumb against the steering wheel.

"We need to talk to Oscar soon. Before the FBI does," Ethan said. I grunted. "Or . . . we let the FBI do what the FBI does, and we take a breather." I stuck out my chin mulishly, and he sighed. "Right. Dumb idea. So what do you think? Could Oscar have attacked you?"

"I don't know. Maybe." I rubbed my thumb along my jaw. Oscar had known Jessi. He was perfectly capable of violence. It was easy to imagine him as the thread stretching between Jessi, me, and Liv. Our monster.

But that would mean that Cass almost certainly lied. And Liv . . .

Could Cass have convinced her to cover for Oscar? I had a hard time believing it. But maybe Liv, in her panic, hadn't seen him clearly. Cass had pulled her away, after all. Oscar fit the basic description they'd given. It was possible that Liv hadn't put it together. Maybe even Cass hadn't.

No. She'd told me she watched the whole thing. She couldn't have failed to recognize her own brother, which meant that if Oscar had attacked me, she'd lied. Lied to Dougherty, lied on the stand, lied to my face, only days ago.

"Naomi?" Ethan asked. I'd been staring out into the distance for over a minute, and my hand was shaking. I tightened it into a fist. Ethan looked at me, his expression open and guileless.

I didn't want him talking to Oscar. I didn't want him finding out the things I'd done or the things that had happened to me. But I couldn't avoid talking to Oscar any longer.

"I'm starving," I said. "Any chance you could go pick us up some lunch?"

"Or we could go sit down like civilized folk," he suggested.

I shook my head. "I'm beat. You go, I'll lie down for a bit until you get back."

"Sure," Ethan said. He hesitated like maybe he sensed something, but he got back in the car. I stood with my hands in my back pockets, watching him pull out. I waited until he was out of sight before I walked over to my car.

The Chester Lumber Company was a ghost of its former self. With the mill shut down, all that was left was a muddy lot filled with trucks and equipment—skidders, loaders, woodchippers that could handle a small elephant. The offices were single-wides on blocks.

Big Jim was out in front of the offices, talking to a grizzled strip of a man with a graying ponytail and stubble you could grate cheese with. The guy gave Jim a nod and headed into the office as I approached.

Big Jim came by his name honestly. He was where Oscar had gotten his massive frame and squared-off features. He loomed literally as well as figuratively in Chester. He'd been mayor for twenty-eight years, and the only person who'd ever come close to unseating him was Clark Jensen, who'd carried three wounded fellow soldiers through a hail of gunfire and still lost the election by six points.

I'd never been sure where I stood with Jim. He didn't like me, but he didn't *dislike* me either, as far as I could tell. Every time I'd talked to him growing up, he'd seemed surprised, like he hadn't noticed I was there. After the attack he'd pulled strings to make sure I got taken care of. He'd even given me a summer job once, filing paperwork in the office. It was mostly code for keeping the pencils sharpened and filling the candy dish, and I'd still managed to fuck it up spectacularly.

He didn't seem to hold it against me. But then, he didn't hire me again either. Now he offered a furrowed brow and a grunt of greeting.

"What can I do for you?" he asked, like I was any customer waltzing up.

"I'm looking for Oscar," I said.

"What do you need him for?" he asked, eyeing me suspiciously. As if I was the bad influence Oscar needed protecting from.

"To see what he remembers about a girl named Jessi Walker," I said. Jim's face transformed from faint puzzlement to complete confusion.

"What's she got to do with you?" he asked.

"You knew her?" It made sense, if she'd spent time with Oscar; he'd been living at home.

"In passing," Jim said, shrugging. He scratched the back of his broad knuckles.

"That's what I need to talk to Oscar about. I know they were friends. I'm just trying to put together a picture of her time in Chester and figure out where she was heading when she left," I said. "I won't take too much of his time."

"Whatever you're looking for, you won't find it in Jessi Walker," Jim said.

"What's that supposed to mean?" I asked, bristling.

He rested a hand on his hip and shook his head almost regretfully. "That girl was a walking disaster. She had a half dozen guys wrapped around her finger thinking they loved her. Oscar just about lost his damn mind over her. Fractured a guy's wrist for pinching her ass in the diner, but she wouldn't give him the time of day."

"He commits assault and she's supposed to drop her panties?" I asked. Jim scowled at me. Interesting that he didn't know they'd hooked up—or maybe it wasn't. Jim wasn't the kind of guy to keep a close watch on his son's love life.

"Look, I'm just telling you the girl liked drama. She made bad decisions and laughed about them. Everything was a game to her." He said it all in a matter-of-fact tone, like he was reporting on nothing more fraught than the weather. "That kind of girl doesn't end up with a happily ever after."

"I don't think she got one," I said. I watched his expression, feeling that familiar sense of not knowing where I stood. He'd had an abysmal opinion of Jessi Walker, that was clear. Yet there wasn't a trace of anger or hatred in his voice. It was like he didn't care at all. That was the way he'd always seemed to me—disconnected. Everyone else seemed to know this affable, charismatic man, but for me it had always felt like talking to a plank of wood, whatever the subject. It was like a milder version of Oscar—I didn't get to see the charm, because I wasn't worth the trouble of putting on a show.

He grunted, done with the conversation. "Oscar's out back. Don't take too much of his time."

With that, he turned and headed into the office. I stood there, teeth clenched. Plenty of people would put me in the category "that kind of girl." The only reason my life wasn't a mess of drama was that I packed up and left everything behind every time things got hairy.

I finally understood why I'd never been able to figure out how Jim felt about me. It was the same reason he could say all those things about Jessi Walker without the faintest flicker of emotion. She was beneath caring about. And so was I. He'd done the necessary steps to fulfill his obligations and play his part—mayor, best friend's father, charitable member of society. And that was it. Except for the moments I intersected with some task he needed to complete, I didn't even exist to him.

Oscar was across the lot when I came around the back of the offices, wiping his hands on a greasy rag, a toolbox open beside him. He looked over and saw me as I approached, but he didn't move. Waited for me to come to him.

I made my way across the rut-striped yard, keeping my steps steady and reminding myself I was a long way from eleven. Oscar was no kind of threat to me now. But it wasn't the gas station I was thinking about as I crossed the yard. It was the shed. That time I'd been entirely willing, and that was what made the memory sting. I couldn't blame anyone but myself for making a mistake like Oscar Green.

"Naomi." He worked the rag over his knuckles with limited result.

"Oscar." I stopped a good eight feet from him. I never stopped being startled by how beautiful his eyes were, even now. Big eyes, the kind of blue people wrote poems about. They tricked you into thinking there was something gentle hidden under that rough exterior.

Oscar gave me a grin, sitting his weight back on his heels. "You get tired of that string bean already?" he asked. He dropped his voice low. "I got a cot in the office if you're looking for an upgrade."

How did he know about me and Ethan? It didn't matter. "Get a new shtick, Oscar. That one's tired."

He chuckled. "You used to like it."

"You were only ever a mistake," I said.

"One you kept on making," he said. He flicked the rag over his shoulder. "What was it, six, seven times?"

It was six. But I wasn't going to let him know I'd been counting. When he'd run his blunt fingers along my scars, had he been remembering the knife that made them? Had it been funny to him? Had it excited him?

I swallowed against a sudden wave of queasiness.

He crossed his arms, inspecting me. "The only use you ever had for me was a good lay. So if you're not here for that, what the fuck do you want?" he asked.

"The FBI was asking me questions."

"So?"

"About you." That got his attention. "They seem to think that you might have been the one who stabbed me." I watched his response carefully.

"What? It was that serial killer," Oscar said, scoffing. Was that surprise in his expression, or a hint of guilt?

"They don't think so. They think we made that up. To cover for you," I pressed.

"Why the fuck would I stab you?" Oscar demanded. "You were an irritating little cunt who thought you were hot shit, but if I killed people for that I'd be neck-deep in cute little corpses."

I blinked, taken aback. That was vicious even for the version of Oscar he saved for me.

"Why are you telling me this, anyway?" Oscar asked. He narrowed his eyes at me. "Not because you want to help me."

I drew in a deep breath, forcing myself to stay calm. If I made it seem like I thought the FBI might be right, he'd shut down. "I'm giving you a heads-up. In return, I want some information," I said.

"About what?" he asked, plainly irritated.

"Jessi Walker."

The name transformed his whole face, surprise opening it up, making him look strangely vulnerable for an instant—and then he locked down again, scowling. "I haven't seen Jessi in . . . what has it been, twenty-five years? Twenty-four? The fuck you want to know about her?"

"My dad said you spent a lot of time together."

"Sure. Jessi was cool. Good-looking. Could hold her liquor." High praise from Oscar. "She was like one of the boys, you know what I mean?"

"She wouldn't sleep with you?" I interpreted. "That's not exactly what I heard."

"We messed around a few times. Nothing serious." He gave a shrug, but there was something angry and wounded in his expression. Cody and Jim had it right, I thought—whatever had actually happened between the two of them, Oscar had feelings for Jessi. Or his version of feelings, anyway. "Anyway, I wasn't her type, turned out."

I raised my eyebrows at that. "Who was?"

"Oh, you know girls with daddy issues." He looked me straight in the eye, dark amusement curling his lips. "Looking for a savior, every one. Somebody to step in and protect them."

"Not Cody," I said.

He barked a laugh. "I was sure it was heading that way, but no. She wouldn't tell me who it was, but trust me, Cody wouldn't have been moping around all the time if he'd been getting laid on the regular. Whoever it was, though, she was head over heels. Two weeks in and talking about how he was promising to marry her. She was smart but she was an idiot, you know what I'm saying?"

"Yes, as subtle as you've been, I get the picture," I said, restraining myself from rolling my eyes. Oscar was trying to play it off like he hadn't cared, but there was real anger in his voice when he talked about her. He hadn't liked being thrown aside, that was for sure. "She wasn't reported missing or anything. Do you know why?"

Oscar frowned, shook his head. "Nah, she wasn't missing. She just took off. Wandered into town and wandered out."

"You're sure about that?" I asked. Not one person had wondered where she'd gone to, why she never got back in touch. She'd been destined to leave since she arrived.

He shrugged. "She told me she was going. Said she was off to a new life or some bullshit like that. A better one than she could get in Chester, but not like that's hard. She said things were going to be different." His eyes darted away. All these years later, he was still upset she'd left. That she'd left *him*. That scorn in his voice when he talked about her lover was covering up a wound that had never healed over, I thought. And the only thing a guy like Oscar knew to do with pain was to inflict it on someone else.

"So she left on purpose? You're *sure*?"

"What else?" he asked. "Why are you asking about Jessi, anyway?"

Ethan had warned me to be careful about who I talked to about Jessi. Here I was running to the least safe person I could think of. But I needed to see his reaction. "I think something happened to her," I said. "Her family's been looking for her for decades."

"Fuck. Seriously?" he asked. He rubbed his palm over his scalp. "I just figured she went to LA or something. You know, some place with sun. And you're asking me about it why? You think I had something to do with it?" he continued, affronted.

"Why wouldn't I? Because you're such a stand-up guy?"

"First I stabbed you, now I killed Jessi. I must've been real busy back then," he said in mock wonder, shaking his head. "What did I do to make you hate me so much?"

I gave him a skeptical look. "You have to ask?"

"Can't have been that bad, if you kept coming back," he said, a lazy grin spreading over his face. "You know, I was just thinking about how funny it would be if Cody knew you'd begged me to fuck you."

The thought sent a jolt of alarm down my spine. "He doesn't know, does he?" I asked.

"Hell, no. After he overreacted that one time, he'd have fucking *shot* me. I mean, Jesus, look what he did because of a little joke."

"You mean shoving a child against a wall and molesting her?" I asked.

"I didn't molest you. It was a prank," he insisted. "You're just as dramatic as he is."

"You deserved everything you got."

He shrugged. "Yeah, probably." I looked at him in surprise, but he left it at that. He scratched his chin idly. "If that's all, I've got some actual work to do. Unless you want to reconsider that cot."

"No thanks," I said with all the venom I could muster. I turned on my heel and marched back to my car with his eyes drilling divots in my back. The fear I'd held in check broke loose as soon as the car door was shut behind me, and my hands were shaking when I went to turn the key in the ignition.

He'd never moved closer to me. Hadn't threatened me. But that old fear remained, etched in my bones. It was the reason I avoided him and the reason I'd kept going back. Because sometimes that fear and that disgust were all I knew how to feel. Oscar Green was always a mistake, but at least I knew why. He didn't hold any surprises.

He'd said he didn't do anything to Jessi—and hadn't attacked me. He could be lying. He'd known Jessi. She'd spurned him. That could have been enough to set him off.

It wasn't enough. I needed more. But first I needed to get back to the motel before Ethan panicked.

I focused my mind on Ethan, on my destination, and tried not to think about what was behind me as I drove away.

When I opened the door, Ethan was pacing. He stopped mid-stride and turned to look at me, anger and relief twinned in his expression. "Where the hell did you go?" he demanded.

"Nowhere." It was still my first, gut reaction—lie, even if the lie was absurd, even if you fully intended to tell the truth. "I went to talk to Oscar."

"Alone? Are you insane?"

"It was broad daylight. There were employees around. He wasn't going to talk with you there anyway."

"You don't know that."

"He called you a string bean," I noted, not as proof, just because it suddenly seemed funny. Ethan looked affronted. "Don't take it personally. He's basically a ham hock with a face. Everyone looks like a string bean to him."

"You're changing the subject."

"Ethan. Relax. I got information, I'm fine, no harm done." I told myself it was true. Oscar hadn't even touched me. And he never had, not unless I asked him first—not since that day behind the gas station. Yet every time he did, it felt like a punishment.

Maybe that was the point.

"What aren't you telling me?" Ethan asked. "You act weird every time Oscar comes up. That isn't 'generic asshole' weird. Something happened."

"It's not important."

"Sawant thinks he's a suspect in your stabbing. He's definitely a suspect in Jessi's death. So it's pretty fucking important," Ethan shouted, his frustration boiling over. He looked away immediately, scrubbing his hand over his face. "Sorry."

I let out a little breath. It was like a tiny crack had appeared in him, and I could see through to the parts of him he tried to keep locked away. It was a relief, in a way.

"I had sex with him," I said flatly.

"What?" Ethan jerked, staring at me. "Just now?"

"Jesus. No," I said, making a face. "A long time ago."

"You said he was an asshole."

"He is. He was," I said. I paced, one hand braced on my hip.

"But you dated?"

"No. Not even remotely," I said, turning back to him. "We don't have any kind of relationship. We hooked up a few times here and there, that's all. But I didn't want you to know. I didn't want him to say anything. I've slept with a lot of people I shouldn't have and I don't mind talking about it, but Oscar . . . I just didn't want that to be what you knew about me."

"When was this?" Ethan asked.

"I don't know," I said, but that was a lie. I knew exactly when the first time was. And the last. I sat down on the motel bed, my fingers finding the scar at my wrist.

"You don't have to tell me," he said. "Really. I shouldn't have asked."

"The last time was eight years ago," I said, ignoring him.

I'd come back to town to be with Liv after she got out of the hospital. She wouldn't talk to me, Kimiko and Marcus would barely talk to anyone, and I'd been suffocating in the silence. I'd gone to the bar I knew my dad didn't frequent, and Oscar had been there.

I took a breath and made myself say the rest. "The first time was eighteen years ago. And a handful of times in between. Every couple years when I was in town and feeling shitty enough that Oscar seemed like an improvement."

"Eighteen years ago you were a kid," Ethan said. Trust him to do the math.

I shrugged and didn't look at him. "Fifteen. It was my birthday."

"That would make him—"

"Old enough to buy the booze," I said lightly. "It was my idea. I made my own decisions every step of the way. They were terrible decisions, but they were mine."

"That's statutory rape," Ethan said. "It doesn't matter that it was your idea. It was his job not to be a fucking rapist."

"I don't—I'm not telling you this to get sympathy or something," I said quickly.

He sat down beside me. "All right," he said. "So why are you telling me?"

"Like I said. I just wanted you to know— I didn't want—" My voice choked off into silence. "I don't know. I've never told anyone before. Cass would kill me. Well, she'd kill him first. Then she'd kill me."

"Is that why you hate him so much?"

"More like it's part of why I hate myself so much," I said. The room was too cold, and my skin prickled with the chill. "There was a reason I knew Oscar would say yes, when I told him to bring a bottle of rum and a condom and meet me in the woods. When I was eleven, right before . . ." I waved a hand. I didn't need to spell it out; *before* was enough. "Oscar was joking around. Shoved me up against a wall and put his hand up my shirt. Scared the shit out of me."

"That goes beyond 'asshole,'" Ethan said. He was working hard to sound calm and factual. I watched him carefully. Even as I kept my own tone casual, I was relieved at the anger in his eyes, the strain of keeping a civil tone. "He should have been arrested."

"His dad is the mayor, Ethan; that wasn't going to happen. Besides, Cody stopped him. Beat the shit out of him, actually."

"Good," Ethan said firmly. "Cody's always had your back, hasn't he? I'm starting to understand why he's so protective of you."

"He's not that protective," I said.

"I thought he was going to take me apart when we first met," he said, eyebrows raised.

I made a feeble attempt at a smile. "The point is, when I asked Oscar to . . ." I had to stop, take a fresh breath. "When we had sex, it was my idea. I knew it wasn't healthy. I wanted to get hurt. It was all me."

"You wanted to get hurt, so you went to someone who'd be happy to hurt you. It doesn't mean it was anything close to okay," Ethan said. "And it doesn't remove his responsibility in any way. You were fifteen. You were a *child*."

"It doesn't bother me anymore," I said. "It didn't traumatize me. Not like Stahl. It's a shitty memory, but I don't think about it much. Bad first sex. No big deal."

"Right. No big deal. Which is why you're shaking."

I bunched my hands tight in my lap to stop the tremor. "I kept going back. I don't think I get to complain if I kept going back."

"You're talking to the son of a battered woman," Ethan reminded me. "And you are never going to say anything to convince me what Oscar did was anyone's fault but his."

"Fuck," I said, pulling my knees up to my chest. "I don't know why I told you any of this. I've never told anyone all of it."

"I told you. I'm good at getting people to talk to me," Ethan said with a half smile. "People tend to trust me. It's . . ." He paused, but pressed on. "It's actually disconcerting, sometimes. It's easy for me to get people to talk or to do little things to help me."

"You are uniquely unthreatening," I told him.

He made a sound in the back of his throat, acknowledgment and discomfort. He looked down at his hands. "When I was in college I was driving home one night. I saw this girl on the side of the road, walking along dragging a suitcase in the rain. I didn't really think about it, I just pulled over and offered her a ride, and she got right in. She said she usually wouldn't, but I had a 'good vibe.'"

"Unless you're hiding your ax-murder side business, you are actually a good guy," I pointed out.

He looked up at me. "But did she trust me because I'm *actually* a good guy? Or is it something else about me, something that *seems* trustworthy but doesn't have anything to do with me, with my character? Stahl—" He paused again. "Alan Michael Stahl convinced at least six women to get into his truck. They got in willingly. He seemed trustworthy. Lots of people said so. The kind of person you told your whole life story to. The kind of person you trusted on instinct."

"You don't murder people, Ethan," I said, unsettled. His gaze stayed fixed on me, and I couldn't look away.

"But I do use them. Get them to tell me their secrets." *Like you have* went unspoken.

"*Should* I trust you, Ethan Schreiber?" I asked him.

"I want to be someone you can trust," he said.

"That's not the same thing," I said, like it was a joke, not sure how to react.

All he said was, "I know."

The knock on my door came just as I was stepping out of the shower. "Hang on!" I called, hastily toweling off and pulling on clothes. I trotted to the door, expecting Ethan, and was taken aback to discover Cass standing on my doorstep instead.

She took off her sunglasses and gave me a withering look. "We need to talk," she said, and stepped past me. I opened my mouth to say something, but all language fled me.

"Cass," I managed. She glowered me into silence before I could say anything more.

"What are you doing, Naomi?" she asked.

"I—"

"You should have told me the *FBI* wanted to talk to you," Cass said. "And you talked to them without a lawyer? What were you thinking?"

"They think we lied," I said.

"Well, you did lie. Which is why you need a lawyer. I don't even know what the statute of limitations is on perjury. Do you?" Cass asked, bracing a hand on her hip. Her mouth pursed, anger in her eyes. Was she really just worried about me? Or was she worried about her own secrets?

"They were asking about Oscar," I said hoarsely, and waited for her reaction.

Her jaw tightened. "What?"

"They asked if Oscar attacked me and we covered for him," I said.

She half turned, her hand coming up in an abortive gesture. "That's—" She turned back to me. "That's ridiculous." Her voice cracked.

"Is it?" I asked.

"You don't think I would recognize my own brother?" she asked sharply. Then her expression went flat. "You think I did recognize him. You think I'm lying."

"No. I don't . . ." I didn't know what I thought. It had seemed plausible, up until I was standing here in the room with her. Looking her in the eyes.

"Fuck you, Shaw," she ground out. "I'm not the liar, remember? Half the things that come out of your mouth are lies."

"That's not true." Not anymore.

"*I left my homework in my locker. I don't know who spray-painted Chief Miller's car. This necklace was a present,*" she quoted at me. "*I saw Alan Stahl stabbing me.*"

My lips peeled back from my teeth, halfway to a snarl.

"Goddammit, Naomi. I'm not going to let you do this," Cass said. And then, to my shock, she stepped forward and wrapped her arms around me. She held me tight, her chin against my shoulder. "I am not going to let you drive me away. I'm not going to lose you, too." Tears quavered in her voice.

I shut my eyes and pressed my face into her hair, bringing my arms up to return her embrace. My throat was tight, my eyes stinging. How many times had I tried to push Cass away? We'd fight, or I'd just stop talking to her, burying myself in my own misery. And every time, she was there to dig me out again. She had never given up on me.

*Except for once,* a soft voice whispered in my mind. *When I lay dying.*

She let me go and stepped back, but her hand cupped the side of my neck as she looked into my eyes. I searched hers, too, desperate for some kind of answer.

"Naomi. What you said when you came to the lodge . . . It made me realize that I can't be sure about what I saw. I've worked so hard not to think about it, and it was a blur even then," Cass said. "But think about it. What reason could Oscar possibly have to hurt you? He's not that kind of guy."

My lips parted. She didn't know. I'd never told her. And I couldn't tell her now. "I'm just trying to find the truth," I croaked.

"About what happened to you? About Persephone? About Liv?" Cass said. I could only shake my head wordlessly. All of it. Any of it. "I heard that you're asking about a girl."

"Jessi Walker," I said.

"She's . . . ?" Cass said, and I nodded. She dropped her hand, stepping back. Her face screwed up like she was trying not to cry, and she stared at the floor for a moment before taking a sharp breath. "You're sure."

"As sure as I can be," I said.

"I remember her," Cass said, her voice sounding distant, and I stiffened. Of course Cass had known her. She was always tagging along after Oscar in those days. And I hadn't known Jessi because I made sure to find somewhere else to be when he was around. "She was nice. She liked to ruffle my hair and she called me sweetheart a lot. Oscar was a complete dope around her. Totally, uselessly in love." A little smile tucked up the corner of her mouth. "I remember Miller dragging him home because he was drunk as a skunk, trying to apologize to her through her apartment door for something. I think singing was involved."

My heart thudded in my chest. Everyone said the same thing— that Oscar was madly in love. Except for Oscar, who seemed intent on downplaying it. Was it ego? Or self-preservation?

Cass gave a little shiver. She folded her arms again and gave me a level look. "I get that you're trying to find the truth, Naomi. But what makes you think you're going to be able to find it if no one else has? You don't even like murder mysteries. You have no idea what you're doing."

"Ethan's been helping me," I said defensively.

She made a disbelieving noise. "So it's true, then. You really are sleeping with the enemy." Bitter amusement laced the words.

"He's a good guy," I told her.

"You don't sleep with good guys, Naomi," she reminded me, so matter-of-fact that I could only wince in acknowledgment. "Just . . . look out for yourself there." She was long past the days of trying to talk me out of bad relationships, and the only thing in her eyes now was weary acceptance.

But Ethan *was* a good guy, I thought. Improbably enough. And I couldn't help the hint of a smile at the thought of him, which only made Cass sigh heavily again.

"The funeral's tomorrow. I don't want us to be angry with each other, not right now. We can't turn on each other, or we're never going to get through this." I nodded mutely. She squeezed my arm and then gave me a fragile smile. "You can't get rid of me, Naomi. You're my best friend, remember? And I've only got one left."

She stepped past me, moving briskly as if she would start crying if she didn't. She opened the door to leave, revealing Ethan, in the middle of raising his hand to knock. They stared at each other for a moment in surprise, then Cass glanced back at me.

"Well. At least he's cute," she said in resignation. "Excuse me." She strode out past the bemused Ethan, crossing the lot toward her car.

"What was that about?" Ethan asked.

I watched as Cass climbed into her car and started the engine. My gut churned. When Cass decided on a reality, nothing could dissuade her. If she'd decided that it hadn't been Oscar she'd seen, she could have convinced even herself. Or convinced herself that lying was the right thing to do.

"Naomi?" Ethan prompted.

I let out a long breath. "Can we hit Pause?" I asked him. "Until the funeral, at least. I can't deal with all of this right now."

"Of course," Ethan said. "We can do whatever you need."

"Thank you," I said. I stepped into his arms, and he held me there, my cheek against his chest. I felt safe in his arms—the safest I'd felt in a long time.

It was starting to scare me.

The day of the funeral, I slipped the case that held Persephone's finger bone into the pocket of my black dress.

The afternoon was bright, with only a few white clouds scraped over the sky. We gathered in the church. I'd gone with Liv and Cass a few times growing up, whenever I spent a Saturday night with them. Kimiko was always there, impeccably dressed, with flyaway hair. Marcus never went, and they gave Liv the option. She liked the ritual. The singing. The way it filled your chest and made your skin tingle when everyone lifted their voices together. But I didn't know that she had ever believed.

Marcus sat in the front pew with his head down and his hands folded around a crumpled program. When Ethan and I entered, the church was half full, but still he seemed to sense my presence. He raised his head and looked back at me, and his gaze seemed to pierce through me. Kimiko turned in her seat to see who he was looking at.

Ethan and I started to take seats in the back, but Kimiko stood and waved us forward. I approached, at a loss for what I should say to her—what I *could* say, that would begin to put words to the loss that shrouded her.

"You were her best friend. You should sit up front," Kimiko said firmly. Marcus made a soft sound and looked away. It seemed like they'd already had an argument about this, and Marcus had lost.

Cass arrived soon after, surrounded by her family—parents, Amanda, even Oscar in a suit that strained around his muscular frame and made him look like the punch line to a joke that hadn't been written yet. Cass guided Amanda up to our pew, the others in tow. Oscar sat at the end and conspicuously didn't look my way. Cass took a delicate seat next to me and pressed my arm in a comforting gesture—while giving Ethan a skeptical look.

Liv had always loved losing herself in the ritual. For me, it was like a fever haze, full of steps I half knew and words that made my lips and tongue feel clumsy. I stumbled through the prayers and hymns, losing the sense of myself as voices merged in recitation, only to jar free of the unity and feel all the more alone.

Kimiko spoke, and Marcus. They talked about Olivia's artwork, her curiosity, her passion. They spoke of her troubles, obliquely, and I was glad that at least they didn't pretend that part of her hadn't existed. It wasn't part of herself that she welcomed, but it had defined so much of her. She wouldn't have been Olivia without having walked through the fire of her own mind.

To my surprise, Cass rose to speak when they were done. They hadn't asked me. She stood at the lectern and cleared her throat, and I braced myself for the polished version of friendship I was sure she would paint.

"When I was five years old, I decided that Olivia Barnes was going to be my best friend," Cass began. Her voice was clear and steady, but she gripped the paper on which her notes were written with a faintly trembling hand. "I wanted to be her savior, but the truth is that we rescued each other. Neither of us was the easiest person to be friends with. But no matter how many times we fought, we always made up.

"Olivia and I went through the usual ups and downs of friendship, but we also faced hardships that no one should. Some of those were inflicted on us by another—by evil that strayed into our community. And some of them came from within. Olivia wasn't just troubled. She was at war with her own mind from the time we were very young. At first none of us saw it. She was quirky. She was odd. She was, to me, magical. Maybe if the horror of that summer had never occurred, she would have had more time to learn how to live with the lies her brain told her. Instead, she was suddenly lost in the woods, and none of us knew how to help her find the way out.

"Olivia believed in me in a way that no one else ever did. And I believed in her. But no amount of faith could fix Olivia. No amount of friendship. And in the end, I gave up. I gave up on her, and on being her friend. I failed her."

She took a shuddering breath. She looked out at the congregation, and her eyes glimmered with unspent tears. "Olivia taught me to believe in magic. I can't bring her back. But I can honor her, by seeing the magic in this world. She wouldn't want us to dwell on the darkness, but the stars she saw within it. And that is what I'm going to do."

She walked swiftly away from the podium and back to her seat, her muscles tense with the effort of keeping everything together. She sat beside me and grabbed my hand and Amanda's, and gripped them both as the next speaker—an uncle—stood and made his way to the podium.

I squeezed her hand back and tried to breathe around the cold, white grief lodged in my throat.

*Is this what Olivia wanted?* I wondered. *For you to be obsessed with her death, obsessed with the attack all over again? Suspecting your best friend?*

Cass was right. It was the last thing Olivia would have wanted. She had wanted to find Persephone so we could bring her into the light, not to destroy us, to mire us in the past. But even as I thought it, I knew it didn't matter. I couldn't let go. I couldn't stop.

I was going to see this through to the end, even if it destroyed me.

We held on to each other until the last strains of the final hymn faded. After the recessional, as everyone gathered up their things, Cass tugged me in close for a hug.

"Will you come by the house? We're having a small gathering," she said. I didn't have to ask to know that *the house* meant her parents' place, not hers. Her eyes cut over to Ethan, who had been pulled into conversation with Marsha in the pew behind us. "Friends and family only. I don't think a reporter—"

"I understand," I said. Ethan would be nothing but respectful, but it was the last thing anyone needed today. And things had been odd between us since Cass's visit to the motel, a moodiness settling over Ethan that I hadn't seen before—and that served to remind me how little I actually knew him. "I'll drop Ethan off at the motel and come right over?"

"Yes. Good," she said.

"Mom?" Amanda said. "We're going now." She gave me a neutral look, like she was trying to remember what she thought of me. She looked so much like Cass at that age—the same wheat-colored hair, the same slender nose and big eyes. Eleven years old. Exactly the same age we had been that summer. It made my breath catch.

As Cass moved away, Amanda went with her, sneaking one last glance back at me. I gave her a quick, friendly smile and then joined Ethan as we trailed out of the church.

Halfway to the exit, I caught sight of Cody. He was standing with an older couple I vaguely recognized as his parents, along with a heavily pregnant, elegant-looking Latina woman I assumed was his wife. He saw me and lifted a hand in greeting, and his wife turned to look at me. Her eyes widened a little in recognition—I was rather distinctive, I supposed—and she broke into a dazzling smile, waggling her fingers in a wave before turning back to the conversation.

That was not a reaction I was used to. The open-mouthed *oohhhh* of recognition, the borderline leering interest, the instinctive disgust, those I'd gotten to know intimately over the years. A smile that bright usually wasn't meant for me.

"I'm going to drop you off," I said. "Cass's folks are hosting a gathering—a reception, I guess? I'm going to go."

"And you'd rather go alone," Ethan said.

"It's not that I don't want you there," I said quickly.

"But for everyone else, I'm not going to be Naomi's boyfriend Ethan, I'm going to be Ethan that nosy podcast guy," he said.

"Is that what you are?"

"A nosy podcast guy? Only when I'm working," he said.

"My boyfriend."

"Ah." He squinted off toward the road. "Slip of the tongue. What would be more accurate? Paramour? Gentleman caller? Booty call?"

"I like *gentleman caller*," I said, and decided not to think about why *boyfriend* sounded so appealing. We got into the car, and I started up the engine. I idled a moment while an elderly woman made her slow way past the back bumper.

"That was an interesting speech Cass gave," Ethan said.

"It was good," I said. "I thought Cass would sugarcoat things, but it was honest."

"I thought it was interesting that she never mentioned you," Ethan said carefully. "If you didn't know the whole story, you would think that something terrible happened to the two of them, and you didn't even exist."

"It's not about me. It's about Olivia," I countered. Ethan shrugged. "What? You think Cass is cutting me out?"

"Why weren't you invited to speak? You said yourself that you and Olivia talked multiple times a week. So why is Cass the 'best friend' and you don't even warrant a mention?"

"This isn't about getting credit," I said. "What are you getting at?"

"I'm just thinking . . . I don't know. You've been gone a long time. Who you are to these people might have changed. Or it might never have been what you thought."

I thought of Meredith Green's anger, Marcus's restrained hostility. I'd been an outcast all my life, until I almost died. Then Chester had embraced me—but had they? Or did they only want the story of the girl who survived and not the prickly, troublesome person inconveniently attached to it?

"Cass can be a bit tricky, but she's one of my best friends," I said. The last one living.

"You're the one who thought she might have lied about seeing Oscar," Ethan pointed out.

I ground my back teeth together. "And?"

"You don't think that anymore?"

"I don't know," I said. I couldn't tell what I thought at this point. "Maybe I'm just seeing things that aren't there."

"I don't think you're crazy," Ethan said. "And in your position, I'd be asking myself if that friendship of yours goes both ways."

We'd reached the motel. I slammed on the brakes harder than I needed to, glaring at him. "I would not have survived without Cass," I said.

"I'm not saying you shouldn't be grateful that she found help."

"That's not what I'm talking about," I said. "I'm talking about after. I could barely function, much less talk about what had happened, and it was all anyone wanted from me. She protected me. She was eleven and she did a better job of getting in the way of reporters and busybodies than my own dad. Liv and I were both falling apart, and Cass held us together with her bare hands and sheer force of will."

I could have told him about the nights she'd sneaked over so that I wouldn't have to sleep alone in my bed or when she'd punched Grayson Talbot in the mouth for calling me Frankenstein. I wouldn't have made it to adulthood without Cass Green.

"You know her best," Ethan acknowledged, but it was half-assed.

"Yeah, I do," I said. I set my jaw. "I'll see you after."

"See you soon," he agreed. I pulled away the second the car door shut.

Who did he think he was? Cass was my friend, always had been.

Almost everyone loved Cass. She was beautiful, charming. She made you work to impress her, and there was something thrilling about succeeding. But there had always been some subset of people who didn't get her. She scared them, or they only saw the hard edges and none of her generosity and charm. They thought she was *bossy*, a term that mysteriously only ever seemed to be applied to girls.

We'd needed that bossiness. Liv and I couldn't make a decision to save our lives, sometimes, but Cass always had something for us to do. We'd gone along with her demands, however outlandish, because she was the best at creating the magic. Making us believe.

Later, it had been a blessing. When I was flunking math, she'd bullied me into doing my homework, showing up with worksheets and a graphing calculator and stealing the TV remote. After Liv got home from the hospital, it had been Cass who was there to boss her into showering and eating until she stabilized and could take care of herself again.

So I'd never much minded that there were those people who didn't get Cass. But it bothered me that Ethan was one of them, and as I pulled up to the house I was glad he hadn't come with me.

The Green family's house was the biggest in Chester. It was an old Colonial-style, wildly out of place in this area. Big Jim had built it back when the mill was in full swing, right after he'd won his first mayoral race.

The drive was clotted up with a dozen cars—the gathering was bigger than I'd expected. I made my way up to the front door, and when

I rang the bell Amanda opened it, looking polished and somber and perfect with her blond hair and little black slip dress, a black ribbon in her hair to match.

"Hello, Ms. Shaw," she said, with painful formality. "I'm glad you could make it."

"You used to call me Aunt Namie," I told her, eyebrow raised. "When did you get all sophisticated?"

She flushed, looking borderline panicked by the attention. She might look like Cass's clone, I thought, but Cass had never been timid. I tried to look friendly, but it wasn't my strong suit. I cleared my throat, thanked her for letting me in, and left before I could traumatize her any further.

The cavernous living room was the hub of activity. Meredith sat on the couch next to a dull-eyed Kimiko. Marcus was over by the side table, a glass of red wine in hand. When he saw me his perpetual frown deepened.

I stood frozen in the foyer. I hadn't been asked to speak at the funeral. Marcus and Kimiko hadn't invited me here—Cass had. Was I even welcome?

I stiffened my spine. Why the fuck shouldn't I be here? I walked across the room, straight to Marcus, and put out my hand. "I'm so sorry for your loss," I said.

He looked down at my hand for a long moment before he reached out and shook it. "Thank you," he said mechanically.

"I'm sorry that I didn't think to ask if I could say a few words at the memorial," I added, trying not to glance over to see who was watching me. Trying not to feel like every eye in the room was trained on me. "Liv was remarkable. She changed my life. I don't know who I would be without her."

His jaw tightened. "She thought the world of you," he said.

I swallowed hard. Tears sprang to my eyes; I willed them away. You didn't cry in front of people. You didn't show how you could be hurt. "I wish that I'd done more to deserve that."

He started to say something, then stopped himself. Kimiko appeared, sliding her hand into the crook of his arm. "Excuse us, Naomi," she said. She drew him away even as a hand fluttered to my shoulder. I managed not to whirl around, but my stomach jolted as I turned.

Cody's wife was standing behind me, holding out a glass of white wine like an offering. "You look like you could use this," she said in a musical voice. I accepted it. I preferred red, but right now I just wanted something to hold so I could look less awkward.

"It's Gabriella, right?" I asked her.

"Gabby, please. And you're the infamous Naomi Cunningham."

"Infamous might be overstating it," I said, taking a sip.

"Infamous to me, at least. Cody talks about you a lot. He likes to keep an eye on you, you know. He's a little bit of an internet stalker." She held up her hand, thumb and forefinger pinched together. I obliged her with a chuckle, though I wasn't sure how I felt about that. "I think it's safe to say he's the biggest fan of your work out there—and getting him to care about *our* wedding was like pulling teeth."

"I didn't realize he'd even seen any of my photos," I said.

"The wedding stuff is great, but I love your other work," she said. "That series of black-and-white photos of decaying things—the one with the mushrooms growing around the deer skull? I bought a print of that one."

I laughed a little, uneasy and flattered at the same time. "He didn't tell me that."

She rolled her eyes a little. "He probably didn't want to make you feel self-conscious, and he'd be completely embarrassed if he knew I was telling you. Honestly, I think he just likes to reassure himself that you're still doing okay. He still can't quite believe it, sometimes. What happened. That you made it out."

"I know the feeling."

She touched my arm. "I really hate the idea that everything happens for a reason, or that you should look for silver linings. What happened to you shouldn't have ever happened. But I can't help but be grateful, in a weird way. Finding you changed Cody. It made him a better man.

If it weren't for you, I'm not sure he could have been the person who convinced me to marry him."

"It still took three tries," Cody said, approaching with a slight wince of a smile. He put his arm around his wife. "Gabriella gets very sentimental in the third trimester."

"There is nothing wrong with being sentimental," Gabby told him. She fit just perfectly under his arm, and next to her glamour all his rough edges took on a sharper quality. Now I could see it. The Cody Benham who'd carried me out of the woods wasn't politician material, but this guy? He was made for it.

"Personally, I'm terrible at it. Sentiment requires sincerity, and that requires vulnerability. Cynicism and sarcasm are way safer," I said.

"Well, at least you're self-aware," Cody said, amused, and gave me a little *cheers* gesture with his glass.

"It's almost as good as being well adjusted."

They both laughed. I was suddenly and acutely grateful that I hadn't made more of a fool of myself, that night I arrived in town. They looked so happy together. If I'd done anything to jeopardize that, I never could have forgiven myself.

"Are you free later today or tomorrow?" Gabriella asked. Cody gave her a puzzled look, but she continued, unconcerned. "I was thinking we could have you up to the lodge for dinner."

"You're staying at the lodge?" I noted, mostly to buy myself some time to think.

"It's remarkable what Cassidy's done with the place, isn't it?" Cody asked, giving me a look that clearly said *I didn't know she was going to ask, and you don't have to.*

"She's remarkable," I agreed, with a note of borrowed pride. "Do you remember what a disaster that place was when we were younger? I can't believe how fast she was able to turn it around. But I have the project management skills of a cranky two-year-old, so I'm not the best judge."

"Oh, a cranky four-year-old, at least," Cass said, coming up behind me. She slipped her arm into mine. "Honestly, though, I was in way over my head. I was just so bored, back home with a baby and nothing to do. If I'd stopped to think for ten seconds I would have seen how ridiculously unqualified I was. Constantly over budget, and the environmental assessments almost kicked my ass. Every single permit seemed like it was going to be the thing that brought the whole project crashing down." She winced at the memory.

"Cody always knew you could do it," Gabriella said. "And it's been a marvelous return on our investment."

"An investment I am eternally grateful for," Cass said. She pressed my arm lightly. "I need to steal Naomi for a moment. If you'll excuse us?"

"Of course," Cody said quickly.

Gabriella gave a little wave. "Don't forget! Dinner! We really need to get together before we leave town," she said, and then Cass was pulling me away.

"I didn't realize Cody had invested in the lodge," I noted as she led me toward the kitchen.

"You would if you ever asked me about it," Cass said, a little snappish.

"In my defense, all that complaining about permits really was mind-numbing," I told her, and she jostled me playfully. But her expression turned serious. "What is it you need to talk to me about?" I asked.

Her lips thinned. "In the office," she said, and inclined her head toward the back hall. She broke away from me as she led the way, and I followed with trepidation. What was going on?

I'd rarely been allowed back here as a kid; the only things back here were Big Jim's home office and his man cave. It was the former that Cass led me to—and to my surprise, Big Jim was already there, standing behind a huge desk constructed from roughly hewn sections of a tree he'd felled himself, a story I knew because he liked to tell it four or five times a year.

"Naomi. Good to see you again," he said, sounding anything but pleased.

"Why am I here?" I asked, looking between them. What could Big Jim possibly want with me?

"It's about Ethan," Cass said.

"What about him?" I asked, trying not to sound defensive right off the bat. "He's doing his job. It's nothing sinister."

"I'm not so sure about that," Big Jim said. "You two have been hassling a lot of people. I've been getting some questions, so I looked into him. Didn't find much at first, but then I discovered something real alarming."

"You looked into him? He's a podcaster. He's just asking questions," I said.

"He isn't who you think he is, Naomi," Cass said gently.

"Please just tell me what you're talking about," I said, panic starting to well up.

Big Jim reached over to the desk and picked up a plain folder. He held it out to me. "Just like he claims, he works for a podcast network and he's written and produced a bunch of stuff on true crime under the name Ethan Schreiber. But he changed his name when he turned eighteen. Before that, it was—"

I stared at the page inside the folder. It was paperwork for having his name changed in the state of Washington to Ethan Schreiber—

From Alan Michael Stahl, Jr.

The words on the page slid out of focus and refused to return. A tight, cold feeling flared along the back of my neck, pooling at the base of my skull, and I tasted something strange and sharp in the back of my throat. It couldn't be true. It had to be a mistake. Ethan wasn't—

"Is this a joke?" I asked, knowing that it wasn't. Neither of them answered me. Ethan was Stahl's son. Ethan had written the letter. He'd lied to me. He'd followed me, stalked me, insinuated himself into my life. He'd made me trust him.

And I'd thrown myself at him.

I choked out a laugh. "He's Stahl's *son*?"

"Looks that way," Big Jim said. "I take it you didn't know, then."

"Of course I didn't fucking know," I snapped. Big Jim gave me a nod, not the least bit bothered by this outburst. I stared at the paper, willing it to transform. How could I have missed it? How could I not have known?

Of course Alan Stahl, Jr., would change his name. If he ever wanted to get out of the shadow of his father, if he wanted to be anything but a serial killer's son, he had to. I'd done it. Why hadn't I assumed he would as well?

Ethan had lied to me from the start. When I'd told him about the letter, he'd worked so hard to calm me down. And it was all bullshit. He'd sent the letter. He'd known that I was lying all along. I'd confessed it to him. Trusted him, the way I'd never trusted anyone.

He was good at getting people to talk to him. Stahl had been good at that, too. He'd talked women right to their deaths.

Cass looked at me with pity. Big Jim's face was as blank as ever. I looked away, shame and embarrassment sliding sickly through me, more pernicious than anger. I should have known. I was a fool.

I thought of the way he'd hinted that I shouldn't trust Cass. Like he was trying to create a wedge between us.

It wasn't just that I'd trusted him. I'd thought . . .

But it didn't matter, did it? Whatever I felt, it was for a man who didn't exist.

"I'll let you two talk in private," Big Jim said. As he passed, he clapped me on the shoulder once. It was the only time I could recall him ever touching me, and it took all I had not to slide out from under his hand, my skin crawling. I didn't want anyone touching me. Not ever again.

The door closed behind Jim. Cass rubbed my arm in a way I'm sure was meant to be comforting. "I'm sorry," she said. "I wish that it wasn't true. I wish that I didn't have to tell you."

"Why was your dad looking into him at all?" I asked. I felt like I was going to vomit, but I forced myself to focus on Cass's face. She always knew what to do. She was always the one in control, and I needed that now.

"I asked him to. I wanted to look out for you," Cass said.

"He lied. The whole time, he— God, Cass, I told him things."

"You told him about Persephone—Jessi Walker, right?" Cass asked. I nodded. "I really wish you hadn't done that. What else did you tell him?"

"Everything," I said. I was an idiot. I'd known he had to be hiding something. He'd all but told me not to trust him. "I told him I lied at the trial."

She looked at me aghast. "You told a serial killer's son that you lied to put his father in prison."

"I'm not sure he was a serial killer," I said, which didn't make it better.

Ethan had been sure, though. Unless that was another lie.

"He must have come to talk to me—but I wasn't even here. No, he came to talk to *you*. And Liv. She said she'd talk to him."

"I didn't know that," Cass said, head tilted, frowning. "Do you know what she told him?"

"Nothing, I think," I said. "But what if he confronted her? She wasn't going to tell him anything until we all agreed, but if he pushed, if he got angry . . ." I couldn't imagine Ethan with a gun in his hands, rage on his face. I couldn't imagine him lying to me like this, either. I had no idea who he really was. What he was really capable of.

Cass's face was pale. "Do you really think he might have killed Olivia?" she asked, voice hushed.

"I don't know. I need to go. I need to— I can't—"

"You should stay. Wait until you're feeling steadier," Cass said.

"No, I have to—all my stuff is at the motel room. I have to go get it. I have to . . ." Shit. I couldn't think past the motel room door. He'd be there. Waiting. What was I going to do? What was I going to say?

"Here." Cass pressed a key into my hand. I frowned at it, uncomprehending. "You're staying with me. As long as you need to. And you're not going to that motel room alone. Go wait at my place. We'll take care of this."

"We should tell Bishop," I said. "Shouldn't we?"

"We need a plan. We need to be smart about this," Cass said. "Go to my place. Don't call anyone, don't answer the door. I have to stick around for another hour or so, but then I'll come right there, and we'll figure out exactly what we need to do, okay?"

"Okay," I said. Cass would figure it out. She always did. I folded my hand over the key, letting it bite into my palm. My mind was reeling. Ethan was Alan Stahl, Jr. He came here because he knew I'd lied before even I did. He'd been angry. He blamed us. He'd come to town. Olivia had agreed to talk to him, and he'd hurt her, and—

What? Why stick around?

To keep an eye on things. To make sure no one else suspected him. To fuck with the person who'd fucked up his life.

"Are you okay to drive?" Cass was asking.

"Yeah. I'm fine," I lied. I took a steadying breath. "It's just a shock. I'd better go."

"Not to the motel," she said firmly.

"I'll go to your house," I agreed. I couldn't think past that, but I could get that far. I folded the page from the file into thirds, then in half, with overly precise movements. I tucked it into my skirt pocket slowly, as if by taking my time I might wait out the pain. Sneak past while it wasn't looking.

Cass got me out the back door. I barely registered getting into my car, starting the engine. I was parked in Cass's driveway before my brain caught up with my body, and when I stepped into her empty house I just stood there, uncertain.

I'd never been in Cass's house alone. It had an antiseptic quality to it. Even the decorations seemed utilitarian, there to create a certain image. Cass had decided who she wanted to be and constructed her life around it. The single mom, successful business owner. She'd clawed her way to normalcy. I could understand why she hadn't wanted Liv to disrupt it.

If we hadn't shut her down, would any of this have happened?

I drifted up the stairs to the bedroom and sat on the end of the bed, feeling ridiculous in my black dress.

I should have known. I only ever went for terrible men. There was always going to be rot at the core of what I had with Ethan. I just hadn't known it would be *this*.

Ethan didn't seem like a violent guy. But his father had had everyone fooled, too.

I wiped my eyes to clear my vision and took a deep breath that didn't seem to fill my lungs. Across from me, the closet door was open. On the highest shelf in the back was a wide wooden box, Celtic knotwork carved along the rim.

She'd kept it all these years. Of course she had. All of us had kept our trinkets. Our pieces of the past. I stood and walked slowly to the shelf. There was a footstool in the corner of the closet, and I maneuvered it under the box and stepped up.

It was heavy, solid. We'd found it at the antique store, coated in dust. The lid was carved with twining leaves and vines. I had been the one who found it. Cass had been the one who kept it. That was the way it worked.

I carried the box over to the bed and opened the lid. It creaked faintly. Inside was a collection of Liv's drawings; a stack of Polaroid photos; a gaudy costume ring I remembered Cass getting from her grandmother; a silk scarf patterned with stars; a cat's collar, "Remington" etched on the tag; a silver cup we'd declared the Goddess Goblet. A small cloth bag held a tiny, hard object; I didn't have to take it out to know that it was a knucklebone.

Cass had taken the bracelet with Persephone's name on it, too, but she'd given it to me at the hospital. A bit of extra magic, she said, to help me get better.

I picked up the stack of Polaroid pictures. I remembered that camera. I'd found it in my dad's stuff when a stack toppled, along with a few boxes of film. The film had been old even then, and the photos had come out washed-out and hard to decipher at times, but I'd hauled it with me everywhere until I ran out of film. I hadn't thought about it since, but I supposed that was the spark that had gotten me interested in photography.

It always came back to that summer, didn't it?

With the passage of years, the poor quality had given the photos an eerie quality. A blurry snapshot of Cass in the woods, holding up the goblet with the starry scarf around her shoulders like a shawl, took on an air of ancient mystery. A shadowed shot of Liv, looking upward, her surroundings indistinct, seemed as if she were emerging from a blackened void. Cass and Liv walking side by side, pinkies hooked together, Liv looking over her shoulder at the camera, at me, with a brilliant slice of smile.

Then a photo of the three of us, together. I was clearly holding the camera. We were sitting on Liv's childhood bed, shoulder to shoulder, and I was in the middle. Cass and Liv were sticking out their tongues, looking at the camera. I was looking at Liv, my eyes shining.

A little breath slipped between my lips, my heart aching. Liv was dead—but so were all three of those girls. The girls we'd been before.

Under the photos were two pieces of notebook paper, folded over, the creases worn with age. I unfolded one delicately, and my breath caught in my throat.

I stole money from Mrs. Green's purse.

I hate my dad and sometimes I wish that he would die. He's a drunk and he's useless.

I cheated on a math test last month.

There were a dozen more lines. I'd written them all. My secrets. We'd all made a page like this—the sixth ritual. The darkest secrets of our hearts, Cass had said. We wrote them down and then we burned them. She'd thrown them into the fire and rambled about purifying our souls with the flames. But then how were they here?

I unfolded the other page. It had to be Liv's—I recognized the hand-writing.

I'm not good enough for the Goddesses. I have to try harder but
I'm afraid.
I'm not a good friend.
I'm weak and I'm a coward.
I can't do anything right.

"Oh, Liv," I whispered. "I didn't know it was that bad." My heart ached for the little girl she'd been. She'd been so vulnerable, and the things that were coming for her were too immense for anyone to handle, much less a child whose demons were starting to wake. But she'd survived them—only for her life to be stolen from her.

I tried to picture it again. Liv by the pond, a gun pointing at her head, and the hand holding the gun—Ethan's. I bit down on a scream, crumpling the papers in my fist. Cass must have kept these. Had she thrown fake pages into the fire? Why?

Probably so that she could read them, I realized, and sighed. She'd always had trouble letting go of control. She'd probably been worried we'd written something about her.

"What are you doing?"

I twisted around, adrenaline spiking. Oscar stood in the doorway, watching me with his usual blunt curiosity.

"Just reliving some old memories," I said. I gestured at the Pola-roids, mouth dry. "I took these. Ages ago."

Oscar leaned against the doorframe. He'd ditched his suit jacket and rolled his sleeves up to his elbows, baring thick forearms. "You were always a nosy little—"

"Can you try to not be a complete creep for thirty seconds?" I snapped.

He grinned. "—kid," he finished. He pushed off the doorframe and ambled toward me. My body tensed but I made myself stay still. He picked up one of the photographs. Cass with a crown of wildflowers, holding a crystal we'd tied to a bit of twine. "You were always doing such weird shit."

"We were weird kids," I said. He was close enough that I could feel his proximity, the shift of air on my skin. I'd never felt safe when Oscar was around. Once upon a time, that was why I'd gone to see him. Danger and pain had felt easier than safety. Now I was all too aware of the strength in those broad hands and of how badly he could hurt me.

"Nah, it was cool," he said. "Weird-ass little witch girls. At least you were interesting."

I stared at him, bile in my throat. "You hated me. The things you did—"

"You really are still hung up on that, aren't you? Yeah, I was a piece of shit."

"Still are," I said bitterly.

"Sure. But I got my ass kicked for it, so let's call it even." He shrugged. Like that was that, pain balanced by pain. Like it didn't leave cracks on your skin, whichever part you played. "Look, it wasn't like I really wanted to hurt you or anything. I was drunk, okay? It was a stupid mistake."

"I was your little sister's friend," I said, not ready to let it go. "She worshipped you."

He snorted. "Hardly."

I stared at him. "Come on. The way she followed you around? You protected her, and she would have done anything for you in return."

"Protected her? From what?" Oscar asked. He was still standing entirely too close, looming over me.

"Your dad," I said. "I know he used to hit her."

He screwed up his face. "Dad? Nah. He beat the shit out of me, sure, but he never touched his precious princess."

"I saw the bruises," I said, confusion overtaking my anger. He had to know. She'd said he stepped in to protect her, so he was obviously aware of what was happening.

To my surprise, Oscar laughed. "Oh, *that*. Cass and her fucking fight club. Yeah, she used to have bruises all the time, but she gave them to herself. She was always trying to get me to lose my temper. She'd fucking *whale* on me, biting and scratching and everything, trying to get me to hit her. A couple of times I had to throw her off and pin her down just to get her to stop, but I never punched her or anything. She'd throw herself against the walls and the furniture and shit so she'd have bruises, though, and threaten to tell Dad I was hurting her unless I did shit for her." He twirled a finger by his temple.

"Yeah, right," I said. "Your seventy-pound sister was a real menace."

"I've been in enough bar fights to know you don't tangle with crazy," he said simply. "Cass didn't worship me. She was always looking for something she could hold over me. But the stuff she wanted was stupid kid stuff, so it was easier just to go along with it. I mean, no one would believe me, anyway. Everyone always loves Cass."

I stared at him, trying to tell if he was messing with me. I didn't want to believe him, but hadn't she done the same thing to me? She'd used words, not fists. But she'd goaded me over and over again until I hit her. *Then* she'd turn vicious, but the fight would be my fault, because I'd started it.

I'd understood it, though—that urge to fight, not just because you wanted to hurt something but because you wanted to be hurt. It had never gone away. I'd just found less visible ways to wear my bruises.

But Oscar was violent, and he was scum. I had no reason to accept his word over Cass's.

"Do you need something, Oscar?" I asked him, my wariness not fading by even a fraction.

"Do you?" he asked.

He touched one thick finger to the underside of my chin, tilting it up. I met his eyes and didn't flinch. His hand slid forward, fingers around my throat. Just resting there. He leaned in close, until I could see every golden speck in the blue of his eyes. The familiar thrum of fear and desire pierced me like a fishhook, and he smirked like he could sense it.

*Why not?* part of me wondered. Was he worse than Ethan? Was he worse than what I'd earned? At least I knew already the shape of the cracks he'd leave on my skin. At least I already knew I hated him.

"Get out," I told him through closed teeth.

His fingers tightened ever so slightly. The pressure cut off my breath for half a second, my muscles tensing in sudden panic—and then he released me. I fought the urge to gasp, to grab for my throat. "No problem," he said, falling back a step. "Cass just asked me to check on you, that's all. Make sure you were here, keep an eye on you, that kind of thing."

Cass had sent Oscar here? This time, when anger flared, it was for her. She might not know the details of what was between Oscar and me, but she knew how I felt about him.

Oscar left at last, leaving me shaky and sick to my stomach. I started to throw the photos and everything else back in the box. There was one more thing at the bottom: a plain manila envelope. I hesitated a moment and then reached for it, shaking it out on the bedspread.

From it spilled a random assortment of photographs and papers, along with a thumb drive labeled "Percy." *With what I've got on the guy, he can't say no to me,* I remembered Cass saying.

I spread out the papers and photos with a slow sweep of my hand, feeling uneasy. There didn't seem to be any clear theme among the documents. A photo showed a man I didn't know, laughing and holding a bong. A printed-out email from someone at a construction company seemed to be discussing wetland delineation and something about drain tile and "Section 404." There were a handful of other photographs, some showing obviously sketchy behavior but most seemingly innocent without context. A duplicate check from Meredith Green to someone named Alicia Barlow for $15,000, dated April 2000.

And at the bottom of the stack, there was one more photograph. This one was older, dented from poor storage. It was a photograph of Jim Green, his hands on the hips of a slim woman in tight jeans and a Chester Lumber Co. T-shirt, what looked like the old mill in the background. His head was bent toward hers, almost kissing her. Close enough that there was no ambiguity about his intent, or hers. The woman was in profile, her face turned away from the camera, but still I recognized her.

Jessi Walker.

Jessi's mystery man was the mayor.

Something like sorrow slithered through me. It wasn't like I'd ever cared much for Jim. He wasn't a surrogate father or a protector. But he'd been a constant presence. One more thing turned foul.

When I'd gotten the summer job filing, it had been Meredith's idea. I'd heard her and Big Jim arguing about it once—what had she said? *This way you won't have to stay late at the office.* I'd assumed she'd meant that he wouldn't have as much work to do. I'd been naïve in my own way, even after everything that had happened.

I gathered everything and stuffed it back into the envelope. The content of the photograph was less of a surprise than the fact that Cass had it at all. What the hell was this? A blackmail stash?

I shook my head. I didn't know what the hell Cass was doing with this stuff, but the implications of it were clear. Big Jim had been sleeping with Jessi.

I'd been focused on Oscar—his jealousy, his rage. But jealousy wasn't the only thing that could drive a man to kill. She'd told Oscar she was going to start a new life with her lover. Which meant she'd thought Big Jim would leave his wife for her. He was going to take her away from this small town and give her everything she dreamed of. Because that's what you tell your pretty mistress before you get bored with her.

But maybe she pushes. She asks for a deadline. She tells him to step up, or she'll tell his wife, she'll tell *everyone*. So things get heated.

Maybe it's an accident, maybe it's on purpose, but either way she ends up dead.

Oscar kills her out of jealousy, or Big Jim kills her out of self-preservation. Whichever one of them does it, though, he has to cover it up. He takes her into the woods, shoves her in a hole where she won't be found.

Except that we found her. The Greens were always in those woods. Hiking, hunting, drinking. What if one of them saw me climbing up out of the Grotto that day, and realized I knew?

Would he have known the others were with me? Liv and Cass had had a sleepover the night before, at Liv's house, but I couldn't go because I had a cold. He wouldn't necessarily have assumed that we'd met up. He might have thought I was alone, or he might not have thought at all—just panicked.

So Cass covers for her brother, or she covers for her father—and either way the result is the same.

I took the paper from my pocket, my finger bumping against the earring case that held Persephone's bone, and unfolded it. The image of the name change paperwork was pasted in below an email I'd barely glanced at. Just *Here's the paperwork you were asking about.* The content didn't tell me anything. But the email was from CalvinS@JCSI.com. Jessup Consulting, Security & Investigations.

They were working for Jim Green. He was the one who'd sent that man to follow me, to break into my hotel room. Protecting his son? Or himself?

I shoved everything back into the box and closed the lid.

Cass had known about Jessi Walker. Had she made the connection to Persephone? Was that why she was so insistent that Liv let it go? She was trying to warn us off because she knew what her father would do if he found out.

Or else she was the one who had told him what Liv knew.

I had to get out of here. I grabbed the box, tucking it under my arm, and made for the front door.

At the bottom of the stairs, I heard a floorboard creak behind me.
I turned, meeting Oscar's eyes. He held a beer in one hand, his arms
crossed. We looked at each other. I wondered for a moment if he would
stop me. Cass had told him to keep an eye on me, after all. Making sure
I was okay definitely didn't include letting me run off unannounced.
But he only nodded once, and turned away. Done with me.

I fled.

There was only one place left for me to go. I parked beside the old Chevy and walked woodenly to the door. I stood on the step, mind blank, paralyzed by the decision of whether to knock or walk in.

The door opened before I could decide one way or the other, and Dad looked at me with his usual blend of scorn and amusement, like it was a big joke I'd wound up back on his porch. Which I guess it was.

"You look like shit," he informed me. "What are you doing crying in a fancy dress?"

"It was Liv's funeral today," I said.

"That's Tuesday."

"It is Tuesday. Can I come in?"

"Not like I can stop you," he said, and walked back inside, leaving the door hanging open. I stepped in. Couldn't bring myself to close the door and shut off my escape route.

"You need something?" he asked.

"No. I just— There's nowhere else to go," I said. My throat felt scratchy, and my eyes were puffy, though I hadn't actually cried.

"That's obvious enough, since there's no way you'd come here otherwise," he said, grumbling, but then he stopped and narrowed his eyes at me. "What the hell happened to you?"

I pressed my lips together and shook my head.

"Are those bruises? Did that pretty boy hurt you?" he asked, and I barked a laugh that turned into a strangled sob.

"I don't even know where to start with that," I said. My grip tightened on the box. "I need to look through some of my old things."

"Go ahead," he said, gesturing toward the back hall. "It's just how you left it."

I suppressed my disbelieving snort. I picked my way past the guest bedroom and discovered it was completely full, stacked five feet high in the back. He'd just been chucking things in for years, not bothering to leave a path, and even the doorway was blocked with a broken bookshelf canted on its side. I crushed a bright pink Easter basket underfoot and kept moving, dreading what I would find in my bedroom.

To my shock, it was almost as pristine as he'd implied. The bed itself had some random detritus stacked on it, but a closer inspection proved most of it was mine. Stuff I'd thrown out the last time I was here. He must have just brought it right back in the house. Old clothes, books, even stuffed animals from when I was a kid.

Everything was still here, untouched. Which meant—

I walked to the closet. It was packed. It took me a few minutes of pulling things out to get at the loose floorboard in the back of the closet. The shoebox, dust-coated and battered, was still inside.

Right at the top was a small cloth bag. I loosened the drawstring and turned it out onto my palm. The white knucklebone was cold against my skin. My good-luck charm. My talisman. My curse.

I'd left it here, like leaving it would mean she wouldn't haunt me.

I set it on the carpet and took out the others. Liv's bone in its earring case, tucked in my pocket. Cass's, in the bag at the bottom of the box. I laid them carefully next to each other. *Hecate, Artemis, Athena.* The prayer, the flowers, the burial, the water. The blood and the fire. Six rituals, when there should have been seven. We'd never reached the end.

I turned to the box again. What else had been important enough to hide? A geode, a feather, a few photographs: of Liv, of Cass. An overwrought self-portrait, eleven-year-old me looking off to the side, her face unmarked by the tragedy that she had no idea was about to strike.

And—God. A photo of Persephone herself. The bones, with lilies in the eye sockets and our trinkets arrayed around her. The photographic twin to the drawings in Liv's sketchbook.

"You seem like you could use a drink," my dad said. I jumped, scrambling around. My back hit the wall before I could claw back a semblance of conscious control. He laughed. "You're such a jumpy little thing."

"Fuck," I said, rubbing the back of my head. Like I needed another head injury. "You know you're not supposed to sneak up on me like that."

"Didn't think I was." He stepped into the room and held out a beer. I leaned forward to take it, then settled back against the wall again. It tasted like stale cereal steeped in water, but it was cold. I drank deeply.

"You're not having one?" I asked.

He hooked his thumbs in his belt loops. "Thought maybe I should cut back."

"Yeah, right. Wait, you're serious?"

He shrugged. "About time, don't you think?"

"Past time." I didn't for an instant believe it was going to stick, but as far as I knew it was the first time he'd even bothered with the pretense of trying. "You know you can't go cold turkey. The amount you drink, it could kill you."

"I said cut back, not stop," he said defensively. But he rubbed the back of his neck and looked away. "I know. I'll be careful. I've done it before."

"When?"

"When you got hurt," he said. "I was drunk as a skunk while my girl was bleeding out. Couldn't even be at the hospital while you were in surgery. So I quit. For a while. Didn't last. But I did it."

"I don't remember that."

"You were a bit distracted by all the holes in you," he said with a wry smile.

I gave a low, broken laugh. "Turns out there's a lot of things I don't remember from back then," I said.

"That right?" he asked. There was an uncomfortable note to his voice.

"Dad, were you there when the police talked to me? When I identified Stahl?" I asked.

"Of course," he said.

"What was it like? What did I say?" I asked.

"They showed you some pictures. They asked you if you saw the man who attacked you, and you pointed him out. Simple enough."

"But did they seem like they were pressuring me?" I asked. "Influencing me at all?"

He sighed. "Shit, Naomi. You were so drugged up that if they showed you a picture of a man in a red suit you would have said Santa Claus stabbed you."

"Dad. Please. Tell me what happened."

"They did it clean," he said. "Had a bunch of photos and showed them to you one by one. You picked him out right away and started crying."

"You're sure?"

"Why would I lie about that?" he asked, but he didn't quite look at me. "Thing is, though. When you woke up, I asked you if you remembered anything, and you didn't. You remembered getting hurt, but that was it. Then right before the detectives came to talk to you, I went down to get some food. When I came back, Chief Miller and Jim Green were coming out of your room. After, you were acting scared, and you kept promising you'd remember and do it right."

"They coached me," I said. Or threatened me. I thought of the sense of doom that had hung over me, the conviction that something truly horrible would happen if I ever faltered. I'd never been able to pinpoint exactly who had said the words that convinced me that horrible things awaited if I messed up. I couldn't imagine what kind of pressure had been on Liv and Cass—the ones who actually knew enough to be a danger.

"That doesn't mean you were wrong," he said. "Besides, it's not like it matters now."

"Of course it matters," I said. "Stahl didn't attack me. That means someone else did. You're sure it was Jim Green in there with Miller?" I wasn't sure whether that made Jim the more likely suspect. He'd done plenty of covering up for Oscar—I doubted attacking me would be enough to break that loyalty.

"I'm sure," he said. He rasped his thumbnail over the stubble just below his mouth in short, nervous strokes. "You don't think he could have had anything to do with it?"

"Do you have a reason to think he did?" I asked.

An animal skittered along the roof above us. He took his time in answering and the words came one by one, like slotting beads on a string. "Well. There was the money," he said.

"What money?"

"For the trust."

"That was from donations," I said. Checks and dollar bills tucked into Get Well Soon cards. Bigger checks from the interviews Dad did. Pound for pound, my body was at its most valuable wounded.

"Some of it," Dad allowed. His thumbnail picked at one red spot on his lower lip now. "But Jim wanted to help out. Get us back on our feet."

"Dad. How much did he give you?" I asked. *Some* money made sense. We'd needed it, Jim had it.

"Thirty thousand," Dad said, and any assumption of goodwill I'd had withered up into itself. "And he took care of the lawyers and everything."

After the hospital, I'd had a succession of lawyers who were with me whenever I talked to the police. Serving as my "advocates." They made sure I didn't have to answer too many questions, that no one upset me. Or pushed me on my story. And Jim Green had paid for them.

"You think Jim's the one that hurt you," Dad said.

"Not just me," I said. If Jim attacked me, it was because of Jessi. "Can you prove where the money came from?"

"I've got the papers someplace," he said.

"So no, then," I said.

He glared at me. "All that stuff ended up in a box. I know where it is, I just gotta get to it."

"It's fine," I said. "Don't worry about it."

"When Jim gave me that money, I wondered if there was something he didn't want me knowing. But we needed the cash," Dad said. Guilt inflected his voice.

"You thought Jim might've had something to do with it?" I asked.

Dad shifted his weight uncomfortably. "I assumed it was Oscar," he confessed.

"You thought Oscar attacked me and you didn't do anything about it?" I asked, not bothering to hide my disgust.

"What was the point of saying anything? You were alive, and . . . well, that money could give you more of a future than I ever could."

Oscar. I'd had the same thought, of course, but that was because I knew about Jessi. "Why would Oscar go after me? He was a psycho, sure. But it seems extreme," I said leadingly.

"There was that thing with you and Cody," Dad said.

"You knew about that?"

"I knew a bit," Dad said. "Oscar was hassling you and Cody beat the shit out of him."

I huffed a breath. "He deserved worse."

"Worse would have killed him," Dad replied matter-of-factly. "If Marsha hadn't called Miller, I'm not sure Cody would have stopped before that boy was dead."

"It wasn't— That wasn't what happened," I said. Except I didn't know, did I? Cody told me to run. I thought the fight was over by then.

"Cody was still on him when Miller got there," Dad said. "Cody told us why he'd done it, but Miller talked me out of making a stink. Convinced me that Oscar got his comeuppance already. I told him I just wished I'd gotten to watch."

I'd thought Oscar was just avoiding me after that. I smirked a little. Yeah, he deserved it. "Why wasn't Cody arrested?" I asked.

"Big Jim pulled strings for him," Dad said. "I think he could see

Cody was starting to turn himself around. Had a chance to make something of himself—as long as he didn't have a felony on his record. Anyway, Oscar going after you might've made some sense after that. If he blamed you."

I nodded. There was violence in him, always. I had tasted it on his skin: salty sweat and bottomless rage at the world. I had felt it in his hands, his fingers when they gripped tight enough to dent my thighs, to bruise my arms. His was a violence of claiming. He could kill me. Every time I had set my teeth to the skin of his throat I had known he could and he would if he wanted to.

In the end, he'd found better ways to destroy me. To ruin the thing Cody wanted to protect.

And Liv? Could he have killed her, too? Absolutely, I thought—if he'd found out she was going to tell the truth about that day. But how would he have known?

I couldn't shake the image of Ethan, pointing that gun at her head. It would have been so easy to lay all of this misery at Oscar's feet, or Jim's, but I couldn't assume I was looking for one killer. Ethan's reasons for being angry with us hadn't changed.

"What's the point in all of this, Naomi?" Dad asked. "You're talking about ancient history. You deserve better than getting dragged around through this stuff again. You should get back to making pretty pictures of fancy people." It was possibly the most supportive thing he'd ever said to me.

"You're a really terrible father," I said, matter-of-fact. "You know that, right?"

"Of course I know it. I'm dumb but I'm not stupid," he said. "It's not like you're winning Daughter of the Year prizes yourself."

"Oh, fuck off."

"Same to you."

I saluted him with my beer and took a long swig. It was already warming up in my hand.

Dad pursed his lips. "You know, I've been thinking. I could use some help around here. Tidy up a bit, you know. Just so that lady cop stops complaining."

"You really think you can part with this stuff?" I asked.

"Most of it's junk anyhow," he grumbled. "There's just too much of it to do it myself." He inspected the carpet at his shoes.

"I can help. I will," I said. "If you're willing, I mean."

"Maybe we'll even find my #1 Dad mug in here somewhere," he joked.

"Could be," I allowed. I knew it didn't mean anything. He'd said that sort of thing before, and it only ever lasted until the first trash bag came out. But saying it mattered. Wanting it mattered. "Dad, I don't know what to do," I confessed.

"You should rest," Dad said. "I may be a shitty dad, but I know when a person's too licked to stand. Take a goddamn nap or something. I'll go get us some dinner."

He stumped his way out of the room. The door didn't quite close behind him, bouncing open when it hit the corner of a cardboard box.

I stood and walked to the window. It faced out back, toward the scraggle of trees, a trailer overgrown with blackberry vines, the rusted skeleton of a bicycle. I drank as much of the beer as I could stomach and set it on the sill, next to the brittle body of a dead fly.

The door creaked. "Did you need cash or something?" I said, turning. But it wasn't Dad.

It was Ethan. My body tensed all at once with an instant awareness of the cage around me. Four walls, one door, the window too rusted to open easily. Ethan, rangy and tall, filling the only exit. Fear was a hand holding tight to the back of my neck.

"What are you doing here?" I asked. I shifted away from the window, trying to get an angle on the door. Like maybe I could run for it, get past him.

For a second, the expression on his face was puzzlement—then understanding washed over him. "You know, don't you?"

"I asked you what you're doing here," I said. I groped behind me and found only the foot of the bed. I gripped it until my knuckles sparked with pain.

"I was looking for you. I couldn't find you anywhere and then I saw your car here, and the door was open," he said. "You never came back. No one would tell me where you were."

"Get out of here," I said. It came out a pleading whisper.

"Why?" Ethan asked. He knew why. A muscle feathered in his jaw.

"Were you just fucking with me?" I asked. Anger surged through me. "Did you think it was funny, sleeping with the woman who put your dad in prison?"

"I didn't mean for that to happen," Ethan said. "You were the one who—"

"If I had known who you were, I would never have let you touch me."

Ethan stepped forward. I stumbled back, and the backs of my thighs hit the mattress. There was nowhere to run. He halted, but his weight was canted forward. The air was thick and close in the room. I had to fight for every full breath.

"I just wanted answers," Ethan said. "You wouldn't talk to me if you knew who I was."

"That letter—" I began.

"I shouldn't have sent that. My father was dying. I was angry at him. At myself. At you. I wanted to know the truth, that's all. I never intended to frighten you." He stepped forward again.

"Don't," I said. "Don't come closer."

But he took another step, and now he was within arm's reach. "We both lied, Naomi. You've been lying all along, to everyone."

"Not to you," I bit out. "I trusted you."

He gave a hollow laugh, and I flinched. "You remember what I told you, about that girl I picked up? How she got into my car because she said I seemed trustworthy?"

"I guess we were both idiots," I said, but he kept talking.

"I couldn't stop thinking about how that was what my dad had done. Over and over, he'd gotten women to get into his truck. Got them to trust him. I started driving around at night. Stopping for anyone who looked like they might accept a ride. A lot of them didn't. But I got better at it. I could tell when they'd say yes because they didn't want to seem rude. When I needed to joke. When I needed to be pushy and when I needed to act like I was sorry to have bothered them."

My skin prickled. "Did you hurt them?" I asked.

His lip rose in a snarl. "What do you think, Naomi? Do you think I'd hurt someone like that?"

"I don't know you," I said levelly. My hand still gripped the foot-board. His fingers wrapped around my wrist.

"Are you afraid I'll hurt *you*?" he asked.

"Of course I am," I whispered.

"That's what I'm afraid of. Every minute of every day," he said. "I kept waiting to want to hurt those women. I enjoyed it sometimes. Convincing them. It was like they were puzzles I was solving. But no, Naomi. I've never hurt anyone like that."

I searched his eyes for a lie. His expression was guileless. It would be so, so easy to trust those words. But he'd taught me better. "I destroyed your life," I said. "Of course you want to hurt me." I could feel my pulse fluttering at the hinge of my jaw.

"I could have spared him," Ethan said. He was so close I could feel his breath against my face. "The day you were attacked, I saw him. He was supposed to be on a trip, but he came back early. My mom was out of town. I was staying at a friend's house for the weekend, but I'd forgotten my Game Boy. I biked home to get it, and I saw him. I didn't want to have to come home, so I left without saying hello. He never knew I was there."

"Why didn't you tell the police?" I asked. "Why didn't you tell them I was wrong?"

"Because you saved me," he said. I looked at him in utter bafflement. "If I let you lie, I didn't have to tell anyone what I knew. He would go to prison, and I would never have to admit to what I'd seen."

His fingers were still around my wrist, but the way he gripped me no longer felt like he was holding me still, but like he was anchoring himself. His throat bobbed. His words, when they came, were barbed wire pulled through a wound.

"He'd take me out with him sometimes. Driving around. Sometimes he had someplace to go for work. Other times we just drove. We'd talk, and I'd fall asleep in the back seat. They were some of my favorite memories. And then one time, we came across this woman. She wasn't going to get in but then she saw me in the back, and I guess I made it seem safer. She was nice. Gave me a candy bar. And then I fell asleep. I woke up because I heard a scream. Except maybe it wasn't a scream, maybe I was dreaming. That's what Dad said when he got back in the truck. There was blood on his sleeve. But maybe that didn't mean anything."

For the first time, he looked away. His fingers had tightened by degrees around my wrist until pain thrummed dully beneath them, but I didn't pull away.

"I knew something bad had happened. I didn't realize exactly what until he was arrested."

"You told me you were sure that Stahl was a murderer," I said. I hadn't understood his insistence, not when the evidence was so ambiguous. Now it made horrible sense.

"That was years before he was arrested," Ethan said raggedly. "He killed three women in that time. Probably more. If I'd told someone, maybe they would still be alive. But I couldn't. So when you lied, I didn't say anything. I'm not angry that you sent my father to prison, Naomi. I'm grateful. You did what I wasn't brave enough to do. I never wanted to hurt you. I only wanted to understand."

"And do you?" I asked, scraped empty. "Did you get what you wanted from me?"

"Naomi, please," he said, two thin words splitting open with the weight of all they contained.

"Get out of here," I told him.

"Please." His hand moved down my wrist, fingers sliding under my palm. I pulled my hand away from his. We stood, inches apart, not touching. My fear was gone. Only the electric pulse of anger remained. Every man I'd slept with had been a mistake of one kind or another. The mistake was the point. You couldn't let someone in without it breaking you, but you could choose the way you broke.

It shouldn't hurt like this. It shouldn't feel like this, unless I had felt something I never let myself feel.

His fingertips brushed the hollow of my throat. He pressed his brow against mine and I let him, a feeling that wasn't quite pain spilling over my skin, tracing the patterns of my scars.

I wrapped his shirt around my fist. I kissed him roughly, my teeth on his lip, his fingers digging into my shoulder in a startled grip, and I pulled him back, pulled him down.

It was rough and fast, anger and hunger and pain. I turned my face away and broke apart, and the cracks were beautiful across my skin.

I twisted out from under Ethan as soon as it was done. We hadn't used a condom, and I swore quietly as I cleaned myself off and yanked my underwear back on.

"Naomi," Ethan said. I hated the sound of my name in his mouth. The way he said it so tenderly, like he was afraid that if he pressed it would split like overripe fruit.

I turned back to him. He sat on the edge of the bed, those earnest eyes searching mine. "Get out," I told him.

"I thought—"

"I want you to leave, Ethan." He'd lied to me. Lied and manipulated and made me trust him. Made me feel for him. I was done. I knew the map of my scars again, the ones you could see and the ones under the surface, and now I was finished.

I watched him get dressed. He avoided my eyes. He stopped one more time in the doorway and looked like he might say something, but he thought better of it. I listened to his footsteps until they reached the front door. Listened to his engine start up and the tires crunch away down the gravel drive.

My body echoed with the ghost of his touch. I had lost nothing, I told myself. A man I'd known for a few days, who turned out not to even really exist.

The mirrored back of the closet doors threw a hash-marked reflection back at me. Some of the scars had blurred and faded. Others remained as ridges and knots. I ran my fingers over them in a roaming inventory.

Ribs—two. Chest—three. Stomach—six. Arms—four. Face—one. I turned to see the single knot of scar tissue on my back, below my left shoulder blade.

It took a long time to stab someone seventeen times. You had to be focused. Or you had to be in such a manic rage that the seconds blurred.

I tried to picture it. Jim seeing me crawl up out of that hole, realizing what it meant. Coming up behind me.

Jim Green was a lifelong Chester native. He did the things men of Chester were supposed to do. He drank hard, worked an honest job, hated liberals, went hunting on the weekends. Jim Green knew how to take a knife to a still-kicking deer and stop its struggling.

I imagined his hand in my hair. Saw the knife swiped once across my throat. Or driven in through my spine. Quick, clean, and finished.

These were not the scars of an execution. This was rage. The person who did this to me wanted me to suffer. Oscar, then.

*He would have wanted you to see him.* The thought came unbidden, but once it arrived I couldn't shake it. Oscar would have wanted me to know it was him and be afraid. To wrap his hands around my throat and feel the fragile crumpling of bones.

I told myself I was being ridiculous. He wouldn't have cared whether he killed me with a knife or by strangling me. He'd just wanted to obliterate me.

I pulled my dress on. Tires on gravel signaled another arrival, but by the time I shoved my feet into my shoes to see who it was, Dad was calling.

"You still here?"

I stepped out into the hall. He gave my disheveled appearance a good looking-over. "Passed that Ethan Schreiber fellow on the way up the drive," he said.

"He won't be coming back," I replied.

"Huh," was all he said. He reached into his pocket, pulled out a folded piece of paper. "Stopped by the bank while I was waiting on the food. Thought I'd get you those records. From the trust."

I walked forward leadenly and took it from him. It was a statement from when the trust was set up, and there it was—a thirty-thousand-dollar lump sum. "I thought you said the money was from Jim Green," I said.

"Sure, because it was. He offered, I said yes, the money arrived. Simple."

"This payment isn't from Jim. It's from Green Mountain Solutions," I said.

"I guess he did it through some company. That's one of his, isn't it?"

"Wrong kind of Green. Green Mountain Services is the name of the Barneses' old consulting company," I said. I stared at the words like they might rearrange themselves into something that made more sense. Marcus Barnes had paid us off, but Jim Green had claimed credit? How did that make any sense? If either one of them had done it, they wouldn't be covering for the other. They hated each other. Famously. "You didn't know?"

"I wasn't exactly detail-oriented at the time," he said, shuffling his feet.

Marcus Barnes. It didn't make any sense. My mind reeled. Could it have been *Marcus* in the woods? But what possible reason would he have to attack me? None of it made any sense, and I couldn't *remember*. I must have seen something. I must have heard something, sensed something—but it was all lost in the fog.

Or maybe I just hadn't tried hard enough, too afraid to go back to that place. Too afraid to remember.

"Where are you off to?" my father asked. I was already past him, already on my way out the door.

"I have to go," I said.

"I got that part," he grumbled, but I didn't indulge him. If I stopped, if I faltered, I would fall apart.

I had to go back to the start.

———

Light lay like fragile lace across the trees, afternoon tumbling into evening. I didn't follow the trail this time. I walked off the path and

straight in among the trees in my funeral dress. I was past sense. Past
logic. I wanted a magical incantation that would sort the world into its
proper order. I did not want to reach the end of the road I was traveling
and find what was waiting there. I wanted to go back. Back before I'd
seen that piece of paper, back before I knew Ethan had lied, back before
the blade made constellations of scars on my skin.

So let me go back to the beginning. Let me stand in the woods
where I'd bled, where I'd almost died, and let me unweave everything
that had followed.

Start again.

This time, I walked as if I knew exactly where I was going. Past
the hidden places where we'd tucked our treasures, past the props and
backdrops of our dramas. Our voices echoed through the trees, and my
own ghost walked beside me. I stumbled in my sensible heels, the wet
of the woods seeping in and leaving my feet numb, but I never slowed.

Here. This had been the spot, more or less. I'd been sitting on that
rock, eating my lunch. We'd had some little argument again, Cass needling me with insults guaranteed to make me run or make me fight.
This time I'd chosen to run. I'd sat alone, stewing on my anger and
eating my peanut butter sandwich, and then—

But the memories shredded into the same confusion as ever. Stahl's
face falsely imprinted over reality. Ragged gaps where pain had oblit-
erated all else. The babble of voices—Cass's and Liv's, the voices of res-
cuers, weaving in and out of each other impossibly, without any sense
of time line.

I strode blindly away from the clearing, chasing my ghost backward through memory. The slip of a girl in her oversized sweatshirt,
marching angrily through the woods. Clambering out from under the
boulder.

They'd been here. I lay on my stomach and wriggled through the
gap, and then I turned back, peering out at the woods. You could just
see the rock where I'd sat. Where the attack had started. They would

have been able to see it—see all of it. Oscar or Big Jim or Marcus Barnes, whoever it had been.

I turned away and wrapped my arms around my knees. The sun slanted down on Persephone's bones. Jessi's bones, I reminded myself. She was never Persephone. She was never anything but a corpse. She couldn't protect us, couldn't heal the wounds of the world the way Cass claimed she could. The way we tried so hard to believe that she would, if only we did what she asked of us.

Liv had believed it most of all, as she always did. And looking back, she was the one who needed to believe it. It wasn't the world that needed fixing, it was her. And Cass had promised her that Persephone would give her the kind of peace she so desperately needed.

And so we'd done the rituals. We'd made the offerings. And all along, she'd been just some poor dead girl who'd dreamed of escape just like we did.

I picked up a string of beads, flinging them angrily away from the skeleton. We'd turned her into this *thing*, an altar for our own unhappiness. We'd never treated her like a person. Like someone who would be mourned and missed. If we'd told someone what we'd found, her family might have answers by now.

Liv might still be alive.

I clawed at the other offerings. Moldering playing cards, a brooch, an earring missing its mate, four wave-polished stones. I gathered them all, moving first mechanically, then with manic energy, shoving them into a pile at the back of the little cave.

I grabbed something smooth and wooden. At first I thought it was just a stick, something that had fallen down here among the bones, but then my thumb brushed against a bit of metal. I looked at it in the slanting light. It was a folding knife. I flicked it open. The blade was caked with something dark. The wood was stained with it, too.

My breath hitched. We'd never left a knife here. It wasn't the sort of thing Persephone would have liked.

I lifted the edge of my shirt, and set the tip of the blade against my skin. Against the ridge of scar tissue just below my ribs.

If I'd been dead, they might have been able to make casts of my wounds and learn exactly what shape the blade had been, but inconveniently, they'd had to stitch up my flesh, had to widen some of the cuts to operate and to check that nerves hadn't been damaged. The exact blade had remained a mystery, so they couldn't match it to any of Stahl's preferred weapons. *Not inconsistent* had been the most they could prove.

I turned the knife in my hands. There was something stamped into the wood at the base. A maker's mark: two Japanese characters inside a circle. I knew this knife. I'd watched Kimiko pull it out of her pocket countless times, to prune a tomato vine or slice open a bag of fertilizer. She took good care of her tools. She kept her knives sharp. A dull blade was more dangerous than a sharp one, she would say. A sharp blade cut what it was meant to cut; a dull blade slipped and cut you instead.

Liv and Cass were the only ones down here. They had hidden, and they had watched it happen.

Except that wasn't right, was it?

They were the only ones down here. The only ones here at all.

Seventeen times I'd been stabbed. Chest and stomach and ribs. Seventeen times, and I hadn't died. A miracle, they always said. Had it been rage that led my attacker to plunge the knife in over and over?

Or had it been because they weren't strong enough to finish me off?

If a man the size of Jim Green, of Alan Stahl, of Oscar Green—or even of Marcus Barnes—had wielded that knife, I would not have been granted the centimeter's grace that kept my heart from being punctured.

Maybe I hadn't survived out of pure luck. Maybe I'd survived because the hand wielding the knife didn't have the strength of those men at all.

I shut my eyes and tried to remember. The blow from behind. The pale sky, my vision blurring. Liv and Cass above me. Shouting. Screaming.

The knife. This knife. Coming down again and again. But the shouting and the screaming, those came after. Didn't they?

Cass, shouting. Liv, weeping.

The knife, flashing. The knife coming down. The screaming and the shouting and the knife, all of it at once, and then silence. Pain and silence and the impossibility of breath.

"Is she dead?"

I didn't know whose voice it had been.

My fingernails dug into the flesh beside the scar on my wrist, memories writhing out of reach.

They'd said they stayed quiet. They watched Stahl attack me, and they hid, because if they made a sound he'd come after them, too. So the shouting had to be after he left. After the knife.

But it wasn't. I'd heard them shouting, screaming, as the knife came down. They hadn't been hiding. They hadn't been hiding, and Marcus Barnes had given my father thirty thousand dollars and never looked me in the face again, and why would he do that? Who would he have done that for, except his only daughter?

Seventeen blows. You had to be angry, to do a thing like that. Filled with hatred. Or fear, and the horrible grip of a delusion that felt like the most powerful truth in the world.

Liv said we'd never finished. We'd done six rituals that summer. We'd never gotten around to the seventh. Cass said we had to think of something big for the final one. Something dramatic. And Liv had been consumed by the thought of it—by the game and the Goddesses. Her illness was a wildfire, and the game was the spark that set it ablaze.

Liv had thought her death would complete that unfinished final ritual. What ritual could be completed by death except a sacrifice?

I couldn't breathe—didn't want to. I didn't want to draw breath in a world where this could be true. Not Liv.

Liv was my best friend. She was troubled, but she had never been violent. The only risk she had posed was to herself. To our too-often broken hearts. Not to me. Never to me.

My certainty fractured. I couldn't remember. My memories had been too firmly overwritten with lies; I couldn't trust them. *Wouldn't.* Because if there was the tiniest sliver of doubt, the smallest chance that Liv had nothing to do with what had happened, I couldn't believe it. I wouldn't betray her like that.

Whatever had happened in these woods, we weren't the only three who would have had to lie to keep up the fiction that my attacker was Stahl. Cass could have lied through her teeth until the day she died, but Liv?

She couldn't have kept those secrets on her own. She would have needed people to protect her. Shield her. Coach her. Marcus Barnes would have known. Kimiko, too, probably.

I couldn't condemn my best friend based on the murky memories I could dredge up. I needed to be sure. I needed to talk to Olivia's parents.

I put the knife in my pocket and walked back toward the road.

I sat on the Barneses' porch, still in my funeral wear, my black dress caked liberally with dirt, my ruined shoes beside me on the step. I had been there fifteen minutes or so when they pulled up. I stood, watching them, as Marcus got out of the driver's seat and Kimiko stepped out of the passenger side. She started forward. Marcus put out a hand, said something I couldn't catch. She waited by the car as he came up the walkway.

Marcus stopped a few steps away. "Naomi," he said. He took in the dirt, the scratches on my arms, the state of my shoes. "You shouldn't be here."

I had practiced a speech on my way here. Words of confrontation and reproach. Eloquent and angry. But now my throat closed tight. All I could do was hold out my hand, the folded knife balanced on my palm.

He stepped forward and took it gingerly from my palm, brushing the dirt from it. "What is this?" he asked.

"You know what it is," I croaked.

He balanced it in both hands, inspecting it like an artifact. "You're a mess, Naomi. You should go home."

"Was Liv the one who hurt me?" I asked.

"Alan Stahl hurt you. You saw him yourself," Marcus said evenly. Too evenly.

"Stop," I said. I stood. My vision blurred with tears I refused to shed in front of him. "I'm done being lied to. And I'm done lying."

"Whatever you think you know, I can't help you," Marcus said.

"No." Kimiko stood behind him. Her gray hair had been wrenched back in a bun for the funeral, its flyaway strands unnaturally tamed. She looked not at me, but at her husband. "It has gone on long enough."

"Nothing good can come of this," Marcus said, and though he was still looking at the knife, he was speaking to both of us. "Leave it alone. Let her rest."

"Our daughter is dead," Kimiko said. "Naomi is still alive, and she deserves to know what happened."

I had hoped that I was wrong. That I had spun some dark fairy tale out of paranoia and grief. That hope crumpled in the face of Kimiko's weary expression, the defeat in her voice.

Marcus folded his hand around the knife, as if it could make it vanish. "It wasn't her fault," he said.

A sob ripped free of me. My knees went weak; I stumbled. Marcus stepped forward quickly and caught me, steadying me, but I thrashed away from him. "Don't touch me!" I shouted, slapping at his hands. "Don't fucking touch me!"

"Naomi, I'm sorry. I'm so sorry," he said. "We didn't— We never—"

"We need to go inside," Kimiko said, coming up behind him. Her lips were pressed in a thin, hard line. She seemed scabbed over with sorrow. "We will tell you everything, but we need to go inside."

I allowed myself to be gently herded through the door, moving in a haze. In moments I was on the couch, a huge marmalade cat bumping his head against my elbow. I sank my fingers into his fur and he kneaded my thigh with enthusiasm.

Kimiko set a cup of tea in front of me. Marcus stood hovering by the mantel, the knife in his hands, turning it over and over. Kimiko took a seat in the chair opposite me, perching on the edge. "You must understand that we did what we felt was best for our daughter," Kimiko said. "We had to protect her. Telling the truth would not have helped anyone. It would not have helped her get the treatment that she needed, it would have destroyed her."

Liv had attacked me. This was the truth, then: an iron nail swallowed whole, the taste of blood and ruin. My throat worked as if to reject it, but it was lodged deep within me. It couldn't be true. She wouldn't have hurt me. Not Liv. She was too kind, too gentle. This couldn't be right.

"We had no idea that Olivia was suffering such strong delusions. She had become convinced that Persephone required a major sacrifice, or something horrible would happen to everyone she loved," Marcus said. "That game you were playing just fed into her illness until it overtook her. She thought she was saving you. Saving everyone."

"You knew about Persephone?" I asked. "Did you know that Liv was trying to find out who she was?"

"What do you mean, who she was? She was part of your game," Kimiko said. "The Goddess Game."

They didn't know about the body. "Who else knew?" I asked slowly. "Cass did, obviously. What about her parents?"

"Jim and Meredith knew," Marcus said, voice tight. "Cass had already lied. There would have been trouble for them. Dougherty had already seized on Stahl. It was Jim who realized we should use that. We could help Liv and stop a serial killer. It was the perfect solution. Jim thought—he agreed that it would only make things worse, if we told the truth."

No, I thought, that wasn't why Jim had come up with his brilliant, perfect solution. He hadn't done it for Liv. He hadn't done it to cover up Cass's panicked lie, something that people would have understood readily enough, would have excused with time. He did it because of Jessi.

I could see the threads now. The line that ran from Jessi Walker to me to Olivia. Three of us in the woods. Our blood spilled. Big Jim had killed Jessi. And when Cass told him what had happened, told him about Persephone, he realized that he was going to be in trouble when people learned that Jessi hadn't just moved on. So: the first lie, and all the ones that followed.

"You were the only wrinkle," Marcus was saying. "We had no idea what you would say when you woke up. But you didn't remember anything—and you were so drugged up. We just kept telling you what had happened, and you accepted it. You even seemed to remember it that way. We never wanted to harm you, Naomi. We were so grateful that you were okay."

"You let me stay friends with her," I said dully.

"She loved you, Naomi. She really believed that Persephone was going to take you to the underworld and then bring you back. She thought she was *helping* you." Marcus's tone was pleading.

I touched my cheek, the side of my face twisted in a permanent grimace. He dropped his eyes.

"She wanted to tell you. There were many times when she wanted to tell everyone the truth and face the consequences," Kimiko said. "Eight years ago, when she tried to kill herself, she said that she was tired of lying."

*I'm tired of lying.* Why did that sound familiar?

"*I hurt Naomi,*" Kimiko said, Liv's voice an echo on her lips. She stared into the distance, her hand holding her cardigan shut at her chest. "It was the only thing she said for almost three days."

"Liv was basically catatonic at the hospital," Marcus added. "They were both covered in blood. There was so much blood." He looked pale at the memory.

Silence settled between us. It lingered, long enough for the conversation to wither, for any sense of connection between us to vanish, until each of us in that room was truly, utterly, alone.

"Naomi, what are you going to do?" Kimiko asked.

I didn't answer. I didn't have an answer. I gave the marmalade cat one last scratch behind the ears, and I walked out, leaving them to their grief and guilt and fear.

I had reached the end. Or my end, at least. I couldn't do this by
myself anymore. I didn't even know what I was searching for, why I'd
thought that the answers I found would bring me some kind of peace.
So Jim was a killer and Liv had almost become one, and there was no
*truth* in any of that. Only sorrow.

The time for keeping secrets was over. I couldn't hold off any longer—
I needed to go to the police. I had to tell them everything.

But I couldn't just walk in there. Not when it was the mayor I was
accusing of murdering a girl—never mind the fact that I'd lied all these
years and sent a man to prison for the wrong crime. I had no idea what
kind of consequences I was facing. I needed help, and there was no one
left to help me.

No—that wasn't true.

Cody Benham's business card was in my glove box. I cast around
blindly for a minute before I remembered that my phone was long gone,
thanks to Jessup Consulting. Instead, I drove until I found a pay phone
at the edge of town, next to a bulletin board warning about keeping
food where bears could get at it. I dialed the number with shaking
hands. He picked up on the second ring with a distracted hello.

"Cody." I gulped against a rising surge of panic.

"Naomi? What's wrong?" he asked, voice sharp with concern.

"At the station, you said that you could help me find a lawyer," I said.
I braced myself, forcing the words out. "Well, I think I could really use

one right about now." I bit back a hysterical laugh and dug a thumbnail into my wrist.

"Are you in trouble?" Cody asked, low and serious.

"I don't know. I don't—" My voice broke off in a sob. "I'm not sure where to even start answering that question."

"Everything's going to be okay," he said, quiet and steady. "Where are you?"

"I don't know. I . . ." I forced myself to focus, look around. "I'm near the Anderson loop trail, I think."

"Good. All right, stay put. I'm going to come to you. Okay?"

"Okay," I said, relief flooding through me. I leaned my forehead against the pay phone's housing.

"We'll figure this out," he promised. "Don't go anywhere."

"I'll be here."

———

The rain had blurred the world outside the car to an indistinct haze of green by the time the SUV pulled up beside me. I clambered out and went over to the passenger side, sliding into the seat next to Cody. "Thanks for meeting me," I said quietly.

"I would have invited you over to the house, but Gabriella is in bed with a headache and a backache and a number of other aches that are all somehow my fault," Cody said. I chuckled like I was in on the joke, but right now domestic bliss seemed more of a fanciful daydream than the goddesses and unicorns of my childhood. "You sounded pretty rough on the phone. What's going on?"

I hunched over, wishing that I'd thought to change into something more substantial than a cotton dress. I couldn't answer at first, but he just put a hand on my shoulder.

"You said you need a lawyer," Cody pressed gently. "Is this about Liv?"

"It's hard to know where to begin," I said. A bird, rendered into a streak of brown by the rainy windows, flashed past. "I keep thinking it started that summer, but it was earlier than that. It didn't even start with me."

"What didn't?"

We'd kept the secret so long. It had seemed impossible to tell anyone, but now I couldn't remember why. I'd told Ethan, and maybe that had been enough to make it easier to tell again, but I didn't think that was really it. It was never that the secret was too powerful to speak. It was only ever that we didn't want to. Too selfish and too timid to even try. Now the words came easily. They'd been there all along.

"That summer, we found something," I said. The wind moved the trees in a gentle undulation, and the sound of the rain was like static, drowning out the rest of the world. "It was a skeleton. A human skeleton. We should have told someone, but instead we made it our secret. We called her Persephone, and we visited her every day. We brought her offerings. We did things for her. It was a game, but it wasn't. We believed."

He made a sound, a startled *huh*, half swallowed like he didn't want to interrupt me.

"After the attack, we kept that secret. We kept it for years. But Liv couldn't live with it. She wanted to find out who Persephone really was. And she did. Her name was Jessi Walker."

A breath went out of him. "That's why you were asking about her," he said. I nodded. "You knew where she was the whole time?"

"She wasn't real to us. Not that way," I said. "We didn't know it was Jessi."

"But when you asked me about her. You knew then."

"I knew. Yes," I said. "I'm sorry I didn't tell you. I wanted more answers first."

He looked away. Silence held for three seconds, four. When he spoke his voice was hoarse. "We hadn't been talking much. At all, really. Not for days. She was angry with me."

"Why?"

"The guy she was seeing. I tried to get her to tell me who it was, but she'd just tease me with it. I knew he was bad news. I tried to get her to break it off. To be honest, I was more than a little in love with her. And because of that, I didn't exactly go about it delicately. The things we said to each other . . . Well. It wasn't surprising that she wouldn't bother to say goodbye. But I never thought . . . You're sure. You're sure it's her."

"She had a bracelet with her niece's name on it," I said. "Everything matches up. The night she left, she never got out of Chester."

"Ah." He rubbed his hand over his mouth. "Ah. I see."

"The person she was seeing was Big Jim," I said, pushing on. "He told her he was going to leave Meredith for her. I think that they argued. I think that he killed her—or Oscar did, because he was jealous. Maybe it was an accident. I don't know. But she died, and she's in those woods."

"You're talking about the mayor. And his son. You'd better be sure before you go after them," Cody said, looking at me.

"I'm as sure as I can get on my own," I said. "I need to tell the police. About Jessi, and . . ." And the rest of it. A part of me still wished the rest could stay silent. No one would have to know what Liv had done. Or what I had done. But I knew that if I kept any piece of this silence, I would never be free of it.

"You have to be careful about how you approach this. Jim's got a lot of power in this town. And yeah, you definitely want a good lawyer. Hiding a body . . ."

"I know it's awful. We were awful. There was so much happening, and then before it seemed like it had been long enough that we could say something, it had turned into too late to say anything. But we should have told. We should have."

Cody put his hand over mine, and I realized that I had been thumping my fist rhythmically against my thigh, over and over. "It's going to be okay," he promised me.

I looked at him helplessly. "I'm sorry to drag you into this," I said. "You've done so much for me already, and all I've done is lie and . . ."

"Don't," Cody said. "You don't need to apologize. I'm glad you came to me. We're going to figure this out. You and me. Just sit tight, and I'll make some calls."

I nodded. I didn't trust myself to speak. He shifted to put his arm around my shoulders and pressed his lips to my forehead, warm against the chill of my rain-slicked skin.

"I'm going to take care of this," he said. And then he opened the door and stepped out of the car, pulling his phone from his pocket. I scrunched down in the seat as he paced away, already putting the phone to his ear. He should be home with his wife, not dredging up old tragedies and calling in favors to protect the fuck-up kid he used to know.

The effort to keep myself from crying had left my eyes blurry and my nose snotted up. I groped around for something I could use as a tissue, hoping for takeout napkins. Nothing. I tried the glove box, but all that was in there was the owner's manual and a phone.

My phone.

The gray cover, cracked at the corner. The peony sticker I'd used to cover up the scorch mark where I'd accidentally held it too close to one of the thousand and one rose-pink candles a bride had insisted on. It was my phone, no question. The one that Jessup Consulting had stolen. And it was in Cody Benham's glove box.

Cody had his back to me, talking intently. I couldn't hear what he was saying from inside the car.

What was Cody doing with my phone? Jessup Consulting had it. He'd have to have gotten it from them.

Cody was starting to head back. I shoved the phone in my skirt pocket and closed the glove compartment with my knee. Cody got in, shaking rain from his hair. "I left a message with the law firm I work with. Their criminal defense attorneys are top-notch. They'll be able to advise you. They're sending someone up first thing tomorrow."

"Okay," I said automatically. My tears had dried, but my breath came sharp and quick. Why did Cody Benham have my phone? It didn't make any sense. Unless.

It took effort to drag myself over the rocks of that *unless*. Unless I'd been wrong. Unless Cody had a reason for keeping an eye on someone who was digging into the past. Finding out exactly what I knew and what Liv might have told me.

"She's really in there?" Cody asked, eyes on the woods.

"Yeah," I said, barely a whisper. "She's in there."

"I always thought . . . I don't know. I liked to imagine what kind of a life she was leading. She was so vibrant," he said. "I guess part of me knew that she didn't have a happy ending. But she was here the whole time?" He sounded lost. He sounded bereft. And I knew liars. He wasn't faking that desolation.

He was Cody Benham. He'd protected me all my life. There had to be an explanation.

"Could you show me?" he asked. He looked at me, imploring. "Could you take me to her? I need to see her."

I did not want to be afraid of Cody, but I was. "I don't know if . . ." I let the thought trail off.

"It's near where I found you, right?" Cody asked. "Near where you were attacked. That's why you were out there?" A nod. He started the car. "It's not far, then."

I gripped the door handle. "You want to go now?"

"If we're going to go, it has to be now," he said. He was already backing up. I could jump out of the car, but then what? There was no one out here. We were alone. And there had to be an explanation. I knew Jim had hired Jessup Consulting. If they'd given Jim the phone, and he'd given it to Cody—but why would he?

"Once you talk to the police, they're going to block it off. They're going to gather her up and take her away. I want to see her before then, Naomi."

"Right," I said, and it was too late now. We were in motion, tires hissing on the wet asphalt. I reached into my pocket and held down the power button on my phone. I had no idea if it turned on. If it had any battery left.

Cody pulled off the road not at the trailhead, but at a small pull-out. The trees shielded the car from the road, keeping it hidden from casual observers. But that wasn't why he'd parked here, I told myself. He parked there because it was the closest place to where I'd been attacked. He knew these woods as well as I did.

Not quite as well, maybe.

We got out of the car. The rain had let up some, but the air still had a bite to it. My dress did little to protect me from the chill.

"Which way?" Cody asked.

I stared at him. I didn't want to believe that he would do anything to me. But the dread in my chest made every breath ache.

I oriented myself. "This way," I said. I angled toward the pond trail. If I could get there, there was at least a chance there would be another human being nearby. And even the chance of it might be some protection.

I still couldn't bring myself to believe I needed protecting from Cody. Not really. "You and Jessi were close?" I asked.

"We were. You remind me a lot of her, actually," he said. "That blend of wounded and untouchable. She didn't have much in the way of support. Her parents were checked out. Her sister had her own kid to worry about, so Jessi was left on her own. And she was managing. But it was messy."

"I can see why I remind you of that," I said. The woods had gone silent with the intrusion of our voices. I wanted to reach into my pocket and check the phone, but Cody was right next to me. "Oscar said that he thought you two might have a thing."

"I certainly would have jumped at the chance. But Jessi wasn't interested."

"I can't imagine choosing Big Jim over you."

"I wasn't such a catch back then," he said with a pained shake of the head. "There was a reason Oscar and I were friends. I spent every weekend drunk off my ass. Most of the week, too. Trust me, I wasn't boyfriend material. If it hadn't been for you, I don't know if I ever could have gotten Gabriella to give me as much as a second glance."

"What did I have to do with it?" I asked.

"I always wanted to protect you," he said. "You were like the little sister I always wanted. Seeing you there, all torn up, and then realizing that you were still breathing—it was like something in me broke and then came back together whole all in the same moment. I promised myself I'd keep looking after you, as much as I could."

The boulder was just up ahead. Another few steps and it would be in sight. "Is that why you asked Big Jim to have Ethan Schreiber investigated?" I asked. He halted, rocking his weight back. I stopped, arms crossed against the chill, and half turned to face him.

"I thought he was just using you to get a story. I didn't imagine he would end up being Stahl's son."

"Then you knew about that."

"I heard, yeah," he said.

"Why have Big Jim hire them? Why not handle it yourself?" I asked. "You've got to have resources, with your work."

"I didn't want to get directly involved," he said, sounding— embarrassed? "It's sort of like meeting your little sister's boyfriend on the steps with the shotgun, isn't it?"

"Were you having me followed?" I asked. I waited for him to deny it. His mouth opened, shut.

"Why would I have you followed?" he asked at last, unconvincing.

"Someone from Jessup Consulting broke into my hotel room. He stole the data cards out of my camera and took my phone. Not to mention almost breaking my nose."

"I would never send someone to hurt you, Naomi," Cody said, shaking his head. He approached me, step by step, and I held my ground. "If I get my hands on that guy—"

"You'll do to him what you did to Oscar?" I asked, head tilted, looking up at him. He had always protected me. Always. "What about the woods? The first night I was in town. After we had dinner, someone was in the woods watching me."

"You're sounding completely paranoid," Cody said. "Listen to yourself. Why would I do any of the things you're saying? What reason could I possibly have?"

"What happened to Jessi Walker?" I asked.

"I'd put my money on Oscar," he replied. "He's always been violent."

"It explains everything," I acknowledged. "Except why you were having me followed."

He sighed, and I saw him shrug off the first lie like so much dead weight. "Look. Naomi. It wasn't anything nefarious. I was just worried about you, that's all. Liv was dead, and there was something going on between you two. I didn't want anything to happen to you, so I asked Jessup to have someone keep an eye out. That's all."

"Why are we out here, Cody?" I asked. I wanted so badly to be wrong. For my monsters to be simple beasts of violence and hunger.

His fingers flexed at his sides. "I just want to see her one last time."

"Is that what you told Liv?"

"For God's sake, Naomi, listen to yourself. You sound completely insane," Cody said. He paced a few steps away, hand to his mouth. Cool rain drifted down, light as mist, coating my skin. I shivered, but Cody was protected by his coat.

"I changed you, you said. I saved you. Who were you before, that you needed saving from it?" I asked. "Did you hurt Jessi? Were you jealous? Were you in love with her, is that it? You snapped and you hurt her, and—"

"It wasn't like that!" he yelled, spinning. The rage in his eyes—I knew that rage. He was looking at me the way he'd looked at Oscar Green, that day behind the gas station. But he took a breath. Held up his hands, placating. "I'm not going to hurt you, Naomi, okay? I swear, I'm not going to hurt you. I just need you to understand what happened and then we can figure this out. Together."

"You keep saying that. But what are we going to figure out, Cody?" I whispered. My hands cupped my elbows. Shivers trailed down my body.

Cody looked at me with the same wrecked expression that I remembered from twenty years ago, when he lifted me up from where I'd fallen. Older now. Lines in his face that hadn't been there. Gray in his hair. He wasn't that boy, and I wasn't that girl.

"What happened to Jessi was an accident," Cody said.

I let out the breath I'd been holding and shut my eyes. My body saw danger in every shadow, panicked at loud noises and unexpected movements, but now I was oddly calm. The certainty of this danger had a kind of comfort.

"Listen. Naomi, listen, I never wanted to hurt her," Cody said. He crossed the distance to me, hands gripping my arms.

I wobbled in my stupid shoes, and only his grip kept me from tumbling. He looked down at me, and I couldn't tell if there were tears in his eyes or if it was just the rain, clinging to his lashes.

"I loved her. I knew she didn't feel that way about me, but I knew that if I was there for her, eventually she'd realize that she was making a mistake, going after this married guy. But then she told me she was leaving. He was going with her."

"What did you do?" I whispered. "Did you hurt her?"

He shook his head fiercely. "*No*. We fought. *Argued*. We said some things we shouldn't have, but I never touched her," Cody insisted. "It was a few days before she . . . That's why we weren't talking to each other, at the end."

"Then what?" I asked. There was nothing left of me to break. No sorrow, no anger. Only the cold.

"Big Jim called me. It was night. He was at the mill. She was there, too. And she was going ballistic, because she'd finally realized what a piece of crap he was. He was never going to leave Meredith. He was never going to blow up his life for a waitress, for God's sake. She was drunk and she was pissed and she'd scratched the hell out of him, so he called and told me to come get her."

"And you did. Because you wanted to take care of her," I said. "You wanted to make sure she got home safe." Because Cody was a good guy, and that's what good guys did.

His hands dropped down my arms, and he took both of my hands in his, looking down at them. "I picked her up. She was still screaming at him when I got her in the car. She was out of her mind, Naomi. She bought every line he fed her, and he just kept stringing her along."

"She never got home," I said. He shook his head. "What happened, Cody?" I kept my voice gentle. I understood the need for confession. Once you began, it was hard to stop.

"She said she was going to throw up. She told me to pull over," Cody said. "So I did. I held her hair while she puked up all that cheap vodka and then she slapped my hands away. She was screaming like it was my fault. She kept saying I thought she was trash. That she was an idiot. I said something stupid, like I didn't think she was trash but she was definitely acting like it. She tried to hit me. I grabbed her wrist, just to stop her, and maybe I pushed her back a bit, and she was in these strappy heels, and she fell. She hit her head on a rock and she just lay there. She didn't move."

"She was dead?" I asked.

He shook his head. "I thought she was. There was blood—there was a lot of blood. But she opened her eyes. I tried to help her up but she kept hitting me. Calling me names. Saying that she was going to get Miller to arrest me."

"Anyone would lose their temper."

He lifted one finger, as if in warning. "No. Not like that. I didn't hurt her. I was so angry. I wanted to hit her. So I left her there, before I did something I would regret. I walked back to the car and I drove away. That's all. I drove away."

"She had a head injury," I said. "And you left her alone. At night. In the woods."

His expression was contorted with misery. He kept touching me—holding my hands, resting his palms against my arms. Like if he could keep hold of me, I could save him from this. "Only for a few minutes. I needed to calm down. I thought she would, too. But when I went back I couldn't find her. I searched for her, I did. But she was gone. I told myself that she'd hitched a ride. When she didn't come back, I tried to convince myself that she was living her life. Somewhere far away. Somewhere she could be happy."

"But she didn't hitch a ride," I whispered. "She stumbled around in the woods, bleeding into her brain. Pressure building up. She tried to find a place to rest. To get out of the rain. She was so tired, and she just wanted to sleep. So she did. But she never woke up."

He sank down into a crouch, his hands laced behind his head. "I didn't even know she was dead, Naomi. Not for sure. I thought she'd show up the next day. Call me a dumbass like she always did. And then when I realized, it was too late to say anything. It would have looked like I did something. It was easier to keep quiet."

"I understand," I said, because I did. I understood the weight of a secret, and the urge to bury yourself beneath it.

I knelt down in front of him. I touched his face lightly, fingertips brushing over his stubble, and his eyes closed briefly, a sigh slipping out of him.

"I've been over that night a million times. I know that if I'd done something different, she might still be here. But none of it was done with intent. I was defending myself, and things just got out of control. She basically did it to herself. You can understand, though, how bad it would be if this came out. I can't prove that I didn't mean to hurt her. I could lose everything. Gabriella, the kids—they can't know about this." He looked at me desperately.

I nodded. "Jessi's death was an accident."

"Yes," he said, as if relieved I understood.

"But Liv's wasn't," I said, ragged as a scream but so soft I could barely hear my own voice over the hiss of the rain. He pulled his hands from mine. He stepped back, his face settling into a hard kind of sorrow. His hand went to his back, lifting up the edge of his jacket. The jacket he'd never offered to me, as I shivered in the rain.

He took the gun from his waistband.

It looked like the one Mitch bought me. Nine-millimeter, I thought. Close enough to the Barneses' gun that you couldn't tell the difference just from the wounds they left. And they'd never recovered the bullet.

My fear was cold and still, the surface of a lake in winter. I could sink forever under it, all sound and sense distant. Shudders racked my body, and I couldn't look anywhere but the perfectly round, perfectly black barrel of the gun. I tried to take a breath. All that came was a short, shallow gasp.

"It wasn't me," Cody said. "Stahl's son—he must have found out that you lied."

"It wasn't Ethan. He wanted his father in prison," I said. "And how exactly do you know he found out we lied? Who told you that? It was Liv. Wasn't it?"

Cody looked down at the gun like he wasn't sure what it was. "You think you know what happened, but you don't," he said.

"You didn't mean for it to happen." Echoing again and again and again. Because nothing was our faults; the universe conspired against us, weaving tight the threads of fate. I'd known the names of the Fates once: Clotho, Lachesis, Atropos. How could I remember that, when I'd forgotten so much?

"I only wanted to talk to her," he said hoarsely. "But she wouldn't listen to me. She wouldn't—she attacked me. I was only defending myself."

"Unarmed? Half your size?"

"She would have destroyed my whole life," he said, voice strangled. "I was just trying to find a way out. That's all I've been doing, all along."

"Was it you in the woods?" I asked him.

"I thought you might lead me to Jessi. I wasn't going to hurt you. I'm not going to hurt you," he said, but he sounded like he was trying to convince himself of it as much as me.

"Then let me go," I said, one last futile thrash of hope as the snare's wire tightened. *I want to live*, I realized, even as survival became impossible. For the first time I wanted more than to outrun the pain, but it had come too late. Even if Cody didn't realize it yet.

"I can't," he said. He half lifted the gun. Not pointing it at me yet. "Sit down, Naomi. We're going to stay here. We're going to wait."

"Wait for what?" I spat out, but he only shook his head and gestured with the gun. I walked three steps to the base of a tree and sat on a protruding root, my back against the rough bark. He kept half an eye on me, half on the way we'd come.

We didn't have to wait long before a figure appeared among the trees, walking toward us.

It was Cass.

W hat the hell are you doing, Cody?" Cass demanded.

I opened my mouth to warn her, to tell her he had a gun—but she could see that herself. He made no effort to conceal it. He didn't point it at her, either.

He'd been expecting her. And she had been expecting this.

Cass was wearing a sensible windbreaker and hiking boots, her hair slicked back in a ponytail. She carried a black duffel bag. As she approached, she glared at Cody, eyes burning with anger.

"She was going to the police. She was going to tell them about Jessi," Cody said.

Cass looked at me, and it was like she'd never seen me before in her life. There was nothing to connect to in her eyes. Nothing but calculation.

"Cass," I whispered, and for one dizzying moment nothing made any sense. She couldn't be here. And then I stilled.

I looked beneath the surface, and I saw what had been there all along.

Cass put her hand on Cody's wrist, pushing the gun down gently. "Give us a minute, will you?" she said.

He nodded reluctantly and paced away a few steps, but he kept hold of the gun. Cass dropped the duffel bag on the ground and approached me, rubbing her palms on her jeans. She crouched down a couple feet away.

"Fuck. This is messed up," she whispered, darting her eyes toward Cody. Making a conspiracy out of the two of us. "What did he tell you?"

I stared at her. She sounded so worried. Almost panicked, and desperately concerned for me. Two minutes ago, her face had been so devoid of emotion it could have been carved from stone, and now I could have believed she was on the edge of tears.

"*I'm tired of lying,*" I said.

"What?" she asked, a line appearing between her perfect eyebrows.

"That's what Liv said after she tried to kill herself, eight years ago. Kimiko told me. It's what she said in the letter, too." The note that proved I was wrong, that Bishop's suspicions and Sawant's insinuations were misplaced. Liv had killed herself. Except she hadn't, so who left the note?

The same person who had known where Marcus Barnes kept his gun. The person who had put the gate code in at 4:47 a.m.

I thought of Liv, glancing back toward the car before slinging herself easily over the gate. Liv at fifteen, skirting the living room because her father had the gun out to clean it.

Liv looking me in the eye. *I'll see you tomorrow.*

Liv never used the gate code—she just climbed over. But Cass knew the code and she knew where the gun was kept.

There hadn't been a note eight years ago. Not that we'd found, at least. That time, I'd known it was coming. We'd all known, hoping we were wrong and terrified we were right. The meds hadn't been helping. They were part of the problem—the high dosage that made her hands shake until she couldn't hold a pencil to draw a straight line. Her notebooks were full of abandoned, sloppy sketches.

Her handwriting had been huge and messy, slewing across the page. Nothing like the tiny, precise lettering she usually had. But exactly like the suicide note.

The note was from eight years ago. It seemed so unlikely—who would have such a thing? After eight years, carefully preserved?

Tucked away in a box of secrets.

Cass frowned at me, uncertainty disrupting her careful mask of concern. "Listen, Naomi. I can try to talk Cody down, but I've got to know what exactly is going on here," she said.

"As if you don't know."

"All I know is that I got a panicked call from Cody saying that you knew something and he was going to take care of it, and I should come meet him," she said.

"And you know about Jessi. You know what he did to her."

"Sort of," she hedged. I could almost see the shift behind her eyes, her lies rebalancing. It was a neat trick.

"He told me what happened to Liv."

Her lips parted. Her head cocked slightly, curiously, as she tried to rebalance again. "What happened to Liv," she repeated softly. Not sure how much I knew.

"He killed her so she wouldn't be able to tell anyone about Persephone. But, Cass, there's no way he could have known that she was about to tell us. Unless . . . unless you already knew," I said.

Cass's lips pressed together. "I knew my dad was fucking Jessi. And I knew what it meant when Cody showed up at our house in the middle of the night, covered in blood and panicking. My dad talked him down. They didn't know I saw."

"And when we found Persephone . . ."

She drew something out of her pocket, staring down at it. Then she held it out to me. A plastic bag. Inside it was a chipped plastic name tag. CODY. A scrap of fabric still hung from the pin, and a splotch of what looked like dried blood marred one corner. "It was raining. I guess Cody gave her his work jacket," she said.

"Why wouldn't you say anything?" I asked, still unable to comprehend what I was hearing.

"Can you imagine what a mess that would have been?" Cass said. She looked back at Cody. "Cody's life would be over. And my dad would get dragged into it, too, and you know this town. Even if he could prove he hadn't killed her, that would be it for him." She looked at me, tears swimming in her eyes, and put a hand on my knee. "Besides, we needed Persephone. We needed something to tie us together before we went to middle school. Keep us from drifting apart."

I nodded slowly, as if this made sense. As if it was anywhere in the neighborhood of sane. "But, Cass, how did Cody know?"

She let out a heavy sigh. "Okay, I'll admit I screwed up there. It was when I was trying to get the lodge up and running. We were out of money. Completely out. I was going to lose everything—all the work I'd put in, all the money my parents had invested. So I called and asked Cody if he could invest some of Gabriella's money. He didn't feel like he could ask her for that much, so I . . . provided him with an extra incentive."

"You blackmailed him."

She rolled her eyes. "You make it sound like some mustache-twirling villain thing. I just reminded him that he owed me and my dad for not saying anything. If you want to get anywhere in life, sometimes you have to get people to do things they don't want to, and it helps to have leverage. I learned that a long time ago."

"You warned Cody that Liv knew it was Jessi."

"I didn't think he'd *kill* her. I thought he'd get a fucking lawyer or something," Cass hissed.

"Bullshit," I said. "You're smarter than that."

Her lip trembled. "I didn't hurt Liv. I wouldn't."

"Then why tell him at all?"

"Don't you think he deserved to know that Liv was about to blow up his life for no reason?" Cass asked. "After everything he's done for you? You're so determined to believe the worst of people. I didn't realize what he was going to do until he called me again. *After* she was dead. He threatened me, Naomi. He said if I didn't help him cover it up—" Her eyes welled with tears, and her voice choked off.

She'd planted the suicide note. A note she'd held on to, just in case. Like the photograph of her father and Jessi, and everything else in that box of horrors. Cass had used the gate code, gone into the house while

Kimiko slept, left the note, taken the gun so that she could make it look like Liv had used it to kill herself.

She'd put in the code at 4:47. It would have taken too long to get up to the pond and back; it would have been daylight by then. There might have been early-morning hikers. She hadn't been able to plant the gun until after the police had searched the pond. She'd raced to the lodge instead, providing herself with an alibi—fudged a bit, maybe, thanks to whatever dirt she had on Percy.

That was why they hadn't found the gun at first. It wasn't there to find. But then Bishop and I had refused to let it go. When had she decided she had to plant it? After I called Cody about Jessi?

"When you helped me look for her, you already knew she was dead," I said. "You pretended to think it would all turn out okay. You *knew* she was at the pond, and you let me go up there alone. You tried to convince me to stop digging. God, that eulogy at her funeral—it was all bullshit. It was all a lie."

"It wasn't a lie. Liv was my best friend," Cass said. "But what could I do? She was already dead. Cody was ready to tell everyone that we were in on it together. I had to protect myself."

I swallowed a laugh. "You should have left it alone. If you'd never helped Cody, it would have been fine, but you wanted to be the mastermind, didn't you? Collecting your blackmail. Pulling everyone's strings. But you're kind of shitty at it, as it turns out."

Her hand whipped out so fast I could barely flinch before her nails were sinking into my cheek, gouging at the knot of scar tissue and raking down to my jaw. I fell backward against the tree trunk with a yelp of pain and clapped my hand to my cheek, feeling a hot trickle of blood beneath my fingers. She looked at me with vicious contempt.

Cody came striding over, looking alarmed. "What's going on?" he asked.

Cass stood, panting slightly between her teeth, the only sign that anything was wrong. Her shoulders straightened. "There's no way around this, Cody. She's never going to keep quiet. But if we hide the body, it'll look like she took off."

Cody flinched. I just turned her words over in my mind, marveling at the way she skipped so neatly over that transition. No mention of killing me. From alive to a body, like it was a process they could have nothing to do with.

"People will look for her," he said.

"Some," she allowed. "But Marcus Barnes called me right before you did. She left his place completely wrecked and acting erratic. Covered in dirt. People will believe that she took off."

"Marcus Barnes? What does he know?" He looked at me. "What did you tell him?"

"It wasn't about that," Cass said. "She found out . . ." She hesitated, like it was painful for her to say. "Liv was the one who stabbed her when we were kids. Had some kind of psychotic break and attacked her."

I thought of all the time Cass had spent with me, after the attack. At the hospital and after. How she'd taken care of being our voice, telling the story again and again to anyone who asked. Taking control of the narrative. And of us.

"What?" Cody said, clearly shocked. I felt a petty surge of pleasure that I wasn't the only one getting blindsided. "That's what Liv meant when she said you lied about Stahl."

"It makes sense that Naomi would be freaked out and take off after finding that out," Cass said, sounding satisfied.

"We can't just kill her," Cody said, voice strained. "I can't—"

"You know we have to. It's that, or you go to prison, and that baby of yours is in college before you get to see her except on the other side of Plexiglas." She sighed. "You don't have to actually do it. I don't mind." She held out her hand for the gun.

Cody stared at her. Looked at me. I was past pleading. I met his eyes and tried to keep myself from shaking. He dropped his eyes and handed off the gun. Cass checked it expertly to ensure it was loaded.

"There's a tarp in the bag. We should lay it down so we don't leave blood behind," she said.

He turned away, mouth set and eyes downcast. He knelt to unzip the bag, and Cass turned her wrist this way and that, as if getting used to the weight of the gun.

"I really am sorry about this, Naomi," she said, sounding tired.

"Fuck you," I ground out. "You can't even tell me the truth when I'm about to die."

"What? I *am* sorry. I would rather not have to kill you," she said, irritated.

"Not about that. You lied about Liv. About that day."

"I don't know what you're talking about," she said. Cody had paused, looking up at us.

"Why did you say it was Stahl?" I asked.

She blinked. "To protect Liv, obviously. Prison would have killed her. You know that."

I let out a sound like a growl, my fingers curled into claws in ineffectual anger. I could believe that Liv thought Persephone wanted her to do it. That she had believed she had to.

Seventeen times, she'd stabbed me. There had been so much blood. Marcus said it himself. And Liv hated blood. Had almost vomited at the sight of it, when I cut myself. Yes, Liv might have thought killing me was what the Goddesses demanded.

But she couldn't have done it.

She wouldn't have.

And only one person had ever been allowed to declare what it was Persephone demanded of us.

"How did Liv get the idea that killing me was the final ritual?"

A shrug. "She was crazy."

I shook my head viciously. "She was never violent. Never."

"Except for stabbing you seventeen times. Kind of a giant exception," Cass said flatly.

"Why would she have decided that Persephone needed a sacrifice?

You were the one who told us what Persephone wanted. You made the rules. It was always you."

Her fingers tightened around the grip of the gun. Her face was bloodless, but her gaze was steady.

My lips peeled back from my teeth. "You made her do it. You told her a story and made her believe it. But I can't figure out why. Why did you want to hurt me?"

"Because she was *my* friend," Cass snarled. "You were both supposed to be *my* friends, but you kept trying to go off on your own. You don't think I noticed? Any time I left the two of you alone together, it was all whispers and holding hands and laughing at your private jokes. I thought if I waited, you'd forget about your stupid little crush and it would go back to the way it was *supposed* to be. But you didn't. You were going to be together and leave me behind."

I gaped at her. "So you told her to *kill* me?" I asked, bewildered, my heart hammering wildly. If I was going to die, I wanted to know the truth. All of it.

"She said that she wanted to be my friend. That she wasn't picking you over me. She had to prove it. I didn't think she'd actually do it. I thought she'd chicken out and then I'd be able to hold it over her. I didn't realize how nuts she was," Cass said, but even now she was lying. I could see the hint of satisfaction in her eye. I could imagine her elation at realizing it had actually worked. Maybe she hadn't expected Liv to follow through, but she'd *wanted* it.

"She stabbed me seventeen times?" I said. "Liv did that?" I couldn't believe I'd ever thought it might be true. One more way I had failed her. Betrayed her.

Cass's lips parted ever so slightly. "You think she was so gentle, so perfect? She did stab you, Naomi. She's the one that stabbed you in the back, but she was too much of a fuckup to even get that right. She panicked. She dropped the knife and stood there screaming. Saying she was sorry, that she took it back. But what were we supposed to do?

You were going to tell, and we'd be in trouble. I had to do something. I was just cleaning up her mess. I still am."

I shook—not with the cold, not with fear, but with rage. Cass had seized on Liv's delusions, her fragile state of mind. She'd manipulated her. Liv would have had to be terrified, to be utterly convinced that what Cass was saying was true—that hurting me was the only way to avert something far worse. And still she hadn't been able to do it.

Cass had tried to make her a monster. She couldn't—but she could make Liv believe herself to be one. And Liv had carried that, all this time.

"The thing is, Naomi, it worked," Cass added, as if she didn't quite believe it. "I saved us. I made it so we would always be tied together, we would always be friends—and Liv would never let anything happen between you that might take you two away from me. And we got to be *heroes*, Naomi. Do you think your life would have been anything but utterly mediocre, if I hadn't done what I did? It all worked out. For *all* of us."

I thought of how brave she'd been, after. How she'd flourished, playing the spokesperson for the three of us, interviewed by serious journalists who spoke to her with deference and kindness. How she'd flung herself into the role of caretaker and protector, and everyone had bought it. Had worshipped her.

And part of me wondered if she was right. If I had never been attacked, had never turned into the miracle girl, where would I be? In Chester, probably. In a dead-end job, a drunk like my father.

But Liv would be alive.

"She was going to tell. She was going to ruin everything I worked so hard to make," Cass said, as if imploring me to understand. As if she truly believed I might.

"I've got it," Cody said brusquely, and Cass glanced toward him. He'd laid out the tarp. The handle of a hacksaw stuck out of the duffel. I looked away quickly, my stomach roiling at the thought of what that was meant for.

"All right. Enough talk. Stand up," Cass said, gesturing with the gun. It was like something she'd seen in a movie. I pushed to my feet. She directed me over to the tarp. "Kneel down," she ordered. Her voice shook now.

She wasn't as tough as she wanted to think she was, I thought. This version of Cass was like all the others. Something that she'd decided on, constructed piece by piece. Friend, protector, mother, cold-blooded killer. A false front, and absolutely nothing behind it. I wondered if she even understood why she did the things she did, or if she was acting on pure instinct and filling in logic after the fact.

And she'd always been like that. The day we met, she hadn't chosen us because she thought we were special. She'd chosen us because one glance was enough to tell her that we were so damaged we wouldn't see the rot already festering inside her.

"I spent my whole life trying to heal from something that never happened," I said. "You were my friend. You *stayed* my friend. You told me you cared about me. You made yourself part of my life after you'd done that to me. What were you thinking when you saw my scars and knew they were your fault? When I told you about my nightmares? When you promised me that Stahl wasn't going to get me? Was it funny to you?"

"A little," she said viciously. Her teeth flashed once. Her eyes were empty and cold, and something primal surged within me, an ancestral instinct birthed before we had words for the thing she was.

Ethan had seen it, I realized. Maybe not right away, but during the eulogy and when he spoke to her afterward, he'd seen that she was the same sort of creature he'd lived with his whole childhood. Maybe he'd only had an inkling. Enough to try to warn me, but I hadn't listened.

"You destroyed her," I said softly. "She was wonderful, and you destroyed her."

"I said kneel down," she repeated, and this time I obeyed, letting gravity overtake me.

She started to lift the gun but hesitated halfway. There was genuine fear in her eyes for what she was about to do—but I knew that fear wouldn't save me. The tarp crunched under my knees. The rain had picked up, a steady hiss all around us. It plastered Cody's hair to his scalp and ran into his eyes.

"Fuck," she muttered. She wrapped another hand around the grip, taking a steadying breath. "Don't look at me," she said, but I stared straight at her.

"Wait," Cody said. "Let's think this through."

"We have to kill her," she said.

He shook his head impatiently. "I know, but you shouldn't be the one to do it. I've already killed someone. If we do get caught, I'm already looking at a murder conviction. Better if it's just one of us."

"Fine," she said. She seemed eager to hand off the gun. Relieved. "Just get it over with quickly, okay? I can't stand this."

Cody nodded, giving her a tight smile, and stepped between the two of us. "Hold on, there's one more thing we should check," he said, turning toward her.

"What now?" she snapped, in the half second before he raised the gun and fired a bullet through her throat.

Cass's body collapsed instantly, dead weight. The mist of blood hung in the air longer, drifting down with the rain as the gunshot faded. A scream lodged in my closed-off throat.

Cody lowered the gun.

He turned toward me.

"She was a monster," he said, but the words didn't penetrate at first. I was still in the moment of the gunshot.

I took a startled breath. I wrenched my gaze away from Cass's body, tried to think through the fog of horror. My mind was filled with the image of the instant the bullet struck. The look on her face—she hadn't even had time to be surprised.

"Yes. She was," I croaked out. She was a monster. She was my best friend. She was dead on the ground and the dirt was stained dark beneath her.

"She hurt you. It was her all along. She did that to you. All that blood—how could she do that to you?" he asked, face contorted in disgust.

I worked my throat, trying to speak. "You saved me," I whispered.

I saw it: The way I lived. The way I walked out of these woods. He didn't want to hurt me. He wanted absolution. He wanted me to kiss his brow and tell him that I understood, that I would keep my silence, that I would save him the way he had saved me.

"You saved my life. Just like you saved me from Oscar. You've always been my protector," I told him, getting slowly to my feet.

I slipped my feet out of my high heels. The tarp was cold and slick under the soles of my feet. Cass's body lay only a few feet from where I stood. Blood still bubbled from the ragged hole beneath her chin. "Cass did this. She did all of it, but you stopped her. Do you understand?"

It took him a moment. There were freckles of blood on the knuckles of the hand that held the gun. He stared at them. "We could pin it on her."

"She could have killed Liv. And when I found out, she was going to kill me. But you stopped her. It all fits. Simple. She's the one who put all of this in motion. You were as much her victim as anyone," I said. Cass's hand shivered with the last electrical pulses of a dying body, but she was gone—her eyes empty, her blood stilled. It was just the two of us, and the gun.

He closed his eyes. His breath plumed in the air, and for a moment I could feel it, the fantasy shared between us—that we would walk out of here, and everything would be okay.

Then Cody shuddered and opened his eyes, and I saw the moment the fantasy shattered. The moment he realized that he couldn't protect both me and himself, and made his choice. "Naomi," he said softly. "I wish I didn't know what a liar you are."

I had lived twenty years and change in a body that knew how to survive when the world turned against it. All the sights and the sounds and the sensations of that day were a hopeless slurry, but survival—that, my body remembered. Without the confusion of hope and trust to muddle things, it remembered it perfectly.

I launched myself off the tree before he finished talking, knocking into him. He went sprawling in the dirt. I scrambled forward, clawing the ground before getting my feet under me.

I ran straight forward, not daring to spend the time to turn back toward the road. Distance would save me. Handguns aren't accurate at long range. Not in the hands of an unskilled shooter. Not with the evening darkness gathering swiftly around us.

Fifty yards and I'd be safe, I told myself, and I knew these woods. Just *run*.

The first shot hit a tree trunk with an explosion of bark. The second zipped somewhere overhead.

The third shot was the lucky one.

People always asked me what it felt like to get stabbed. Turned out it felt a lot like getting shot. The impact first, not the pain, a punch to the back that took my legs out from under me. I collapsed as Cody tramped toward me. I lay still, facedown. It didn't hurt. Adrenaline, I thought. The adrenaline was masking it. The pain would find me soon. It knew me too well not to find me. But maybe I'd get lucky. Maybe it wouldn't have time.

Cody reached me. He stood over me, panting. "Goddammit, Naomi," he said. He knelt down and grabbed my shoulder. I held my breath, which was easier than breathing, anyway. I didn't like what that said about what the bullet might have hit.

I stayed limp as he flipped me over.

"Fuck," he said. There were tears in his voice. It was getting harder to hold on to the world. I risked opening my eyes to slits. He was looking away, wiping at his face with his sleeve.

"Dammit," he whispered again.

He was crouching down. The gun was in his right hand, resting on his knee. His grip on it was loose. He wasn't stupid. He wasn't going to leave without making sure that I was dead. And the pain was coming now, around the edges of that blessed numbness that the galloping adrenaline brought with it.

I had nothing left in this world. Not one thing to fight for. Nothing except myself.

It was enough. Somehow, it was enough.

I pushed myself up from the ground, and with the movement came the pain at last, roaring in as blood gushed from the hole the bullet had bored through me. Cody jerked. The moment of shock was all I had—and all I needed. I wrapped both hands around the gun and twisted as he lifted it to fire again.

The bullet ripped through my fingers and tore through the meat of

Cody's leg. Blood burst in a mist; I could feel it on my eyelids, taste it on my tongue. Cody screamed. So did I, a strangled yell as agony ripped its way up my arm. But the pain was mine, and it was proof that I wasn't dead, so it didn't slow me. I rolled. Shoved myself up on my elbows.

I half crawled, half staggered away as Cody howled in pain. I didn't look back. I shoved the bloodied stumps of my ring and pinky fingers against my opposite arm and held my forearm tight to my body to stop the bleeding as best I could, and I barreled forward. It felt more like falling than running.

I plunged through the trees. The boulder was up ahead. I veered for it. I knew where it was without thinking. Without having to look. That dark mouth had been calling to me for twenty-two years. I had forgotten how to listen, that was all. I had forgotten the sound of her voice, but it was all around me now. In me.

The Goddess of oblivion was calling me home.

The darkness of the cave welcomed me. I slung myself beneath the stone and scraped at the soft mud behind me to obscure the slick of blood I left. Gravity won out over my failing strength and I slid down the small slope, coming to a rest on my side, staring at Persephone's bones.

I could hear Cody moving. Limping along. He called my name. I squeezed my eyes shut. I had to have left a trail of blood. He could follow it if he saw it. But I hadn't told him about the boulder. I hadn't told him about the cave. He might not know.

He might not know, and so I would be able to die here, die with the bones of another lost girl. And we would rest, shrouded, together.

"He killed you," I whispered. He hadn't meant to. It didn't matter. He'd let her die and he'd let her be lost, all these years. The secret had stayed lodged under his skin like a splinter, and infection had festered around it. Until we found it, and pricked our fingertips with that diseased bit of wood, and the infection had entered our blood as well. Had wrapped our lives around these bones and wrapped Liv's fingers around the knife.

That secret had driven the knife into my back. It should have killed me. Cody had no idea as he wept over my bleeding body that he'd set this in motion. Not until Liv's guilt had driven her to go digging for that splinter, that secret, slicing open the silence. All that pus and rot came spilling out, and the secret had killed her, too.

And there were other infections, too, all spreading from that first push, the crack of Jessi's skull against the rock.

Ethan, growing up knowing that his father was condemned for the wrong reasons, unable to bring himself to admit to either truth: the one that would have freed his father or the one that would have put him away years before. That might have saved some of those girls whose names he carried now, a talisman of his guilt.

Marcus and Kimiko, gripped with fear that they hadn't done enough to protect Liv. That the truth would come out—or that it wouldn't, and she would hurt someone else, and it would all be for nothing.

And Jessi's niece. The real Persephone. Not a goddess. Not bones in a cave. Not a story we'd told, but a girl who'd loved her aunt, and who missed her. Who'd never known what had happened so that she could properly grieve.

A mistake had killed Jessi Walker. Silence had killed Liv. And the truth had killed me now. And I would be lost, too. There was no one left who knew where Persephone's bones lay. And that seemed right. I wanted to stay here forever with her. The seventh ritual. Everything would be in balance again.

But if I was lost, Marcus and Kimiko would never know that it hadn't been Liv's fault. I needed to tell them.

Cody's calls were moving away. He'd lost my trail. He'd backtrack soon, but I might have a few minutes first.

My phone was a hard lump against my thigh. I pulled it out and squinted at it, the screen blurring. There was the tiniest shred of signal. I stabbed at the screen, managed to pull up the last number dialed. Ethan. I couldn't hold the phone up anymore. I pressed the button to call and let my arm drop, holding it propped on the ground beside my ear.

It rang twice, and then Ethan answered. His voice dipped in and out, and I couldn't tell if it was the poor signal or unconsciousness grasping at me.

"—there? Hello?"

"You have to tell them," I said. There was blood in the back of my throat; I coughed on it.

"Naomi? Is that you?"

"Listen. Listen." I swallowed against the blood. "Tell them it wasn't Liv. She didn't do it. You have to tell them." I tried to take a breath and choked, and a whine of pain slipped between my teeth. Ethan was talking but I couldn't understand the words. I hadn't explained properly, but I couldn't think of how to tell him what he needed to know. "I have to go now," I said.

"Naomi, don't hang up. Tell me where you are," Ethan said.

"It's okay. She's here with me," I said. I let go of the phone; it tumbled from my fingers.

I pulled myself closer to the bones and rolled over onto my back. I shut my eyes and saw again the image of Cody above me as the pain in my back began to register. The way he'd knelt over me, horrified, grief-stricken. Like it was a thing that had happened to *him*.

His face swam. Blurred. Other memories crowded it. Oscar's fingers dug into my abdomen. "You and me were meant to be," he crooned. His fingers punched through my skin, wriggling in my innards. Then he yelped as Cody pulled him away, was kneeling over me again, face streaked with tears. Young again.

"No, please no," he said, pawing at my neck. "Please don't be dead." I tried to tell him I was alive, but I didn't believe it. My fingers curled against the bark. His face hardened. "I wish I didn't know what a liar you are," he said, and drove a knife into my cheek.

I writhed in pain. My breath rattled, and there was a slurping feeling every time I gasped. The stones above me fractured into light-dappled branches.

"What are you doing?" Cassidy screamed, her young voice high and furious.

"I can't. I can't. I can't," Olivia chanted.

"We have to! You promised!" Cassidy yelled.

The knife flashed. I raised a hand to ward it off, striking out weakly at the person looming over me, but a firm hand caught my wrist and held it. "It's okay. We've got you. She's down here!"

Memory ceded reluctantly to the present. Cass's hand, Cody's, Oscar's—they collapsed into reality, brown skin and a solid grip.

I blinked blearily up at Officer Bishop. "I'm starting to think I should have just arrested you," she told me. She pressed her palms to my abdomen, sending a fresh wave of pain through me. I coughed and tasted copper.

I had to tell her about Cody. I tried to speak, but I only coughed again, and she shushed me.

"Just keep breathing," she told me. "Just stay awake and keep breathing. You're going to be okay."

For once, I didn't mind being lied to.

I stayed awake. I fixed every moment in my memory as best I could. I wouldn't forget again. I might die, but if I lived, I would remember this.

Ethan was there when they hauled me out, strapped to a backboard. He tried to talk to me but the words were all slushy. I wanted to tell him I forgave him for lying, but the EMTs got testy when I tried to talk and then they were putting me in a helicopter.

"You've really got to stop doing this," one of the EMTs joked, yelling over the sound of the blades.

"Last time, I promise," I mumbled, and he shushed me again.

And then, despite my best efforts, I faded.

Consciousness seeped back slowly, punctuated by the soft beeping of a monitor. With my eyes closed and my body cocooned in the half oblivion of morphine, I might have been eleven years old again. Except this time, my dad was there when I woke up.

"Hey, kid," he said when he saw me open my eyes.

"Hey," I replied weakly. It came out like a shoe scraping over asphalt. "I'm not dead."

"Go figure," he said.

I looked down at my right hand. Even with the thick bandages, the shape of it was obviously wrong, the last two fingers gone almost entirely, the middle finger ending at the second knuckle. "Thought I still had that one," I said, irrationally irritated at its absence.

"The surgeon wanted a souvenir," Dad said. I gave him a blank look, unable to process the humor. He cleared his throat. "It was damaged. They had to amputate."

I hadn't even noticed. "What about the rest of me?"

"I hope you didn't have an emotional attachment to your spleen. And a sizable piece of intestine. You're basically a soup of antibiotics and narcotics with a few chunks of meat to provide texture, but you'll live."

"That's good," I managed. I tried to wet my cracked lips, but my mouth was just as dried out. "What happened?"

"You don't remember?"

"I mean after. Did they—is Cody—"

"He's been arrested," Dad said. "Even these chuckleheads have managed to put two and two together. Plus you kept saying 'Cody Benham shot me' over and over again."

"That part I don't remember," I confessed.

"Yeah, you were pretty loopy," Dad said. He leaned forward and patted my good hand. "Anyway. Glad you're not dead. You, ah. Should really stop getting hurt."

"Wasn't planning on it," I said. My eyelids were getting heavy.

"Naomi, I—"

I drifted. I dreamed of a gleaming snake slithering down my throat and a black-eyed woman biting down on my fingers, dull teeth grinding their way through my flesh.

I woke alone.

---

I had plenty of visitors. Bishop, Sawant, other cops. Dad. Even Marcus and Kimiko.

Ethan never came. I wasn't sure if that was a disappointment or a relief.

There were loose ends to wrap up. I told my story countless times, and after the hundredth repetition or so I finally got some information in return. Marcus Barnes, as it turned out, had indeed been worried about my mental state when I left the house. Worried enough that he called around trying to find out where I was and make sure I wasn't going to hurt myself. Bishop and Ethan were already on their way to the woods when I made the call—and a good thing, since Cody probably would have found me first, otherwise.

Cass hadn't been lying about Cody threatening her, as it turned out. After years of her blackmail, he'd started recording their phone conversations. Including the one the day that Liv died, when she told him that he needed to come back to Chester and "deal with the situation." Maybe she'd convinced herself there was another way it could end; maybe she'd known exactly what she was setting in motion. Either way, the result was the same. My two best friends were dead.

As news spread, other stories emerged. People she'd blackmailed came forward—or were forced to, as her life was turned inside out and evidence uncovered. Others, presumably, kept their silence and hoped their sins wouldn't be unearthed along with hers. The Greens got a lawyer and didn't speak to anyone. They had a small, private funeral for Cass. As strange as it was, I wished I could be there. I hadn't gotten to say goodbye—to Cass, or to the person I'd thought she was. I couldn't stop thinking about Amanda. She was living with her grandparents now. I'd taken her mother from her.

But then I remembered the timid way she watched the world and wondered what it had been like, to have a mother like Cassidy Green.

The day before I left the hospital, Bishop came by one more time to speak to me. They'd released Jessi Walker's remains to her sister.

Persephone had made it out of the forest at last.

———

I was in the hospital for three weeks before I was well enough to be discharged, and by that time the life I'd had was gone for good.

Between the hospital bills and the fact that I couldn't work, my savings dried up in the blink of an eye. This time around, no one was sending Get Well cards packed with cash. I couldn't go back to weddings. I was the wrong kind of almost famous now.

So I did what Mitch had always told me to. I turned my pain into art, and I sold it. *17* opened at a gallery in Seattle the same week Cody took a plea deal, sparing me another trial. The synchronicity led to a flurry media interest, and before the show even opened I'd sold half the prints for more money than I'd ever thought possible.

Seventeen photographs, one for every scar, the broken pieces of me against the backdrop of the forest, the cracked asphalt behind the gas station, the rusted junkers in my father's yard. Each one was like cutting myself open all over again. Each time, I healed a little cleaner.

I sent Mitch an invitation, a message scrawled on the corner. *Dear Mitch: You were right, it turns out. So fuck you.*

He showed up with a girl who cried when she talked to me. They were perfect together.

I wondered if Ethan would show, but he didn't. I'd searched for his name sometimes, but he seemed to have vanished again, and I didn't look too hard. After the gallery show I stood in front of the bathroom mirror, stripped down to my skin, and splayed my mutilated fingers under the whorl of scar tissue the bullet had left on my stomach on its way out of my body.

*Eighteen*, I thought. *Nineteen.*

But the numbers were a lie, like everything else. The cracks on my skin were too many to count.

---

Ten months after the second time I almost died, we were cleaning the house again. It was a lurching process, steps forward followed by frantic backsliding, but Dad was still trying.

The sun beat down, a rare day without a cloud in the sky. I tossed the trash bag I was carrying onto the pile by the front steps and peeled off my gloves. Dad was already outside, hands on hips, squinting at the old Chevy.

"I think I could get this running again," he said as I made my way over.

"But you won't," I told him.

"But I won't," he agreed. He sighed and scrubbed at his patchy scalp. "You think we could burn it all down and start over?"

"We could do that," I replied amiably. It was only about the thirtieth time we'd had this conversation and that he'd suggested that particular remedy. "But then you'd always wonder what you'd left buried."

"You really think there's anything worth saving?"

"You asking about the house, or about you?" I asked.

He snorted. "I get enough of that crap from my shrink, I don't need it from you, too."

Wheels crunched on gravel. I shaded my eyes with my hand. We didn't have much in the way of visitors these days, and I didn't recognize the car. "Expecting someone?" I asked.

"Hell, no," Dad said.

The car parked. The door opened, and Ethan stepped out, wearing a black T-shirt and jeans.

"Should I get the shotgun?" Dad asked.

"Dad." I gave him a look. "Maybe the baseball bat. Just in case."

He chuckled. Ethan hadn't moved, standing by the car with one hand on the door. I approached slowly, arms crossed.

"Hey," he said. He'd lost weight since I last saw him, the hollows of his cheeks deeper. He was holding a little stuffed hedgehog, which he held out to me. "I got you this," he said, not meeting my eyes. "When you were in the hospital, at the gift shop, but then I never . . . Anyway, it made me think of you."

I stepped forward, just close enough to snag it with the tips of my fingers. The hedgehog was clutching a heart between its paws that said "Get Well Soon." "It made you think of me," I said. "Because I'm prickly?"

"No, see, I have a subtle and insightful metaphor that proves I know you deeply," he said, rubbing the back of his head.

I raised an eyebrow. "It's because I'm prickly."

"It's because you're prickly," he confirmed, wincing.

"You didn't come. At the hospital. Or after," I said. "You didn't call. I never heard from you at all."

"I wasn't sure you wanted to," he said. "The way we left things . . ."

"I don't know if I would have wanted to see you, either," I said. The question hung in the air between us—was it different now?

I didn't know the answer to that, either. When I'd thought I was dying, I'd wanted to forgive him. Now I wasn't sure. Anger and relief and affection and betrayal fought tooth and claw for dominance.

I shook my head. "I want it to be easy to forgive you. But it isn't."

"It shouldn't be," he said. "Things like this should never be easy. That's how you know it's real, if you manage it."

I held the hedgehog in both hands, wiggling its paws idly. "Cody was my hero," I said. "He saved me. And he turned on me. How am I supposed to trust anyone ever again?"

"That's the thing about trust, isn't it?" Ethan said. "You gather all the evidence you can, use your brain, weigh character and past actions. But the final inch of it—that's faith. Trust means believing in someone. It's not just a conclusion. It's a choice."

"That's a pretty way of putting it. You know, you should be a writer or something," I said. "Maybe start a podcast."

He gave a dry chuckle, though it hadn't been particularly funny. "I'm working on one, actually," he said.

"Serial killers of the Pacific Northwest?"

He shook his head. "This one's more personal. It's about my father, but it's more about me. It's about the crimes my father committed, and the ones he didn't, and what it means to me. I have most of it written already. There's a big piece of it missing, though."

"What piece is that?"

"Yours. That day changed our lives. My father might not have attacked you, but from that point on we were connected, you and I. I can't tell the story of what didn't happen without the story of what did. And that belongs to you. I need your help if I'm going to do this right."

"Ethan . . ." I folded my arms over the hedgehog. The sun hit my eyes, giving me an excuse to look at the ground. "We only knew each other for a few days. And that whole time you were lying about who you were."

"You're right. You don't actually know me, and I don't know you. I'm not asking to be your boyfriend, Naomi. I'm not even asking to be your friend."

"Then what do you want?" I asked.

"A trade," he said. "A question for a question. Just the way we started. But this time, we'll both tell the truth."

I looked off down the road. The way it curved, you couldn't see far before the trees swallowed everything up. Anything could be around that corner, and I could never decide if that felt like a threat or a promise.

Trust was a choice, he said. A matter of belief.

I looked back at him.

"Naomi?" he prompted.

"Ask me a question."

# ACKNOWLEDGMENTS

When I was in elementary school, my two best friends and I spent all our time lost in an elaborate game—the first rule of which was that we never acknowledged it was a game. Spells and potions, monsters and magic, they were all real—and so were the dark forces hunting us because we knew. The thing I remember most is the desperate wish that if we acted as if it was all real, it would *become* real. We believed enough to scare ourselves, sometimes—like when we found a perfect stripped skeleton of a bird in the middle of a field or when we sensed something huge and malevolent lurking in the thick fog beyond the apple tree. This book wouldn't exist without those days and years of surrendering ourselves to our imaginations, so thank you, Katie and Audrey, for being the best friends a girl could ask for.

I also owe a debt to the incomparable Jay Ridler, who told me years ago that I should be writing thrillers; it took me a while to get around to it, but you were right. The No Name Writing Group is a constant source of support and insight, so thank you to Shanna Germain, Rhiannon Held, Corry L. Lee, Erin M. Evans, Susan Morris, and Rashida Smith—with a special thank-you to Erin and Susan, who were in the trenches with me from the start with this book, and to Rhiannon for her help on environmental compliance details. Dana Mele and Amelia Brunskill also provided invaluable feedback on drafts along the way. My agent, Lauren Spieller, transformed the manuscript with her keen editorial eye and championed it on submission, finding it the perfect home.

My editor, Christine Kopprasch, understood this book immediately, and her insights shaped and honed it into its final form. It has been an absolute joy getting to work with Christine and with the whole team at Flatiron—thanks especially to Megan Lynch, Maxine Charles, Claire McLaughlin, Erin Kibby, Jolanta Benal, Erin Fitzsimmons, Kelly Gatesman, and Susan Walsh.

A special thank-you to my son, who tells me that I write boring books and they should have pictures in them—someday you'll think I'm cool. And to my daughter, who does think I'm cool, but mostly because I give her Goldfish crackers. I love you to bits.

And always, always, always: thank you to my spouse, Mike, and to the rest of my brilliant, funny, generous, creative family. I couldn't do it without you.

# ABOUT THE AUTHOR

KATE ALICE MARSHALL writes horror and thrillers for all ages, from middle grade to adult. Her books for younger readers include *I Am Still Alive*, which was nominated for a Washington State Book Award, and *Rules for Vanishing*, which was nominated for a Bram Stoker Award. She lives in the Pacific Northwest with her family. *What Lies in the Woods* is her adult thriller debut.